THE SUMMER HOTEL
LOVELY BAY

POLLY BABBINGTON

POLLY

PollyBabbington.com

Want more from Polly's world?

For sneak peeks into new settings, early chapters, downloadable Pretty Beach and Darling Island freebies and bits and bobs from Polly's writing days sign up for Babbington Letters.

1

Nina Lavendar got to the door to the building of her flat, keyed in the numbers on the pad, nudged the bottom of the door with her foot, and scooted up the stairs as fast as she could. She was in no mood to see Mrs Gilbert from the flat on the opposite side of the landing. Slipping off her shoes by the mat, she shrugged off her coat and hooked it over the bannister post. She then took the two further odd half steps up to the sitting room and then went around the meticulously tidy flat, turning on the battery tealight candles until pretty much the whole place was twinkling. She needed something to sparkle in her life because her *actual* life was rather dull around the edges. Throw in a bit of sadness just alongside the dullness and perhaps sprinkle on a little bit of grief, too. Another Friday night on her lonesome, with the only things to keep her company being Mrs Gilbert's blasting of Radio 4 floating across the hall, and every three and a half minutes, the trundle of the underground train below.

She opened the fridge, closed it again, peered into the bread bin, hoping to find some inspiration, and sat at the kitchen table staring out the window for a bit. Another three and a half minutes went by as she felt the tube rumble underneath, sloshed a half measure of gin into a gigantic glass, sliced some lemon, poured in a very generous serving of tonic, and mooched her way to the bathroom. Half an hour later, she emerged in her oldest, saggiest, best friend pyjamas, sheepskin-lined slippers, and her cosiest, shaggiest cardigan over the top. A long night of Friday night fun with a screen as a companion, and the only thing ahead of her on the cards was what to watch next. At least work was finished for the week. There was that, she supposed.

Nina endeavoured to stay upbeat, but, really, if she was honest, it wasn't actually working. Her most pressing decision of the weekend would be whether or not she could be bothered to clean the already clean flat, if there was anything else in her life that could possibly be decluttered, and how she would dry her washing because the weather forecast was more than abysmal. She had five work blouses to make sure were clean and ironed, and the same number of knickers. Her Friday evening entertainment consisted of two main options – watch Netflix at the kitchen table or watch Netflix from the sofa. Life was that good in Nina Lavendar's world.

With a mahusive sigh, she took out a portion of curry from the vat she'd defrosted the day before, tipped it into a saucepan, put on some rice, and then stood by the worktop looking out the window over the rooftops of London. Grey sloping slate roofs matched a dark grey sky, shiny droplets of rain slid down the glass, and the little ledge outside her window, where she grew potted herbs and anything else she could think of, had gathered its usual three puddles where it wasn't quite level. Plop-plop-plop went the same old drip she'd been watching for years as it dropped from the gutter. A rumble from the train deep underground caused the window panes to shudder a little bit. Another three and a half minutes of her Friday night sliding past.

Just as she was sitting watching the same droplets running

down the window and wondering if her rosemary would thrive its repotting, her phone buzzed. Her best friend Sophie's name slid from right to left across her phone screen. Sophie didn't realise that Nina realised that Sophie always phoned about the same time on a Friday night to check in, just to make sure Nina was okay. Was Nina okay? Probably. Did she really have a lot of choice in the matter? Nope. She shoved a forkful of curry into her mouth, reflected on how good it was, made a mental note to try to remember what combination of spices she'd used, and pressed to answer. Sophie came onto the screen. Sophie was her usual upbeat self. She had the smile on her face that Nina had come to refer to as the Pity Smile. She'd seen it in many guises many times before even though Sophie thought she was really smart and tried to wrap it up in lots of different ways, most of which didn't work.

'Hiya! How's your week been? What have you been up to?' There it was again, right after Sophie had finished her sentence – the Pity Smile doing its thing.

Nina pretended her week had been good. To be frank, it had been like any other week – dull with a side of boredom and a sprinkle of sadness. Though, to be fair, she'd not let the sadness settle this week. She'd had a gutful of it already at the beginning of the year and she'd told herself she was no longer prepared to be sad. She was going to do something about this life she still had and make something of it; she just wasn't sure what. Time for big-girl pants. She smiled and pretended to be happy. 'Hi. Yeah, it's been good, thanks. You?'

'Fabulous! What's been going on with you?'

As she did every single time Sophie asked her, Nina racked her brains to try and think of something, *anything* that had occurred in her week other than *going* to work, talking to Mrs Gilbert when she came *in* from work, reading in her break *at* work, and trying new recipes *after* work. She could ramble on about the books she'd read that week – a very far-fetched and much-hyped story about an old people's home where the residents solved murders, an autobiography of a woman who married a politician twenty-five years older than her, and a cookery book from 1960 about a woman who moved from Berkshire to live in a Spanish cave. Sophie wouldn't be interested in any of that.

Suddenly, Nina remembered something that had happened in her week that could possibly be considered news. She had looked at joining a gym. A new one had opened just down the road from her flat. It looked pretty fancy and Nina's jeans told her she needed to go to a gym or do something other than read and eat. She'd even signed up on the gym's website for a trial lunchtime Pilates class. She'd put her trackies and trainers in her bag one morning and forced herself to go along in her lunch hour. It was not one of her better moves. The Chelsea Collective was not for the Nina Lavendar gym-goers of the world. The Chelsea Collective had a few prerequisites. Firstly, it helped if you were slim, borderline see-through. Nina might have passed for that at one point in her life. Not these days. Secondly, you needed to be dressed from head to toe in white and it was preferable if you had a white-blonde rinse on your exquisitely highlighted hair. Nina's tracksuit was a washed-out-seen-better-days black with a bleach stain just past the knee. You needed a blow-dry to attend a class and the right logo on your leggings. Nina's gym top was about ten years old, and the logo had long since worn off.

Nina had arrived at The Chelsea Collective in a fairly positive frame of mind, determined to get fit and start something happening in her life. She'd checked in and gone to the changing rooms and it had slowly slid downhill from there. As she'd sat on the bleached wood Scandinavian-designed bench, she'd stared at a huge olive tree in a white pot nestled in the corner of the white room and asked herself what she thought she was doing as the positive frame of mind slipped out the window. She'd soldiered on, taken her joggers out of her bag, and more or less wanted to cry as she realised how she was so in the wrong place. A woman with a bouncy ponytail, fantastically expensive eyelashes, and a sculpted midriff clad in white leggings came out of the cubicles and beamed. The woman had been friendly and happy and bouncy and *nice* which had made Nina feel a billion times worse. Once the girl had gone, Nina had stuffed the trackies back in her bag and sloped away past the huge pale wood reception desk, where another olive tree sat in another white pot, as quietly as she could. The Chelsea Collective had not in any shape or form made Nina Lavendar feel good. Her muffin top continued to grow.

Nina flicked her brain back to Sophie and the call. There was no way she was going to tell Sophie about the gym. She'd then have to listen to a whole long list of reasons why Sophie thought it would be good for her to join a gym. *Get a life. Get fit. Get some friends. Do you good. Good for your mental health.* Blah, blah, blah. All of it would be generously interspersed with the Pity Smile. She heard herself saying she was busy. 'Busy at work. You know how it is? How about you?'

'Looking after the needs of two tiny humans and addressing the needs of one other large human,' Sophie joked.

Nina laughed. Sophie had gone from being super high up in a marketing job for a FinTech firm to falling pregnant twice in the space of just under two years and moving out of the city down to the coast. She was now pregnant again and loving it. Nina joked back. 'You did it to yourself.'

'I certainly did, and I'm doing it again. Glutton for punishment, I reckon.'

'Who would have thought, eh?' Nina remarked fondly. She loved that Sophie was happy and content.

'I know. What happened to the woman who spent her evenings working and her weekends shopping for Gucci?'

Nina chuckled. 'Hopefully, she'll be back at some point. How's Nick?'

'He's fine when he's here.'

Nina wasn't quite as sure as Sophie about Nick being fine, but it seemed that Sophie was happy, so she kept her mouth firmly shut. 'Good. Has he been away again this week?'

'He has. Sometimes, I think he goes away to escape the madness of the house.'

Nina nodded to herself. *Of course he did.* Never a truer word said in jest sprang to mind. She chided herself inside. Who was she to be judging the whereabouts of Nick? It was none of her business, whatsoever. Was she bitter and twisted? A horrible person inside? She joked, but she wasn't actually sure if it was funny. 'He leaves you to the delights of the little people. That's your job now.'

'Yep. I'm not complaining, though. I *love* being home with them. Love it. Oh, that reminds me! The funniest thing happened today. I was scrolling through Facebook, as one does, and I came across a post and straightaway, I thought, Nina. This would be good for my Nina. You know how much you love organising and suchlike.'

'Oh?' Nina raised an eyebrow. *Here we go,* she thought. Another one of Sophie's schemes to get Nina 'back on track' as Sophie called it. The thing was, Nina felt as if deep down she was never, ever going to get back on track. Grief did that for a girl.

The Pity Smile was in residence as Sophie chatted. 'Someone posted looking for a sort of house-sitter thing for...umm, like an old B&B or hotel, I think. I drive past the town on my way to Parents and Bubs. On the bay side of Lovely I think it is – you know, just down the dual-carriageway from me. It looks like it's been empty for a while, from what the post says.'

Nina wrinkled up her nose. 'Yeah, sounds delightful.'

'No, I reckon it would do you good.'

'Sorry, what even is it?'

'House-sitting in a former B&B hotel while the owner is overseas on a gap year. You need something to...' Sophie stopped herself. 'I'll forward you the post.'

Nina's phone dinged as the notification came through. She clicked on it while still listening to Sophie describe the building and where it was, in a place called Lovely Bay.

'The whole place looks like it hasn't been updated in a long time, but, I don't know, the views are something else. Someone at Parents and Bubs was telling me that it was once a thriving place and that the owner has a whole load of these B&Bs up and down the country, but she's gone into a care home. Or maybe she's no longer with us...one of the two. Yeah, anyway. I think she said the daughter is in charge of it, but she's away in South America or somewhere like that. Maybe it was the niece, not the daughter. Sorry, I've got pregnancy brain.'

Nina really, *really* wasn't interested, but Sophie was trying to be nice. She pretended to be interested and tapped on the post. 'Sorry, where is it?'

'Lovely Bay. You know, we drive past it on the dual-carriageway on the way to my place.'

Nina didn't know. She squinted and shook her head. 'Nope.'

'We were going to go there when I first had Lilly to get ice cream. I told you about it. It has a pedestrianised area through the middle with loads of old shops and lots of little greens. There's that chocolate shop I told you about last Christmas with the chilli chocolate. Come on Neens, get with the program.'

'Nup. Sorry.' Nina shook her head. She couldn't remember it at all. She scanned the post Sophie had sent her with mild interest.

House-sitter needed for seaside B&B. We need a house-sitter for one of my late aunt's B&Bs on the bay side of Lovely. It's an old building and we need someone to move in, keep an eye on the place, and make sure

*it's looked after while we're travelling. As any Lovelies will know, it's a
bit run down though very cosy, with amazing sea views, but it has not
been up and running as a B&B for quite a while.*

*Everything is provided and includes accommodation in the living
quarters which encompasses a gorgeous kitchen with an Aga, fab old
fireplaces, a wrap-around verandah overlooking the sea, and access to
a resident's only beach. Responsibilities include keeping an eye on the
property, clearing out the living quarters (decluttering and organising),
doing the garden, and maybe some upkeep (a dab hand with a
paintbrush would be good), bringing in mail, etc. We're looking for a
house-sitter who doesn't mind an old, draughty building in need of
some TLC. You'll have the whole place to yourself. Utilities included
including internet. Lovelies are preferred but not required. *Pls note*
This is NOT a paid position. Apply by DM or to the email address (in
the comments below) and let us know why you'd be a good fit.*

Sophie continued, 'Anyway, the post has loads of comments
on it, but she's edited it to say that they still haven't found
anyone who can stay long enough. It says that she doesn't want
to have to work out the logistics of people coming willy-nilly
for a few days or a few weeks. They want someone to commit to
it for a couple of months until they decide when they are
coming back from South America.'

Nina swiped to the picture of the property. 'Interesting. It
does look cosy, I'll give it that.'

Sophie let out an exaggerated gasp. 'Does that mean you'd
consider it?' The Pity Smile appeared.

Nina stared at the image on her phone screen. There was *no way*
she would consider it. Not in a million years. Sometimes Sophie
irritated her when she did the Pity Smile and acted so concerned.
'No! Why in the name of goodness would I want to house-sit for
someone in a dusty old mansion in a place I don't know from Adam
when I have a perfectly nice flat here? I also have a job to attend.'

'Have a change of scenery,' Sophie fired back. 'They've said you can work from home a few days a week, you can extend that, and you love decluttering and organising. It's your gig, Neens. You are the only person I know who likes clearing out airing cupboards. Need I remind you that you had yourself a very good small business by way of word of mouth doing just that.'

Nina ignored the fact that Sophie was right. She had done very well with a little side hustle business decluttering for rich people in St John's Wood and Knightsbridge, but she'd slowly let it fizzle out because of the grief. 'I don't need a change of scenery, and I don't need to get away either before you say it.'

'Maybe it would be good to get away from your fabulous life in the city,' Sophie teased. 'I've just sent you the email address that's in the comments.'

Nina rolled her eyes. 'Yeah, thanks Soph, it would possibly be good to get away. But to be quite honest, I'm more up for a week in Tuscany in warm weather than someone's old B&B on the coast. I might be a bit lonely, but I'm not desperate. Not yet anyway.'

Sophie brushed over Nina's response. 'I think you'd love it. It's so different out of the city. People talk to you, say hello, and you could be part of a little community. Honestly, it's the best thing we've done. You could come down here and read and cook to your heart's content. This would cost you nothing, and you could, well, umm, you know, heal.'

'Yeah, you've said multiple times. You also live in a beautiful house in the country's answer to Notting Hill and you live next door to a famous actor.' Nina squinted at the pictures Sophie had sent her. 'This does not look in the same league in any shape or form.'

Sophie ignored the bit about the famous actor. 'Don't you think it's time you tried something new? You've been in a bit of a rut lately. A change could be just what you need to hit the reset button. A change is as good as a rest, as they say.'

Nina sighed. She was fine, and there was one thing she'd learnt about grief; it liked to come up and smack her on the head when she was on her own, which was why she didn't really like the weekends and why she wouldn't be going to Lovely Bay on her Jack Jones anytime soon. The last thing she needed was to be in a house in a seaside town on her own where she knew no one and had no routine. 'I don't think Nowheresville is going to get me out of a rut. Not that I'm in one.'

'It would be an *adventure*. You might love it so much you'd stay down here and be nearer to me.'

'Nup. Sorry, the odds of me, one, going and, two, thriving in a remote isolation like that are slim to none.'

'You'd be nearer to me and the children,' Sophie persisted.

Nina frowned. 'How far is it then?'

'Like twenty-five minutes' drive when the traffic's bad, which it is often, and there's a train. In fact, there are two stations. Lovely and Lovely Bay.'

'Right.'

'You could just let yourself *do* something for a change. You are still allowed to have a life, Neens, even after...'

Am I though? Nina thought. 'I know, I know.'

'Say you'll consider it.'

There was no way in the world Nina was ever going to go to Lovely Bay. Not on your Nelly. 'Okay, I will.'

'You won't. I know that face.'

'I will, honestly.'

'Neens.' Pity Smile.

'I will.'

Sophie made a more serious, pointed noise and turned around to a sound behind her. 'Ahh, someone is awake. I'm going to have to go. Have another read of that post.'

'Will do. Have a nice night. Give those bubs a kiss from Aunty Neens.'

'See you later. Love you.'

Nina sat staring out the window for ages, poured a second, more generous glass of gin and tonic, dished out another serving of curry, and put it on to warm up. As she stood with her back to the worktop with her phone in her hand, she pulled up the message from Sophie again and idly read through. Another message came in from Sophie with a link to the WebMD page on Lovely Bay, which actually sounded as if it was quite nice.

Lovely Bay was mentioned in the Domesday Book (1086) as a fishing port, and with its River Lovely brought trade to Lovely in the 15th century. The town received its charter from Henry VII in 1489. The grant of the charter is marked by the annual Lovely Fair, when it is read out by the Town Clerk.

As the microwave pinged with her rice, a crack and boom of thunder sounded outside, and a snap of lighting bolted right down the centre of the window. Nina tapped to close the image and put her phone in her pocket. House-sitting in Lovely Bay in an old B&B? Pah. There was no way she would even *think* about doing that.

2

Exactly a week later, Nina was sitting on the park bench she sat on every day during her lunch hour. Well, the lunch hours when she didn't make disastrous trips to attend trial sessions at gyms. She shook her head as she felt the waistband of her trousers dig in. She needed to do something to get rid of what she called the 'grief weight', but the white gym, which bred olive trees in pots, wasn't going to be the place the weight fell off, that she knew for free. She tutted out loud to the ducks in front of her and shook her head. She should have known by the name. The Chelsea Collective. Grrr. She hated the name 'collective' anyway. Collective this, collective that. What even was a collective? She didn't really care. She did know she was never in her wildest dreams ever going back. She would not in her lifetime ever step in a gym, white or not, again. She shuddered at the thought.

She balanced the little glass container with her lunch in her left hand and Kindle in the other, then started to eat the spicy noodles she'd brought from home and nodded. So good. If there was one thing Nina wasn't bad at, it was comfort eating and cooking. So good, in fact, that it was showing all over her face. Mostly in her jowls.

Many of her work colleagues had told her many a time that she should do something with her recipes. But like what, though? Sell them on the street? That wasn't going to be happening anytime soon. She did now bring her trial recipes into work and leave them in the fridge for anyone to grab should they so want to. There'd been fights over them and even an email from Sue in Accounts, who had seriously got the hump when she'd missed out on one of Nina's extra-hot Sri Lankan curries. Now there was a spreadsheet on the shared Google Drive and a hard copy on the front of the staff fridge for Nina's cooking. The spreadsheet made Nina laugh out loud. It was hilarious that there were fights over the things she made. She'd started learning to cook when grief had had her around the neck. Before that, she'd been quite good at beans on toast and very good at Uber Eats. One night she'd picked up one of the cookery books that had sat on her shelf as a display book, and she'd tried out a recipe for store cupboard curry. That had been the start of her comfort cooking, and she hadn't really looked back since.

She sat by the pond reading her book, got to the end, clicked her Kindle off, and put it and the little glass dish beside her on the bench. The tall, lanky, handsome man from the office next door came along the path and smiled. His trousers were too short, his face was very handsome, the ring on his left hand glinted, and she wondered, as she always did, how he could stand being outside without a jacket. 'Hi, Nathe. How are you?'

Nathan sat down on the other end of the bench and splayed his long legs out in front of him, making his trousers play around way above his ankles. 'Keeping out of trouble. You?'

'Same.'

'What were your delights today for lunch?' Nathan asked, flicking his eyes to Nina's lunchbox. 'Something spicy?'

'Asian noodles, and yes, very spicy.'

'Nice?'

'Yup.'

'Good enough to be going into your monthly rotation?'

'Possibly.'

Nathan laughed. 'What have you been up to?'

'Absolutely nothing. Same as usual. Reading and cooking. You?'

Nathan tilted his head to the left at a funny angle and pretended to consider. 'Now let me see. Hmm. What have I been doing with my exciting life? Oh, I know. Nothing new.'

Nina chuckled. 'You and me both.'

'Though I did have to go to the christening of one of my brother's babies, which, although fairly pleasant, meant I had to talk to people for pretty much six hours straight.'

'Eew.'

'Precisely.'

'How's the channel going?'

Nathan had somehow accidentally found himself at the helm of a very popular gaming channel, whereby he basically broadcasted himself to the far corners of the world playing war games. He'd started gaming when his wife had left him, taking their two children with her and moving in with his best friend. 'Yeah. Millions of views.'

'Right. That's good. I bet that's worth a few bob.'

Nathan nodded. 'You wouldn't even believe it, and here I sit on the same bench in the same park by the same pond I've been sitting on for, what, ten years, is it? Yeah, something like that.'

Nina turned her mouth upside down. 'Well, I mean, you could *do* something with your life now. Couldn't you?'

'Like what?'

'I don't know. What's the trendy thing to do these days? I know. Van life. Yeah, you could have a go at that.'

'What in the world is van life when it's at home?'

'Get a camper van and drive it around the country. Add a few fairy lights to the van, make chai lattes every night, and look out over the moors with a wistful look on your face.'

'Yeah, right. That sounds like fun. Not.'

'You can game wherever you like, right?'

'Well, technically, yes.'

'But?'

'But I have two children.'

'Ahh, yes. That could put a spanner in the works.'

'I'm stuck here, whatever way I look at it. If I want to be in their lives, I get to be faced with the fact that my ex-wife now lives with my ex-mate, and they have a baby of their own, and get to look after mine seventy per cent of the time.'

'Ouch.'

'I know.'

'Which is why you're on this bench every day of the week.'

'Correct.'

'Ahh.'

'I also need to start looking for somewhere to live while the building my flat is in is completely rewired and the asbestos is removed.'

'Can't help you with that.'

'My life really is crap,' Nathan stated morosely.

Nina started to gather up her things. 'Right, well, on that note, see you tomorrow.'

'Yep.'

'I might bring you some noodles if you're lucky.'

'Can't wait.'

As Nina walked away from the bench and made her way around the pond, she stopped, as she always did at the willow tree, and watched for a bit as a few ducks went past. The conversation with Nathan went idly through her mind. She thought he was a bit crazy to stay at a job he didn't like when he had the opportunity to do all sorts with his life. She pondered it for a few minutes, then blinked and nodded over and over again as a realisation hit her. She was precisely the same. Admittedly, *unlike* her, Nathan's partner hadn't died, but the *same* as her, he was grieving for a life that wasn't going to be. Nina thought about it more and realised that she liked to think that she would do something different if she were in his shoes, but would she? Would she really? What was stopping her from doing something with her life? Her mind flicked to the conversation the week before with Sophie and the post about the house sitting thing. She pulled it up on her phone and read through it again. She shook her head. Stuck in the middle of nowhere in an old B&B sounded about a million times worse than her dull little life in her flat. Terrible idea. Dreadful.

3

A few hours later, Nina was at her desk. She kept repeating the conversation on the bench with Nathan in her head. It had made her feel all out of sorts. After she'd made a cup of tea halfway through the afternoon and was on her break, she found herself googling Lovely Bay.

Nestled right down in a little corner of the unspoilt south coast, the small Georgian town of Lovely Bay is a nostalgic, quintessentially British seaside dream. Just that bit quieter than our neighbours, our pretty seaside town (the third smallest in the country) is the perfect place for a bucket and spade day out from days gone by. With its sandy beaches and beach hut-lined promenade, Lovely and Lovely Bay are just wonderful any time of the year to enjoy a little paddle, an ice cream, a pint, maybe a pub lunch, and a stroll along the prom. Our idyllic seaside areas are home to lots of picture-postcard greens surrounded by pastel-coloured cottages, cafés, pubs, and shops. Walk over one of the many little bridges connecting our town, take a boat trip, have a look at the lighthouse, pop in the chocolate shop, or have a wander out across the dunes and enjoy Lovely Beach.

Lovely and Lovely Bay occupy a prominent position on the South Heritage Coast in a designated Area of Outstanding Natural Beauty. Set around numerous greens, our small town offers a range of boutique shops, our very own renowned Lovely Chowder, is home to the famous Lovely Brewery and has its own unique picture palace cinema. Lovely also has a listed train station, two sailing clubs, and the surrounding area is celebrated for its coastal and countryside walks. Pop down for the day. We guarantee you'll love it.

Nina nodded to herself. When you looked at it like that, it didn't sound too bad. She clicked on the next website down and read more. The town was tiny but housed the country's smallest pier, along with a white lighthouse that appeared nestled among a row of houses. Lovely Bay itself was complete with mudflats, a yearly crabbing competition, meadows, and marshes that served as a home for many birds, otters and deer. She could work with that.

Long after her tea was finished and as her colleague Mariana was pretending to work but was really browsing the holiday section of the Next website, Nina was still deep down in the depths of the World Wide Web, googling and reading about Lovely Bay and its sister Lovely itself. Every single time she read something, she kept thinking that it couldn't get any better, and then she found something else. On and on it went until she was swimming agog in all things Lovely Bay.

Later on, when she'd trudged up from the underground as she nudged open the door to the hallway in the flats, she stopped to chat with Mrs Gilbert over the way, stroked her little dog, Charly, picked up her post, and made her way inside. She shrugged her coat off, hung it over the bannister, slipped her shoes off by the door, and did the same routine she always did. At least it was Friday, though, which meant that she could have a G&T. She was also looking forward to one of the accounts she followed on Instagram doing a live book review on a book she'd had her eye on for a while.

Half an hour later, she was sitting in exactly the same position she'd been in the week before, only this time she'd waited for Sophie's check-up call to go to voicemail. The weather was the same, too, and she squinted out the window at her plants through droplets of rain running down the window. With her chin in her hand, she sighed, picked up her phone, and read through the message she'd written in response to the Facebook post that afternoon. She'd done it, first of all, just to see what she would write if she were going to apply to the house sitting post. What had happened had surprised her because it had been much harder than she'd thought and it had taken her at least four attempts. In the end, she'd scrapped everything and written the truth, not that she was going to send it anyway but she'd done to pass a bit of time.

My name is Nina Lavendar. My friend Sophie told me about your post on FB about a house-sitter in Lovely Bay. To be honest, I have to say from the outset that I'm not sure I'm the person for you. Frankly, I've written this a few times and also deleted it a couple of times, too. I even Googled how to respond to a house-sitting post. I mean, really? Can you imagine? Apparently, one is meant to say that they do yoga and go to the gym. You have to pretend that you love animals and are responsible. Let me tell you one thing that is absolutely the truth – I don't go to the gym and won't be starting anytime soon.
So, why would you want me in your house/hotel? More importantly, why would I want to come and stay, right? Okay, well, I'm single and fairly level-headed; I have a job I can do remotely should I require it. Although it is really boring and extremely low paid, but a job is a job these days so I've been there way longer than I should (does this make me responsible? I think so).
I'm in my late thirties, and a few years ago, I lost my husband. I always think it's weird to say 'lost' because I haven't misplaced him. I

didn't go into M&S one day to get an egg and cress sandwich with him beside me and came out without him because he'd got lost. He's dead. Meaning, I am a widow. That in itself comes with a whole lot of stuff attached to it. Trust me, you don't want to be a widow in your early to mid-thirties (as I was) these days. It's not just the sadness and the grief; I reckon at some point you can sort of come to terms with that – oh no, it's more that people can be very strange when they find out. If you ever experience it, you'll learn the look that comes over a face when they hear that you've lost (not in M&S) your husband. It's sort of a cross between empathy, pity, sadness and, to be quite frank, fear.

You see, the word 'widow' and being in your thirties doesn't really go, and people think that you've probably not dealt with any of it well. To be fair, I've not done too badly compared to some of the people I've met at the grief group (that is a whole other story altogether).

Anyway, I met Andrew at school when I was fifteen, nearly sixteen (he was the new boy, he'd moved from overseas) and I'd been with him ever since. We moved to London together, bought a flat together, tried for a baby together, you get the gig. Only it didn't quite pan out as I expected. Burying him wasn't part of it nor was paying the mortgage off with the life insurance, though that part of it was a bonus (?), if indeed we can call it that.

Sorry, I've really blabbed on now. Anyway, my friend Sophie thought it would be 'good for me' to have a change of scenery. I'll just quickly tell you what I'm into. I love organising and decluttering (let me at your spices, sheets, and airing cupboard, ha ha). Since Andrew got lost, I rediscovered my love of reading. I like lots of different genres but mostly I'm into domestic noir and autobiographies and some cookery books but not 'recipe' books as such. Speaking of recipes, I dabble in what I call comfort food (also since losing Andrew). I'm also quite into growing stuff. Let me expand on that; I have a small balcony garden (it's more like a ledge to be honest) and I grow things in pots (it was recommended to me by the grief group leader). Supposedly, it's therapeutic and can be healing.

I really don't think I've sold myself here. As I said, Sophie said a

change is as good as a rest. Also, she lives a twenty or so minute drive away from Lovely and she's been my best friend since I was six, so there's that. Right, I'll go. No doubt I won't hear from you, but if you're absolutely desperate, you know where I am.
All the best. Nina Lavendar.

Nina underlined and bolded 'absolutely desperate', selected the email address from Sophie's message from the week before, opened her emails, popped the address in the email address bar, then copied the text to her clipboard and pasted it in the body of the email. In the subject line, she wrote – Nina Lavendar for house-sitter post. Before she knew what she was doing, she thought stuff it and clicked on *Send*.

Immediately, she regretted it. What in the world was she thinking? The woman would think she was bonkers. There was no way she'd ever get a reply, not that she wanted one. So it didn't really matter. There was also no way she was going to the back end of the country to a little coastal town to house-sit for someone who was gallivanting all over the planet on an adventure. Why would she even consider it? She was quite happy with her superbly organised little flat, her lost husband, her newly found love of reading, and the plants on her rooftop ledge, thank you very much.

4

Monday morning rolled around. Nina's weekend had been the same as the one before. The weather had been the same, the washing conundrum the same, and the gin and tonics were the same. The only excitement had been that Mrs Gilbert's sink had sprung a leak, and the plumber who had come to fix it had fallen over his toolbox and broken his arm. Mrs Gilbert had proceeded to have a panic attack over that, and Nina had spent the afternoon making cups of tea, feeding Mrs Gilbert's cat, and liaising with the plumber's wife so she could come and collect his tools.

As she did every weekday, Nina sat on the bench by the pond with her lunch and her Kindle. The book reviewer she followed on Instagram, Lotta Button, had recommended a crime book, and Nina had blindly bought the book and hoped for the best. Since then, she'd not really been able to put her Kindle down. She was finishing off the last few chapters when Nathan came along, as usual, jacketless and not looking full of beans. Inside, Nina knew that once Nathan got himself together, he'd be okay. He was just in the early stages of his trauma.

'Hello. How was your weekend?' Nathan asked as he sat

down and splayed out his long legs with their too-short trousers in front of him.

Nina slipped a glass container with a blue plastic lid out of her bag and passed it over to him. 'Yeah, fine. You?'

'Not bad.'

'How were the children?'

'The same. I miss them when they go back.'

'Any gaming?'

'Oh yes. I call it PTSD gaming.' Nathan chuckled. 'There was plenty of that.'

Nina could tell there was a lot of truth behind Nathan's laugh. 'Oh yeah, how'd that go?'

'Twenty thousand viewers watched my stream live.'

'So that was good.'

'Pays the bills.'

'Ha! Just a bit. I remember how much you said you made when you had one thousand viewers.'

'I know.' Nathan sighed really loudly. 'My life's still crap, though.'

'Ahh, it'll get better.'

'It can't get a lot worse.'

Nina wondered. Was seeing your ex-best mate with your ex-wife worse than having a dead husband? Inside, she shuddered. Defo on a par. 'No.'

'What did you get up to?'

Nina glanced at Nathan and shrugged. 'Mrs Gilbert had a minor meltdown when her sink started leaking, and the plumber fell and broke his arm.'

Nathan's eyes widened. 'Drama! Is the plumber alright?'

'Oh yeah, just a broken arm, I think. But you know Mrs Gilbert, I've told you about her before. Total drama queen. She was freaking out, worried she'd get water damage or mould or something if her sink wasn't fixed immediately. I had to go over and make multiple cups of tea while we waited for the plumber's wife to come and get him.'

Nathan chuckled. 'It all goes on. I didn't have anywhere near that excitement.'

'She had a panic attack too.'

'At least you were there to help.'

'I tried my best. She's nice, really, just a bit prone to getting herself in a tizzy. Anyway, how about you? Do anything fun this weekend?'

Nathan sighed, picking at a thread on his trousers. 'Not much. Had the kids Saturday, which was nice. We went to the park and got ice cream. Basic dad stuff. Ordered a pizza and watched movies in the evening. But then they went home and the loneliness settled back in, which is why I gamed for more or less the rest of the weekend. Plus, I need to sort out somewhere to live because they're coming to do that asbestos removal I was telling you about.'

Nina knew all too well the feeling of emptiness at the weekend. 'Sounds sad.'

'Just wish I could see them more often.' Nathan turned his wrist to glance at his watch. 'Speaking of which, I should get back to the office. But thanks for listening and for the noodles. Thanks for the lunch, Neens.'

'Anytime. I want a full report. It's a new recipe.' Nina smiled. 'See you tomorrow.'

'Same time. Same place.'

Nina gathered her things and strolled away from the bench towards the pond. She mulled over their conversation. She understood Nathan's feelings and possibly how sad he was. Though she had no clue what it would be like to watch your best friend with your kids. After losing Andrew, she'd grieved not only him but her whole future. All of it gone in one fell swoop as if someone had zapped her and flicked a switch, meaning an end to everything she'd thought her life was going to be. Strangely, it was the little things that had been the hardest. No more lazy Sundays being brought breakfast in bed, no one to just chat with after work and watch Netflix with, no one's laundry at the end of the bed to tutt at and throw down to the laundry bin by the door. Loads of small, little, precious, inconsequential humdrum moments gone forever. All of it crumbled around her head. She stared at a duck and squeezed her eyes tightly shut. She wasn't going to even think about it. She didn't have the energy to go there again.

~

The following day, Nina was running late for work. She'd been up half the night reading and had lost track of time, meaning she'd got up late. As she hurried down the hall from her flat, juggling a coffee, her handbag, and her phone, she nearly collided with a man coming out of Mrs Gilbert's doorway.

'Oh goodness! Sorry,' Nina exclaimed as a slosh of coffee landed on her blouse.

The man gave her a friendly smile. 'Not to worry, no harm done. You must be Nina from next door. I'm Rob, Mrs Gilbert's son.'

Nina blinked in surprise. She hadn't realised Mrs Gilbert had any family living nearby. She'd never seen him or indeed heard of him before. Nina glanced anxiously at her watch. 'Is your mum okay?'

'Yep, she's fine.'

'Rightio, great. Look, I'd love to chat, but I'm running criminally late for work. Lovely meeting you!' Nina bustled away down the stairs, making a mental note to ask Mrs Gilbert about her son later. It was all going on; broken arms, mystery sons, leaks in sinks. It was the most that had been going on in her life for ages.

There certainly wasn't much going on at work, and her day

passed in its usual monotonous blur of emails, meetings, and mind-numbing spreadsheets. By the time Nina switched off her computer at the end of the day and found herself back at her flat, she knocked to see how Mrs Gilbert was, then went into her place, closed the door, and let out a sigh.

She popped the kettle on to boil, and as she washed her hands and then waited, she scrolled idly through her phone. She had a few notifications from Instagram and Facebook, plus a reminder about the grief group meeting the following week that she had zero intention of attending. Nothing interesting on her phone. There never really was. She scrolled through a Facebook reader group she was in looking for book recommendations and perused a few posts on container gardening in small spaces. Then, with a cup of tea in hand, she curled up on the sofa and tried to decide what to watch. She was debating between a new crime documentary or a subtitled French film when her phone pinged with an email alert. She squinted as she looked at the first line and then at the sender's address. She wrinkled her nose, not knowing who it was from. Sick to the back teeth of spam and concerned after reading an article about leaving spammy emails undeleted, she clicked on the email with the intention of then reporting it and scanned the first line. She then bolted upright, nearly spilling her tea and dropping her phone.

Hello Nina,

Thank you for the message about The Summer Hotel, in Lovely Bay. I appreciate you taking the time to share a bit about yourself. My name is Jill, and I'm the niece of the owner of the property. I have to say, your email made me chuckle. You sound like a lovely, real person, which is precisely the sort of person we've been looking for. You wouldn't believe the number of house-sitters who profess to spend their day doing yoga, ha ha. They also seem to think our place would be great for padding their Instagram feeds with content.

The property is/was my aunt's (she recently passed away). It used to be a B&B back in the day. She owned (still does at the moment) a string of them, and this one, sadly, hasn't been open for a while. It was at one point a hotel and still officially carries that name today. It hasn't really been fully updated in decades, but the views are stunning and it holds many happy memories. I usually oversee most of the properties, depending on what part of the country they are in (some of them are now full-on Airbnb businesses). I've been travelling for a while and the Lovely Bay property needs overseeing - just so you know there is a view to sell in the future. So far, I've not had much luck with the house-sitters.
Based on your email, I think you could be a great fit. Are you able to have a video call to chat further? I'm in and out of Wi-Fi coverage but can make it work. Let me know what you think!
Warm regards,
Jill

Nina read the message twice more, then put her phone down in shock. She honestly hadn't expected to hear back, much less receive such an enthusiastic reply. She made a funny face as her mind whirled, and she tried to process the email. The responses must have been really bad if this woman wanted to chat with her. There was no way she'd expected a reply from her overly honest, oversharing email. It seemed Jill had read her ramblings and liked the sound of her. How very, very strange. What were the odds?

Nina's gut reaction was an off-the-bat, emphatic no. The idea seemed ludicrous. Why would she even consider inhabiting a remote property in a place she knew nothing about and didn't know a single soul? She was happy enough on her own; she was used to the widow label these days, and she thrived on routine and the familiar comforts of her London flat, her little plants, reading, and cooking.

Yet, something about the reply made something happen to

her inside. A feeling she hadn't felt for a very long time. A tiny part of her was intrigued. Maybe fate was doing something here? Not that she believed in fate. Maybe a change *was* as good as a rest, as Sophie had said. She *did* have quite a lonely existence. Her brain started to play the what-if game. What if she went? What if she stayed? Would she regret it? What if she had a good time? What if she hated it? What if she *did* need a change? What if she threw caution to the wind?

Nina mused it for a few minutes, reread the email, went to call Sophie, and before the practical side of her brain could talk her out of it, she typed a quick response.

Hi Jill.
Thanks for your reply.
I'd love to have a chat. Thank you so much for considering me. I have to confess I'm quite surprised but flattered that you think I could be a good fit after my initial email.
I can do any evening next week or anytime on Saturday. Looking forward to chatting about Lovely Bay.
Best,
Nina Lavendar

With her heart racing and without being sure why she was doing it, Nina hit send. Too late to back out now. She'd officially committed to at least having a chat with this person named Jill, who she had no clue about. The whole scenario felt surreal.

Nina's thoughts raced as she tried to concentrate on Netflix, then she gave up and poured herself a glass of cordial. All she could think about was Lovely Bay. She glanced over to the fireplace and the long line of pictures of Andrew. She waited to feel the familiar prick of tears at the corners of her eyes but oddly, they didn't come. Was the real, raw part of the grieving over? She knew it would never, ever entirely go away like they'd assured her in the grief group it would. She knew she'd always be sad, but whatever it was about this Lovely Bay thing, she was feeling different.

Nina squeezed her eyes shut, thought about it and opened them again with a start. She knew what it was. Since the day she'd got the call from Andrew's work to say he was not in a good way at all, it had been as if someone or something had dropped her down into a well. She'd lived in the well ever since. Dark, lonely, and weighing down on her at all times. But the Lovely Bay thing had made a tiny bit of light appear at the top of the well along with a small, minuscule little dot of something deep down in the pit of her stomach. As her eyes focused on the picture on the mantelpiece of her and Andrew on honeymoon, she knew what the feeling was – hope.

5

'Sorry, darling, I don't think I heard you correctly. Where did you say you were going again? Was it near Padstow? Cornwall, wasn't it? Marjory next door has a little cottage down there. Remember, we went there when you were little? Lovely part of the world, Cornwall, and so nice in some parts of it, if you know what I mean. Other parts, I've heard, not so much. Lots of economic problems down there these days. And drugs, too, what's the name of that drug that's rife again? The one that makes you like a zombie? Anyway, I blame it on Blair myself.'

Nina sighed. Her mum, along with her sister, had selective hearing. Nina, sadly, wasn't particularly close to either of them. Not that she would ever tell them or anyone that. It had just always felt as if Nina was the odd one out. It was fine. She could deal with it. 'Lovely Bay. It's just down the road from Sophie's.'

'What, where that film star lives? Hugh Grant, wasn't it?'

Nina shook her head and tried not to get irritated. She'd told her mum her plans multiple times. 'It's not Hugh Grant. No, it's about twenty minutes from Sophie's.'

'Sorry, where is it again?'

Nina relayed the location again, enunciating each syllable clearly.

'Darling, I don't even really know where that is. It's like the back end of nowhere. Why would you even go there?'

Nina kept her sigh quiet. 'I've already explained this. Sophie thought I could do with a change, and it all kind of fell into place as if someone was telling me to go there and see what happens. I just have this feeling as if it's something I'm meant to do. Fate or something. I don't know.' Nina was going to say hope but changed her mind. That would open a whole can of worms.

'Don't be *ridiculous*, darling.' Nina's mum scoffed. 'You know what I think about fate. People use the fate word to make excuses about all sorts of reckless things. There is no such thing as fate.'

Whatever. Nina rolled her eyes even though her mum couldn't see her through the phone as she closed the top drawer on the dresser in her bedroom. 'Well, I'm going, fate or not. I can't change my mind now. I would really let the woman down.'

'Darling, it's just a silly little thing on Facebook. You don't owe anyone anything.'

'It's not silly, Mum,' Nina said, trying not to let frustration seep into her tone.

'I still don't understand why you'd want to spend time in some little backwater town. You have to be *so* careful these days, you really do. I blame that on Blair too. His lot are going to get in again soon, too. Meaning we're all going to have to be really careful not to mention what's going to happen to the economy. Honestly, Nina, with that in mind, you really should be thinking about battening down the hatches, not going off to remote parts of the country. And at this time of year, no less! Won't it be dreadfully gloomy and cold?'

'That's part of the appeal. It might be really beautiful there at this time of year. It'll be quiet and peaceful. It will give me a chance to...'

Her mum made a little harrumphing noise. 'Well, I can't say I understand it, darling, but you always were a bit odd.'

Nina shook her head. She was well aware that she often perplexed her very mainstream, suburban mother. 'I'm going to go for it. A chance to get some perspective and clarity. Since Andrew...' she trailed off, throat tightening.

Her mum was quiet for a moment. 'I know how much you've struggled. I just worry about you rattling around all alone in some creaky old, nasty B&B. Are you sure being isolated is the best thing? I was watching something about mental health the other day. You really do have to be careful with it.'

Nina shook her head. Her mum didn't know how much she'd struggled. No one did. Sophie had half an idea. 'I won't really be alone as such. Sophie is just down the road, so I can see her anytime. And I think peace and quiet could be just what I need.' Nina wasn't sure she did need peace and quiet but her mum didn't need to know that.

'Well, it's your decision, darling. What's happening with the flat again? You did say.'

'Nathan is staying in it. The bloke who works in the office next door. I did tell you. His building is having asbestos removal, so I said he could move in until it's finished.'

'Ahh, yes, you did say. At least the flat will have someone living in it then.'

'I'm only planning to stay for a bit. It's not like it's forever.'

'Alright, darling, keep me posted on how it goes.'

'Will do.'

'Let me tell you, though, you won't last long down there. Honestly, Nina, mark my words. I don't think you're doing the right thing.'

Nina nodded, eager to get off the phone. 'Noted.'

6

Nina felt almost removed from the world as she looked out the train window as snatches of countryside trundled past in a blur of colour. She fiddled with her engagement ring which she now wore on her right hand, her wedding ring was tucked away in her bag, and watched as more people got off the train. The closer the train got towards Lovely Bay, the fewer people were left in the carriage. She'd changed trains about halfway into the journey, and as it had made its way south, it had slowly emptied itself of most of its passengers. She re-read the instructions from Jill and realised that she should have listened to what Jill had said about the journey. Jill had given her two ways to get to The Summer Hotel. One was to take the express limited stops service from St Pancras and then hop on a bus. The other route was to change trains and get on the riverboat. Jill had said the second route was slower but much prettier and a pleasant way to arrive on a nice day. Nina had decided to go for that option, but it was really dragging and it wasn't a nice day. The sky was grey, it had been drizzling since she'd left her flat in London, and she'd already exhausted the little flask of coffee and homemade flapjacks she'd packed for the journey.

Taking out her phone, she flipped through the pictures Jill had sent her after their third video call and read through the detailed instructions about the property. Using her finger and thumb to enlarge the pictures, she nodded. It looked nice enough for a place to get away from it all for a while. Jill had said it was a little bit tired inside and needed some TLC here and there, and Nina was actually quite up for that. Some therapeutic decluttering and cleaning would do her the power of good. She stared at the pictures as the train took off again. The little private beach didn't look too bad, nor did the Adirondack chairs on the left side of the property underneath a tree. She read through Jill's notes about the electricity box and trip switches, the few paragraphs about the history of the place, and how the front section seen from the road today was in fact a timber addition added in the late thirties to the older property that rambled its way down to the sea. She read about how the living quarters needed to be cleared out and packed up of what remained of Jill's late aunt's things.

She flicked to her emails and scanned down, then frowned at an email from work. Strange, she had a few weeks of holiday to use up and hadn't expected to hear anything from them at this point. She read through agog. She definitely hadn't expected to hear via her inbox that she and most of the department's jobs were being made redundant. *She was redundant.* What the actual? Nina read the email three times, shook her head, dropped her phone in her lap, and stared out the window. Redundant, no job, given the flick just like that. That was the end of that then. Nina was a bit numb, but funnily enough, she didn't actually care that much. Yeah, she'd need to find another job because she needed an income, but Andrew's life insurance had paid off the flat and their other property, so though she was far from rolling around in money, as long as she was *very* careful it wasn't paramount for her to get a job right away. She'd get by.

The train continued on its journey as Nina read more about

Lovely Bay until the guard came over the tannoy, instructing passengers for Lovely Bay to alight. Nina heaved her overfull backpack onto her back, clicked up the handle on her case, secured her handbag over her left shoulder, and balanced a large duffel bag on top of her suitcase. She'd told herself she wouldn't come with much, but as she'd packed, she'd more or less thrown in the kitchen sink. In for a penny, in for a pound.

She stepped off the train, loaded down with her belongings, and wondered where to go. As the train pulled away, she stood for a second and looked at the pretty Victorian station in front of her. An old station house with two chimneys, beautiful fretwork, and at the top still displaying its old advertising signs from years gone by. She watched pretty stripy blue and white bunting flapping around the station house and platform signs for Lovely Bay. Ambling over towards the exit she stood and read the plaque on the wall telling her that the Lovely and Lovely Bay and District Railway Station Museum, built in 1858, with the only moveable platform in the country was open on Fridays, Saturdays, and Sundays. She turned to look for a moveable platform and raised her eyebrows in surprise as she spied it on the other side of the tracks. The plaque told her that the platform had been installed in 1888 to cope with the increasing length of passenger trains heading to the coast and resort of Lovely Bay in the summer. It wasn't possible to extend the platforms due to the lie of the land, so moveable platforms were devised to swing across the track. Quaint.

Through the constant drizzle, Nina inhaled as she looked around. Quite nice. In fact, very nice. Fresh coastal air with a side of seaside rain. She examined her map, looked up and over to the other side of the station, and made her way to the exit. Struggling with the weight of her bags and pulling her case behind her, a very attractive woman with coral-pink lipstick and deep brown eyes in a railway uniform and hat came out of the station house. 'Morning.'

Nina wasn't sure if it was still morning, and she wondered if the woman was actually speaking to her. She felt as if she had been travelling all day. 'Morning.'

'Brought the kitchen sink to Lovely with you, have you?' The woman chuckled.

Nina reciprocated with a chuckle. 'Feels like it.'

The woman shrugged on a blue wax raincoat with a stripy lining in the hood and a white emblem on the breast pocket over the top of her railway uniform. 'Where are you off to in Lovely Bay with that little lot, then?'

Nina raised her chin in the direction of the river. 'I'm staying over on the other side of Lovely Bay, actually.'

The woman flipped over her left wrist and frowned. 'You'd better get a wriggle on if you're going to be getting on the boat.'

Nina shook her head. 'No, no. The website timetable said it comes every half hour, more for the commuters in the mornings and evenings.'

The woman locked the door to the stationmaster's house behind her and tucked a huge bunch of keys onto the loop of her belt. 'It might *say* that on the timetable online, yep, but it's Friday.'

Nina frowned. Was the fact that it was Friday meant to mean anything to her? 'It says on the website, Monday to Friday it runs on the hour and the half-hour, more in the commuter hours, rain or shine, and that it runs to a Sunday timetable on, well, Sundays.'

'Indeed, but not on Fridays. Clive is at his French lesson and Colin goes to lunch on Fridays down the coast here. A little island you get to by ferry. Yeah, a girl, well not a girl these days, who used to live here in Lovely moved down that way. He thinks none of us realise. He reckons he goes to some café called Darlings because of the quality of the coffee. We might look stupid and have a bit of an accent, us Lovelies, but we're not. Remember that.'

Nina wasn't sure why she was being told something about an island and coffee or who Colin and Clive were. 'Right, sorry, so what are you saying about the boat timetable?'

'I'm saying that Colin won't be back for the next run until school time, meaning unless you want to walk with all of that lot the long way round, you're going to need to hotfoot it there and get on the next boat, which leaves very soon. There won't be another one for a while after that.'

'I see. Thanks for letting me know.'

The woman took a few steps, opened a side gate, craned her neck, and looked down the road. 'Here, come through this way; it's quicker. Go over that footbridge and you'll see it. I'll What-sApp him and tell him to wait for you.'

'Oh, right. Okay. Thanks. How will he know it's me?'

The woman made a funny face. 'Trust me, he'll know. We don't get many like you at this time of year, loaded down as if they're about to climb Mount Everest.'

Nina wasn't sure if the woman was being nice or not. She seemed friendly enough. 'Thanks for your help.'

'No dramas. Name's Nancy if you're interested. I'm sure I'll see you around if you're staying for more than a week, which by the looks of you, you are. Yeah, since COVID we get a few more like you at this time of year. Never last long.' Nancy flicked her thumb to her fingers in a quacking movement. 'Blah, blah, blah, they're going to work from home by the sea. Yadda, yadda, it's so idyllic working here. Digital nomads, they call themselves nowadays. Really? Then they get fed up with it when they can't get this, that, or the other. What was it? Batch brew coffee or something. Hah, hah, hah. Anyway, work is work is work if you ask me. Passive income, they always say.' Nancy rolled her eyes. 'Work-life balance my left foot. They soon get fed up with us and go back. Most of 'em anyway.'

Nina went to explain that she wasn't staying for a week, nor was she working from home. She considered for a brief second revealing about the house-sitting, that she needed a change of scene, that Andrew was dead, that she'd just been made redundant, that she could do with a bit of perspective on what the heck she was going to do with the rest of her life. That she'd lost her husband and lost her way. There was no way she was going to go into that, and no way this extremely attractive woman was going to be interested in the slightest. 'Thanks.'

Nancy typed with her thumbs like lightning over her phone screen. She looked back up. 'There you go. He's waiting for you.'

'Thank you again, err, Nancy.'

'My pleasure. Have a name, do you?'

Nina wasn't sure what to think about this Nancy or giving her her name. It wasn't very often Transport for London staff even looked in her direction, let alone asked her her name. 'Umm, Nina.'

'You sure about that?' Nancy chuckled as she waved a lunchbox in front of her face. 'I'm off for my lunch. Oh, by the way, make sure you have the Lovely Chowder, you must have read about it, oh and go to the chocolate shop and tell Birdie I sent you if you go to the chemist. Yeah, don't forget the chowder – a stay here in Lovely Bay is nothing without it. You won't forget it. We all live on the stuff in this part of the world. While we're making our passive incomes by the sea, hah hah hah.'

Nina smiled. She hadn't had chowder for a long time. 'Thanks, I'll look out for it.'

'You do that. You won't miss it. I'll send Colin another message and tell him you'll be there shortly. Enjoy the delights of Lovely Bay.'

'Thank you very much. Will do.'

7

I n the constant drizzle, Nina hurried away from the station across a small dead-end road, past the back of the afore-mentioned moveable platform, and onto a path. She could see glimpses of what she assumed was the River Lovely up ahead. She struggled to pull her hood up with her left hand and looked around. The only other person she could see from the path was a man on the far side of the river with a dog and what looked like a café with one person sitting outside also with a dog. Her case wheels bumped on the path as she dragged it along and made her way towards the river.

She tried to get her bearings and attempted to remember where the bay was in relation to the main part of Lovely, and the prom, and the other part where the dunes went down to the sea. Now that she'd arrived, it all felt quite different from what she'd imagined in her head. The weather wasn't helping, though the colours on the river were amazing and the sky seemed to go on for miles. A smudge of beautiful greys, blues, and purples almost lit it up as it continued to drizzle. As she got closer to the river, the colours changed again as if perhaps she was standing in a muted watercolour painting on a wall.

Nina followed the path as it veered to the left, and she felt herself taking in big lungfuls of the air. She frowned; how odd – the air felt so fresh and so clean. What even was it? She couldn't quite put her finger on it. She'd read about the Lovely Air from her desk at work and had fully rolled her eyes that it had a name. Now she was wondering if there was such a thing as Lovely Air. Was what she'd read in fact true? She decided she didn't really care, wondered if it did any good for grief, and took another deep, full lungful as she continued down the path.

As she hustled along with her suitcase behind her, she passed a couple of what looked like day-trippers with matching red anoraks and backpacks. On the right, a small car park backed onto a narrow sliver of river beach where a camper van had its boot door up and a couple were sitting in big jumpers, beanies, and with steaming mugs of tea in their hands. Two, what she thought might be windsurfers were dragging some kind of board up the strip of sand and a woman wearing the same coat as Nancy in the train station was pushing a double buggy and chatting away to her children.

Nina took it all in as she made for the riverboat. There were more people around near the river than she thought there was going to be; though it was hardly pumping. In the distance, she could see the lighthouse she'd seen in the pictures looking as if it was protruding from the tops of roofs, and could see on her left a little line of squat, timber-clad shops in the pastel colours she'd read about.

A few minutes later, she could see the River Lovely fully. Every few metres or so, jetties snaked out into the water. Loads of them lined up to attention as far as the eye could see. The river glinted and she could see a boat at the end of the jetty in front of her. As she got closer, a sign told her to 'Please Queue Here. Dogs Welcome.' Nina hurried over the timber-slatted boards underfoot. Her case clattered, her handbag strap slipped off her shoulder, and the duffel bag on top of her case slid around from its position to hanging behind the case and drag-ging along the ground. She could see a few passengers sitting on the boat and a man standing in a small shed-type building at the end of the jetty. As she finally got to the shed, the man stepped out. Nina took him in – a navy blue seafaring jumper, oilskin trousers, a pair of sunglasses on his head, the same blue wax coat as the one Nancy had been wearing, and a works-outdoors tan. The man beamed and chortled. 'Ahoy, there. You made it across land to get to us. Brought the kitchen sink with you, have you?'

Nina wasn't sure if the man was joking or not. She was a bit breathless from hurrying with the weight of her bags. 'Thanks for waiting for me.'

'No worries.' The man held out his hand for her case. 'Colin. Welcome to Lovely.'

Nina coughed, struggled to get the duffel bag from the case, and then handed it over to him. 'Thank you. Sorry, I had every-thing planned so that I could take my time. I didn't realise you weren't running on Friday lunchtimes. I was going to have a sit here for a bit when I looked at it on the Google thingy. You know, when you drop the little blue man and you have a look around. However, I was hoping for sunshine or at least for it to be dry. I mean, really, who was I even kidding?' Nina stopped, realising she'd been blabbering.

'All good.' Colin lit up a weathered smile.

'Thanks. The woman at the station said she'd message you.'

'Yes, our Nancy. We do that down here, us Lovelies. You know, wait for each other and stuff.' Colin winked. 'It's not hard.'

'Right.'

Colin picked up Nina's case as if it weighed nothing and popped it in the back of the boat. He then did the same with the duffel bag and Nina's backpack. Chuckling, he held out his hand for Nina to step onto the boat. A few minutes later, Colin was at the back of the boat, Nina was sitting on a bench with her duffel bag on her lap, and the boat was puttering away from the jetty. Nina watched the far side of the river as a few houses came into view and started to slowly slide past. In the far distance going the other way, she could see the dunes she'd read about and wondered if there really were deer and otters. As the boat chugged along, they went past lots of the same jetties and so many boats tied up almost everywhere. Owning a boat around this place was clearly a thing.

As she sat and stared, she tried to get her bearings and take it all in. With the motion of the boat, she found herself thinking about the previous few years. She thought about the flat, Mrs Gilbert, Nathan, and the people at work. All of them were nice enough, but there wasn't really much else in her life. The scenery changed and a line of houses backed onto the river. She could see in the far distance the lighthouse she'd seen raved about on TripAdvisor, an RNLI lifeboat station, the back of what looked like an old industrial warehouse of some sort, and a church spire poking up into the purple-grey sky.

Colin tapped the back of the bench. 'Know your way, do you?'

Nina nodded. She didn't really know the way, of course. She'd never set foot in the place in her life. She had no clue really where she was going or what she was doing. Part of her wasn't sure why she was there at all, but it did look quite pretty. 'I do.'

'Right, good job. Weather's coming in later.'

Nina frowned. What did that mean? 'What, a storm?'

'Not a storm as such, no, but we're forecast for a bit of a rain battering. When it rains, it pours in Lovely and Lovely Bay.'

'Thanks for letting me know.'

'Meaning we might well get a power cut, just so you know. If you're needing to make dinner or going anywhere, like down the pub or anything.'

'Thank you.'

'Chances are we'll be fine, but you never can tell down here in our little neck of the woods, see. The power cuts come and go. Every year they tell us it's all fixed. Every year, we get cut off when it rains hard. They reckon the computer says it's not that at all. Doesn't matter what we say about it being linked to the rain. Nah. We know nothing, us Lovelies. Thick as mince, they think, see.'

Nina noted that the first and only two people she'd met had both referred to themselves as Lovelies. Was that charming? Possibly or just odd.

The boat puttered along, passing more little jetties extending from tall white properties backing onto the river. Nina watched another woman in one of the blue wax coats with the striped hoods and a fluffy white dog walking along the shore path. Behind the houses, trees swayed in the wind, and she spied more of the same bunting she'd seen at the station.

From the front of the boat, Colin called out to the woman in the coat on the path, 'Alright, Daph. How was it?'

The woman waved, beamed, and did a thumbs-up sign. 'I have the all clear!'

Colin shouted back. 'Great! Fantastic news.'

'Tell Clive for me.'

'Will do.'

Colin caught Nina's eye. 'You'll be needing one of those jackets she's wearing if you're staying a while.'

Nina side-eyed. 'Will I?'

'You get 'em in the shop on the corner by the chocolate shop, but you'll have to put your name down. Sold all over the world. You might not know it yet, but you'll need one. Put one of those on and it'll get you through any weather. Ask me how I know.' Colin laughed at his own joke. 'If anyone asks you to go on the waiting list, do it.'

Nina had no idea what Colin was talking about. He loved the sound of his own voice. 'Thanks for the tip.'

'We know weather in Lovely. We get four seasons in one day, any time of the year. Our coats are designed in Lovely and made in Lovely. We know a lot about sun, rain, wind, and patchy weather forecasts in Lovely Bay. Us Lovelies know weather.'

Nina looked around and realised that a person in the row in front of her was wearing the said coat. And one in the row in front of that and a toddler who was standing on his mum's lap was wearing a mini version. She turned her mouth upside down and considered as she felt the dampness in the insides of her elbows. Colin could possibly have a point if the weather didn't improve.

Despite the drizzle, the river was pretty and something about the colours and the sky made Nina feel a little bit excited about her decision to get out of London. She took a deep breath, inhaling the scent of the shore mingled with briny sea air. For the first time in ages, her lungs felt as if they were taking in all sorts of goodness. She sat and just stared out at the water, lost in a world of her own as Colin navigated around clusters of boats moored on either side of the river as they bobbed around and glinted in the drizzle.

She saw Colin catch her watching him calling out to people walking along the side of the river. 'You'll find folks around here are mostly a friendly bunch. We look after our own in Lovely Bay.'

Nina nodded. Probably a load of old hogwash, but from what she'd seen so far, people appeared to be amiable enough. Not that she really cared. She was just after a bit of a change for a couple of months. She hardly needed people to be friendly to her. She wasn't really going to be talking to anyone anyway.

After passing under one of the many little bridges Nina had read about, Colin steered them towards a dock on the right riverbank and she checked her phone that she was in the right place. Colin manoeuvred the boat against the dock and hopped ashore to tie them off. Two other passengers, one of them an elderly woman wearing one of the blue coats with the striped hood, gathered their belongings and tottered onto the landing. Nina stood, balanced herself, and slung her duffel bag over her shoulder. She grabbed the handle of her case and flipped the hood on her now very damp coat up so it covered her head.

'You sure you'll be alright finding your way from here?' Colin asked. 'Ask anyone if you get lost.' He pointed into the distance. 'This side is Lovely Bay and the river, that side over there is Lovely itself and the prom, the main shops, and picture palace. We intersperse Lovely with Lovely Bay a lot. Make sense?'

Nina nodded. She'd studied her phone map for long enough and had thought she knew where she was going. Now, not so much. She wasn't going to be telling anyone where she was going or asking for directions, though. First rule of a woman on her own in a strange place. 'I'm sure I'll manage. Thank you so much, though.'

'Right. Well, enjoy your holiday! Give a shout if you need anything. See you on the way out when you leave.'

Little did Colin know that Nina wasn't on holiday. He didn't need to know that.

With a smile, Colin untied the boat and puttered off down-river. Nina balanced her case for a second, checked her phone, and then set out in the direction he had indicated, wheels bumping on the uneven pavement. The path followed the shoreline for a bit and then turned to go through buildings and a row of pretty shops. A sign above the door of a pale pink building announced 'Lovely Bay Cakes', a weathered old bench sitting under a pink scalloped awning invited a sit-down. She kept her eye out for the chocolate shop but didn't see it. What she did see were a fair few people in the striped hooded wax coats. As she continued along, the shops gave way to a little green with a bench and what looked like a war memorial, rows of neat brick cottages in pastel tones of pale blue, lemon, and pink. Window boxes overflowing with pansies punctuated the greys and purples of the drizzle, and a tabby cat washing itself in a window paused to watch Nina pass with slitty green eyes.

Nina continued to follow the directions on her phone and as she turned down the road for The Summer Hotel, she wasn't sure what to expect. Just as she was ambling along, feeling as if she had a sack full of bricks on her back, a woman came out of a door a few doors down. 'Yoohoo! You must be Nina! I'm June. So pleased you found us alright. Jill said you'd be here about this time, and you are. I've been looking out for you.'

Nina quickly deduced this friendly woman was the neighbour Jill had detailed in her notes.

June touched the elbow of Nina's soggy coat. 'Dreadful weather, isn't it? I was hoping we'd have sunny skies to show the place off to you when you arrived. Never mind, the colours on the river are pretty when it's like this. It won't last long, it never does in Lovely. We get four seasons in one day here. The sun will be out tomorrow. They're saying a lot of rain tonight, though.'

'Yes, sunshine would be nice.'

'You need a Lovely coat if you're staying, which Jill said you will be.' June touched her chin for a second and tilted her head. 'You'll find an original or two in the depths of that house somewhere.'

Nina was beginning to realise that the coats were a thing. 'Someone else told me about the coats, too. Something about a waiting list?'

June chortled. 'Oh, you won't get far around here if you stay longer than a few weeks without one of our coats. Sorts us out from everyone else. You might be lucky enough to go on the waiting list, or as I said, there are a few in the house.'

'Ha, right, I see.' Nina didn't really see.

'Anyway, if you need anything, just knock.'

'Thanks, yes, you're in the notes.'

'Not sure what good I can do,' June said with a smile.

'Hopefully, you won't need to do anything.'

'Nope. Jill mentioned you're going to be clearing out the living quarters…'

'Yes, I am.'

'Good luck with that. The old place itself hasn't hosted guests in a long, long while. I was trying to work out how long it's been. Sad really. The last few sitters have not really been, how can I say? Not really suitable for Lovely. Anyway, it makes a nice escape from the city down here.'

'Yes, a change is as good as a rest, as they say.'

'Oh yes, and you might meet a few ghosts of guests past over there.'

Nina smiled, not sure she liked the sound of that. 'Eeek.'

'Joking of course! Gorgeous view from the back there; I never tire of watching the water. The way it goes on forever, constantly changing, but always the same. One of the best things about Lovely Bay, if you ask me.'

Nina nodded. 'I was thinking the same thing earlier when I was on the boat. It makes your problems feel smaller somehow.'

June regarded her with kind eyes. 'Exactly, yep. So, how did Lovely find you?'

'Pardon?'

'Ach, sorry, I mean, how did you find our Jill's post?'

'Umm, it was sort of by accident actually. A friend passed it on.'

'Yeah, thought as much. That's normally how it goes.'

'What do you mean?'

'The old wives' tales of Lovely Bay say that if you were meant to find this place, you will. You know? Lovely Bay is a bit off the beaten track, but we're gooduns down here. Lovelies will always have your back.'

'Ahh, yes, right.' Nina wondered if June had lost her marbles. She'd have to try and steer clear of her.

June pointed into the far distance. 'The sea on that side and the river on this side have their way of working their magic with you down this way too; you mark my words.'

Nina nodded. Did the Lovely water work with lost husbands? Did it zip up broken hearts? She doubted it. She'd need more than a bit of seawater to work its magic on her that she knew for a fact.

8

Nina stood in the road looking at The Summer Hotel. Umm, yeah. She didn't know what she'd been concocting in her head, but this wasn't it. Obviously, she'd seen the pictures but she'd embellished them somewhat. In her head there was a gorgeous, if a bit tatty, hotel, a blue sky, and a pale sandy beach in the background; it must have magically disappeared. She stepped three steps to the left and squinted. Yeah, okay, check, the river beach was there just about. In the drizzle, the sand was rather dull. Then there was the front of the building that lived in a pretty greetings card picture inside her mind – clad in timber, painted a pale blue, shutters, an open door, pots of flowers. Oh dear. Granted there were timber shutters, however, in the picture in her head, none of them were falling off. The imaginary place had bunting strung across the font. She wasn't sure where that was from, but it definitely wasn't fluttering in the breeze on the building in front of her; dead weeds were.

Then, of course, there was the fact that the actual building itself was much bigger than she'd thought. And sort of much more imposing. The pictures she'd seen on Google were clearly from a long time before, and they all showed mostly the front section of the house, which Jill had told her was an addition. She retraced her steps along the pavement and walked to the other side of the street so she could see more clearly. It looked as if random bits had been bolted on willy-nilly, here, there, and everywhere.

The whole of the front garden was completely overgrown. So much for a little bit of tidying up and upkeep. The porch verandah she'd secretly swooned over in the pictures was covered in ivy, and one of the balustrades was missing. Nina stood in the road, squinting up at the rambling old building. She tried not to let her heart sink. This wasn't exactly what she had envisioned when she'd been sitting on her sofa in her flat thinking about house-sitting by the sea. In her mind, she'd pictured a quaint, postcard-worthy seaside affair with pretty blue paint and freshly whitewashed woodwork. The shutters in her Pinterest-worthy version were in pristine condition, window boxes spilled with healthy plants, and the whole place had radiated a sort of cosy, fuzzy, mend-her-broken-heart, seaside escape.

Reality wasn't quite the postcard dream. The paint was faded and peeling, the roof shingles weathered and patchy in places. Several shutters hung crooked or were missing slats entirely. Definitely no cheerful flowers or bunting in sight. Standing in the drizzle, Nina tried to think good things. There was at least a windswept beach at the back, even if the blue ripples in her head were actually a dirty, quite unfriendly, and definitely English slate-grey.

Nina didn't go in the gate but walked around to the far side of the rambling structure. The building's full size and haphazard additions were at the fore. She shook her head, not quite sure what to think. The pictures she'd seen online were nothing like what was in front of her. The images must have been cropped to show the building directly front-on. In real life, the place was easily three times larger than she'd expected, with mismatched wings sticking out at odd angles all over the place. Jill had mentioned the main section was an old house that had been added onto over the generations. Jill hadn't been telling porkies about that.

She made her way back to the gate; the persistent drizzle continued to land on her now wet coat and luggage as she stepped onto the path and looked at the garden. What greeted her wasn't too pretty; knee-high grass, weeds choking the flower beds, vines engulfing just about everything. The porch was a joke – she'd dreamed about sitting on a chair with a hot chocolate and a rug, where she'd ponder what the heck she was going to do with her life. She wouldn't be doing that from this porch, that was for sure. She'd be sitting amongst an ugly tangle of dead vines and missing rails.

Standing in the rain contemplating the chipped paint and missing balustrades, she turned back to look down the road and considered walking straight back to the train station or calling an Uber. Clearly, the old place had fallen into more significant disrepair than Jill had let on. She should have guessed any old seaside building dating back to the early 1800s, that had been more or less empty for a while, wouldn't be exactly in pristine condition, but she'd let herself fall for something that wasn't true.

What had she let herself in for? She stopped a prick of tears at the corner of her eyes and straightened her shoulders. She must *not* get sad. So it wasn't quite what she had conjured up in her mind. So it needed more work than she had bargained for – so what? She'd told just about everyone that she hadn't come looking for a holiday. She'd said that she was having a bit of a change that would be as good as a rest. Healing, that's what she'd told herself in the middle of the night when she'd been lying awake with grief.

Perhaps, in a way, the old, slightly decaying hotel was fitting. It looked like she felt. Something in her head was telling her to stay one night. She'd almost certainly made a mistake, but she'd deal with it. Somehow there was a tiny bit of her still saying that Lovely Bay was the right thing to do. Even though the hotel looked dreadful, borderline scary, and she was nervous, anxious, really missed Andrew, and didn't fancy spending a night alone in the place, there was a little bit of her that somehow still felt the hope she'd first felt in the flat. What even was that? Something sort of strange and a bit twirly in her stomach. Maybe it was just fear. Nina couldn't really tell.

She did know that since Andrew had passed away, she'd not done anything much other than go to work. She'd never been on holiday, never got a new job, never taken a different route on the tube, never bought anything much. This was the first thing she'd done that wasn't part of the Nina and Andrew story. Even the death bit had been about him and her. This wasn't. Lovely Bay wasn't. Andrew wasn't part of it. Nina felt the wham of grief start to rush towards her, the old familiar spasm on the right side of her chest, but she stopped it before it got a grip. Bugger that. She wasn't going to let that happen, at least not tonight. She told herself she'd give it one night.

She looked down the road again, thought about the journey, decided she had little choice now but to stay, and picked her way up the weed-choked path to the weathered front door. She'd email Jill the next morning and tell her exactly what she thought.

9

Nina opened her phone as she got to the front door, reread the instructions, left her suitcase on the porch, thumped down the steps, turned, and walked down the side of the house in search of an elusive 'tradesman's door'. She squeezed around a conservatory with huge amounts of peeling paint and walked past a green gate in an old Victorian brick wall. The drizzle continued to fall, her jeans were now soaking wet, and her feet squelched in her trainers. A happy camper, she was not.

Finally getting to the door, she half expected someone to jump out and tell her the whole thing was a joke. She was more than surprised to see what appeared to be a newly installed keypad by the door. It was more the sort of house where, in a book, the key would be under an upside-down terracotta plant pot or the place would be so quaint and crime-free that the door would simply be unlocked. This was the 21st-century version, and the door was very much opened by a pad to the left side of the architrave. The number was long and apparently the numeric version of Lovely Bay plus a few extra zeros. Nina keyed in the code, the lock clicked, and she squelched in. She stood for a minute on the mat and peered around. There was not a smile on her face. She hauled her duffel bag inside, leaving it and her handbag by the door as she paused to take in her surroundings.

The first thing that hit her was the musty, dusty smell in the stale air. A five-star hotel lobby pumping out cherry blossom scent through the air conditioning system this was not. Clearly, no one had cared for the place in a while. Cobwebs stretched across the corners of the hallway, and a layer of dust covered every surface. Nina read Jill's words again that this entrance led off to a self-contained living quarter section to the left.

She turned left past a staircase beside walls with faded brocade wallpaper and opened a door. She raised her eyebrows, not sure what to think. An inner hallway had further rooms off it; a bedroom and box room, a bathroom with a roll-top bath and old-fashioned chain toilet, a large kitchen with a tiny scullery, a what might once have been a pretty sitting room with French doors to a terrace.

Nina felt as if someone had dropped her into another world. The Summer Hotel's living quarters were so much bigger than she'd anticipated, and the little space she inhabited in her flat. Somehow, despite a lot of both clutter and dust, it was sort of cosy and comfy, or at least it had been at some point. She stood in the kitchen and stared at an Aga on the right-hand side. It sat in a little nook, a Sheila's Maid hung over the top, a long line of whitewashed pine units flanked windows looking out onto a private garden, and a fireplace with a wood burner was tucked in on the other side. A floral-covered chair was nudged up next to the fireplace, a tartan blanket over its arm. It looked as if someone had started to make a cup of tea, got up and left and never come back. A newspaper was open on a large scrubbed pine table, a chair was pulled out as if someone hadn't bothered to tuck it back in, and a mug was sitting by the kettle with a bottle of gone-off milk by its side.

Nina opened a few cupboards; boxes of cereal, jars of cheap

coffee, a vast collection of glasses, and packets of pasta by the dozen. She pulled back a pair of heavy gingham curtains on a window going out to the side and despite the grey drizzly day, light flooded into the kitchen at the same time as dust billowed into the air. In a double-width Butler sink a load of dirty plates, knives and forks, saucepans with congealed food, and a heap of dirty glasses were piled in haphazard stacks. Nina had never seen a worktop with quite so many things on it – jars, at least six salt and pepper mills, an open, mouldy jar of jam with a knife stuck into the top, two toasters, bunches of dead flowers in jugs, three biscuit tins, and the place looked as if it was growing spoon rests. So many display plates adorned the walls, and mugs of every size and shape hung from hooks anywhere there was space for one.

Nina grimaced and thought about the kitchen she'd left in the flat. She liked the flat to be tidy, orderly, and clean. She had ironed tea towels, labelled shelves, and colour-coded containers. She screwed her nose up and peered in the sink. The place wasn't a health hazard as such, but by golly it was grubby and it could do with a kitchen spray or six.

She leaned over the sink, pulled an old-fashioned window latch to the left, yanked it out, and pushed. Nothing happened. She gave it another go. Zilch. With her right hand on the handle and her left hand on the window frame, she gave it a bit of force. The window sprung open; the momentum carried it, and it swung around in the drizzle. Nina leaned over, inhaled at the same time, and put the window on the latch as fresh air whooshed in. The air made the kitchen a tiny bit more palatable, though it did nothing for the clutter.

Strolling back across the kitchen, she went in search of the bedroom. The same thing was going on in the bedroom. Bits and bobs, knick-knacks, lamps, books, clothes, and paraphernalia everywhere. Jill's aunt or the previous house-sitter clearly had a penchant for high-end lotions and potions by the looks of what was displayed on the top of the dresser. Everywhere she looked, there was clutter, lotions and potions, books and magazines.

The smaller box bedroom was, as Jill had put in her notes, a different matter. It was tidy, neat, and mostly clutter-free. Nina sighed and walked back into the main bedroom, sat down on the edge of the bed, and bounced a little, testing the mattress. It felt surprisingly good, and the pure white heavy cotton duvet cover with crocheted edges felt nice as Nina ran her hand over the fabric. A stack of books with a pair of readers perched on top was on the bedside table, and a bookcase under a large window was filled with more books in lopsided rows. Jill's aunt had clearly enjoyed winding down in the evenings with a good book. On the top of a tall dresser, trinkets and silver-framed photos, seashells, pottery figurines, jars of buttons, and ribbons all jostled for space. A large tray full of dust-covered fancy perfumes was perched on a shelf. Clutter and things everywhere.

Nina sighed, went back to the smaller bedroom, leant down, and sniffed a pile of sheets stacked on the end. She recoiled; they were clean but not that fresh. There was no way she was sleeping in musty sheets. She peered out the window at the rain, put her hand on one of the old-fashioned radiators, picked up the pile of sheets, and went in search of a washing machine with no idea how she was going to get the sheets dry.

A few minutes later, she was standing in a small scullery off the kitchen staring at the buttons on a washing machine and tumble dryer. Both machines appeared to be in working order. She flicked the sheets out, shoved them in the machine, and studied the panel. Quick wash, daily wash, or sanitise? She wondered if it would even work and deduced by the fact that it had orange glowing lights and that there was a packet of washing capsules, wedged in amongst the clutter on the side, that it would do the job.

Just as she was peering into the drum and listening to it fill with water for the quick wash cycle, her phone buzzed. She pressed and held the phone to her ear. 'Hi Soph.'

'How is it?'

'Umm, put it this way; I'll be emailing Jill later. I'll stay tonight.'

Nina could tell that the Pity Smile had arrived by way of the tone in Sophie's voice. 'What? What do you mean?'

'It's just, I don't know, much bigger than I thought and much sort of grottier. It just feels so unloved and draughty. Grim. It's dusty and full of clutter. It's a no from me. I shouldn't have come here.'

'Err, you knew that, didn't you? She put that in the post.'

'True. I underestimated it, though.'

'The weather probably isn't helping. Is it grey and drizzly there?'

'Yeah, it's been raining since I left home,' Nina said as she peered out the streaked, filthy scullery window at the drizzly grey day.

'Classic British seaside weather to welcome you to the coast. Probably not helping your first impressions of the place.'

'No, it's definitely gloomy. Adds to the whole feeling of the house being sort of forgotten and unloved, you know?' Nina wandered back through the cluttered kitchen as she talked, dodging around mismatched chairs and scanning the jumbled counters.

'What's the B&B side of it like?'

'I haven't got that far. There's just stuff everywhere here. It's like whoever lived here last left mid-task and never returned. Dirty plates by the sink, half-read newspapers, dead flower arrangements. It's weird. A bit creepy.'

'Oh no, that doesn't sound very cosy. Didn't the listing mention it needing some TLC though?'

Nina ran a finger along a cobwebbed windowsill and

grimaced at the dust. 'I guess I didn't fully appreciate just how much TLC it needed until seeing it in person. I can't believe people live like this.'

'Surely it just needs a good clean. I'll come and give you a hand.'

'You have two children, a husband who is away a lot, and you're pregnant.' Nina walked back to the scullery to check on the washing machine's progress. 'Like, there is dust on every surface. Clearly, no one's done a proper deep clean in ages. I'm almost scared to see what's lurking in some of these corners. There's so much stuff, too.'

Sophie chuckled. 'Maybe don't go poking under the furniture then. But look on the bright side – at least you won't run out of things to do! You love decluttering. It's in your blood; that's why I thought about you for this in the first place.'

'Too right. I could probably spend a month just scrubbing and still not finish cleaning this place from top to bottom.'

'Jill said the last house sitter was useless, didn't she?'

'She did. She wasn't wrong.'

They continued chatting as Nina walked around. The washing machine beeped, signalling the wash cycle was complete. Nina tucked her phone in between her ear and her shoulder and transferred the sheets to the dryer, hoping the drier worked.

'Anyway, how's the bedroom?' Sophie asked.

Nina started the dryer and wandered back into the kitchen. 'It's alright, I suppose. The aunt's actual bedroom, though, is completely packed with stuff. Knick-knacks and perfume bottles and fancy soaps. Boxes full of John Lewis things, crates full of beauty stuff, clothes, books everywhere. Weird.'

'Sounds like my kinda John Lewis delivery,' Sophie joked.

'Ha. Way more clutter than I could ever live with, that's for sure!'

'I can picture you getting twitchy just looking at all that clutter.'

'Yup.'

'That's why you're there.'

'Ugh, I know. I didn't think it through properly. What was I thinking?' Nina swore as she gingerly picked up a storage canister to find a decade's worth of dust on the bottom.

'Just close the door to most of it and start with the kitchen,' Sophie suggested.

'I don't know what I'm going to do. There's no way I'm staying here and Nathan is in my flat. I can't ask him to leave now, what with everything he's going through.'

'No! You can't leave. It will look better tomorrow.'

'I'll send you pics and then see what you say.'

'You'll be fine. Do you want me to come and get you if it's that bad? The spare room is made up.'

Nina liked the sound of Sophie's spare room. She couldn't be doing with the Pity Smile, though. 'Nah, I'll be fine.'

'Just take it one little project at a time. Celebrate every little victory, like having clean sheets tonight. You'll get there.'

Nina tried to have some perspective. It didn't work. The Summer Hotel was *horrible*. She hated it. She pretended she was fine and made attempts to get Sophie off the phone otherwise Sophie would start the need-a-change lecture, and she was in no mood for that. She didn't need any more of the Pity Smile either.

After she'd hung up, Nina washed out a mug, refilled the kettle three times, boiled it once and sloshed the water down the sink, and put it on again. She made a cup of tea with the teabags she'd brought with her, had it black, and listened to the tumble dryer going round and round. ***** *my life.*

With the rain continuing and not many options, Nina decided she could at least do something to the room she would be spending the night in. She put her bags by the door, took out her pyjamas, and gave the room a thorough sweeping and dusting. She opened the window to air it out and sprayed so much lemon cleaner on the surfaces it made her eyes water. She stood back at the end of it to survey what she'd done. She needed to get a grip; it had hardly been filthy in the first place, but now it at least felt as if it was somewhere near 'her' level of clean.

After she'd taken the sheets out of the tumble dryer, noted on the John Lewis label that the sheets were in fact made in Portugal and after ironing them to within an inch of their life, she made the bed. Slightly better. Actually quite nice.

In the bathroom, which clearly had a second life as an outpost for Sephora, she shook her head at the dust. Half an hour later, she'd scrubbed the roll-top tub until her fingers pruned, washed away toothpaste spatter and soap scum from the pedestal sink with a grimace, and poured cleaner down any and all plugholes she could find. A thick layer of dust and hair came away when Nina swiped a cloth over the mirror and wiped out the cabinet behind it.

Once she'd had another cup of black tea, the initial overwhelmed feeling had faded a tiny bit. At least she would be staying the night and not having to look for a hotel or room in a pub. Of course, she could have pitched up at Sophie's, but she couldn't be dealing with the fallout after that. Poor Nina this, poor Nina that. The Pity Smile looking down on her.

As she was sitting staring out the window, watching the drizzle and the grey sky, a WhatsApp message pinged.

Jill: *Hi Nina. I've heard you've arrived. Thank you so much. I hope you're finding everything okay. I'm out of mobile coverage at the moment – we're in South America in a rainforest but the place we're camping at has really patchy internet at the main property so I hope this comes through. As I said in my message, I've got someone coming to service the boiler check dates on my spreadsheet as I'm in a different time zone (sorry) and the chimney stacks also have someone coming to assess them as discussed in our email conversations. Thank you so much. I'll be back in touch when we're on Wi-Fi again.*

Nina started typing out a reply and then deleted everything she'd written. The woman was in a rainforest. The last thing she needed was a message from the house sitter she'd found to tell her that she was welching on the deal. What did she really care, though? She'd leave the next day, and when she was back in London, she'd send Jill a message then. There was no way she was going to stay.

10

Nina put her phone in her pocket and walked outside to assess the weather. There was no change, it was just a constant, not too offensive drizzle that looked, possibly, as if it was never, ever going to stop. The kind of British drizzle that made you think you wouldn't really get that wet, but if you stayed out in it too long, you absolutely did get wet or soggy more like. A particularly English sogginess with a bit of dampness on the edges. Nina decided she could handle a bit of sogginess. In for a penny, in for a pound, and she needed to get her bearings at the very least. She may have to end up staying a few days to work out what she was going to do.

A few minutes later, The Summer Hotel was behind her and she was making her way into Lovely Bay itself. She'd read a lot about Lovely Bay; how one of its larger houses had been a hospital in WWI, specifically chosen for the recuperation properties of the Lovely Air. She'd learnt about the lighthouse, the listed train station, and the workings of the river. As she'd sat with her tea in the kitchen, she'd learnt how the specially designed coat had a Lovely spin on it, fit to handle the elements and the great delights of an English sea. Lovely Bay was apparently the third-smallest town in England, with Lovely itself across the river not far ahead of it. According to the local information centre's website, many Lovelies, as they liked to call themselves, considered Lovely Bay to be a large village. Lovelies seemed serious about the outdoors, where many miles of track meandered by the River Lovely, which wound its way through woodland, in and out of dunes, across marshland, and made its way through the odd fruit orchard too. Lovely Bay had many little greens, each complete with a pub, cottages, and shops.

All of it was apparently very, as the name suggested, *lovely*. Nina expanded the map on her phone and read a bit more as she stopped in the drizzle on the side of the pavement. A few minutes later, she was walking along a long line of what a blue plaque fixed to one of the house fascias informed her were fishermen's cottages. She stood at the end and gazed up at the unusual scalloping of the roof tiles, counted the chimney stacks, and took in what she was now realising was the town sign which she'd seen everywhere.

Ambling along in the rain, Nina got to the main street and peered at the shops. Stripy blue and white bunting gathered from a central point and fluttered through the purple-grey sky. A pub with more of the scalloped shingle roof tiles stood in the centre and down to the left, just as she had read about, was one of the many greens. Nina walked a bit further, stood on St Lovely green and mused what was in front of her. It was as if it had been lifted straight out of a watercolour seaside book from the forties. The sort of book that you flick through in an old bookshop but never quite believe was actually once a thing. She touched the back of a bench that sat to the right of a gigantic flagpole – it was definitely real; she was not, in fact, lost in the pages of a watercolour book. Then, of course, to add to the surreal feel was the lighthouse which stood tall and white against the grey sky as if it was looming down and watching over the town. Nina lost herself in the lighthouse's old-world charm as its white paint gleamed. She stood with her head raised up and considered how the lighthouse looked as if that very morning someone had been up on a ladder with a paint-brush giving it a quick fresh coat of brilliant white paint.

She peered at a long row of houses in hues of ice-cream pastels. A yellow door, a blue door, a pink house, the bricks and paints soft and weather-faded, and all of them looking as if they were competing for the 'Loveliest Cottage in Lovely Bay' award. Nina found herself daydreaming. It seemed like the sort of place where people left their doors unlocked and someone might just pop round for a cup of tea without an invite. It was a lot nicer than The Summer Hotel.

A flag with a stripy background and the Lovely Anchor sign flapped away in the salty sea breeze, and a couple of seagulls soared overhead. Nina vacuumed up the peace of it all. A sort of peace she hadn't felt for a long time. It was as if it was seeping deep into her bones. The feeling kind of disarmed her. What even was it? Her heart and her stomach were doing funny little skips every few beats. The sea air, the new town, the slow rambling nature of the place, the colours in the sky, the feel of the sea air in her hair. She squinted and examined the light-house again and tried to work out what was happening to her. For a second, it fleeted across her mind; a tiny part of her was relieved that was what it was. She wasn't with Andrew, and it felt okay. That in itself was very, very strange.

Nina stood, staring at the Lovely Lighthouse for a little bit longer, and then she made her way further along the street. Little shops with paned windows looked back at her, bunting fluttered across the top of the street, and despite the drizzle, the whole of the area looked pretty and somehow soft. Nina passed a deli café where an old couple sat in the window with steaming cups of tea, a little dog was tied up outside a co-op, and a book-shop with a stripy awning had a bench outside chock full of second-hand books. She stopped and stared outside an old-fashioned hardware store, where timber trestle tables lined up against the shop window were stacked with old fishing baskets full of hardware items. A charity shop's door was propped open and a woman with a baby in her arms stood chatting by the counter.

All of it seemed very quaint, old-fashioned, and from another time. Nina came to a bow-fronted shop with bunting hanging across the top of the door. A chalkboard sign with fancy white lettering told her that Lovely Bay chowder was available. She stood for a minute as bunting haphazardly tied around the top of the chalkboard flapped in the wind, and she considered what was on offer. Three different varieties of chowder, including what the sign was telling her was the famous Lovely Bay crab chowder.

As she continued on her walk, she got soggier by the minute, but something was making her feel slightly better, despite the disappointment of the hotel. When she had arrived, the place seemed friendly, and as she'd first thought on the boat, something about the air felt nice. Nina came to a small pub, setback at the end of a row of shops. A sign above swayed in the wind, bunting was hanging from the gutters, and the sign over the door told her that The Drunken Sailor was open 365 days a year. She cupped her hands over her eyes, ducked her head, peered in the window, and spied a few people sitting inside. Not sure what she was doing really, it had been a very long time since she'd been into a pub on her own; she opened the door and stepped in. The pub was dry, warm, and friendly. A couple of men were sitting at the bar with pints. A woman on the far side had a toddler beside her on a chair, and another woman who sat with a friend, both of whom had knitting needles in their hands, were chattering away over cups of coffee.

Nina walked up to the highly polished bar, taking in the multitude of vintage anchors pinned across the top. A woman came around the side of the bar and Nina did a double-take.

Unless she was seeing things, it was the same woman who had been at the train station earlier that day. The woman chuckled. 'Yes, it's me again.'

'I thought I was seeing things.'

'Our Stephanie has gone over to Lovely, so I've stepped in here for an hour until our Shirley gets here. What can I get you?'

Nina didn't even know what she wanted. It was way too early for an actual drink. She pointed to the women with the knitting. 'Any chance of a coffee?'

'Of course. Take a pew and I'll bring it right out. What sort of coffee would you like?'

'Cappuccino would be lovely.'

'On the way.' Nancy squinted. 'You're looking a bit damp.'

'I've been on a long walk. I really needed to get some fresh air and get my bearings.' Nina didn't add that she would be going back whence she came the next day. This Nancy, from what she had already gathered, felt proud of the third-smallest town in England, no point in bursting her bubble. She wasn't going to tell her that she'd made a huge mistake and that she needed to get back to the familiarity of her real life.

'Right you are. Will I be adding a bit of whipped cream to the top of your coffee?'

Nina smiled. 'I wouldn't say no.'

'Chocolate shavings from next door?'

'Sorry.'

'Homemade chocolate from the shop along the street there.'

Nina chuckled. 'You know how to treat a customer.'

'All part of the Lovely service. I'll bring it over to you.'

Nina took her damp coat off and sat down at a table right in the corner by a window that looked out onto the pavement. Pansies in a window box outside danced in the wind, and she sat lost in a world of her own, letting her eyes slowly take in the tiny cottages opposite. She found herself daydreaming about opening the pale-blue stable door to the pink house opposite as if she lived there. The little pots by the door would greet her and, in the picture in her head, there was a little girl in a raincoat and wellies. Dreamy Nina and the girl were laughing; Dreamy Nina put a shopping basket over her shoulder, and they made off down the road, leaving the pink cottage behind. Nina sighed. That ship had sailed when she'd buried Andrew. It took two people to make babies as far as she knew, and there'd been a distinct lack of anyone capable of making babies in Nina's life for a long time. About the nearest she'd got to a baby maker was sitting on a bench with Nathan talking about his ex-wife.

She shook her head to rid the daydream as Nancy arrived at the table and put a large mug of coffee on the table with a flourish. There was coffee, and then there was coffee. The whipped cream on top was covered in chocolate shavings, and there was a small piece of chocolate on a little dish in the saucer. Nina's eyes lit up. 'Ooh, thanks.'

'We're talking freshly whipped cream and the best ever chocolate. We do a few things well in Lovely, just so you know – coats, chowder, and chocolate. All the Cs,' Nancy joked.

'Wow, thank you.' Nina picked up the spoon and dipped it into the chocolate. 'Oh my goodness!'

'I know, right? I thought you looked as if you needed a bit of Lovely chocolate.'

'I didn't know it, but I did.'

Just as they were chatting, a man in a navy blue work shirt, cargo pants with some sort of straps and belts attached to them, and work boots walked into the bar. Both Nancy and Nina looked. *Flipping heck.* Nina may have just set her eyes on someone she wouldn't mind being the other part of the baby-making machine in the daydream about the pink cottage across the street.

Nancy beamed. 'Hi Robby. How are you?'

Nina's first impression changed when Robby didn't smile too much, and he sounded much more well-to-do than she'd anticipated by the way he was dressed. 'Good. Yeah, did Jase leave his work jacket in here?' Robby asked, completely ignoring Nina as she felt herself staring, trying to keep her jaw from dropping and drool from running down her chin.

Nancy shook her head and started to look around the pub. 'No idea. I'm covering for our Steph. Where'd he leave it?'

'If I knew that, I wouldn't be in here.'

'Good point.'

'What sort is it?'

'One of our Molly's.'

'Eeek, colour?'

'Yellow. It cost me an arm and a leg, and it's the second time he's lost it.'

'Soz, no idea.'

'Forecast is for more rain, and he's on an overnight job in Poppleswick. I said I'd come in on my way home.'

'Sorry, can't help you.'

Robby didn't look too chuffed. 'Right.' He then turned around and thundered out of the pub.

Nina's eyes widened. She wanted to ask who the rock star with the straps around his legs was. She wanted to know quite what the straps were doing. She may just have imagined herself being caught up in the straps. She restrained herself. She didn't have to worry, Nancy was all over it. 'Sorry about that. Yes, I know what you're thinking, and yes, he's extremely good-looking and ignores visitors. We do try to keep him out of the way as much as possible. Don't want to frighten people away.'

'What was he looking for?'

Nancy flicked her hand back and forth. 'Oh, it's a Lovely thing. The coats are made by a family who have lived here for generations. There's only one of 'em left now – our Molly – and her staff hand make everything. They are really expensive and really sought after if you're from around here. Well, it's not *just* that they're expensive. You can't just rock up and buy one. You have to first go on the waiting list, and then you get fitted for one, and it takes months. Most of them are blue, but you get the odd yellow one here and there, which is what he's looking for.'

'Oh, okay, I see.' Nina wasn't really sure what the big deal was about a coat, but she'd heard it a few times now.

It was as if Nancy was reading her thoughts. 'It's a big deal, and you don't lose 'em. You have them for life, pretty much. They're handmade and oiled right here in Lovely Bay and don't you forget it,' Nancy joked. 'Which is why our Robby there wasn't too happy.'

Robby, hmm, nice. Very nice. Robby with the straps and nice accent. 'He certainly doesn't look it.'

'Ahh, we give him a pass after what he's been through, though that was years ago now.' Nancy sucked air in through her teeth. 'Life deals you with some crap sometimes, eh?'

Nina had definitely been dealt some of life's crap. It fleeted through her mind that it was a good time to play the widow card. Sometimes she laid it on the table as some sort of warped trump card. She decided against it. Nancy was way too nice to make her feel all uppity and uncomfortable.

Nancy looked at her watch. 'Okay, well, I'm done. Shirley should be here any minute and I'm back to the station. Enjoy your coffee.'

Nina watched Nancy walk to the bar and someone else in one of the blue coats with the striped hood, who was obviously Shirley, came in. She smiled as she took another sip of her coffee. The place seemed friendly enough, but she didn't really want to know. She would be going home tomorrow as far as she was concerned.

11

Things were not going that well for Nina as late afternoon turned into early evening. The drizzle of rain that had been her constant companion since she'd stepped foot outside her flat had decided it might like a change. It had decided it would like to provide the residents of Lovely Bay with an absolute downpour. Nina thought about the message with Jill and kicked herself for not responding right away. She should have gone with her gut in the first place and gone right back to London. How was she going to explain to Jill that she wasn't staying? Jill potentially might not get the message for ages.

Rain hammered on the roof of The Summer Hotel, and the more Nina thought about it, the more she desperately wanted to go back to the comfort and familiarity of her flat. She cursed Sophie for ever suggesting the whole madcap idea in the first place.

She also couldn't stop thinking about Andrew, the fact that he was gone, and the fact that while she'd been in the pub she hadn't missed him. She was on her own on a very strange path, a path she hadn't even wanted to be on in the first place. She was in an unfamiliar, rainy, grey place at the bottom of the country without Andrew. She knew no one. She didn't even have the delights of Mrs Gilbert and her blaring radio to keep her company. She felt like packing her bag and heading to the train and never looking back. The problem was she had no flat to go to unless she wanted to share a bed with Nathan, and she had no idea whether the train was running. It would probably not be running on a Friday or something ridiculous like that.

The pounding rain matched the pounding in Nina's heart as she sat in the darkened property. Despite what had happened in the pub, most of the time she still missed Andrew terribly, and it had been years. She told herself all the time she was better. She wasn't really better, though these days she wasn't breaking down in tears every five seconds, so there was that. Other people had insisted she would be able to put it behind her; she was still waiting for that to happen. It was especially bad on lonely nights like this. Andrew would have known what to do. The creaky old hotel only seemed to amplify her grief and longing. The musty rooms, strange sounds, and isolation mirrored what she felt. As the rain poured and poured, the more morose she felt.

She sat for ages with her Kindle in her hand and her phone charging on the worktop beside her and tried not to think about it. It was *one* night. She was utterly catastrophising. She could get through one night in a strange bed – heck, she'd survived losing her husband.

About fifteen minutes later, things got a lot, lot worse. There wasn't much warning either. Not like a big storm or a huge clap of thunder or howling wind. Just pouring rain and a flicker of the lights. Nina looked up from her Kindle at the lamp on the other side of the kitchen and let out a sigh of relief when the lamp stayed on. It didn't last. It flickered again, the fridge beeped, there was a sound from the washing machine in the scullery, and the whole place was suddenly in darkness. Nina sat motionless for a second, absolutely petrified, listening to nothing other than the rain. Then she said a silent prayer that she'd put her phone on charge, felt her way around the kitchen table, and snatched up her phone. A door banged somewhere in the building and, as Nina put the torch on on her phone, she wanted to cry. Rain lashed the windows, and she shivered, feeling suddenly vulnerable in the unfamiliar house.

She swung the phone light around the shadowy room. 'Okay, Neens, get a grip,' she muttered to herself. 'And breathe. Just find some candles and you'll be fine. You are fine. Fine, fine, fine.'

She aimed her phone at the dresser by the side door and ran her hands along the cluttered surface. There were more than a few candles; at least that was one thing for all the clutter. She picked up a couple of aromatherapy candles in pretty frosted jars and put them on the kitchen table. On a shelf above the Aga, she found a mismatched collection of votive candles and a candelabra. She then scooted out to the sitting room, rifled through sideboard drawers and found another scented candle and a vintage hurricane lamp.

Back in the kitchen, she ducked down and opened the cupboard under the sink. Her chin dropped in shock at the plethora of cleaning sprays and paraphernalia, and she started to root around for some matches. Tucked beside an oven mitt still in its packet, she discovered a box of matches and nearly wept with relief. With her hands trembling, she quickly lit the aromatherapy candles and a few dinner tapers, and the kitchen lit up with a glow.

The flames cast dark shadows on the walls; she was now even more scared, but at least she could see. Not quite sure what to do next, she took the candles into the bathroom and turned on the tap in the bath. Feeling overly happy that piping hot water came out of the tap, she found a bath bomb in the multitude of supplies in the dresser, ran the bath, and dropped in the bomb. As the weather got worse and rain lashed down, she sat marooned in the tub with her Kindle as if she was the only person in England, let alone in Lovely Bay, and tried not to think about what was going to happen in the night.

Finally getting to a time when she could go to bed to try and shut everything out, Nina hastily put her pyjamas on. She tucked her phone under the pillow, and got into bed as periodic creaks around the house made her jumpy, the rain continued to pour outside, and the power stayed off. Nina Lavendar was not in a good way at all.

12

The next morning, Nina woke up to not only sunshine outside the window but the realisation that the strangest thing had happened. She'd actually had the best night's sleep in a very, very long time. The night before, lit only by her phone torch, she'd opened the window a tiny bit letting the air whoosh around the bedroom, climbed into the fresh sheets on the bed, and gone to sleep listening to the sound of the sea in the distance and the pouring rain battering the window. The next thing she'd known, she'd woken up nearly nine hours later in a bit of a daze. She hadn't had a sleep like it since Andrew had died. Stranger things happened at sea.

She pulled her dressing gown out of her open case on the floor, put her feet on the floorboards, recoiled at how cold it was, found her slippers, and stuffed in her feet. A few minutes later, she was standing in the kitchen by the Aga looking at a whole different place to the drizzle-filled space she'd witnessed the day before. Sunshine pooled on the floor and, without the grim, constant drizzle of rain and depressing light, the place was a tiny bit brighter. Not a lot but a bit. Realising that the electricity was on, she filled the kettle, found a pot of unopened and in-date instant coffee, shuddered at the thought of poisoning herself with instant coffee, and spooned a heaped teaspoon into the same mug she'd used before for her black tea.

With her mug in hand, she went back into the bedroom, fished around in the bottom of the duffel bag for the waterproof clogs she'd put in at the last minute and usually wore to take out the rubbish at the back of the flats, pulled on a thick pair of pale pink socks, tucked her pyjamas in the socks and went back out through the kitchen with her coffee in her hand. On the back of the door on the other side of the kitchen, Nina spied one of the infamous coats with the stripy lined hood. Dubious about putting it on but feeling as if it would be cold and damp outside despite the sunshine, she pulled it on over her dressing gown and trekked out to the garden.

Everything in the garden glistened from the rain and now the sunlight. Fallen twigs and leaves littered the grass, and mud spattered the paths. She'd thought the front was overgrown, but this was much, much, *much* worse. The view down to the water, though, was so unbelievably nice it took her breath away. She instantly went to say something to Andrew. As usual, he wasn't there. He hadn't been for years.

She looked around at the rambling old house and felt weirdly emotional. It felt almost as if the house was sad. As if it was waiting for someone to care enough to nurture it back to its former self. Nina stood looking up at it as she drank her coffee. She frowned and screwed up her nose. If she wanted to, maybe she could be that person who brought the house back to life. Her phone pinged with a message.

Nathan: *Morning. Just wanted to say again thank you so much for getting me out of a stitch. I would have been in a hotel otherwise and not been able to see the kids properly for ages. This really helps me out. How's it at the seaside?*

Nina swore. Nathan's text was the last thing she needed. How could she now tell him that she'd changed her mind, that she was coming back, and that he needed to leave? She couldn't do that to the man. It would finish him off. She would be responsible for a death. She already lived with one daily. She didn't need another death in her life at this stage of the game.

Nina: *Ahh. You're welcome. Stay as long as you want.*

Nina grimaced. What the? So now she was the one who was going to be living in a hotel.

Nathan: *Seriously, I appreciate it. Hope the sea air is doing you good!*

Nina stared at the message, conflicting emotions churning inside. She couldn't ask Nathan to leave when he had nowhere else to go. But now she was essentially homeless if she didn't stay at The Summer Hotel.

Nina: *Stay as long as you need. The fresh air is nice here, but the place needs a lot of work.*

Nathan: *Yikes, that doesn't sound ideal. Is it one of those situations that looked better in the photos?*

Nina: *Ha, yes, you could say that! It's bigger and older than I realised.*

Nathan: *Oh.*

Nina frowned at the phone, conflicted.

Nina: *Not a problem.*

Nathan: *Sorry, gotta run, one of the kids is calling. But keep me posted!*

Nina: *Will do, thanks Nathan.*

As she walked back into the house, she put her phone back in her dressing gown pocket with a deep, troubled sigh. Her choices now were to give up and go home in defeat, meaning she'd have to oust Nathan or put her feet under the table and get on with it. The thought of retreating back to her homely London life made Nina's chest tighten. She glanced around the now sunny kitchen, picturing it without as much clutter and after a deep clean. She downed the last of her coffee and nodded her head in resolve. No more moping. A dusty old house wasn't going to kill her. She'd had worse hits from life. Time to stick to her word and pull up her big girl pants. Apart from anything else, something was telling her that the place deserved a second chance. Maybe, in a way, she did too.

Nina decided not to waste any time. If she was staying, even just for the weekend, she needed to do something about the state of the kitchen. Just to make sure, she read through Jill's PDF again. The notes told her that Jill wanted the house cleared and that nothing, except for photos and books, was sentimental. Everything else could and needed to go. With that knowledge tucked safely in the back of her head, and still in her dressing gown, pink socks and gardening clogs, she got to work in the kitchen. She started by unloading the dishwasher, filling it up again, and working out how to turn it on. As she heard it filling with water and it hummed away merrily, she found herself doing the same.

She plugged her phone charger in, stuck it in her phone, turned on a playlist, and before she knew it, she was clearing the work surfaces like nobody's business with Take That songs as a companion. She found all sorts of strange things as she worked; a family-sized, unopened tub of Vaseline, a dish of cotton reels, four Chanel nail varnishes, many rolls of kitchen towel, three cans of odour eliminator spray, two jars of Eve Lom face cleanser, empty egg boxes by the dozen, a tin of out-of-date Roses and two pairs of sunglasses. The mind boggled.

Once the worktop contents were either in the bin or on the kitchen table, she started on the cupboards, binning anything perishable or past the expiry date. The number of dusty cans, old bottles, and expired spices was astonishing. Nina was a bit disgusted. She had to admit that sometimes the contents of her gigantic spice collection got out of control, but this was on a whole other level. Twenty-year-old baking powder and way out-of-date herbs and spices were left, right, and centre. Clearly, no one had done a proper clear out in years, if ever. She scooped the whole lot into a bin bag to deal with later.

After feeling guilty about how much of it had gone into bin bags even after recycling as much as she could, most of the pantry cupboards were at least workable. By mid-morning, all the worktops were clear and, at worst, resembled a functional space. Next, she opened the under-the sink cupboard and shook her head in disbelief. Just like the boxes of toiletries in the bathroom, someone who'd been in the house clearly liked cleaning sprays and accoutrements. She counted twenty-three sprays alone. The person, however, didn't quite follow through and use them. The irony was that nearly all of them were sealed and had never seen the light of day. She opened a spray from somewhere called The Laundry Lady and sprayed away for all she was worth all along the worktops and sprayed and wiped to her heart's content. An hour or so later, the kettle was back on the worktop, one of the toasters was in a cupboard, the other was on the side, and not much else was out on display at all. The Aga was clutter-free and shone.

Next, she clambered up on the worktop, pulled down the striped curtains, took a chance, and stuffed them in the washing machine. Still in her dressing gown and with the kitchen windows open, she sprayed a fancy spray over the sink. Realising that the spray looked good, smelt good but was more or less useless at stubborn stains, she rummaged around in the back for some that was formerly known as Jif. Liberally squirting the sink, she scrubbed and huffed and puffed until things improved.

She stood back and smiled as the sink shone, and she realised she hadn't thought about Andrew all morning. Boy, did it feel good. Maybe this place could be a good thing. As Sophie had said, perhaps the clearing and cleaning and fresh coastal air would be the perfect therapy for her after all. She could but wait and see.

13

An hour or so later, Nina was still humming, which in itself was both odd and good at the same time. She'd take it as a bonus on a trip that had gone wrong that she was trying to make the best of. She grabbed one of the huge bin liners full of out-of-date spices and attempted to pick it up. Luckily, it didn't split, but she could barely lift it off the floor. Dragging it to the tradesmen's door, she heaved it over the step and looked up and down the side path for a wheelie bin. Unable to see anything like it and assuming the bins were on the other side of the house she hadn't explored yet, she peered out towards the road. Deducing that at some point the bins would be collected from the front, she dragged the bag towards the front gate.

It was not an easy job, and she struggled with the heavy bag of spices. Her dressing gown had fallen open, her hair was in her face, and she was now realising why she should have joined The Chelsea Collective gym. A Pilates class or three wouldn't have gone amiss. She pulled and heaved past the front door and finally got to the fence. Balancing the bin bag, unlatching the gate, and holding the gate open with her foot, she yanked the bag in the direction of the gate, at which point the bag split and its contents spilled all over the place and a large pot of paprika deposited powder just about everywhere.

Nina actually laughed out loud. Another strange thing. She was smiling and laughing at herself. 'Hah, hah, hah.' She singsonged as she started to gather out-of-date oregano pots from the grass and started to scoop up paprika from the path. She started stuffing the pots back in the bag, and with red hands from the paprika, grabbed a load of cinnamon sticks and shoved them in the bag. She was, in fact, quite enjoying herself.

With everything back in the bag, she set about going inside to get the next one. After repeating the same scenario, she was back in the street with her heart pumping and feeling quite pleased with herself. She looked down at her dressing gown and chuckled at what a sight she must look in the pink socks, dressing gown, and gardening clogs. It wasn't even important. What did she care? Firstly, there wasn't a single soul around and, secondly, she didn't even know anyone anyway. If there was a thirdly, it was that she wasn't going to be hanging around that long either. She'd get through the weekend and reassess at the start of the week.

As she stood with her hands on her hips, nodding at a job well done, the neighbour June she'd seen the night before came out of her house and along the pavement. She frowned and wrinkled up her nose. 'I thought I heard something. Hope you were okay with the power outage last night.'

Nina lied. 'Yes, thanks. I was okay. How about you?'

'Oh yeah, fine. It often happens when it rains here. We Lovelies are used to it.'

'Yes, I was told that on the boat or at the station, one of the two.'

June frowned at Nina's face. 'Sorry, what have you been doing?'

'Clearing out the cupboards. I've never seen as many spices in my life.'

June raised her eyebrows. 'I bet that hasn't been done for a long time.'

'You're not wrong.'

June looked at Nina's dressing gown, which was covered in paprika. 'Nothing like getting on with something.'

'I took the bull by the horns.'

'I can see that.'

June looked down the street. 'I'm just waiting for my nephew. He's dropping off something.' A van came along the road. 'Oh, here he is now.' June frowned. 'Oh, he's in one of the work vans. That's weird.'

Nina turned to watch the van pulling into the kerb and continued to look as a man got out. Tall, chestnut hair and really blue eyes. Not that Nina was looking at all. He was dressed in what she could only describe as smart working combat trousers with straps around the tops of the legs and a neatly pressed navy blue shirt with the same anchor logo she'd seen on the boat on the river and on the coats. **** *me dead.* June's nephew was gorgeous. It was the thundering man from the pub. For a split second, Nina wasn't sure what day of the week it was as her world tipped upside down, where she was or who she was talking to. She could barely remember her own name. Or Andrew's.

'Robby, this is Nina.' June gestured to the hotel. 'Next door.'

Robby made a bit of an effort to smile but not much. 'Another house-sitter?'

Nina coughed. 'Err, yes.'

'I wonder how long this one will last?' Robby joked with his aunt.

Nina felt a rod of irritation shoot up her spine. ******* 'Nice to meet you, too.' She looked down at her hands and realised that, like her dressing gown, they were covered in red powder from the spilled paprika. She tried inconspicuously dusting them off on the pockets of her dressing gown. It didn't work, but just made the dressing gown muckier.

'Sorry, I'm a bit of a mess,' she said with an awkward laugh. 'I was just saying to your aunt, I was clearing out the spice cupboard and had a bag split open.'

Robby eyed her dishevelled appearance coolly. 'Right. Well, just as long as you don't make a habit of dumping rubbish in the street.' He sort of said it jokingly, but Nina wasn't sure. He was strangely unreadable and definitely a bit distant. 'The last one thought it was fine to fly-tip her stuff everywhere, including down the back by the water there. Guess who ended up sorting that out?'

Nina bristled at his condescending tone. She heard herself explaining. 'It was an accident when the bag broke. I was cleaning it up.'

'These old places in Lovely need a careful hand. Not someone barging in tearing things apart.'

'Sorry! I'm not tearing anything apart, I'm just organising and cleaning!' Nina shot back defensively.

'Robby, what in the world? What has got into you this morning?' June chided. 'Don't mind him, dear; he's just protective of the area. We all are.'

Nina managed a tight smile. 'It's fine. I'm protective of myself, thank you very much. Plus, I don't like to be insulted.' Nina would tell this jumped-up idiot with his RP accent to stick his Lovely Bay where the sun didn't shine. She didn't care if he was unfairly handsome. He didn't seem perturbed in the slightest. In fact, the bright blue eyes now glinted with annoyance.

'Just offering some friendly advice.'

'You failed. That wasn't friendly as far as I'm concerned.' Nina crossed her arms, fighting the urge to argue. Who was this idiot to judge her after a two-minute interaction?

June continued brightly, 'Robby helps me out around the

house. He can turn his hand to anything. Electrical, plumbing, carpentry – you name it, he can fix it.'

'Jack of all trades, then,' Nina said crisply. *Friendly clearly isn't one of them. Super handsome however is. Certainly very handsome.* Nina hated herself for noticing. She shooed the thought away. Then she took in the straps.

'Right, I should get on with it. Lots still to do today.' Robby said to his aunt.

Nina managed a strained smile. She gulped at the straps. 'Yes, me too.'

Nina walked away, her irritation simmering. So much for friendly small-town vibes. She was too sorry for herself and mentally exhausted to stay worked up, though. Plus, she'd be gone in a few days, and besides, she was too concerned with trying to remember how to get oxygen to enter her body after witnessing the sight that was Robby in the middle of the road. Back inside, she walked through the house to the bathroom, peeled off her dressing gown, glanced at her reflection in the mirror, and nearly screamed. No wonder this Robby bloke had seemed judgemental and rude. She looked like she'd just escaped from somewhere. She was still in her pyjamas, her hair was wild, red paprika dust was splattered on her right cheek and above her left eyebrow and there were spice stains everywhere.

'Well, can't make a worse impression than that,' Nina muttered to herself. She had basically confirmed every suspicion Robby might have had about fly-by-night house-sitters breezing through Lovely Bay.

Nina pulled the lever on the shower and stood under the water for a good five minutes. There was one thing she knew about the place. The hot water was nice. After choosing one of the fancy shampoos and matching conditioners in the shower rack, she scrubbed her hair, attempting to rid it of any paprika, washed out the suds, slapped on some conditioner, and cleaned her face while that did its job.

After getting out of the shower, she dried herself off, and with a towel wrapped around her and a turban towel on her head, she padded into the spare bedroom and pulled out a clean pair of jeans from her bag and a white shirt. She then dried her hair off, directed a huge blob of CC cream onto her face, and rubbed it in. She added loads of mascara, a tiny bit of blusher and left it at that.

She forced herself to forget about the arrogant but handsome Robby and focus on herself. She'd actually thoroughly enjoyed her morning decluttering and cleaning. It had been therapeutic, quite rewarding, somehow peaceful, and strangely cleansing. She'd quite like a bit more of that in her life.

14

Nina walked along the road and reread the texts from Nathan. There was no way she was going to be able to tell him that she was coming back. She wasn't really sure what she was going to do but with the sun out, although it was quite chilly, she decided she'd stay in Lovely Bay for a few days or so at least. Other people from what she'd seen so far all over the internet seemed to like Lovely Bay. In fact, people loved it and raved about its charms. It couldn't be that bad. She'd also quite enjoyed the therapeutic properties of clearing out the kitchen. What she'd done so far was hardly what she would call a deep clean, but in terms of getting satisfaction from chucking away someone else's clutter, it was up there with fantastic.

Just as she was trying to decide whether or not to go towards the dunes, to get on the boat and go to the station museum, or go to have a proper look at the lighthouse, June was coming the other way.

'Ooh, blimey. You look a bit better than you did earlier!'

'Thanks. Sorry about that. I didn't realise I was covered in paprika, and I was still in my dressing gown. I must have looked like I'd had a fright.'

'Not a problem. It takes all sorts. Where are you off to?'

'I'm going for a walk.'

'There you go. I can recommend the marshes if you're into nature.'

'Is it really true that there are otters?'

'Oh yes, if you're lucky.'

'Hopefully, I will be. Have you lived here long?'

'Forever.'

'What's the best thing about Lovely Bay, then?'

June beamed. 'Oh, where do I start? How long have you got? The community's lovely, everyone knows everyone. The bay's gorgeous, especially at sunset and in the warmer months and you want to be here at Christmas. The whole town goes mad for Christmas lights. And there's always something going on – festivals, markets, you name it.'

'Sounds nice,' Nina mused, her thoughts drifting to what she'd left behind and how she hardly knew anyone in her building, let alone in the community. 'A bit of a change for me. Not quite the hustle and bustle of the city.'

'It's peaceful here, but not boring, you know? There's a charm to it. You'll get to see it if you stay a while. Plus, there are the C's. Have you heard of those? Chocolate, chowder and coats.'

'Yes, someone in the pub told me the same.'

'We live on them.'

Nina looked up at the sky. 'It's a lovely afternoon for a walk.'

June made a clicking sound with her tongue. 'Yes. I've been telling myself I'll walk more this year. Every single year, I say I'll lose the weight. Every single year, it doesn't budge.'

Nina laughed. 'I said the same thing this year.'

June rolled her eyes. 'In the past, I used to tell myself that I would join a gym. At least I don't even bother lying to myself about that these days. Too long in the tooth for all that malarkey.'

'Too funny. I actually did go to a gym a few weeks ago.'

'Oh, right. How did it go?'

'Absolutely terrible. I didn't even enter the class itself. Pilates it was.'

'Really. Why not?'

'I should have realised by the name The Chelsea Collective.' Nina winced. 'Everyone was head to toe in white. I needed a mortgage just to be kitted out in the right gear.'

'You see, this is why I don't go myself. That's my excuse, and I'm sticking to it anyway.' June chortled.

Nina patted her tummy. 'I've piled on the weight, though, so really I do have to do something about it at some point. I feel like I need to be fitter, too, which is why I'm heading out on this walk. That and the fresh air.'

'What about that thing where you listen to a podcast thingy and it instructs you?'

Nina wrinkled up her nose. 'Sorry, I don't know what you mean.'

'My friend's daughter did it. You start off walking for like five minutes, then you jog for thirty seconds. Yeah, something like that. She entered a marathon at the end of last year, that's how good it was. The weight absolutely dropped off. We're talking she's a size eight if she's a day now. Like it fell off her just from doing this app thing.'

'Wow. What just from walking and running?'

'Yep. I know. My days of trying to run are over. Just goes to show. Totally free too. That's the whole reason why she started it in the first place. She had no money to go to the gym or classes. This was free on her phone.'

Nina's eyes widened a bit. 'That sounds doable. And free's always good, especially after my gym fiasco. It was an arm and a leg for the fees to go there every month, and there was some dodgy lock-in contract.'

June nodded enthusiastically. 'Exactly! And you can do it

anywhere. No fancy equipment or gym memberships. Just you, your trainers, and the great outdoors which we have a lot of in Lovely. You're so in the right place for that.'

'I might have to give it a go.'

'Right, well, I must get on.'

'Yes, sorry, I'll let you go.'

'Enjoy your walk, and who knows? You might just spot an otter.' June laughed, 'I might see you jogging past later.'

'Chance would be a fine thing.' Nina laughed at the thought of her *actually* jogging. 'See you, thanks for the heads-up on the marshes.'

Nina strolled down the road, and her mind turned over the conversation with June. She wouldn't mind seeing an otter. She then thought about the conversation about jogging. She looked at her phone and put walking jogging in the search bar. The first app she saw had hundreds of thousands of reviews. Apparently it was designed for beginners and was not only easy but would have you running in 12 weeks. Nina laughed to herself. It was even more preposterous than The Chelsea Collective. She hadn't run since primary school sports day, when she'd come last in the egg and spoon race. She felt her muffin top resting over the top of her jeans and decided that downloading the app wasn't going to harm anyone. A few minutes later, it sat on her phone. She listened to the first ten seconds, promptly turned it off, and continued walking along the road.

Deciding on a route, she made her way through the edge of the dunes, took a path through the marshes, ambled over a few small bridges, marvelled at the beautiful colours of nature and ended up on the far side of Lovely Bay ready to make her way back through the town. She stopped at a couple of greens, had a sit on a bench as she let the world go by and spent ages staring at the bright white lighthouse punctuating the sky.

By the time she had finished her walk, she was hungry. She checked her phone for places to eat in Lovely Bay and read a few reviews for a café right on the water. The more she read, the more she nodded to herself. Gushing online reviewers had uploaded many photos of the place's interior, of the views, and of the chowder. It looked good enough for her. About fifteen minutes or so later, she was standing outside a café overlooking the river and harbour. She mused to herself whether or not to go in. Just as she was trying to make up her mind, Nancy from the station and the pub walked along the road, coming the other way. 'Oh, you again!' Nancy called out.

'Ha, I've only been here five minutes, and I've already seen you three times.'

'I get around. If you live here, you get used to it,' Nancy joked and pointed to the café. 'If you're after chowder, this one is not bad.'

'Apparently, you can't come to Lovely Bay without the chowder in this establishment, according to the reviews. A must-stop destination located in the heart of Lovely Bay is what it says by those in the know.'

'Ahh, yep. Though, if you stay here a while, you'll be able to go to have one of our secret ones.' Nancy smiled with a glint in her eye. 'I didn't tell you that, though.'

Nina wasn't sure if Nancy was joking or not. 'Ahh, sounds interesting. Secret chowders?'

'Yup. Has anyone told you about them yet? Although they shouldn't have, that's the whole point, so I don't know why I'm asking.'

'Err, that would be a no.'

Nancy chortled. 'Something for you to learn. There's a very nice one in a house in your road. You never know you could get an invite.' She tapped her nose. 'Well, enjoy, and yes, might see you again. If you play your cards right, we might let you in on the chowder secret at some point.'

15

Nina shook her head as she pushed open the door. She wasn't expecting what greeted her in any shape or form. She stopped in a small timber-clad entrance area and wriggled out of her coat. She just stood and stared for a second at how pretty it all was. Antique fishing rods made into coat hooks were full of the coats with the striped hood, on the right a distressed teal dresser was stuffed full of umbrellas, exotic plants spilled from bottle-green pots, and a long line of shelving on the left was stacked with shells and things collected from the beach. The smell took Nina's breath away. She inhaled deeply, lifted her ribs, and held her breath in for a minute as lovely scents filled her nose – essential oils, flowers, the sea, and what was clearly the chowder wafting around the whole place. Divine.

Peeling off her coat and nodding at the lovely smell, Nina hung it on one of the hooks on the fishing rods in between two of the navy blue coats with the stripy hoods. She pushed an inner door open and stepped in, hardly able to keep the smile off her face. She'd been expecting something like a fish and chip shop with a few melamine tables, industrial-sized bottles of vinegar galore, some jars of pickled gherkins, and not a lot else. She hadn't expected to be sitting in a movie set. Lovely old, weathered green Bentwood chairs were tucked underneath tables, a wood burner was flickering away to itself on the far wall, and a battered leather Chesterfield sat along the wall on the other side.

Nina raised her eyebrows as she looked towards the back, where old, weathered shutters ran all the way from left to right on the windows looking out towards the sea. On dumb waiters painted in the same green as the chairs, piles of vintage dishes, glasses, and huge water jugs stood ready for service. Nina didn't know where to look first – little lamps stood everywhere, over-sized bunches of dried coastal flowers spilled from wicker baskets, and large Kilner jars of sea glass were dotted all around.

A girl in a white shirt and chinos with a tan oilcloth butcher's apron, similar to the look of the coats she'd now seen every-where, caught Nina's eye and directed her to a table near the old shuttered windows. Nina sat down and stared at shelves lined with a mismatch of old photos showing Lovely Bay from days gone by, piles of history books were dotted here and there, and baskets piled with mismatched fabric napkins sat on the tables. Sprigs of greenery were rammed into vintage bottles, sweetie jars were filled with faded driftwood, and behind her Nina craned her neck to have a look at a gathering of pots holding so many ferns and palms that the whole lot appeared as if at any moment it would all end up on the floor.

Nina swung her gaze from the wood burner to the sweeping views of the sea, the River Lovely in the distance and the light-house poking up into the sky and felt as if someone had waved a magic wand and transported her to somewhere where she felt warm, safe, and strangely happy. A large chalkboard sign dangled from a thick rope on the ceiling detailing a seafood chowder of the day. Nina read the three chowders on the menu and decided that any of them sounded nice.

The woman in the tan oilskin apron hustled over. 'Okay. We have a good chowder on today. It won't last long. All you need to do is order over there; you'll get a number, and then we'll bring your food over. Table for two, is it? Is someone joining you?'

Nina swallowed. How many times had she heard that since Andrew had died? Too many. Way, way too many. Being on her own in Lovely Bay, though, hadn't bothered her as much as it usually did. Was it something about the Lovely Air? Who knew? She'd be happy if it didn't rear its ugly head again. 'Just me, thanks.'

'Okay. So shout if you need anything.'

'Will do. Thanks.'

Nina took her time as she went up to the counter to order. When she was back at her table, she sat with her chin on her hand and just stared out at the sea and suddenly sat up straight as she spied someone outside. Not only had she seen Nancy three times, but the same thing had happened with June's nephew, Robby. Only Robby was a little bit more interesting to her than Nancy. Actually, a lot more. So very interesting indeed.

Robby was with another man about the same age; both of them had been in the water. Both barefoot and in wetsuits. Just looking at them made Nina shiver with cold, but it didn't seem to bother them. Robby's wetsuit was unzipped at the top. Oh my. Swimmer's shoulders, gulp, the tan hadn't come from Lovely. Nina rummaged around for her sunnies – the ones with the prescription lenses in. Things got better. Dripping water from wet hair, muscular thighs shaping the wetsuit fabric along with other things. Nice.

Nina ripped the sunglasses off. *Ridiculous!* She had to remind herself that she wasn't interested in anyone, let alone this god, no matter how good he looked or whether he wore straps around his nether regions or not. But she continued to watch as the two men walked away. About ten minutes later, she was surprised to see them come back the other way and walk in. They stood chatting to the woman in the apron, and another woman joined them. Clearly, everyone knew everyone in this little town and just as June had said, people seemed friendly.

Nina shocked herself as she could barely stop looking at this Robby person. She squeezed her eyes shut and shook her head in quick little movements. Who was he? What was he doing to her? Who was *she* more like? She'd not felt whatever it was she was feeling in such a long time, she wasn't even quite sure what it was. He wasn't even her type. What was her type these days? Did she even *have* a type? Goodness only knew. Her old type was dead and buried, but this one? Hello. This one was tall, the shoulders were oh-so-wide, oh my gawd, the back of the neck. All of it made her tingle. She was tingling from the other side of the room about a man she'd probably never see again. *Wind your neck in, Neens*, she told herself. But she didn't do that at all. She didn't wind her neck anywhere, and certainly not in. She, rather, stuck it out and gawped.

From her pew by the window, she quite enjoyed herself and continued to watch. The best thing about it was that Robby had no idea, and nor did anyone around him. Nina Lavendar was just another faceless run-of-the-mill Lovely Bay visitor as far as anyone here was concerned. Which was precisely what she was – a visitor. She didn't care because no one knew her. She would look. And look again. It wouldn't hurt anyone. A girl could dream.

16

Nina had had another night's sleep like no other. After two of them in a row, that in itself was perhaps a reason to stay in Lovely Bay. She hadn't slept without waking up at least three times in the night for years. Years and years. Her head had hit the pillow and the next thing she'd known she had woken up not in her bed in the flat without Andrew but with the curtains at the window blowing back and forth in the wind, birds tweeting outside, John Lewis Made in Portugal sheets all around her, and the distant sound of what she now realised was the sea. Nice.

After giving herself a gigantic pat on the back at the state of the kitchen, Nina had enjoyed a long and leisurely cup of coffee in the bath. The bath coffee date was nearly as nice as waking up in the John Lewis sheets. She'd mused how when she got back home she'd somehow put a roll top tub into the bathroom in her flat, as she'd soaked and sipped.

Out of the bath, she pulled on a pair of khaki combat trousers and an oversized white shirt, put her hair up into a ponytail, and pulled the magic CC cream out of her makeup bag. With that firmly in place on her face, she didn't quite glow as it had promised, but she no longer looked as if she was about to join Andrew, so that was a plus. Orgasm blusher was fluffed on next. She smiled at her reflection as the blusher performed a magic trick, and she didn't look half bad. The blusher proposed to give you *that* glow that came after, well, you know what. Nina Lavendar had most definitely forgotten what *that* glow was. The nearest she got to it was whatever was on the end of her blusher brush. Going through the hallway, she stopped to look in the enormous gilt-edged full-length mirror and assessed. Not too bad as widows go. Definitely in need of joining a gym, but the white shirt was doing a darn good job of hiding her gym-less body. Her hair wasn't too bad either. She chuckled to herself as she remembered someone at work who had asked her where she got her balayage done. Nina had frowned at that, not knowing balayage was a thing. The woman had explained precisely what it was, and Nina had snorted that her balayage had not found itself on her head by way of a hairdresser. The honey-coloured light gold ends on her hair were a result of the nice weather in the summer when her hair always lightened in the sun and the dark blonde bits at the roots had been given to her at birth. She was a walking, talking embodiment of balayage DIY.

After making another coffee and putting it in a travel cup, she opened the back door and made a grimacing face. The garden needed much more help than she could give it. Clearly, Jill had no idea how badly the string of house sitters had left the place. She stepped gingerly across the block-paved terrace with wide eyes at the sight of weed upon overgrown weed. It was like stepping into a small, self-contained wilderness. The remnants of what was once a tidy Victorian garden were now engulfed by rampant, overgrown plants just about every which way she looked. What she presumed was once a lawn was a tangle of weeds and long grass. Scraggly shrubs lined a Victorian wall. She could barely make out the shapes of what used to be flower beds, overrun with weeds, creeping vines, overgrown trees and plants. Fallen branches lay scattered around, a whole bank of hydrangeas was brown and shrivelled, and they appeared as if they might have given up the ghost.

Nina let out a long breath, her mind racing at the thought of tackling the jungle in front of her. It was certainly a challenge. She took out her phone and frowned as she reread Jill's words in her initial email about what was expected in return for staying in the house. Jill had written that there was some light gardening involved. Pah, Jill was having a chuckle. Even if it was in a tidy state, the garden was huge, and it certainly wasn't light gardening by any stretch of the imagination. The work needed to get the garden back to something workable would be enough to keep an actual gardener in a job for a while. As Nina continued to pick her way through the undergrowth, something about it, though, felt as if it had promise, as if at one point it was loved and pretty and nice. A bit like her, really. The air too seemed full of something she couldn't quite put her finger on - thick with the scent of plants, the sea and nature.

Nina continued to stand still and observe the state of the overgrown garden, mug of coffee in hand. She walked further to the other side of the cracked terrace, surveying the scene before her, shaking her head at the amount of work involved. On the right side of the house, more of the same greeted her: knee-high grass and weeds obscured crumbling garden paths. An ancient brick wall clad in ivy and moss enclosed the space on one side. Along it, overgrown boxwood shrubs and gnarly woody plants merged into a tangle of green. Wisteria snaked up the side of the house and an empty rusted plant stand had toppled to the ground and virtually disappeared beneath tall grasses.

Nina shook her head in dismay. Clearly, the grounds had been neglected for quite a while. Stalks of long-dead flowers poked up randomly, here and there, and a leaf-filled stone urn overflowed with rainwater. Weeds sprouted abundantly from beds, and tucked under a timber archway, an ornate metal bench was nearly obscured by vines. A mossy sundial sunken into its stone base looked ready to topple, and a crumbling bird-bath was covered in lichen.

As Nina gingerly picked her way along what remained of a path, wet grass soaked her shoes. She wrinkled up her nose and inhaled air heavy with a pungent scent; soil, decomposition and salty sea. Stakes that once held up climbing plants poked up crookedly, and an archway tangled with dead vines sagged in the middle. An empty stone-lined pond occupied the centre, now brimming with rainwater.

Nina made her way to a double-width dead-looking shed where the wooden remnants of a cold frame leaned askew at the side. As she got closer, she could see the shed's door hanging off one rusted hinge. Everywhere she looked, there was something to do. She stepped around piles of wet leaves and overturned plastic pots, yanked the loose door, and opened it with a creak. She turned her mouth upside down at the same time as raising her eyebrows. There was certainly no lack of tools for her to have a go at a few tasks. A jumble of abandoned tools lay all over the shed: shovels, rakes, pruners and hoes, all tarnished and dusty with disuse. Someone at some point had clearly taken the gardening of The Summer Hotel seriously. A multitude of trugs hung from the shed roof, gardening baskets spilled over with coils of ancient garden twine and empty seed packets were scattered all along a long timber bench. A shelf along the back held dusty glass jars; balls of string and terracotta pots were piled up everywhere.

Wrinkling her nose at the musty air, Nina stepped back out into the garden. In one far corner, a dilapidated greenhouse hunkered beneath sprawling ivy. Many panes in its metal frame had shattered, leaving jagged shards. Inside, broken clay pots and shrivelled plants lay strewn across benches. Nina chuckled to herself as she looked around and thought about her little ledge in her flat. And she'd thought she was a gardener. Ho, ho, ho. The work needed to restore order in the garden she was looking at would take months, if not longer.

Not sure if she was the person for it, she made her way back to the house, stepped gingerly over a cracked section of block paving and headed for the side of the house. To the right, an arched wooden door was set into an old brick wall. She went to test the old latch. Finding it stuck fast with rust, she bashed it with a closed fist and pushed it with her shoulder. She managed to shove it open and found herself standing in what had obviously once been a kitchen garden. Stakes that likely once held up runner beans or peas stuck up here and there. Empty frames stood skeletal against the old walls, and a crumbling brick path wound around the beds. Nina ducked beneath trellises that supported remnants of dead vines, passed a compost bin near collapse and a potting bench whose surface had warped and split and stood for ages just looking. Something about it was doing something to her. Something unexpectedly stirred, making her emotional. The nearby sea, the scent of the earth, the multitude of green things. She imagined how lovely the garden must have once been. It was almost as if it was a little sanctuary that had been waiting for her. A robin hopped nearby and looked at her with a beady eye, as though wondering quite where Nina had appeared from.

Nina felt quite out of sorts. A strange and odd kind of hope and optimism she hadn't felt in ages had descended as she'd walked around. After not quite believing what she had seen and that there was an actual old-school kitchen garden with the remnants of all kinds of herbs and vegetables she went in, made a cup of tea headed right down to the back garden and sat lost in thought for ages looking out over the water.

Just as she was standing by the water contemplating whether or not to take off her shoes and paddle in the river beach, she heard something behind her. As she whirled around at the noise, everything lit up. Her morning had just got about a million times better. Robby, sadly not in a wetsuit with the top down but in a heavy-duty canvas work shirt and combat trousers, was standing not too far away from her. It appeared as if he'd been working. A little bit sweaty possibly, clearly someone who worked outside, maybe on the water. Big hands, big shoulders, everything just sort of big. Nina couldn't quite believe that her pulse was actually speeding up. The same tingles from the day before made themselves known in regions long since dead. Nina felt mildly alarmed. She clearly fancied this bloke; she just about remembered what fancying someone was about. This was it. Quite worrying. She knew nothing about him. Also, she'd never thought in a million years that she might ever be attracted to someone ever again – male, female, or identifying as anything. Her mum had mentioned that there were plenty more fish in the sea, and Sophie had tried and failed many times to get her to even consider meeting a few people. Sophie had even set her up on a blind date with one of Nick's divorced friends. Nina had simply *just not* been interested in relationships. Not even a little bit. That had changed by way of a man in a small coastal town and owner of fabulous eyes and very nice hips. The thighs weren't bad either. She was so interested, it wasn't even funny. She felt guilty about the tingles.

'Oh, hey,' Nina heard herself say and felt herself stand up straighter. She felt her ribs rise, her stomach get sucked in and her head seemed to be moving of its own accord; it did a strange slow movement and ended up cocked to the side. A smile she'd not had on her face since she was in school appeared. It said 'I'm friendly and nice, and you might like to get to know me'. It didn't really work.

'Hi.'

Nina heard herself continuing. 'Nice day for a spot of gardening.' She cringed inside. *WTAF. Idiot.*

'You're funny.'

Nina frowned, 'Sorry?'

Robby jerked his thumb to the back of the house and garden. 'That will take more than a "spot of gardening".' Robby held his fingers up to demonstrate speech marks around the spot of gardening bit.

'Ahh, yes. I was just thinking that. It's quite overgrown. I just discovered a little kitchen garden at the side there. So nice.'

'I bet you did.'

Nina was irritated by Robby's sarcastic tone. 'Sorry, what *is* your problem?'

Robby looked very taken aback at Nina's tone. 'What do you mean by what is my problem?'

Nina shook her head. 'I've seen you like twice and you've been rude both times. To be quite honest, get lost. Don't bother to talk to me. Go on. Shove off.'

Robby stifled a smile and raised his eyebrows. 'Interesting.'

'No. Not interesting. Go away. Don't even look at me. Go on. Get lost.' Nina then swore at him. Quite badly.

'I'm standing on my aunt's property. I don't need to get lost.'

Nina sighed and shook her head. The tingling was going ballistic, but she was going to ignore it. Who even was this bloke with the attitude? 'Whatever.'

'I'm just not keen on freeloaders. The last one conned my aunt out of a fair whack of money, and we haven't seen her since. This whole house sitting thing gets my goat. Just rent a place already, like the rest of the world has to. You know, get a mortgage, pay some rent...'

Nina shook her head. 'I do have a house, thank you very much.'

'Of course you do. That's why you came down here to "house-sit".' Again, the speech marks went around the last two words. Robby rolled his eyes. 'Born yesterday, do you think we are?'

Nina also put her hands up in speech marks. 'I'm house-sitting for a change of scenery.'

'So where's this supposed house you own?'

'It's a flat actually, and it's in London. Actually, there are two of them, so there.' Nina retorted and winced at the fact that her voice had just taken thirty odd years off her age. *Pathetic.* She even considered playing the widow-in-your-thirties card. But she hadn't used the W-word for ages, and she was probably going to keep it that way.

'There you go. Bully for you.' Robby turned back to the house. 'Right, well, apologies if I was rude, but yeah, as I said, freeloaders are not my thing.' He started to stride away.

The magically moving-on-its-own head turned to look at the bottom, which was walking away from her. The bottom (small, tight, outstanding) did not disappoint. The tingles were now coming in waves. She was, in fact, perhaps going to keel over. She might have to have a bit of a lie down. Nina heard herself calling out. 'No worries.'

17

It was a few days or so later. Nina had spent full days in the garden, not seeing a single soul and listening to books while pulling out weeds, and she'd *thoroughly* enjoyed herself. She'd completely bypassed going into Lovely Bay, not really in the mood to see anyone and finding just being at The Summer Hotel strangely comforting. After looking at short-term lets on Right Move with Nathan in mind, she'd realised that she would probably be staying in Lovely Bay for a few weeks at least. Since Andrew had gone, she'd not really had any interest in property prices or anything like that at all, and she hadn't realised that a short-term let was, firstly, like gold dust, and secondly, more or less extortion. She'd also realised that her flat, which when they'd bought it had been in a quite rough area, was now apparently 'up-and-coming,' now clearly de rigueur and the place to be. The flat's value had shot up exponentially and so had renting anywhere around it, meaning turfing Nathan out wasn't going to be easy. She'd considered staying with her mum or Sophie until Nathan had gone home but hadn't been able to stomach asking so had canned that idea.

Her delve into the property market had been a surprise. In

all the time she'd been on her own, it had not even really crossed her mind what the investment property might be worth. Andrew had insisted on taking out an insurance policy on the properties which had paid off the mortgages when she'd lost him, and she hadn't thought about the property value much since. Both flats were tiny, she didn't really have much savings, and the financial adviser at the bank had told her to rent the investment out and start getting the money into a pension fund before it was too late. That was one of the many things she missed about Andrew. He'd just always got on and done the boring things; mortgages, insurance, car stuff when they'd had a car, holiday bookings, rates, bills – you name it, he'd done it. Nina had completely taken it for granted, and when she'd had to learn, and fast, she'd realised just how much he'd taken care of.

So, realising that it would be a pain in the backside for Nathan to try and rent somewhere for a short term, she'd decided to seize the day and get stuck into the kitchen garden at The Summer Hotel. At the very least, it would give her a bit of exercise and a learning curve for when she got back to her gardening ledge. What had actually happened had surprised her; she'd found it all very satisfying. The garden still had a very, very long way to go, but even with a couple of days of work, the change and potential it held was quite astonishing. Maybe she'd been a bit harsh about Jill's words, that it only needed a bit of a tidy up. Perhaps she'd been looking at it with her city-girl eyes. She'd found all sorts in the kitchen garden: lovely timber beds under weeds, herbs hanging on for dear life, things emerging from the soil, thriving rosemary bushes, and onions by the dozen. She'd uncovered beautiful iron Victorian cold frames swallowed by weeds and found vintage gardening tools lying about discarded all over the place.

Something The Summer Hotel was doing to her made her feel good deep down in her bones. As if with her fingers in the soil, her nose in the air, and her head in the clouds, a new Nina was beginning to emerge. She felt better than she had in a long time, and she was going to hang around for a bit and see how, or if, it continued. She might as well, especially since she'd been made redundant; there didn't seem to be much to run back to London for.

She sat down with a cup of tea and spent way too long scrolling through Instagram. How did people even get lives like that? Where were the widows of Insta hanging out? Pouring out another cup of tea, she tapped the Gmail app and was surprised to see that there was an email from Jill. There must have been Wi-Fi at Jill's latest destination.

Hi Nina,

I hope you're getting on well with the place. I wanted to let you know a few things.

We have been waiting for official stuff with my aunt's estate, and things have now finally come through. We have decided that we are going to cut our losses and put the property up for sale at some point in the future (just waiting for the final official things/solicitor's work).

I was wondering if you would be interested in a paid position in sprucing the place up for sale. I know our arrangement at the moment consists of you sorting the living quarters, but the rest of the place, too, will need work to get it ready to go to market. We are going to try and market this place as an Airbnb, seeing as all the red tape stuff is already in place.

Let me know if you're interested first, and we'll go from there.

Thanks so much.

Jill

Nina read the email twice more and then again. Was she interested? She leaned back in her chair, reading over Jill's email a fourth time. Her mind raced as she processed this new development. A paid position at The Summer Hotel? The notion of getting the place ready for sale felt a bit daunting, but nothing she wasn't up for, and at the end of the day, there was only so long she could go without a job. She needed an income and something to do. Plus, if there was one thing Nina quite relished, it was a challenge and The Summer Hotel was most definitely one of those.

On top of that, she was enjoying herself. Even in the short time she'd been there, she'd loved the satisfaction derived from getting rid of clutter. Sophie had been telling her for years to get her little organising business back up and running again, but she'd never had the oomph. It could, in fact, be the start of that. She sat back, her mind whirring with the implications of Jill's email. The idea of sprucing up The Summer Hotel for sale intrigued her a little bit. She'd already found herself wondering what it would be like with some care and attention, and she was even already a little bit attached to its walls and gardens. The thought of it being sold made something somewhere in the back of her head twinge with sadness.

She sipped her tea, pondering the offer. Would she be up for it? Anyone could see it was not a job for someone who shied away from hard work. Decluttering the place alone was a lot of graft. On one hand, taking on the project could give her a sense of purpose, something she hadn't felt in a long while. On the other, it meant investing her time and effort into a place that wasn't really anything to do with her. Could she realistically oversee and take that on single-handedly? Where would she even begin?

Nina mulled it over with her tea. She wondered if the whole thing was fate. Sophie seeing the post, her spontaneously applying, the implication of the Nathan problem, losing her job, and now this. Maybe Jill's proposal was a good one. Possibly, The Summer Hotel could be her anchor for a little bit, as Sophie had said, to get her out of a rut.

Her gaze drifted over the garden, and she realised just how much she'd enjoyed her time outside. She'd relished getting well stuck into the removal of weeds, discovering things in the kitchen garden and seeing plants coming back to life. There was so much potential, so much that could be done to transform The Summer Hotel or, more rightly, give it back its life.

Was she interested? Yes, she kind of was. However, a little part of her was asking if it was a good idea. Did she really want to buy into something that was a fleeting thing in her life? Something, however, was whispering to her, telling her she should have a go. Telling her there was hope.

18

Nina squinted at the running app she'd downloaded on a
whim, puffed out her lips, let a whoosh of air out and
shook her head a little bit. She'd found the app after her conversation with June and after mulling it over for a while she'd
decided that her stay in Lovely Bay would be the time when she
finally took her fitness by its neck, stopped making excuses and
made getting fit happen. She flipped to the first session and read
through. Surely it couldn't be that hard, could it? It was just a
short amount of time. An itsy-bitsy twenty minutes of exercise.
She could manage that, couldn't she? Anything had to be better
than working out with the goddesses dressed in white inhabiting The Chelsea Collective. At least this way, she was on her
own and didn't have to bother with anyone else at all. She
nodded as she read through. It sounded simple enough; begin
with a brisk five-minute walk, then alternate one minute of
running and one-and-a-half minutes of walking, for a total of
twenty minutes. Too easy. A breeze. She would be fine.

Tying on her trainers, Nina looked down at her running
gear. The goddesses would cringe at her attire. Although to be
fair, her workout top was white, so she'd sort of fit in wearing

that. Well, at least it was once white, now not so much. It was now more a grey-ish white and most of the elastic had stretched, so it was no longer quite performing its job as a bra quite as well as it might once have done. The leggings were slightly better, if still a bit see through. Sophie had given them to Nina because she'd ordered the wrong size, not realised, taken the label off and then ascertained that they were way too big. Shame, the same didn't apply for Nina - the leggings were far from too big.

Nina was determined, though, to give the running app a go despite what she was wearing or how she felt. She had a pair of trainers, and she could walk well enough, so she could surely manage one-minute runs interspersed with walking, couldn't she? People ran marathons, for goodness' sake. People survived sprinting up mountains and across continents. People ran for hours for fun. She could do a mere twenty-minute walk with a few runs thrown in for good measure.

She scraped her hair up into a ponytail, put her earphones in, and headed out into the road. Once standing on the road, she had second thoughts. There was no way she was going to try and run in broad daylight on the pavement for all the world to see. She was going to have a go, granted, but she'd have to do it somewhere a little bit more secluded. Taking a left turn, she headed down towards the river and the path she'd seen walkers, cyclists and all sorts on. Other people used the path for their fitness pursuits; she'd join them and no one would take any notice of her whatsoever.

About five minutes later, Nina was on the path and raring to go. Actually not quite raring, more like bracing herself. She listened to the American in her ears, who was telling her that in a couple of months she would transform from a couch potato to a runner. She would no longer *feel* like a potato, either, apparently. Simple. Easy-peasy.

'Begin with a brisk five-minute warm up walk.' Nina listened to the instructions. The voice told her she needed to walk at a brisk pace, as if she was late for something but still be able to hold a conversation. She stopped and sat on a bench for a minute, gearing herself up for it.

Pushing herself up from the bench, she pressed play again and started to briskly walk. Too easy. She shouldn't have even doubted herself for a second. Four minutes in, the voice told her she should be very proud of herself and that she should keep up the brisk pace. *Yes, sleek collective-type body shape, here I come.*

'If you have been lying on the couch for the last week, don't worry! This is for you. If you have been intimidated by running, this is for you! If you've been intimidated by super perfect people in the gym, we've got you covered! You're going to love this. Get ready to feel good about getting fit, couch potatoes out there.'

Nina nodded. The voice was speaking to her soul. She had been all of those things. She strode determinedly along as her pulse quickened and she warmed up. The voice instructed her to swing her arms and start thinking about some running form. 'Don't forget to breathe and have fun.' Run tall, it said. 'Tall, soft, breath, fun,' it repeated a few times.

Nina nodded. She could do it. Though fun wasn't quite what sprang to mind when thinking about running, even for a minute. Torture felt more appropriate.

A woman in very fancy exercise clothes, a white branded baseball cap, and huge headphones came the other way. The woman was definitely tall and soft, was breathing, and by the beam on her face, appeared to be having fun. The woman waved a happy little hand at Nina. Nina did a funny grimace-smile back.

'You have a minute to mentally prepare your body that it is going to run. Our bodies are ready for the workout we are about to do. You're going to run couch potatoes!'

Nina swore.

'Ten, nine, eight, seven, six, five, four, three, two, one. Let's go. We're running! You are officially now a runner.'

Nina started to jog and felt as if she was going to keel over. She plodded along, one foot in front of the other, as her whole body appeared to be wobbling of its own accord. Her skin and fat had, in fact, taken on a whole new lease of life. She was now a jelly. However, she was doing it. She was the slowest, wobbliest, jiggliest jogger on the planet, but she was able to run along the path. Quite unbelievable.

'Okay, take it down to a walk. Whatever is a nice pace for you. We'll be here for ninety seconds, and then we'll run again.'

Nina balled her hands into fists and did little fist pumps in front of her. Seb Coe, eat your heart out. She couldn't quite believe it, but she'd just completed a one-minute run. Woohoo.

She took a deep breath, steeling herself for the next upcoming minute of running. The woman's cheerful voice was not infectious; it was fairly annoying, however, Nina felt a flicker of optimism. 'If she can enjoy it, maybe I can too,' she mumbled to herself.

The voice in her earphones counted down. 'Three, two, one, start running!'

Nina broke into another tentative jog, her feet pounding on the path beside the river, the beach and sea in the distance. She focused on keeping her posture tall and her steps light. Neither of them happened; she wasn't tall or light, she was heavy, wobbling like a jelly, out of breath, but she was doing it. Her breathing quickened further, her cheeks felt on fire, and she reminded herself of the voice's advice – breathe deeply, run tall, stay soft.

The minute of running felt like the longest minute of her life, but as she neared the end, she found herself feeling oddly exhilarated. The voice in her earphones chimed in, 'Great job! Now, slow down to a walk for one-and-a-half minutes.'

Nina obeyed, slowing her pace to a walk and breathing in

quick little puffs. She could feel her heart pounding in her chest, and she was hot all over. She wasn't quite sure if she liked running yet, but she didn't hate it, which was a start.

As she walked, she reflected on the changes she had already made since arriving in Lovely Bay. The old Nina would never have considered doing something like this. She would have made loads of excuses. But here, now, she was giving it a go, pushing herself out of her comfort zone.

The voice brought her back to the present. 'Ready for your next running minute? You can do this! Guys, this is flying by! In thirty seconds, we're going to run again. Make yourself proud. You will not regret doing it. Don't quit now, couch potatoes.'

Nina braced herself and started running again. This time, it felt a little easier or maybe harder, she wasn't even sure. She did know she was less focused on her surroundings and more on the sensation of moving, of her muscles working, of wobbling from head to toe.

The pattern continued as she made her way along the river path, alternating between running or very slow jogging in her case and walking, with the slightly annoying voice offering encouragement and advice. By the time she got to the last segment, Nina felt as if her skin was dropping off. Everything wobbled, her bottom, her cheeks, the tops of her arms, her inner thighs, her outer thighs. The bra really was not doing its job. Had her boobs actually hit her stomach all of their own accord? Possibly.

'Remind yourself why you're here. You have the ability to do this. Feel the power of your body.' Finally, the voice announced, 'Last run minute coming up. Give it your best shot!'

Nina plodded along at not more than a fast jog-walk as the voice encouraged. Maybe, just maybe, she could become one of those people who actually enjoyed running. Yeah, maybe not.

'I'm super proud that you are here with me! Your goal might seem out of reach, but before you know it, you will be a runner.'

Sweat was pouring from any and every place it could. Nina's top was around her waist and the grey-white crop top was on show for the world to see. Touching the back of her right hand to her face, Nina felt a boiling hot cheek. Her breath was coming in fast gasps, her legs felt like lead and as the voice instructed she slowed right down to a stop. Putting her hands into the small of her back, she raised her head up and looked up to the sky. Taking her hands from her back and still with her head raised up, she made fists, punched the sky and cheered herself. She'd only actually gone and done it. She shouted up to the sky. 'Yessssssssssss! Yes, yes, yes, yes, yes.'

Bringing her hands back down, she cringed and wanted the ground to open up and swallow her whole as she heard clapping coming from the river. The riverboat was chugging past and Colin was holding up his hands in front of him and clapping. 'Way to go!'

Nina didn't need any more redness to hit her cheeks, but some more landed there anyway. She wasn't sure what to do as she looked at the river, at the boat and at the people watching who had all clearly just witnessed her fist pumping the sky and congratulating herself at how well she'd done. Nina just blinked rapidly and pretended she was fine as her blood pumped, her head felt as if it was about to explode, and she was wondering if she would ever breathe normally again. She made a wincing gesture, nodded a little bit and did a little embarrassed wave back. It was as the back of the boat was sliding past, when she'd just put her hands into the small of her back and was trying to recover her breathing that she saw Robby sitting on the other side of where Colin was standing. He was smiling but not waving. Nina just sort of looked, not sure what to do. She'd never felt so undignified in her life.

19

After spending a good five minutes reading through the community noticeboard with a smile on her face, Nina walked away from the green with its pretty Lutyens benches, war memorial, and plethora of rose bushes and made her way along the high street. As she got to the main thoroughfare, rows of shops interspersed every now and then with cottages whose front doors opened right onto the pavement and people strolled along in the sunshine full of the joys of spring. From a central point, bunting cascaded back and forth across the street and hanging baskets filled with flowers halfway up old-fashioned lampposts swung back and forth in a sea breeze. Pretty awnings snaked out over the cobbled pavement, a woman cycled by on an old Raleigh bike, and there somehow seemed to be cheerfulness in the air. Nina smiled as someone in the Lovely wax coat with a huge bouquet in her arms smiled and said hello as she bustled out of a flower shop. Nina reciprocated and then stood for a minute gazing at the flowers, wondering whether or not to treat herself to a bunch.

A few minutes later, she was about halfway down the high street at another parade of shops. She stopped to look at what was on offer on tables outside a deli and had a little nose in the window. Timber boxes were rammed full of homemade chutneys, locally sourced honey, little loaves of sourdough, marmalades, and relishes. Another table held what appeared to be small batches of homemade biscuits. Inhaling the smell wafting from the door full of the aroma of freshly baked bread, aged cheese, and herbs, Nina couldn't quite get enough. Inside she could see platters of antipasti, large wheels of cheese stacked in lines, gigantic dishes full of olives, pork pies, sun-dried tomatoes in tubs, and bunches of bay leaves hanging from above. In lines across the top of the counter, a variety of cured meats and garlic braids hung from the ceiling on gigantic hooks and baskets laden with fresh, crusty loaves. Tucked here and there, little tables and chairs were perched between everything. Nina was in artisan food, window shopping heaven.

Ambling to the shop next door, Nina stopped at an old-fashioned chemist sign, and squinted at the sign writing over the door where it told her the proprietor was L. Hong Pharmacist. Peering in at the old-fashioned timber shelves, she smiled and then frowned. Unless she was very much mistaken, the Shipping Forecast was blaring from the inside of the chemist; not quite your local branch of Superdrug. The next shop made her jaw drop as she came to the door and stopped in amazement; an *actual* handmade chocolate shop. Just inside the window sat piles and piles of chocolate truffles in little trays, melted chocolate poured from a fountain, and as Nina squidged her nose almost to the glass, she realised the huge revolving copper drum in the corner was full of chocolate.

'I could get used to this,' she said to herself as she stood transfixed by the paddle going around and around on the top of the machine.

A woman in a Lovely coat came hustling out of the shop with a huge wicker basket in her arms. The woman smiled. 'Hello. How are you?'

'Good, thanks,' Nina replied, chuckled and pointed to the chocolate in the window. 'I've just been lusting after the chocolate. I might have to move in.' She then squinted and strained her ears; she was either hearing things or the Shipping Forecast was coming from the vicinity of the woman's left shoulder. *On behalf of the Maritime and Coastguard agency. There are warnings of gales in Viking, Dogger, Fisher, Trafalgar, Hebrides, and Faeroes,* the left shoulder said. Nina shook her head, thinking she was hearing things. She squinted towards the woman's shoulder, trying to fathom what was going on.

The woman completely ignored her left shoulder and laughed. 'It's a common problem on this street. You might want to take a chocolate souvenir home with you and think of us when you have it with a cup of tea. Lovely chocolate is the best, not that I'm biased, of course.'

Nina shook her head. 'Oh, I don't need a souvenir. I'm just down the road here.'

'Oh right, an early holiday. The weather's good for you today.'

Nina shook her head. 'Actually, I'm here for a while.'

'Oh, right you are. A long holiday for you, then? Where are you staying?'

'No, no. I'm not really on holiday, though I am getting away for a bit. I'm looking after a hotel.'

The shoulder continued to broadcast. *The general synopsis at one eight double oh.* The woman's eyes lit up in recognition. 'Ahh, right, of course. Jill's?'

'Yes. How did you guess?'

The woman chortled and tapped the side of her nose. 'The Lovely grapevine made me aware that you had arrived.' The woman shook her head. 'Sorry, I should have realised as soon as I laid eyes on you.'

'Ahh, I think that grapevine likes me at the moment.'

'The last house-sitter took a Lovely local for a ride, so we've been looking out for you.' The woman laughed heartily. 'Be aware; you are being observed.'

'I've heard about that.'

'It wasn't nice. The last house-sitter conned one of our own out of money.' The woman held out her hand. 'Li, or as I'm known around these parts, Birdie. It's a long story. I'm the pharmacist, so if you get anything wrong with you, you know who to call.'

'Oh, right.' Nina pointed back to the pharmacy and the flat above. 'That's your place, is it?'

Birdie smiled. 'Yes. Guilty as charged. I hear you've got a lot of decluttering on your hands.' The shoulder spoke. *Showers good, occasionally poor.*

Nina widened her eyes. 'You could say that.'

'Bit of a mess in there, is it?'

'Nothing a good clear out and deep clean can't sort out. It'll just take a bit of time, and I like nothing better than a good decluttering.'

'So, you, err, do house-sitting for a living, is that right?'

'Gosh, no! It was all a bit spur of the moment. I saw a Facebook post, and yes, well, now I'm here.'

'Ahh, right. I see. Some people do it for a living...'

'What?'

'House-sit, couch-surf, pet-sit, all that sort of thing. They go all over the place, or so I'm told.'

'Interesting. Well, no, that's not me. It's my first time.' Nina wondered whether or not to say that she'd not really been anywhere much for years. She couldn't be bothered to launch into it all.

Birdie looked up at the sky. 'Sun is out for a bit. You've probably already gathered that we get four seasons in a day here in Lovely.'

Nina laughed. 'I think I have. When I left, it was drizzling, then the sun came out, and now it's windy. All in the space of no time at all.'

Birdie pulled at the corner of her coat. 'That's why we all have these. Best thing ever.'

'I think I might need one.'

Birdie made to move. 'Right, well, I hope you get on well with the decluttering. I'll see you around then probably. If you need anything at all, just pop in.'

'Yes, okay, thanks.'

'Oh, and if you go to the chocolate shop, tell them Birdie said to give you the Lovely treatment.' The shoulder continued, *Biscay variable two to four.*

Nina frowned. 'The Lovely treatment? What's that?'

Birdie cackled. 'You'll find out, haha. Our very special treatment for Lovelies, and if you're in the hotel over there, you sort of qualify as a temporary Lovely.'

'I like the sound of special treatment. Is it similar to the secret chowders?'

Birdie frowned and rolled her eyes. 'No idea what you're talking about – secret Lovely chowders, what are they?' Birdie was clearly pretending not to know. She tapped the side of her nose. 'We don't talk about those, but no doubt if you're here for a while, I'll see you at one.'

'I hope so.'

'There's one down your road, or so the rumour goes. You might get an invite,' Birdie said with a chuckle at the end.

'Thanks.' Nina laughed.

Birdie hustled away. 'See you later.'

'See you.'

Nina frowned as she walked away. The whole episode had been accompanied by what sounded like the Shipping Forecast coming from Birdie's left shoulder. Nina screwed her eyes up and tried to make sense of it. Birdie's phone had appeared to be tucked in her left bra strap under her top and coat and the Shipping Forecast had been playing in her ear. As Nina smiled and then continued along the street, she stopped to look in the window of a bustling little hair salon with two Lovely flags in holders by the front door. She thought about the conversation with Birdie and the secret chowders and whether it really was a thing or not. Whether it was or not, she did know that people seemed to take it all very seriously indeed.

20

Nina had been up to her eyes in clearing out the hotel. She'd got well stuck into the clutter, had ordered for the delivery of a couple of skips to aid with removal of some of the old B&B furniture, and she'd focused a lot on the garden. By the end of the third day of working almost solely on the garden and clearing out the scullery, she had decided seeing a human might be a good idea. So, early evening after reading more about the Lovely Bay chowders, she set off in search of just that.

She hopped on the riverboat, wandered through the town and just as she was peering into the window of the local bookshop, a woman came out of a bistro coffee shop on the other side where tea lights flickered in the windows, and the shop looked as if it was open. Nina crossed over, wondering if she might go in. The sign on the door, however, said it was closed. She cupped her hands to her eyes and peered in. Candles flickered, a countertop wood burner was lit, and an old-fashioned chandelier with fabric shades glowed. The place gave the appearance that there was life, but the door was definitely closed. She squinted through an archway where she could see movement, more candles, and a couple of people sitting at a table.

'Peeping Tom now, are you?'

Nina nearly jumped out of her skin. She whirled around to see Robby getting out of the van he'd been in when she'd seen him at his aunt's. 'You're funny.'

'What are you up to?'

'I've been attacking the garden, and I thought tonight I'd go out in search of something to eat. I'm trying to find somewhere to have some Lovely chowder.'

'Right, you are. Well, you're in the right place for chowder.'

Nina pointed to the bistro. 'Is that place open?'

A funny look crossed Robby's face. 'Not really.'

'Not really? What does that mean?'

'Sort of.'

'Am I missing something? Is it open or isn't it?'

'Yeah, umm, for Lovelies.' Robby coughed.

'What? For Lovelies? It looks open, but the sign says it's not...'

'As I said. It is and it isn't.'

'You're not making much sense. So it's not open?'

'It's not open, but yeah...'

Nina wasn't sure what Robby was going on about and then it dawned on her. The thing Nancy had said about secret chowder. She wrinkled up her nose. 'Ahh, right. Is it the secret thing?'

'It might be.'

Nina burst out laughing. 'Are you *actually* serious?'

Robby joked. 'It's not a laughing matter, Miss-I've-got-a-flat-in-London.'

Nina swore. 'So, I can't go in there?'

'Officially, it's closed.'

Nina turned to walk the other way. 'I'd better go to the pub then or get fish and chips, assuming I can go in there and that's not officially closed.'

'Hang on. Look, I'm going in there, so, well, if you want to come in with me.'

'What and try the secret chowder?'

'Yeah, do you like chowder?'

Nina wasn't sure. But if Robby was asking her to go in with him, she liked chowder. She'd eat frog's legs wrapped in cardboard, to be quite frank. 'I do. I love chowder. Absolutely adore it.' She felt her head do the turn thing. She touched her hair. Her eyelashes were batting for England.

'Because that's all that's on offer.'

'What, literally?'

'Yes.'

Nina hesitated, second-guessing herself and wondering if she should accept Robby's offer. The whole thing was most bizarre, and there was no doubt that she was curious about this 'secret' chowder spot. Mostly, though she couldn't really give a stuff about chowder, secret or not, it was the company she was interested in. She did give an absolutely gigantic stuff about Robby. Her head did the weird thing again, where it turned on its side. 'Are you sure it's okay for me to tag along? I wouldn't want to intrude.' *I so want to intrude. I would like to get lost in your straps.*

Robby seemed a lot more cordial than he'd been when she'd first met him. Maybe he wasn't quite as grumpy and up himself as he'd first appeared. 'Not a problem at all. They won't mind an extra guest, I don't think.'

'You don't think?'

'Nah. It'll be fine. Follow me.'

Nina followed Robby a few shops along, past the pharmacy and the chocolate shop and then turned down a narrow alley, to a small back courtyard area completely covered in fairy lights. He turned left and stopped at a door, and gave a quiet knock. After a moment, Birdie, the woman Nina had met outside the pharmacy, opened the door. 'Our Robby. Wasn't sure we'd see you tonight. How are you?'

'Are we good for another one? Summer Hotel,' Robby explained.

Birdie beamed and ushered them inside and quickly shut the door behind them. 'Ahh, Nina! So you found one of our secret venues.'

'I might have known you'd already met Nina,' Robby said with a chuckle.

'You know me. Nothing gets past me in this town.' Birdie laughed.

'She gets a pass to come in even though she's not officially a Lovely?' Robby asked.

'I'll grant her access even though I'm not in charge here.' Birdie chuckled.

Nina swallowed. These people were serious. 'Thanks.'

Nina realised the Shipping Forecast was coming from the direction of Birdie's shoulder. *Dogger, Fisher, Portland, Plymouth, west, five to seven. Rain then showers, good, occasionally poor at first.*

Nina looked around and realised that they were now in the back room she'd seen when she'd been looking in the window on the pavement. She felt as if someone had dropped her into a whole other world of strange, joyful, perfectly curated chaos. Tealights and candles flickered on the tables, on a mantelpiece over a fire, along the windowsills, and on a picture rail going around the whole room. Two chandeliers with fabric lampshades hung from the ceiling, antique rugs in pastel colours lined the timber floors, watercolour pictures of the River Lovely were haphazardly placed on the walls, and a pale blue velvet armchair was tucked in the corner. Little vases of fresh flowers were dotted here and there, flickering tea lights in amber glass holders glinted from the tables, and in piles everywhere stacks of well-loved books and magazines appeared as if they might topple over and fall.

Robby led her over towards the window to a table tucked in an alcove. Not really sure where she was, Nina sank gratefully onto a cushioned chair and peered out the window into a small courtyard where a couple sat at a bistro table with a little dog snoozing underneath. As Robby chatted, Nina soaked up every detail of the pictures on the crowded walls around her depicting Lovely Bay through the decades; fishermen standing on the sea wall, shop owners, and local families posing in front of boats, storefronts, and lovely Victorian homes, and loads of snapshots of daily life – a horse-drawn carriage clip-clopping down a lane, ladies strolling with parasols along the seaside promenade, a crowded market day on the village green. Sepia-toned images of the winding river, the lighthouse standing tall beside quaint shops.

'This is so nice,' Nina said, touching the edge of a crocheted curtain at the window.

Robby agreed. 'Yeah, it is. You are now sitting in a Lovely Bay institution. Tourists don't often get to see this place out the back here. You have to be a Lovely.'

Nina lowered her voice. 'Sorry, I thought Birdie was the pharmacist.'

'She is.'

'And she owns this as well?'

Robby laughed. 'The Lings own many places in the town, including this place and the deli where you'll sometimes find her. She pretends she doesn't though. She's not usually in here or the deli, but everyone is short staffed. She's mostly just in the chemist, but at the moment you'll find her everywhere.'

'Right. What and they have one of these speakeasy chowder places, too?'

'Everyone does. It's just that this place is the one on rotation tonight.'

Birdie bustled back to the table. 'Good to have you. How are you getting on in the hotel?'

Nina wasn't going to say that at one point she'd been thinking about calling it a day and going back to London. No one needed to know her business. 'I, err, I'm enjoying it so far.'

'You're working hard, so I've heard. That must be a job and a half. Gives you something to get your teeth stuck into anyway.'

Nina thought about what she'd done so far in the kitchen. 'Yes, for sure. I'm enjoying it, actually.'

'Good luck with it.'

'Thanks. I've done well in the garden. There's a kitchen garden at the side.'

'Indeed there is.' Birdie nodded.

Nina squinted. 'Oh, you know it, do you?'

'Everyone knows that old place. Or I should say anyone from Lovely knows it. The developers would love to get their hands on it. Lovelies hopefully will put a stop to that.' Birdie rolled her eyes. 'Goodness knows how many council meetings there have been about it.'

'Okay, wow, interesting. I didn't know that about developers.'

Birdie looked at Robby. 'Luxury flats and all sorts.'

Robby nodded, 'Yep.'

Birdie's voice turned more serious as she turned back to Nina. 'Anyway. Just you make sure you take care of it. Drink?' Nina tuned in to the Shipping Forecast, not quite sure what to make of it. *Rain or showers, good, occasionally moderate. Biscay east or south-east, four to six.*

Nina wasn't sure what to think of Birdie's serious tone. 'Yes, please.'

'Lemonade, wine, beer or shandy. Lovely lemonade. Ale from the brewery.'

Nina gulped. Sounded like gin and tonic wasn't on the menu. 'Umm, yes, please, a beer.'

'Great.'

Nina whispered over the table to Robby, 'How do we order food? Where are the menus?'

'We don't.'

'Oh.'

'You get chowder. That's it. That's why I asked. Like it or lump it.'

'Right, okay. I see. Sorry, so we just get what we're given, do we?'

'Pretty much.'

'How does that work, then?'

Robby smiled. 'It goes back to the old seafaring days, and it's said it first came from the Breton fisherman who used to come here. Fishermen's families used what was left over from the trawl and served the chowder in or with bread. Depending on where you are, you'll get mussels, cod and salmon chowder to eat in a bread bowl or a slice of Lovely brown bread.'

'Nice.'

'It's an old Lovely tradition.'

'Sounds good. What's the secret thing?'

'That also goes back to seafaring days and smuggling. There are loads of old superstitions around it, but yeah, it was something to do with fishing tax and building levy and so they went a bit underground and the tradition still exists today.'

'How funny. What, so there are loads of these establishments? Like chowder speakeasies?'

'Not officially no but yes. You get secret restaurants and secret clubs in people's homes all over Lovely Bay.'

'Oh wow.'

'There's a rotation - it changes venues most nights. You wouldn't know about them if you weren't with someone from Lovely or unless someone invites you like I just did out the front there.'

Just as Nina went to speak, a plate with a small sourdough loaf filled with a creamy thick soup landed in front of her, together with a glass of beer. It seemed like a whole lot of fuss about nothing. Surprised at the bread as a bowl thing but pretending she was totally cool with it, she followed Robby, picked up her spoon and dug in. She swore. 'Oh my word, that's incredible'

Robby laughed. 'Good?'

'Flipping heck. I wasn't expecting it to taste that good. No wonder it's a thing!'

'Yep.'

Nina took another spoonful. 'Goodness. Outstanding!'

'Each place has their own special ingredient. This is one of the best. Birdie's grandparents put their own spin on it back in the day. She's not usually here actually. Her staff normally run this one but you might see her over at the deli too.'

'Really?'

'Yes, indeed.' Robby chuckled at her reaction. 'Told you it was good. A recipe handed down through generations. It's a well-guarded Lovely Bay secret.'

Nina took another bite. 'No wonder you all keep it to yourselves. I can see why it's legendary.'

Robby chuckled. 'We're very serious about it.'

Nina continued to tuck in and looked around. 'This place feels like stepping back in time. I love the cosy vibe with all the antiques and photos and stuff.'

'The community here has a long memory. Traditions run deep.'

'You must have grown up here, then? Nice.'

Robby was a bit on the cagey side. 'I didn't actually grow up here. It's a long story. My family has been around Lovely Bay for generations, though.'

'It seems like a nice place to have memories.'

'Yeah.'

'You live here now?'

Robby gave a small shrug. 'Lovely Bay has a way of calling you. The roots and all that is what they say.'

Nina thought about her own lonely flat in London and about Andrew. 'That must be nice, having such a connection to a place.'

Robby changed the subject. 'How's the rest of your chowder?'

'Oh my gosh, amazing. I may have to beg for the recipe.'

'Good luck. It's guarded like a national secret. You have to live here for a long time and then one of them might bend,' Robby teased.

'That's me out then.'

Nina and Robby continued to chat as they finished their food, and the time seemed to fly by. Nina couldn't quite believe how easy another few ales had slipped down and what a nice time she was having. It was as if someone had dropped her into another pretty little world from days gone by. There was no grief in this world, and it wasn't quite as lonely. This world was fun and happy.

Robby downed his beer. 'I should apologise for seeming unwelcoming before. Lovely Bay is close-knit. Outsiders take some getting used to, especially at this time of year, and that last house-sitter took my aunt for a ride. She made my blood boil. I shouldn't have tarred you with the same brush. I was rude. Apologies.'

'It's okay. I'm a big girl. I'll survive.'

Robby pushed his chair back. 'Fancy one for the road in the pub? I'll leave the car, and then I'll walk you home or we can hop on the riverboat later.'

Nina went to say no, then she felt the tingle that zoomed into regions long forgotten. She heard a strange sound come out of her mouth. She had, in fact, giggled, too. 'Love to.'

21

I t almost felt as if it was someone else walking along a street in Lovely Bay beside a handsome man and not Nina Lavendar at all. Who was this happy person chatting away as if it was going out of fashion? As they got to the pub door, Nina flipped the hood down on her coat, wiped her feet on the mat by the door, went up a little step and followed Robby into the main bar of The Drunken Sailor pub. It was busy, with most of the tables full and a few empty spots at the bar. A few people turned around and looked in Nina's direction, a couple greeted Robby and said hello, and all of a sudden Nina felt as if she'd made the wrong decision. She'd got carried away with herself and a little bit complacent because of the strong locally brewed ale. What was she doing in this place where everyone knew each other? She was the odd one out, sticking out like a sore thumb. She suddenly felt not only as if she was being a bit stupid, but at the same time, the loneliest she'd ever felt since Andrew had gone. As she followed Robby in and out of people, she realised why: since Andrew had passed away, she'd not really let herself get into situations where she was out of her depth or alone. She'd got the local job she'd seen on a Facebook community

board not long after Andrew's funeral, and she'd been there ever
since. Apart from the grief group, the only thing she did was go
to work, speak to her mum, chat with Nathan on the bench,
FaceTime with Sophie and go down to see her at weekends
sometimes, and go to Sainsbury's. The rest of the time she
stayed in her flat watching YouTube, fussing with the plants out
on the ledge, and cooking things, some of which lasted her all
week.

She looked back towards the pub door, wondering what
excuse she could make up so that she could leave. As if sensing
what was going on in her head, Robby raised his eyebrows. 'You
okay?'

'Yeah.'

'Are you sure? Do you want to go now? Not a problem if
you do.'

Nina felt a bit taken aback by how nice Robby was being and
how quickly he'd sensed her mood change. The other Robby,
the grumpy one she'd first met, seemed to have left the building.
A little voice was telling her to stay. 'No, no, I'm fine.'

'What would you like?'

Nina didn't know whether to continue with the ale or to
have a gin and tonic. She'd swayed so far from her regular
Friday night half measure scenario, she wasn't sure whether she
was coming or going. She decided mixing her drinks was the
last thing she should do. 'I'll have another one of the brewery
beers, please.'

Robby nodded and took a step closer to the bar. Just as she
was standing a bit in No Man's Land, she realised Nancy, from
the train, was standing next to Colin from the boat and a couple
of other people. Nancy smiled. 'Hey, you again? How are you?
How are you finding life here?'

'Good, thanks. How are you?'

'I'm good. What have you been up to then? Rumour has it
you've been getting stuck in at The Summer Hotel.'

'Ahh, yes, I have.'

'You didn't say you were going to be staying there when you first arrived at the station.'

'I didn't realise...'

Colin butted in, 'Yeah, no secrets in Lovely Bay apart from the chowder.' He roared with laughter. 'We know all your business already.'

'Not really a secret,' Nina replied, not sure whether these Lovelies, as they liked to call themselves, were being serious or not. Plus, where she was from, she was hardly likely to announce to any random stranger she met in the street where she was staying. You didn't do that where she came from. 'I didn't realise anyone would know about the place.'

'Ha! You're hilarious. You're having a giraffe.' Colin again roared with laughter. 'You can't move around here without someone knowing about it. Lovelies are born with a nosy streak. Get used to it! Plus, you're being watched! We're all observing you, so you'd better not put a foot wrong.'

Nina nodded. 'Ahh, right, I see.'

'You'll get to know that we all know everything if you stay around for a while.' Colin chuckled, and the skin at the corners of his eyes creased. His ruddy complexion seemed to get redder as he continued to laugh at his own jokes.

As Nina was chatting to Nancy about the moveable platform at the railway station and how it attracted loads of trainspotters throughout the year, Robby arrived with her drink. She smiled, took the drink and Robby then stood next to her between her and Colin. Nina felt as if Nancy's eyes were boring into her as Nancy watched intently.

Nancy beamed. 'So, you're with us for a while, are you? Not like the last one. She was a royal pain in the behind.'

Robby rolled his eyes. 'Let's not talk about the last one. She'd better not be seen around these parts again.'

Nina was too scared to say she'd considered leaving, and that she wasn't sure whether the bay and the hotel were really for her. These people seemed to love where they lived and were seriously proud of it. 'Yes, I am. I'm, errr, loving it so far.'

'You're sure about that?' Colin laughed again.

'I am, yes, definitely.'

Colin then spoke to Robby about something that had happened on the boat, and Nancy turned ever so slightly and started to chat. Nancy asked Nina a few questions about her flat, Nina told Nancy about her job, and how Nathan was in her flat until the asbestos had been removed from his. She didn't really want to divulge too much information about herself. 'How about you? How long have you worked at the station? Have you always lived in Lovely Bay?'

'I went straight from school to the station. My dad used to work there before he retired. We keep it in the family here.' Nancy laughed. 'My nana owned the little kiosk on the platform there and passed it down through the family, but it's closed for now. It's seasonal. It's manic when the trainspotters come to see the moveable platform.'

'Married?' Nina felt annoyed with herself for asking the question. It irritated her whenever people asked her the same thing, not that she met many people but still.

'God no! No such luck. I'm quite happy in my little cottage on my own. No one would have me! You?'

Nina shook her head. She wasn't going down the avenue of explaining the whole Andrew thing especially since she'd had a few drinks. She'd been there, got the t-shirt, and learnt that in most situations it wasn't worth bringing it up and having to stand there and wait for the pity and the sad looks wasn't fun for anyone, least of all her. She also didn't trust herself not to start blubbing. 'Nup.' Saying no though made her sad. As if she was denying the memory of Andrew altogether.

'Enjoying yourself here, are you?' Nancy asked.

'I am, actually, yes. It's different from how I thought it was going to be. Good different.'

'Well, seeing as you're here, and you walked in with our Robby.' Nancy jerked her thumb towards Robby. 'I am officially inviting you to Lovely Lighthouse Drinks.'

'Drinks?'

'Yup. We have Lovely Drinks in various old institutions around the town – the lighthouse, the old town hall, the library building, the RNLI headquarters, etcetera, etcetera. Lovelies only.'

'Pardon? Lovelies only?'

Nancy batted her hand. 'Oh, nothing. I'll send you a ticket.' Nancy tapped away on her phone and then raised her eyes up in question. 'Nina's iPhone?'

'Sorry?'

'Airdrop. Do you have it turned on?'

'Oh, yes, yup, that's me.'

'Right there you go. Lovely Lighthouse Drinks invite for you.'

There was no way Nina was going to go to drinks at the lighthouse. Not really her scene standing around making small talk with people she didn't know. She sounded enthusiastic on the outside though. 'Thanks.'

Nancy's eyes widened and flicked in a flash towards Robby. She then raised her eyebrows as if in suggestion. 'Heard you went for secret chowder. That's a bit of a turn-up for the books.'

Nina frowned. How in the name of goodness did Nancy know she'd been for the secret chowder? She attempted to ignore Nancy's loaded look in Robby's direction. 'Sorry, what is a turn-up for the books?'

'Getting asked by our Robby to go to the bistro.'

Our Robby? Nina's heart went nineteen-to-the-dozen. She attempted to sound non-committal. 'Ah, yes, I just bumped into him on the street there when I was peering in the window.'

'You may well have done, but our Robby doesn't take just *anyone* into a Lovely chowder bar, especially not that one, that I know for sure. Nor do any of us, for that matter.'

Nina spluttered a bit. 'He doesn't?'

Nancy sort of cackled. 'Oh no. No, no, no.'

Nina wasn't sure how she was supposed to react to that. 'Ahh, well. It was just a spur-of-the-moment thing...'

Nancy continued, not really stopping for breath and speaking very quickly. 'And then he not only does that, but he then brings you into the pub, too.' Nancy held her hands out. 'Big, huge in fact.'

'Is that so unusual?' Nina asked. To be quite honest, it was so long since she'd been on a date, that she wasn't sure what was what. Not that it had been a date anyway. She'd just said yes to the chowder because she had fallen into the idea that it was secret and all a bit underground. It had nothing to do with Robby at all. Course it didn't.

Nancy threw her head back and laughed. 'Ooh yes. It's very, very unusual for our Robby. Lots to tell about our Robby.'

'Really. Like what?'

Nancy hooted. 'I'll let you find that out for yourself. Bit of a catch, though! Just you wait and see.'

22

It was an hour or so later, and Nina smiled as she leant against the bar. She wasn't sure what it was, and it might well have had something to do with the brewery ale, but she was feeling fuzzy and warm and just sort of happy all over. She really could get used to it. She was out and about and chatting with people and things were simply just nice. The warmth from the bustling pub seemed to be seeping into her bones, or was it Lovely that was working the magic she'd read about on her? Who knew? Probably just the alcohol talking. Then, of course, there was Robby, standing close enough for his elbow to occasionally brush hers. That was nice. She'd take that for the team.

Robby raised his eyebrows in question. 'Another drink or do you want to head off?'

Nina hesitated, aware that the beer was already making things feel a bit hazy; very pleasant but certainly hazy. Something made her change her mind about going down the sensible route and not having another drink. Perhaps the pub, the laughter, the clinking of glasses, or perhaps the tingles that were currently zipping around her body with a mind of their own. 'I really shouldn't, but go on then. We said the last one was one for the road, so what does that make this one?'

Robby's smile widened, and he signalled for another round. As they waited, Nina could barely take her eyes off him in the low-lit pub. What was happening to her? His earlier standoffishness had disappeared, he was being very nice, and she was *loving* it. She liked his smile, the way his eyes crinkled when he laughed. She hadn't looked at much else. Of course she hadn't.

'So,' Nina said and felt her head doing the odd tilting thing again. 'What's your story? We didn't get much further.'

Robby chuckled at the same time as definitely being a bit cagey. 'Not much to tell, really.'

'No? What do you do for a living?'

There was a slight pause. 'Short answer is I abseil down the side of skyscrapers.'

An image of the straps flashed at the front of Nina's brain. She swallowed. She hadn't seen that coming. Nice, very, very nice. 'Okay. That must keep you fit.'

Robby laughed. 'That's one way of putting it.'

'Keeps you, umm, busy, too, does it?'

'Extremely busy. We can't keep up. I just put my head down and get on with it.'

'And what about Lovely? There aren't many skyscrapers...'

'No, not here, but I love it by the sea. So yeah, I've made it work. I have a small office here where all the admin side of it gets done, and then we're all over the place in the vans. Up in your neck of the woods a lot, obviously. Plus we have a couple of depots elsewhere and, yeah, contracts all over the place including abroad.'

Nina nodded. 'Oh, right, wow.'

Their drinks arrived, and Nina wrapped her hands around the glass, the condensation nice against her skin.

Robby clinked his glass lightly against hers. 'To Lovely Bay. Oh and to house-sitters. Nice ones.'

'Yeah, to Lovely Bay and to new adventures,' Nina added, her voice more wistful than she intended. In her head, she giggled and thought, *and men with straps.*

'That's why you're at The Summer Hotel, is it? For an adventure?'

Nina sighed. Was this the time to drop the Andrew thing into the conversation? Probably not. There was never a good time. She was enjoying herself, and it would really dampen her spirits and undoubtedly his, too. 'Not really. I don't really do adventures, to be quite honest. I just needed a bit of fresh air and a different perspective and this sort of fell into my lap, so yeah...'

'You're in the right place for that.'

'I'm surprised, actually. I didn't realise what a rut I was in, you know?' Nina actually wondered if someone like Robby could ever be in a rut. He looked suspiciously successful and rut-less.

'Yeah. I know what you mean. You're doing okay at The Summer Hotel? It's a big place for one person.'

Nina sipped her beer. 'I am. It's a lot, but I'm managing. It's strangely satisfying, uncovering stuff. I lost my job just as I left for here. So I don't know, it's somehow therapeutic. When I say I lost my job, I got made redundant but really it's the same thing. The company made loads of us redundant basically because of a new piece of software that does the job of ten people in about ten minutes. Artificial intelligence.'

'Ouch. Doesn't sound nice.'

'I'm, err, strangely happy with it. I got the job because it was close to where I live, and I should have left ages ago...'

'Right, well, maybe it was meant to be.'

'Possibly. I like it here too, so yeah, change is afoot. Lovely Bay is the start of new things. Ha! I do love a challenge and getting stuck into things.'

'It's a special place if your face fits. It's full of history, and community and with the river and sea and all. Lots of little quirks and stuff, but it's done me good being here.'

'Hopefully, it will do the same for me.'

'Jill's selling the hotel now. Is that right?'

'Yes, she is. There are a few things with the solicitors and legal stuff causing delays, but yes. I've actually taken on getting it ready for when it goes up for sale.'

'Big job.'

'Bigger than I anticipated. A couple of the B&B rooms are a mess. They need clearing out. Two skips arrived, but the problem is how to get stuff into said skips. Heavy lifting is not my skill set, so I'm going to have to figure out how to sort that out. That's what Jill is paying me for - to sort out the logistics of it all. I'll need to find some muscle in Lovely Bay. Jill's out of Wi-Fi for the next week or so according to her last WhatsApp message, so I'm not sure what her budget is. Anyway, yeah, I'll sort it out.'

Robby squinted. 'I can get a couple of my blokes to come and give you a hand if you like. We had a job cancelled next week. I've already slotted another one in, but it's not as big, so we'll have an afternoon free or a few hours at least.'

'Really? Wow, that would be amazing. I'm not sure how Jill will be able to pay.'

'Nah, don't worry about that. It doesn't work like that in Lovely.'

Nina frowned. 'What do you mean?'

'We all help each other out. Jill helped my aunt out quite a bit back in the day when she was having problems with her house. A bartering system, as it were.'

'I see.' Nina wasn't really sure she did see.

Robby turned his hand in a circular movement. 'What comes around goes around. I'll text you my number and let you know.' Robby tapped his phone and then looked up at Nina for her to give him her number. She fired off her phone number and felt her phone ping.

'So, what you'll let me know, will you?'

'Yup, not a problem. We'll sort it.'

Nina swooned at the way Robby sounded so capable. *Nice.* 'Okay, thank you. That's great.'

The last bell rang, and Robby glanced at his watch. 'Looks like it's time to call it a night.'

Nina stood up straight, feeling the weight of the evening in her limbs. 'Thanks for the drinks and for welcoming me to Lovely Bay. Oh, and the secret chowder. It's been a really nice evening, actually.'

Robby shrugged on his jacket. 'It's what we do here. Look after each other if we think you might fit. Plus, I needed to make up for my rudeness the other day. I thought about it afterwards and realised I was bang out of line.'

Colin and Nancy, who were still standing nearby, were also making a move. Colin bellowed. 'Off so soon, our Robby?'

'Which way are you going? We're heading out as well.' Nancy asked.

'I'm going to see Nina to the boat.'

Colin chuckled, slapping Robby on the back with a thud. 'I bet you are, our Robby.'

Nancy looped her arm through Colin's as they made their way to the door and laughed in the direction of Nina. 'Take care of our Robby.'

Nina chuckled. 'I will.' Nina felt a flutter in her stomach as she pulled her coat tighter around her. 'Thank you all for a lovely evening. It's been fun.'

Nancy turned to go the other way. 'See you at Drinks.'

Colin roared again. 'You've invited the newcomer to Lovely Drinks! Wow! I'm noting that down on the town minutes. Did you get approval from Birdie?'

Outside in the street, it was quiet except for a few people coming out of the pub. The air felt crisp compared to the warmth inside the pub, and the sea rumbled in the distance. Nina felt a little bit awkward and unsure of herself. As they walked in the direction of the river, Robby's hand brushed against hers. She couldn't quite believe it when she felt a ripple of what she believed to be lust zip through her. She glanced at Robby and shook her head to herself.

'Right, just down here and there'll be a boat along shortly.'

Nina felt the effects of the night as the fresh air hit her. She was a bit deliciously tipsy and happier than she'd been in so long that she couldn't actually remember when. 'Good. I'm ready to get home.'

The water lapped against the wharf as they arrived at the River Lovely where a couple were sitting on a bench, a man was standing with a dog on a lead, and an inky black sky sat above the whole scene. Nina's breath misted in the air in front of her, the cool night air making her pull her coat tighter around her. As she looked around the little wharf with its community noticeboard, she got lost for a minute in how nice it all was. Tiny lights flickered from the other side of the river, a boat creaked past, and the moonlight glinted off the water. The sky appeared to go on forever as the river turned to the right. Nina stood and watched as the riverboat puttered to the wharf, its fairy lights strung around the cabin twinkling and little lanterns hanging down the sides swung in the breeze.

'It all looks so pretty. Just a bit better than the night bus, that's for sure.'

'I should say so.'

As Nina stepped onto the bobbing boat, she thought she was seeing things in the soft glow of the cabin lights. She did a double-take at the skipper's face. Colin from the pub appeared to have popped himself onto the boat, put on a Lovely coat and was now skippering. She frowned in confusion and whispered to Robby, tilting her head towards who she thought was Colin in the Lovely Bay wax jacket, 'Isn't that...? How did he get here before us?' She shook her head in confusion. 'What? Am I seeing things?'

Robby followed her gaze. 'That's Clive, Colin's identical twin. They own the boat company. Easy mistake to make. It confuses you until you hear them open their mouths, and then you'll know who is who.'

Nina blinked, and she mouthed a silent 'oh' as she processed that Colin had an identical twin. As she settled into a seat, she couldn't stop looking at Clive. He and his brother were so identical it was bordering on creepy. 'So, Lovely Bay not only has secret chowder spots but also twins who lead double lives?'

Robby chuckled, resting his arm along the back of the seat behind Nina. 'Something like that. Clive's more of a night owl, prefers the quiet of the river to the noise of the pub. So, yeah, it's usually him at night depending on which way you're going, of course. He's sort of French.'

Nina wrinkled her nose. 'What? What's sort of French?'

Robby tapped the side of his head. 'He loves the whole Breton thing and speaks with a bit of a French lilt.'

'Oh, okay, I'll keep an eye out for it.'

Clive raised his eyebrows in recognition of Robby and began to ease the boat away from the wharf, and Nina gazed out at the river and over towards the sea. She took in a deep breath as the boat gently rocked, the stars above twinkled, and the occasional hoot of an owl sounded from somewhere on shore. 'It's so pretty here and just so peaceful too. Like it lulls you.'

'It is on a night like this. It's a bit busier come the warmer months. You're here at a good time of year.'

A boat went the other way, and someone waved. Clive did a mini salute and called out, 'Bonsoir.'

Nina giggled and heard herself whisper-laughing. 'It's so quaint. Does he really pretend to be French? The coat thing, too, everyone is wearing them. I mean, really? Hah, hah, hah.' Nina enunciated her words, ridiculing in a nice way. 'It's all so ridiculous!'

Robby laughed and Nina continued on a roll, her softened edges making her giggle. 'And the third-smallest town in the UK thing, ha. Plus the greens, everywhere you look there's a little green or a tiny bridge.' She laughed at her own joke. 'Ha, ha, it's like Lovely Bay morphs greens left, right, and centre. At first I thought I was seeing things. Now there are twins on the boats...'

Robby tapped Nina's leg. She tingled like crazy. 'Yup, we like our coats and greens here. Lovely Bay's full of surprises. You just never know what—or who—you might come across.'

'I'm starting to see that. It's a bit different from where I live. No one gives you the time of day! It's like I've stepped into a storybook here.' Nina giggled again. 'And the secret chowder thing. I mean, really? Why bother with all that farcical secret stuff? Soooooooo funny!'

Nina watched the little lanterns swinging back and forth, casting light on the water, and felt as if everything around her was a little bit fuzzy. Could somewhere really be this quaint and nice? Was she so hardened by London life that this place felt as if it wasn't real? Secret traditions, strange little quirks, friendly locals, actual chocolate shops, pretty boats and the lighthouse, all of it seemed to bobble around her head. She wasn't sure what to make of it as she heard herself chatting away to Robby without a care in the world. Who even was she?

The boat pulled into a wharf and Nina realised they'd gone past the back of The Summer Hotel and were now not far from it. Robby held her hand as she hopped off, and the tingles again made themselves known. As they got closer and closer to the hotel, the more and more awkward and strangely nervous Nina felt. Part of her just wanted to sprint to the front door and not look back.

As she popped her hand over the top of the gate and flipped

up the lever, she heard words coming out of her mouth. 'Fancy coming in for a coffee? I make a mean coffee.' She had to stop herself from narrowing her eyes and shaking her head as she processed what she'd just asked Robby. Her own words tumbled through her head on repeat. *You make a mean coffee? Really?*

Robby didn't miss a beat. 'Love one. Coffee sounds great.'

Nina led Robby up the overgrown path, along the side of the house and in the tradesmen's entrance to what Jill had called the living quarters. As she opened the door, Robby's eyes went wide. 'Flipping heck!'

'What?'

'You've worked hard. I can barely recognise the place. It actually smells clean too. Blimey, you've transformed it!'

Nina frowned. She hadn't really done that much; she'd tidied the hallway, run the hoover round, admittedly for hours, hung the runner outside for a day to air, cleared the clutter, had a proper deep clean and had washed the curtains and cleaned the windows until they'd sparkled, hardly renovating. She frowned and narrowed her eyes as she took her jacket off. 'How do you know?'

'Ahh, I came in with my aunt a few times to check on things when Jill was looking for someone to house-sit. As I said, the last one was here for a while and let it go to rot. Filthy woman. I'll have to fill you in on that one day.'

Nina opened the kitchen door, flicked on one of the lamps on the dresser, and Robby exclaimed. 'Blimey!' He looked around and shook his head, 'This explains the way you were looking the other day when you had red powder all over your face.'

'What do you think?'

'Astonishing. You must have worked your socks off.'

Nina didn't feel as if she had at all. She'd just got her head down and got on with it. It was hardly rocket science. She was not shy of hard work, though, and that was evident by the look of the kitchen. The whole place had just needed a dirty great clear out and a good scrub. Whoever had lived in it the past few years had been allergic to a dishcloth. 'Err, not really. It just needed a good clean.'

'I don't think so. It looks like you've been grafting. You've done a great job.'

'I'm told I'm obsessive by some. Who wants to live surrounded by dirt and clutter, though?'

'Like who?'

Nina fluffed over another occasion where she could have mentioned Andrew. 'My best friend, for one. In fact, she has me organise her house for her when I go there. At one point, I had a little organising business. Not really a business... Well, I got paid for it, so I suppose it was. Yeah, it started by word-of-mouth and took off, but then...' Nina stopped mid-sentence, *but then I lost my husband.* 'But then it fizzled out, and I got a job.'

'Well, you need to restart your career because you've done an amazing job.'

Nina made a coffee, and they sat at the kitchen table. Most of the chat was about what Nina had done to the kitchen already and how she was getting on in the garden and Jill's plans to sell the hotel.

Once the coffee was done, Robby pushed out his chair. 'I'll be off then,' he said eventually. He rinsed the mugs and placed them in the sink. 'You'll be alright?'

Nina led him to the door. 'I will. I'm fine, thanks for walking me home,' Nina replied, her quickening pulse taking her by surprise. 'I've had such a nice evening.'

As Robby stepped across the threshold, he paused and turned back towards Nina. Her breath caught in her throat as he leaned in and kissed her. Nina wasn't quite sure what to do. Her heart thudded so loudly she was sure the whole of Lovely Bay would be able to hear it. Her heartbeat and its pace would make the ten o'clock national news. Robby smelt amazing and whatever it was enveloped her. She inhaled deeply, her hands finding their way to Robby's chest, and his fingers rested lightly on her waist.

With a charge running through the air, she pulled away, a bit embarrassed, and Robby stepped down onto the path. He said goodbye and turned, and Nina closed the door, walked back to the kitchen and sank down onto one of the chairs, with her heart and just about everything else racing. Something very odd had just happened. For a long time in her life, it was not only Andrew who had died, but something in her had too. Now something had just occurred, and she couldn't quite believe it; she'd never felt more alive. Nina Lavendar – welcome back to Planet Earth.

23

Nina opened her eyes, turned over, turned back the other way, and felt a bit of a heavy head; she wasn't really sure what day it was. She pushed herself up to her elbows and then plonked back onto the bed again. Definitely a bit on the dusty side. This was precisely why she had a strict rule about only drinking half measures and only drinking those on a Friday night unless it was Christmas or someone had died. Neither of those had happened the day before. She'd drunk a few more than her usual half measures, which was why her head was a bit heavy, and she felt like she needed a bacon sandwich or six. Really? She was a lightweight.

She tried to tell herself that she was fine and that all she needed to do was go back to sleep and sleep it off. There was something very un-fine, though, about the feeling on the inside of her head. She rolled over, fluffed up her pillow, and closed her eyes. It didn't work; all she could think about was a cup of tea, some fresh air, six pints of water, and a bottle of Lucozade. She laid still for a bit, trying to force herself to go back to sleep, but failed miserably. She shook her head and tried to calculate in half measures how much she'd actually drunk with

Robby in the funny secret bistro. Surely it hadn't been that many?

Giving up on sleeping it off, she shrugged on her dressing gown, shuffled along to the kitchen, winced at the light coming in the windows, ran the tap, poured herself a glass of water, flicked on the kettle, and sunk the water down in one. She felt it travel down her body as if it was hydrating parched, cracked cells on its way down.

She remembered the night before after the chowder, when she'd walked into the pub with Robby as if she hadn't had a care in the world. Standing chatting at the bar with the lovely Robby with the lovely hips and nice eyes and general all-around gorgeousness. She remembered thinking at that point in the evening that she'd had more than a few half-measures, and she should call it a day. She recalled shoving her serious, sensible voice out the window and having another one of the local Lovely brewery ales. She remembered being silly and flirty and not like the widow she'd become at all. She remembered how nice it was just to be Nina without the widow label slapped on her forehead.

She rummaged around in her dressing gown pocket for a scrunchie, scooped her hair off her face and tied it up in a bun, then poured a pot of tea. Sun streamed in the window and she looked outside as she waited for the tea to brew and thought about what a funny off-the-cuff evening it had been. Opening the door, she stood on the step and took in deep inhales of fresh air hoping it would do something about the state of her fuzzy head.

After pouring a cup of tea and dunking biscuits in one after another, she felt better, and she ventured out into the garden and stood about halfway down with her hands around the mug, thinking. She cringed as she overthought the night before, remembering how she'd giggled and said that she thought the Lovely coat thing was silly, how the little greens all over the place were odd, and was it really a good thing that Lovely referred to itself as the third-smallest town in the UK?

Robby flashed into her mind on a long loop. He'd offered to walk her home, put his arm around her waist when she'd wobbled getting onto the boat, and laughed in all the right places. Nina shuddered a little bit, realising that she'd not only broken her own rule of only drinking in half measures, but that she'd also not been careful about getting home. She'd been stupidly careless and in a place where she knew no one, too. She could have woken up with a very different story. For her, the story was fabulous with the end of the evening working out fairly well as far as she was concerned, but in safety terms, she'd acted completely out of character.

As she stood watching the river and drinking her tea, she couldn't stop thinking about Robby. Or Andrew. Mostly Robby, though. That in itself felt strange. It had been a long time since she had thought about little other than Andrew. Let alone thinking about another man and how she might like to get caught up in his straps. She went over the kiss; how nice it had been, how it had made her feel. How she absolutely wanted it to happen again. Come on.

Right after the swooniness of how wonderful the kiss was, she felt something else slap her in the back of the head. There was one simple word for it; embarrassment. She'd got a little bit tipsy and broken all her silly little usual rules about everything. She recalled sitting on the boat feeling as if she was in a dream as the boat had puttered along the river, the fairy lights and lanterns twinkling. She remembered joking about how quaint Lovely was and how it was as if it gave birth to greens and how funny Clive's faux French accent was.

She thought about how Robby had put his arm along the seat, how tall he'd seemed as she'd walked along beside him in the night air, how she'd chatted away with him as if she'd known him forever. Mmm. Just. So. Nice. So nice but also silly.

As she stared out at the water, she had second thoughts about what had happened. What was she doing? Flirting with fun and having a life was what she was doing. It was a good thing, wasn't it? She started thinking about the what ifs and analysing how she'd behaved. She shook her head to herself. She wasn't going to start worrying about it, that would get her precisely nowhere. She cringed a bit, though, at her behaviour. She'd invited him in for coffee. What in the world had she been thinking? She went cold as she thought about him saying yes. Had he thought she was offering more? Nancy had said that there was loads to tell about 'our Robby'. Like what?

Nina suddenly felt really embarrassed and really small. Stupid Nina the Widow. She shook her head and resolved not to let it bother her. It was just a kiss, nothing more, nothing less. She'd bury it and get on with doing the job she'd come to do at The Summer Hotel and take it from there. She didn't care less about our Robby anyway.

24

After what felt like sixty-five cups of coffee and a lot more thinking, Nina emerged from the shower and wrapped herself in a towel. Her mind constantly replayed the previous evening, and it flipped between embarrassment at what she felt was her brazen behaviour and some sort of exhilaration that made her smile despite herself. The whole thing, to be quite frank, had taken her completely by surprise. Not just the kiss, yadda, yadda and the getting a bit tipsy, but more the going out, flitting around happily, *doing* something with her life, chatting and drinking and just *being*. It had felt so blooming well refreshing and simply just pleasant. She was going to damn well make the most of it. Maybe The Summer Hotel and Lovely Bay were a turning point in her life. A fork in the road of grief she hadn't seen coming. Was this the thing they talked about in the grief group where things suddenly got better? Maybe she'd run with it and see where it ended up. It felt nice just to have the opportunity.

As she got dressed and made herself another drink, she nodded to herself. Yes, it was nice to have an opportunity to do things, and she needed to make the most of it. No more Nina of old with not many options on the table. No more wallowing about Andrew. The night out had made her see where she wanted her life to go. She needed decisions, an action plan, and forward-thinking about her future. She would focus on what needed to be done to move forward with her plans for The Summer Hotel which in turn would spur her on as to what she was going to do with the rest of her life.

As she sat, feeling quite smug with herself that she'd had a nice evening out and had decided to stay in Lovely Bay for a bit, her phone buzzed with an incoming FaceTime call. Nina tapped 'Accept' and Sophie's face popped up on the screen, her hair and makeup perfect as always.

'Hi, Neens! How's my best friend? Wow, looks like Lovely Bay is treating you well!' Sophie exclaimed.

'Does it?'

Sophie narrowed her eyes. 'Hang on, wait, what? What have you done?'

'Nothing.'

'Bloody hell, Neens! Have you had relations? You have!'

'I have not!'

'I have not seen that look on your face for years, and when I say years, I mean years and years. What in the name of goodness is going on?'

'Nothing! Don't know what you're talking about.'

'You're glowing.'

'I am not.' Nina laughed. 'I was just thinking about calling you. I may have news.'

'Ooh, intrigue! I knew there was something just by looking at you.'

'There might be.'

'This sounds promising. Dish!' Sophie prodded and rubbed her hands together.

Nina laughed and couldn't stop a blush from creeping up her

cheeks. 'I might have had a little trip to the pub last night,' she confessed.

Sophie wrinkled her nose. 'Really? Who with?'

'I ended up going for dinner with...'

Sophie interrupted. 'What the actual? Who even are you?'

'With that bloke I told you about who was next door.'

'I can't speak. I'm *that* surprised,' Sophie said as she shook her head from left to right.

Nina raised her eyebrows. 'You're not the only one.'

'Fill me in. Oh, gosh, this is gold. Who is he again?'

Nina launched into the story. 'Okay, so he's June's – the neighbour here's – nephew. He was a bit standoffish and rude initially, but we got chatting, and well, I ended up inviting him in for coffee.'

Sophie held her hand up and widened her eyes. 'Wait, wait. What? Start at the beginning.'

'I went for one of those secret chowder things and then to the pub.'

'What, he invited you? You didn't say!'

'No, I was standing peering in the window of a place in town because it looked as if it was closed, and then yeah, well, it went from there. We had the most amazing chowder bread bowls. Everyone knew him, it was sweet. Then we popped into the pub for a nightcap. I got chatting to a few different people. It was a really good evening, actually.'

'This is unheard of! Wow.'

'I know.'

'You said yes to going into somewhere with someone you don't know! I'm gobsmacked. I can't even get you to go out with me half the time.'

'You and me both.'

'Ooh, this is so promising...'

'Not really. Everyone is nice here, it seems. You said it might get me out of a rut, and I didn't believe you.'

'True. So, what else happened? What explains the glow?'
Sophie giggled.

Blushing, Nina went on. 'We talked for ages. Yeah...' she
trailed off, suddenly shy.

'What?' Sophie demanded. 'Don't leave me hanging!'

'Yeah, it was...'

'Then what?'

'I had a bit too much to drink.'

'You did? The mind boggles. What, you broke your half-
measure rule? Flipping heck. Someone must have died,' Sophie
joked. 'Oh, wait, no, that's already happened.'

'And then some.'

'So?'

'So he brought me home, and I invited him in for coffee and
then yeah...'

Sophie's eyebrows shot up. 'Coffee! You! That's a new
euphemism for you. I'm more or less not sure if this is you I'm
talking to. This is so exciting! Then what?'

'That was it, really.'

Sophie didn't miss a beat. 'Yeah, you think I believe it ended
there? You have that look on your face... You can't pull the wool
over my eyes, Neens. I have known you for a very, very long
time.'

Nina giggled. 'There might have been a kiss right at the end.
Just a small one, though. It wasn't really a kiss. I don't know.'

Sophie swore loudly and shook her head. 'What sort of a
kiss? Like a snog?'

'No, I don't know. It was nice.'

'Blimey. I didn't see this coming. I mean, I know I was the
one who initiated the Lovely Bay thing, but still.'

'Nup, you're not the only one. It was probably nothing...'

Sophie let out a little scream. 'Trust me, this is *not* nothing!
Your first kiss in Lord knows how long! With a gorgeous local
to boot.'

'I know! The whole night was good, actually.'

'Will you see him again, do you think?'

Nina twirled a strand of hair around her finger. 'Dunno. I'm sort of embarrassed, but it is what it is.'

Sophie sighed dreamily. 'Oh, Neens. I just knew this was going to be good for you. Lovely Bay must have sprinkled its magic fairy dust on you.'

Nina had to agree. She was still slightly stunned at this new development herself. It seemed almost too good to be true. 'I was thinking that. Maybe you're right,' she mused. 'I can't properly explain it, but for the first time in ages, I feel hopeful. Being here, I'm remembering parts of myself I thought were gone forever. It's like I have just existed in the flat and going to work and not much else since Andrew, well, you know all of it. I don't need to tell you.'

'It's called living again, babe! I've been telling you for ages, you need to get out there. And now look!'

Nina shook her head. 'I'm just going to not think about the kiss and not think about it, though.'

Sophie wrinkled her nose and frowned. 'What? Why would you do that?'

'I just am. What will be, will be. I'm going to concentrate on my life. I'm going to get stuck in here and see where it goes before I start looking for a job back at home. I feel I'm at a bit of a turning point.'

'Right.'

'I have no job and not much in my life in London anymore. What do you think?'

'That's brilliant,' Sophie encouraged. 'I *do* think it would do you good. You can't live the rest of your life mooching in that flat on your own.'

'I've got to do something about a job in the long term but starting applying for stuff online gives me the dreads. This paid thing here will tide me over. Plus, I can spruce this place up with my eyes closed. You know how much I love a good clean and organise.'

'And you've got that killer view in the background while you're doing it,' Sophie added. 'Plus, you're closer to me.'

'I know. I'd be mad to go back and get another dead-end job and go back to working five days a week and doing nothing else. I only got that job in the first place because it was near the flat.'

'I have been telling you this for the last, at least, five years.'

'I know you have.'

'The time has finally come. Woohoo!'

'Thanks for giving me the push.'

'What are best friends for?'

'Ha.'

'Right, I'll love you and leave you. I'm coming over at the weekend. Speak later.'

'Bye.'

As Nina sat thinking about the call, she felt a strange, renewed sense of purpose, as if the evening out, The Summer Hotel and the job for Jill had flicked a switch in her. There was a long-gone little spark inside her, more of an ember really, coming back to life. She wasn't totally sure what it was but something was giving her a good feeling about Lovely Bay. She decided she'd give it a chance and run with it. What could possibly go wrong?

25

It was a few days or so later and after more sorting of Jill's aunt's belongings, Nina was standing in the front garden of The Summer Hotel, wondering where to start with the weeds. She'd taken a good hard look at the front of the place and decided that clearing the front would make the whole place look a lot better. It couldn't really look a lot worse.

Standing on the old cobbled paving stones, she looked left to right, trying to decide what to do first. She had to laugh – when she was in the flat and tending to the pots on the ledge she'd sometimes thought of herself as a gardener. Hah, hah, hah. She now knew she was no gardener with not a lot of experience at all. She really was way out of her depth. Weeds were everywhere around her, and so high, she wondered quite what might be lurking. She wrinkled her nose at strange brown patches in clumps in the weeds here and there. It looked as if someone, possibly the useless house-sitter before her, had stood on the path and randomly sprayed weed killer willy-nilly. The result being large chunks of dead brown weeds sitting among rampant brambles. Nina went to the shed, grabbed various tools, but none that looked particularly impressive, and struggled back to the path, wondering quite how she'd found herself in this job in the first place.

Deciding to just get stuck in and see what happened, she bent down and started to yank out weeds. After pulling at the brown clumps about fifteen minutes in, she was making good progress and some of the dead foliage was in a pile on the path. Suddenly, she squealed as a gigantic load of spiders came out of a nest. The air was blue, and she jumped up and back in fear. Just as she was standing looking aghast at the spiders and shaking her head, a car pulled up, and she frowned as Birdie, from the chemist, jumped out. The shipping forecast blared from the car's speakers.

'Ahoy there. I thought it was you. I was passing on my way to my dad's and saw you out the front.' Birdie looked over the fence. 'Looks like you're busy. Everything okay?'

Nina made a face. 'Oh, hi. I just ran into a spider's nest. Revolting.'

'Euh. That explains the look on your face.'

'Not my favourite thing. I'm not keen on spiders.'

Birdie looked left and right at the weeds. 'Looks like you've got your hands full. You need a strimmer by the looks of it.'

'There's a strimmer in the shed, but I plugged it in and it was as dead as a doornail.'

'I do my dad's garden just down the road here. I can drop you in a strimmer if you like.' Birdie pointed into the car. 'We're on our way there now. Dad's got all sorts of power tools in the shed. I'll run one down if you want to borrow one.'

Nina wiped her brow, still eyeing the spot where the spiders had emerged. 'That would be amazing. These weeds are a nightmare... I'd probably get it done a lot faster with the right tools.'

'Yeah, definitely. Rightio, then, I'll just pop back and grab the strimmer. Won't take long.'

As Birdie drove off, Nina surveyed what she'd done. It was

going to be a long, slow task, and having proper tools would be a game-changer.

About ten minutes later, Birdie was back. She hopped out of her car, pooped the boot, and pulled out a strimmer. Nina opened the gate and smiled.

Nina watched as Birdie showed her the buttons. 'It should make short work of that lot.'

'Thanks, Birdie. I really appreciate this.'

'No worries. Just pop into the shop if you need any more help. My dad's shed is a treasure trove of garden tools. He used to be a power tool fanatic back in the day.'

'Right, good to know.'

'Oh, I nearly forgot.' Birdie picked up a Tupperware box from the car. 'I brought you some of my dad's chowder. Guard it with your life, and if anyone asks you where you got it, it wasn't from me.'

Nina chuckled. 'Where did you get it?'

'Dad makes it by the gallon. Rumour has it he makes it for a few places around here. He's old-school and harks back to the fishermen. They literally pass on the recipe when they die. It's a Lovely old wives' tale.'

'Ooh, I love this whole secret thing.'

'I know, it's a bit strange.' Birdie lowered her voice. 'Dad's house is one of the speakeasy places, not that you got that from me. It's really only Lovelies who are meant to have that information at their fingertips.'

'Secret's safe with me. What, so he sells chowder, does he?'

'Not as such. You can't legally sell it without all sorts of red tape. Anyway, you'll get to know if you stay for a while. That's if we like you, of course, which, from what I've heard, we like you. It appears our Robby likes you.'

Nina felt a shudder of embarrassment. Who knew about what had happened right at the end of the night? 'Oh, right.'

'Hear you're coming to Lighthouse Drinks too, and you are in possession of a ticket. Guard it with your life.'

Nina had forgotten all about the ticket Nancy had airdropped her. She smiled on the outside at the same time as thinking on the inside that she wouldn't be attending a drinks evening on her own. Been there, done that, got the T-shirt, not had a nice time. 'Hmm.'

'Our Robby will be there, of course.' Birdie chortled and wiggled the Tupperware. 'Anyway, must get on. Shove this in the fridge. Trust me, you'll love it.'

'Thanks will do, and thanks for this,' Nina said, holding the strimmer aloft.

After popping the Tupperware in the fridge, a few minutes later, Nina attacked the weeds with gusto. Like a woman possessed, she strimmed back and forth as large patches of dead, brown clumps were cleared. As she worked, her thoughts drifted to Robby, Andrew, and the conversation with Sophie. By the time she stopped for a coffee, most of the front lawn was no longer knee-high, and Nina was feeling it in her lower back. Bit by bit the place was looking better. Her muscles ached, and she now realised that she should have made the gym a priority over the years since Andrew. As she stood and put her hands in the small of her back and looked around, she felt quite pleased with herself. She was grabbing her life by the balls and doing something. It felt amazingly good. She mulled over the Lighthouse Drinks event, opened the invite, scanned it a few times, and slipped her phone back in her pocket. It actually sounded quite nice. Maybe she would continue whilst she was on a roll and make an effort to go after all. It wasn't as if it would do any harm.

26

A day later, Nina was flat on her back under a double bed in the first B&B room trying to ascertain whether or not the bed slats could be fixed. She wasn't sure. Her phone pinged from the other side of the room, so she wriggled and slid her way back out, more or less crawled to the window and picked up her phone. When she saw who was texting, she smiled. Tingles. Handsome Robby with the wide shoulders, nice eyes, and of course the straps. Not that she'd looked at those, no, no, no.

Robby: *Just coming into Lovely Bay if you're there at the moment – if you open the side gates, we can pull onto the drive. I've got Jase and Tommy with me. Cheers.*

Nina totally panicked. She'd completely forgotten about Robby's offer of help. If she had remembered, she wouldn't have been in her tracksuit, with no makeup and looking as if she'd just crawled backwards through a hedge or out from under a bed. **** *my life.*

Nina: *Great, I am. Thank you so much.*

Feeling slightly flustered, Nina hurried to the gates and grappled with the latch, her heart racing not just from the effort but also at the thought of seeing Robby again. The kiss was front and centre; it lingered in her mind, and she cringed as she huffed and puffed to get the huge old gates to open. Just as she was securing a bolt down into the ground, she heard an engine and turned around to see a Mercedes van indicating to turn. She stood back and smiled as the van pulled up onto the drive behind the two skips. Robby was at the wheel, with who she assumed was Jase beside him and another man, probably Tommy, beside the window. Nina stood awkwardly, smoothing down her hair and tracksuit. She kicked herself for not doing something to her face and hair that morning and cringed at her dishevelled appearance.

The engine came to a halt; Robby hopped out and started to pull off a climbing harness that was fastened over cargo work trousers with reinforced knees. Nina felt faint.

'Hey,' Robby said with a smile and held his hand up in greeting.

Nina's heart skipped five hundred beats. 'Hi, Robby.' She attempted to sound more composed than she felt; her heart felt as if it was galloping down the road of its own free will.

Robby gestured towards the other two men. 'This is Jase, my colleague, and Tommy, also a colleague but also a wizard with DIY. I mentioned them when we were out.'

Jase, a burly man wearing a yellow version of the Lovely wax coat, waved at her. 'Pleased to meet you, Nina. Heard you're doing well with the old place.'

Tommy, who was slightly shorter than the other two, nodded in greeting. 'Happy to help out.'

Nina smiled back, grateful and totally self-conscious because all she could think about was the kiss. The straps too. 'Thanks for coming, guys. I really appreciate the help.' She was sure Robby's gaze lingered on her for a moment but tried not to think about it. Her thoughts raced back to the aftermath of the kiss. She felt a blush creep up her cheeks as she bustled around.

'Let's get to it then. What's the plan?' Robby asked.

Nina led them back around the house, through the living quarters, and into one of the old B&B rooms. She flipped her phone out and looked at the list Jill had sent her. 'The main task is getting rid of the stuff I've labelled – mostly it's things that are broken. Jill wants to totally get rid of them. Then I need to check what is salvageable, and she's going to try and sell it or get me too, ha. What else? She wants the carpets gone. Then the fridges need to be taken out. I need to check how to dispose of them. Yeah, the list is a long one...'

Jase and Tommy began assessing a few things and discussing potential repairs. Nina pointed to an old dresser. 'That's got a broken door, and it's damp, so that is to go, but the wardrobe there is going in the other room which Jill wants staged for the sale.'

Jase whistled loudly as they lifted the old dresser. 'This thing weighs a ton. They sure built things to last back then.'

'I know, I couldn't even shift it when I tried to barge it with my shoulder.'

'This place is a goldmine,' Tommy said as he looked around. 'So much potential.'

Nina indicated to the carpet in the corner of the room she'd pulled up and attempted to roll. 'That's for the skip, so if you could lift that out there I'd be grateful, and the gripper rods need removing.'

Jase grimaced at the state of the carpet, retrieved a tool from his belt, and pulled up a gripper rod. He raised an eyebrow at the hardwood floor. 'Wow, don't make 'em like this anymore.'

Nina nodded. 'I know. I couldn't believe it when I saw it. I didn't expect to find such well-preserved wood under there. I bet it would cost a fortune to get a floor laid like that these days.'

'I should say so, that's even if you could get the materials.' Robby nodded.

As they started to drag out the rolls of old carpet, Nina tried to concentrate on the task at hand, but her mind kept drifting back to Robby. Tingles ran up and down her body. She had to force herself not to keep stealing glances at him.

About two hours or so later, one of the skips was full, and the fridges were stacked and ready. Nina was feeling it. She went and made four cups of tea, brought them out and the four of them chatted as they sat out the front near the skips with the tea. Nina caught herself having a strange feeling; she felt oddly as if she belonged somehow. Here she was a newcomer to Lovely Bay, and these blokes were helping her out as if they did it for people every day of the week.

Robby jerked his thumb to next door. 'June's got a pile for the tip. I'll pop around and chuck that in the bit of space left in the skip, if that's okay.'

'Of course.'

Jase nodded. 'Yeah, you do that.' He looked at Nina. 'Was that the kettle I heard on again?'

Nina laughed and a few minutes later she was standing, leaning on the worktop and chatting to Tommy and Jase, who were sitting at the table. Tommy gestured around the kitchen. 'So, you were house-sitting here, weren't you?'

'I was, yeah. Well, I still am, but now I'm working here.'

'Now it's going up for sale. Is that right?' Jase asked.

'Yes, I got an email from the owner. Apparently, she just wants shot of it because of the state it's in. She's just waiting on a few things from the solicitor.'

'Shame really,' Jase said. 'It's a lovely old place.'

Tommy frowned. 'Didn't someone say something about developers trying to get hold of it a few years ago or was that somewhere else along the river here?'

Jase shook his head. 'Dunno. You might be right.'

'Needs a local to buy it.' Tommy noted.

'Yep. You offering?'

'Ha, if I had the money, mate. I'm surprised our Robby hasn't got his eye on it. Right next door to June and all that.'

Jase snorted. 'Like he needs another property to add to his portfolio.'

'Nah, true. He'd just buy it cash, though, right?'

Nina leaned back slightly, her arms folded casually in an attempt to portray that she wasn't interested in what they were saying about Robby. She was *so* interested, it wasn't even funny. 'Robby has a couple of places around here, does he?'

Jase chuckled, nodding. 'Oh yeah, just a few. He's got a few places around Lovely Bay and all over the show. Smart with investments, that one. Smart with everything, really. Don't be fooled by the work gear and window cleaning shtick he likes people to believe.'

Tommy took a sip of his tea. 'He's got an eye for potential and a business mind, plus he's ruthless if he wants something. Takes no prisoners.'

Nina raised an eyebrow and swallowed at the same time. 'Right.'

Jase leaned back in his chair. 'Yeah, and he's not just about the money. Cares about the community, too. Doesn't want to see Lovely Bay lose its charm.'

Tommy nodded in agreement. 'True. He's always been all about keeping the place special, not just making a quick quid or too.'

'Right.'

'I mean, how many of us does he employ now?' Jase asked, looking at Tommy.

'What branch you talking?' Tommy asked with eyebrows raised. 'Then there's the overseas lot...'

'Good point.'

'Yup, anyway so this place. It wouldn't take much work to turn it around. Looks a lot worse than it is, especially with the state of the outside areas,' Jase noted.

'Really?' Tommy said with narrowed eyes. 'It looks quite a mess from where I'm standing.'

'Roof's good, walls are solid, chimneys look okay, and the position couldn't be much better. From what we've seen of the floors, they've stood the test of time, too. It looks pretty hideous particularly because of the outside paintwork and because it's so dated, but most of it's cosmetic.'

'You're right actually,' Tommy acknowledged.

'It's grunt work and not a lot else.'

Nina frowned. 'You reckon?'

'I don't reckon, I know. I've flipped enough houses in my time, just not ones as big as this admittedly. I'm talking two ups, two downs, but it's the same principle. You look at a few things and purchase something with that in mind. It's got a name in the flipping game.'

'What do you look for?'

'What I just said. Steer well clear of dodgy roofs, floors, or walls, never go anywhere near black mould. You can work with most other things. I can rip out a crappy kitchen in a day, and put in a new bathroom. Yeah, it's how I'm slowly moving up the property ladder. Not quite as nice when you're living in it twenty-four seven.'

Nina nodded. 'Interesting.'

'What about you, Nina? You're from the big smoke, aren't you? Got a property up there, have you?'

Nina wasn't going to bother to go into the investment property. 'Yes. I've got a tiny flat. It's very small, but it's fine. No garden or anything, well I do have a ledge with plants.'

'Right. So, what, you wanted to come down here for a bit of a change? Get some Lovely in your bones, did you?'

'Something like that. It was all funny timing, really, as now I'm doing this for Jill as a paid thing. Initially, it was a house-sitting gig, but then she decided to sell.'

'That'll tide you over then.'

'Yeah, exactly. I think this is the start of new things for me.' Nina paused for a bit. 'I couldn't see the wood for the trees, you know?'

Tommy nodded. 'A change is as good as a rest, as they say.'

Jase stretched, standing up from the table. 'Well, we'd better get back to it. That skip won't fill itself.'

Tommy followed suit, pushing his chair back. 'Yeah, let's crack on.'

Nina stood up as well. 'Yep, thanks so much for this. I'm really grateful.'

Jase quipped. 'Nothing to do with us. We do what we're told. Robby's the one paying the wages.'

As they left the kitchen and Nina cleared away the mugs and wiped down the sides, she pondered the conversation. There was clearly a bit more to Robby than met the eye. Nina Lavendar really wouldn't mind finding out more. A lot more. Loads.

27

It was a couple of days later and the skip filling had made a real difference, Nina had got well stuck into further clearing the hotel. She stood in one of the bedrooms in what was once the B&B. Stale musty air hit her in the face, but apart from that, it wasn't actually too bad. The bed looked like new, the sitting room area was dated but okay, and the bathroom needed a good clean but the nuts and bolts of it weren't too bad at all. The dreadful feature wall with the bright red poppy design on the wallpaper would need to go at some point via whoever bought the place, and the curtains had seen better days, but none of it was too bad. Whoever bought the hotel would, in the long run, get a lot of bang for their buck.

Nina opened WhatsApp on her phone and hit the video call button to call Sophie. As the call connected, Nina's face appeared on the screen, framed by the dated backdrop of the B&B room.

'I'm in the B&B. I thought I'd let you have a looksie,' she said as Sophie appeared on the screen. Nina turned her phone around, giving Sophie a panoramic view of the room.

Sophie's eyes went wide with interest. 'Oh wow, yeah, it's definitely dated. Spacious though.'

Nina chuckled. 'Spacious and stuck in the nineties,' she replied, panning across the room.

'It's got potential, though. Someone could totally transform it. I mean, look at those windows – so much light! The ceilings are so high.'

Nina moved towards the windows, showing off the view of Lovely Bay. 'Right? I was thinking the same. Whoever buys this has a lot of work to do, but imagine waking up to this view.'

Sophie nodded enthusiastically. 'Absolutely.'

'I have loads more clearing out and getting rid of the clutter and broken things to do, but it's getting there.'

'Crikey, it really could be something special. A bit of paint, some new furniture…'

Nina moved around the room, focusing on various details – the old sitting area, the outdated but sturdy furniture, the bathroom that needed a good clean. 'Yep, it could be nice if you had a bit of time and a bit of money.'

'You should buy it!'

'Don't be ridiculous. I currently don't have a job, and oh, about zero savings and a pathetic pension.'

'You have a flat worth a fortune and an investment property, plus this is a business with an income. Or it could be,' Sophie reasoned.

'Nah, not for me. Way too hard work. I'll be interested to see who buys it and what happens to it, though.'

The conversation continued as Nina moved through the other rooms, each in a similar dated state. 'I reckon there's so much potential there,' Sophie repeated.

'For someone willing to take it on, yes.'

'You should think about it. You said you're loving it down here already.'

Nina guffawed. 'What and run it as a hotel? Do I look like a hotelier to you?'

'I was thinking more just Airbnb it, like Jill has with the other properties.'

'Hmm, good point, but no, not for me.' Nina shook her head. 'It's a big commitment, and I know absolutely nothing about it.'

Sophie's face on the screen was thoughtful. 'Even more reason – give you a bit of a challenge. Think about it. You've got an eye for this sort of thing. And with your flat in the city, you've got a safety net. You could just rent it out once Nathan's gone. Not go back there to all that, well, you know...'

Nina paused. There was no way she would rent her flat out. It was her and Andrew's place. Full of memories. His clothes were still in the wardrobe. 'Guests, bookings, cleaning... Nope, not me at all.'

'You could hire someone to do that,' Sophie countered.

Nina sighed, looking out of the window at the view of Lovely Bay. 'It's a beautiful location, no doubt about that.'

'Exactly! Plus, it's so much nearer to us. You said you were enjoying it.' Sophie's voice was encouraging.

'I am. It's grown on me. But I'm never going to permanently move out of the flat. It's where... you know.'

Sophie nodded. 'That place could be a good for you, though.'

Nina leaned against the wall, her mind whirling with possibilities. 'It could be. You are actually right. The blokes who helped with the moving said that the other day, too.'

'What's stopping you?'

My dead husband. 'Ahh, I don't know. It's a lot to think about.'

'Don't dismiss it. You've got the skills, Neens. And I bet you could negotiate a good deal with Jill,' Sophie advised.

Nina chuckled. 'Negotiate with Jill? That'd be a challenge.'

'Since when have you backed down from a challenge?' Sophie smiled.

Nina smiled back. Little did Sophie know that she'd not had a challenge for years. 'True.'

'Anyway, what else is happening with you? You've got that drinks thing to go to, haven't you? Isn't that this evening?'

'I don't know. I've changed my mind about it, I think.'

'What? Why? After the kiss, I thought...'

The truth of the matter was that Nina had mulled over the thing with Robby and had a change of heart. Plus, the few things she had been to on her own since Andrew had passed away, including the grief group's Christmas party the year before, had made her feel terrible.

She always felt like crap after going to things on her own and so had decided with the Lovely Lighthouse Drinks she probably wasn't going to bother. She hated small talk and spent most of the time counting down the minutes until she could go home, so what was the point in the first place? The Lovely Lighthouse Drinks thing she'd been invited to by Nancy was just probably a pity invite anyway. And then there was the whole Robby thing on top of it all. Now she'd learnt a bit more about him via the blokes who worked for him, she'd realised he would not see anything in someone like her. Plus, he'd not mentioned it to her when he'd come for the skip filling or texted her or anything. She actually felt more than stupid about the whole thing, as did he, she assumed. 'I don't know. I've just got a funny feeling about it now. I don't think I want to go.'

'You're going. Don't be bloody ridiculous!'

'Ha.'

'I will not let you not go to this. You need it, Neens.'

'I'm fine,' Nina said adamantly.

'You are not fine and you are going. The end.'

'No, it will be a waste of time. I hate turning up at stuff on my own. No.'

'Yes, I will not let you not go.'

Nina nodded, and before the Pity Smile appeared, she

pretended that she would go, but she'd more or less made up her mind that she wasn't going. She wasn't going to put herself through another Billy No Mates event where she stood around waiting until she could make a swift exit and toddle off home. She'd so had enough of that.

28

Something, however, had made Nina force herself to get ready to go out. As she stood by the front door, wondering how she was going to get to the lighthouse, her stomach fluttered with butterflies. This was why she didn't bother going to things on her own these days. Too much effort.

She looked at the river timetable, shoved her bag under her arm, and began to jog to the wharf to make sure she didn't miss the boat. As she ran, she thought about the gym again. This was precisely the sort of occasion where being fit and agile would have helped her out. The running app was clearly doing something, though, as she didn't feel too bad. About five minutes later, she was standing on the jetty just as the boat puttered along the river. She smiled as it pulled up and she got on. She wasn't sure if it was Colin or Clive. She realised it was Clive when he opened his mouth and started to speak with the strange faux French accent just as if he'd just stepped out of 'Allo 'Allo which wasn't French anyway, but you get the picture.

'Bonsoir!'

It was definitely Clive. 'Evening. How are you?'

'Lovely evening on zee river,' Clive said in the accent. 'Where are you off to?'

Nina showed her phone with the drinks invitation. 'I'm going to the Lovely Lighthouse Drinks. What is the best stop to get off at for that?'

Clive, in his exaggerated faux accent, replied, 'Ah, the lighthouse soirée, très chic! You'll want to get off at St Lovely green. It's a short walk from there if you go around the back there.'

Nina nodded, tucking her phone back into her bag. 'Thanks, Clive. I appreciate it.'

'No problem at all, mademoiselle,' Clive said as he steered the boat away from the jetty. 'It's a beautiful night for it. So, you got an invite – that's pretty impressive.'

Nina chuckled. 'It is?'

'Yes indeed. Lovelies don't invite any old one to the lighthouse. Our Nancy, was it?'

'Yep.'

'Even more impressive, mademoiselle. You must be doing something right.'

'Really?'

'Oui. We don't let any old one into a Lovely event, especially not one at the lighthouse. But I heard you got into the chowder the other night with our Robby. So it follows.'

Nina wondered how everyone in Lovely seemed to know her business. 'Ah, yes, I did.'

'Well, there you are then. Lovely doors are opening. Drinks are a big deal here. The lighthouse always has the best gatherings, in my humble opinion. You'll have a bien time.'

Nina smiled at Clive's strange interjection of French words into his sentences. 'I hope so.'

Clive didn't realise quite how much Nina hoped she was going to have a nice time. She'd forced herself to get ready and go and couldn't stomach an event where she stood on her own feeling like a spare part.

The lights from Lovely Bay twinkled in the distance as the boat glided smoothly along the river and Nina gazed out at the water with a funny mix of nerves, dread, and worry. The feelings were precisely the reason she didn't go out much. Once she'd started accepting invitations after the initial grief from Andrew had dissipated somewhat, it hadn't taken her too long to realise that she didn't have much appetite for socialising on her own. Now not only was she on her own, but here she was doing it in a strange town to boot.

Clive turned to the side and addressed her, 'Still a bit of a nip in the air. You'll be fine once you get there.'

'I've never been to a do at a lighthouse before,' Nina said, trying to make conversation.

Clive chuckled. 'Oh, Lovely events are great. Good food, good company, and the view is spectacular from up the top. If you get a chance to go up. It depends on whether Birdie is there or not to open up. It's quite the climb, though.'

Nina leaned against the railing, watching the ripples in the water. 'I'm not usually one for these things. Kind of out of practice with social gatherings.'

'Well, everyone's friendly around here. You always meet a few interesting characters at a Lovely event. People make you feel welcome if they like the look of you.'

The boat approached its stop, and Clive skilfully manoeuvred it towards the jetty. 'This one's for you. Here we are, mademoiselle. Enjoy your evening at the lighthouse. Literally, as you can see, straight down this road. Be good. Bonsoir.'

'Thanks, Clive. I'll do my best. Bonsoir.'

Nina followed her nose with the lighthouse in front of her. She'd never seen anything like it before, not that she'd seen many lighthouses in her life. Rather than on a cliff, as she assumed lighthouses always were, the lighthouse towered from a long, squat building seemingly right in the middle of the town.

As she got outside, she stood for a second and read the information board.

The Lovely Grade II listed lighthouse, which is a prominent local landmark, was commissioned in 1899, and was automated and electrified in 1937. It survived a fire in its original oil-fired lamp just six days after commissioning and today operates a 180-watt main navigation lamp. Today, this lamp has a range of 22 nautical miles. The lighthouse is 30 metres tall, standing 36 metres above sea level. It is built of brick and painted white, and has 113 steps around a spiral staircase. Two keeper's houses were built next to the lighthouse in addition to the lighthouse hall which was used in World War I, and large living quarters being made in the lighthouse itself.

Nina gazed up at the looming lighthouse and suddenly had second thoughts about going in after all. What was she doing? Where was Andrew? He was lost, and right at the second, Nina felt as if she was too. Here she was again on her own outside a gathering, really wondering whether or not she should bother. She took a deep breath, gripped her handbag strap, straightened her shoulders, and walked towards the entrance. A few seconds later she was standing in the foyer; the place was deathly silent and there was not a soul to be seen. She felt her heart sink; she couldn't even get herself to the right place. A few seconds later, she decided to turn around and head back in the direction she'd come from, get herself home, and have a nice evening in the company of Netflix. Just as she was opening the door to go back out again, Nancy came the other way with her arms full with bottles of wine.

'Ahh, you made it. We're not in this building. We're down there in one of the old halls. Sorry, should have told you that. The heating isn't working up here at the moment, and it was way too chilly.'

Nina paused, her hand on the door handle, turning to face

Nancy. 'Oh, I was just about to leave. I thought I was in the wrong place.'

Nancy, struggling slightly with the bottles, smiled. 'No, you're exactly where you should be, but just down there a little bit in the old hall. Loads of us are here tonight. I'll introduce you to a few people.'

Nina hesitated for a moment, then her determination to put herself out there overrode her instinct to flee. 'Okay, lead the way. Do you need a hand with those?'

'That would be amazing, thank you,' Nancy replied, handing over a couple of wine bottles. 'Nice evening for it. We were hoping the weather would play ball, and it has. You never know in Lovely. We get four seasons in a day. You must have been told that a million times already. Oh, and how if you live in Lovely you need a coat. Ha ha. We're full of ourselves and our silly old superstitions.'

Nancy led Nina down a path that wound its way past the main section of the lighthouse. The old hall came into view and as they approached, Nina could hear chatter, laughter, and the tinkle of music. She felt her stomach swoop, and again she wondered what she was doing. The hall sounded full of happy people with happy lives, happy friends, and happy chatter. She wondered how many of them might have lost their husbands.

As if Nancy sensed her misgivings, she beamed. 'Right you are. Come and chat with Colin. He can talk the ass off anyone. I bet you probably just had a chat with his brother if you came on the boat,' Nancy said, pushing open the door to the hall. 'Everyone's been looking forward to meeting the person who is currently turning around The Summer Hotel, so you won't be short of people to talk to.'

Nancy led Nina over to a group of people where she could see Colin and the woman who had been in the bar on the first weekend. 'Colin you've already met Nina. Everyone, this is Nina, currently in charge of The Summer Hotel.'

Nina couldn't quite believe it as she was greeted with a chorus of friendly words and smiling faces. Before she really knew what was happening, she had a mini sausage roll in one hand and a glass of wine in the other. Not that she really drank wine much, but that didn't matter. She pretended that she did and sipped away happily.

Nina felt Robby before she saw him. It might have had something to do with the electric jolt that rampaged through her body, sending tingles to just about every part of her being. She was even in possession of tingling eyelashes. He touched her elbow from behind, and she smelt him right away. She turned and smiled and inside danced and swooned. She pretended to be casual, as if very handsome men approached her from behind every day of the week. She heard herself make an odd chirping sound. 'Oh, hiya.'

'Good to see you made it.'

Nina continued to be nonchalant and casual, breezy even, so very happy. 'Yeah, almost didn't, but Nancy intercepted me just in time. I started off over the other side there, and it was deadly quiet. I didn't realise it was in this hall.'

Robby laughed, his eyes twinkling. 'That's Nancy for you. She'll always be the one to find you, especially when you're up to no good.'

Nina swallowed, gazed upwards, and felt a little bit dreamy. All she could really concentrate on and think about was the kiss. Something felt as if what she was feeling was reciprocated, but then again, perhaps she was imagining it. 'Right, yes, I've gathered that.'

'What have you been up to?'

The chirpy voice continued to chat. 'You know, more of the same.'

'What's the go-to with the hotel?'

'Just to continue with getting it ready for sale.'

'Did she say whether or not there's been any interest in it? Jill, I mean.'

'I don't really know. Her email did say that the estate agent is putting feelers out already, but so far, no interest; I don't think. There aren't any photos or anything yet. It was too much of a mess for that.'

'Interesting. I guess you've got to be a certain kind of person to take it on. Goldmine though really. A lot of investment too, though.'

Nina thought about what Jase had said, but didn't let on that she knew anything about Robby. 'Yep, if that's the sort of thing that floats your boat.'

Nina stood and chatted with Robby for ages; more sausage rolls came around, various other people chatted, and surprisingly Nina found herself having a nice time. After getting Nina another drink, Robby smiled and his eyes searched hers. 'I err, I wanted to follow up on before.' He coughed. 'Well, you know, the thing that happened.'

Nina felt a flutter through her stomach and the tingles made themselves known. 'Oh! Yes, of course.' The kiss on the doorstep had been front and centre of her mind since it had happened. She so didn't want to look too keen. She took a too-hasty gulp of wine.

Robby shifted his weight. 'I, umm, I hope I didn't overstep. You're new and everything, yeah.'

Nina felt excruciatingly embarrassed. Her toes were nigh-on, folded back inside her shoes with cringe. 'You didn't, not at all. It was very, errr, nice, yes, nice.'

'Good. I mean, okay, I'm glad we're on the same page.'

Nina was hyper-aware of Robby's nearness, his scent, and just about everything about him. There was no doubt that her radar was very rusty, but it seemed as if he'd liked what had happened too. She wanted to do a fist-pumping lap of the room, instead she stayed rooted to the spot, gazing upwards. Just as

Robby was about to say something, Nancy bustled over and butted in. She jerked her thumb to the opposite side of the building. 'Lighthouse is open if you're going up. Birdie's just been in. Have you been to the top yet, Nina?'

Nina shook her head. 'No, not yet.'

'Oh, you *have* to go. It's amazing up there, isn't it, our Robby? The views are phenomenal, especially on a night like this.'

Robby tilted his head. 'Yep, the view up top is stunning this time of evening. Want to go up?'

Nina didn't hesitate. She nearly bit Robby's hand off and set down her wine. 'I'd love that.' She was more than happy to leave the drinks behind for a private tour with Robby to the top of a lighthouse. She'd had worse invitations in her life. Robby was her kind of tour guide.

~

A s Nina ascended the spiral staircase of the lighthouse, following closely behind Robby, she wasn't quite sure what to feel; excitement, apprehension, or what. The wide stairs wound around and upwards, their steps echoed and the pristine white walls of the lighthouse seemed to glow in the dim light. Something about it felt magical.

'Careful on these steps, they can be a bit of a challenge,' Robby called back over his shoulder. 'Just watch out you don't trip. One hand for the rail.'

Nina nodded and then looked up. The staircase seemed to stretch endlessly upwards. As they climbed, the sound of the sea and the distant chatter from below grew fainter and fainter. Nina's hand gripped the smooth timber railing, and she started to feel the number of steps in the muscles of her legs as they got closer to the top. Finally, and a little bit out of breath, they arrived at the top and emerged onto a viewing platform. Nina raised her eyebrows at a breathtaking panorama of Lovely Bay.

She couldn't quite believe it. Her achy legs were worth the shimmering view where the sea met the sky in the distance, the lights of Lovely Bay twinkled and everything took on a whole new meaning. Nina stepped closer to the glass, taking in the view.

'Wow, worth all those steps. It's like another world up here.'

'I always say the same thing. It's beautiful, isn't it?' Robby said as he stood beside her, following her gaze.

'It really is incredible,' Nina replied, her eyes fixed on the horizon. 'I had no idea the view would be this stunning up here. I should have realised that, really. Gosh, we're really high.'

'Thirty metres up.'

They stood in silence for a moment, and Nina gazed out lost in the twinkly lights and the strangely quiet, ethereal atmosphere. The panoramic view of Lovely Bay felt as if it had dropped her somewhere else entirely. 'I could stare at this view all day long.'

Robby followed her line of sight. 'It's one of my favourite spots in Lovely Bay. It gives you perspective, doesn't it?'

'Yeah, it makes you see things differently.' Nina pointed. 'Right, I'm getting my bearings. So that must be the train station over there and the railway line and the river there.'

'Yep, and over there are the dunes. You could spend hours up here pointing out things,' Robby noted.

For a moment, they both stood there and said little, but the air around them felt charged with something Nina certainly hadn't been part of for a very long time. Just as she was wondering what was going to happen regarding the tingling and as if it was the most natural thing in the world, Robby moved closer, put his hand on hers, then leaned down and kissed her. Boom. Nina Lavendar got in a spaceship and headed for the moon. She felt a surge of emotions she hadn't thought she'd ever feel again. A mix of things but mostly excitement, a strange sort of longing, and somehow via the tingles, a sense of being alive. As if, before, in an odd sort of way, it hadn't been just Andrew who had died but something in her had too. Now it was coming back to life. No longer dead to the world, but heading for the moon and tingling like crazy.

An almost drunk feeling slammed into Nina as the world around her appeared to fall away. As if they were the only two people in the world standing at the top of the lighthouse, surrounded by the beauty of Lovely Bay, zooming back and forth to the moon. She never wanted it to end.

29

Nina sat in bed with her head resting back against the headboard, a cup of hot chocolate on the bedside table beside her, a cool breeze blowing in through the open window, and the only light in the room, a little reading lamp in the corner. She stared at the window and watched the curtain moving back and forth in the wind. The sound of the sea floated around her, and she could hear the hum of the dishwasher from the kitchen across the hallway. With her phone in her lap, she relived the whole scene in the lighthouse with Robby in her head and let her mind drift deliciously back to the evening. How nice it was. How good she'd felt. How the lights around Lovely Bay had twinkled far below. How she'd not felt as happy in a very long time. How fabulous it was to be out-out. How she'd rocket shipped it to the moon and back. How she'd tingled for England.

She stirred the hot chocolate around and around with a spoon and then took a sip and let the evening's happenings whoosh through her brain. What a turn-up for the books. She'd kissed a fabulously handsome man at the top of a lighthouse. Ding blimming dong. She thought about Robby as she swirled the chocolate in her mug. He'd been charming, easy-going, and funny and nothing like the grumpy, rude bloke she'd first met. She smiled at the thought of him, the way he had looked at her, and the way he made her feel. It all felt so deliciously nice and somehow just right. It hit her that she hadn't felt guilty about Andrew while she'd been standing next to Robby, looking out at the water; that in itself was a first.

The curtain fluttered again. She heard a rustling outside and then, somewhere in the distance, a boat puttering along. As she sat there musing the whole dreamy evening, Nina realised both how much she had needed a proper evening out and also how long it had been. Just doing something other than being in her flat and alone with nothing and no one for company except her books, her cooking, and her laptop had been really nice. She'd been out in the world chatting to people, smiling, laughing, and had actually enjoyed herself. How nice. Her phone pinged.

Sophie: *Hey. Are you back? How was it? I'm itching to know, lol!!*
Nina: *Just got back. It was actually really nice.*
Sophie: *Ooh glad you enjoyed it. Where are you?*
Nina: *Sitting in bed with a hot choc.*
Sophie: *Tell me everything! Was he there?*
Nina: *Yup.*
Sophie: *And???*
Nina: *We climbed to the top of the lighthouse..*
Sophie: *Aww, that sounds amazing! How was it?*
Nina: *Very good.*
Sophie: *Did anything happen?*
Nina: *There may have been another kiss.*
Sophie: *Yesssss!!!!!* Sophie added a fist pump emoji.
Nina: *I'm trying not to overthink it. Just enjoying the change of scenery.*
Sophie: *My kinda tree change, haha.*
Nina: *Seriously. I need to not analyse this and go with the flow.*
Sophie: *Good idea. No pressure, right?*

Nina: *Exactly. But it was a lovely evening. The lights of Lovely Bay below us, the sea in the distance... very picturesque.*

Sophie: *You're living the dream, Neens! So happy for you.*

Nina: *I wish! Anyway, off to sleep now.*

Sophie: *Alright, sleep well. Keep me updated on the Robby saga. I'll take a nice big fat payment for making you make this change in your life. You're welcome.*

Nina: *I'm glad you made me. Night.*

Nina let her phone drop in her lap and thought about the lighthouse's wide spiral staircase, and how the view from the top had taken her breath away. She put her empty cup on the bedside table, plugged in her phone, turned off the lamp, and for a bit just laid in the darkness thinking. As her eyes adjusted to the light, she traced the silhouettes of the furniture with her eyes as her brain continued to wind down from the evening. She then snuggled under the covers and closed her eyes, with the image of the twinkling lights of Lovely Bay and Robby filling her mind. As she started to drop off, she hugged herself. Things in Nina Lavendar's life appeared as if they were on the up. She couldn't wait for another trip to the moon.

30

Since Andrew had passed away, Nina had not really slept properly and certainly not all the way through the night. Sometimes she'd felt as if the *thought* of sleeping alone actually suffocated and panicked her a bit. In the night in her flat, she'd wake up so many times that she'd begun to give the occasions names. There was the time around one when the bloke from downstairs got home from his shift at work, the 3 a.m. slot where she'd often thought she could rent herself out to parents with newborns, the four-thirty-ish slot when someone leaving for work on a motorbike just down the street butted into her sleep. Then there was the time about 5:45 a.m. where she'd have little arguments with herself on whether or not it was worth going back to sleep. In addition were the other random times when she'd lay awake and wonder what would have happened if her life had gone a different way and how it would now be if Andrew was still around.

The strange but not unwelcome thing in Lovely Bay was that none of the early morning awakenings had occurred at all in her room in The Summer Hotel. In fact, it was completely the opposite. The moment her head hit the pillow, she was more or less dead to the world and had woken up nine glorious hours later feeling as if she'd been dropped into a box of long, dark, delicious sleep.

For so long she'd been so used to surviving on the horribly broken night's sleep that at first, when she'd slept through the night, she hadn't known what to make of it. She'd pondered why she was sleeping so well and, more importantly, analysed how she was going to ensure it continued. After thinking about it for a bit, she'd realised it wasn't rocket science and had put it down to the physical exercise, the coastal air, and the fact that she had things going on around her other than wallowing in a load of overdone grief. Whatever it was, it was certainly working for her, and she wanted to keep it that way.

This morning was no different to all the other Lovely Bay mornings, and she woke up from a delicious night's sleep with the curtains billowing and a cool breeze rushing through the room together with a patch of sunshine landing on the floor. Shuffling to the window, Nina pulled back the curtain, shoved the window up, and felt a cold breeze along with a bright sunshine. A flurry of clouds marched across the sky and a flock of birds way up above floated as she yawned, stretched her arms above her head, and shifted her weight from side to side.

Pulling her dressing gown on, she shoved her feet into her sheepskin-lined slippers, tied her hair up in a scrunchie on the top of her head, and went into the kitchen. A few minutes later she'd put the kettle on, lifted the lid on the old Aga and was frying bacon in a pan. About ten minutes after that, with a huge mug of tea in her right hand and a bacon sandwich in the other, she struggled with the back door, stepped down the side of the house, and walked all the way down the garden to the end. Perched on an old outdoor table, she sat looking at the river and watched as a few boats went by and people on the path on the far side of the river went about their days. She watched a man in a business suit hurry along towards the riverboat jetty, a woman with a pram and a dog stopped and chatted with another woman with a pram, and a jogger with no shirt made her shiver.

As she enjoyed the bacon sandwich and tea in her little spot at the end of the garden, she thought about Robby, wondered what would happen next, checked her phone about a trillion times to see if there was a message and felt disappointed when there was nothing.

Half an hour later, she'd decided to walk to the shops and see what happened. She put on a slouchy beanie, decided it was warm enough not to wear a coat, wrapped a scarf around her neck, and slipped her feet into her Blundstone boots for a walk into Lovely Bay and a trip to the shops. Her mission was to pop in to get the bits and bobs to make a curry recipe which she'd found in an old cookery book from the seventies living on a shelf above the Aga.

Five or so minutes later, with the wind in her hair, she walked down by the river, past a lovely row of old cottages, around the back of one of the churches, and stopped here and there looking around at Lovely Bay doing its thing. The sun dipped in and out from fluffy white clouds, the river glinted between buildings, and just as she was walking past the main green on the right, she bumped straight into Colin from the riverboat in his regulation navy blue waxed Lovely coat. Colin had a dog beside him on a lead, a shopping bag on his arm, glasses propped on the end of his nose, and a stripy bobble hat on his head.

'Ahoy there. How are you? It's a gorgeous day this morning. Warm weather is in the air. Hooray for that. Couldn't come sooner if you ask me.' Colin's dog sniffed Nina's foot and wagged his tail.

'Hi. Yes, it's so nice today.'

'How did you get on last night? Enjoy it, did you? Your first Lovely Drinks, was it?'

Nina nodded. 'It was.'

'Ahh, you're right in now. Our Nancy clearly likes the look of you.'

Nina chuckled. 'I think so, yes.'

Colin jerked his thumb in the direction of where Nina had come from. 'I bumped into Jase in the deli. He said you've been clearing the place. That's right, is it? I didn't get much chance to chat with you last night.'

'Yeah, it's a big job, but I'm getting there slowly.'

'I bet. I don't think anyone's touched that place for years since the old girl went into a home. Just various house-sitters along the way, none of whom seemed to give a damn about it. I never could quite work out why Jill did that. Weird, if you ask me. Anyway, each to their own, as they say.'

'Yep. It could have done with a cleaner over the years. The trouble is, when you leave something for so long, the job becomes huge, if you see what I mean.'

'Totally get you. On that note, I have one of those industrial vacuums if you're interested – might help you out.'

Nina nodded. 'Hmm.'

'It's brilliant. Jase said there's a decade's worth of dust in the old B&B rooms. It would do the trick.'

'He's not wrong.'

'I'll drop it off if you like.' Colin put his shopping bag down, whipped off his glasses, took a pair of reading glasses out of his top pocket, perched them on the end of his nose, and tapped his phone. He turned his phone around to face Nina. 'Yeah, this is it, plus I have one of the robotic ones too. Set it and forget it.' Colin chuckled. 'It's not bad as it goes.'

'Thanks, that's really nice of you. That would help out, actually. I've been doing it with the vacuum, which really has seen better days. I was thinking about emailing Jill to say she should get a new one sent. You have a robot one, too?'

'Oh yes. I mean, it's not as good as getting stuck into it on your own, but it will break some of the back of it for you. Do you want to borrow them?'

Nina was surprised at the generosity. 'Yes. Thank you.'

Colin picked up on the surprised tone in Nina's voice. 'We're a generous lot down here. You'll get used to it if you stay. We Lovelies help each other out, you know?'

Nina was getting used to the way Lovelies operated. 'Yes.'

'Have you heard much from Jill?'

'She's in and out of coverage, so not really, mostly instructions via email and that's about it. I'm getting it ready for sale while the last few red tape bits go through.'

Colin dipped his head, wrinkled his nose, and looked at her over the top of his glasses. 'A good buy that place, if you want my opinion. My brother thinks so, too. Just needs someone capable in charge of it.'

Nina nodded. 'I was just thinking that earlier as I was having my tea. It really does have potential for whoever is willing to take it on.'

'You're not wrong. Plus, around here it wouldn't be hard to rent it out and get it back to its glory days. My places are rented out year-round, more or less.'

'Right, you have holiday cottages, do you?'

'Flats, yep. Ach, a lot of us Lovelies do, though we'll never let holiday places overtake the locals like you hear about in the news. The mix is just right to keep our little economy buoyant.'

'Right, I see.'

'Would you think about taking the place on? Seems like Lovely Bay suits you so far.'

Nina adjusted the scarf around her neck and looked at Colin thoughtfully. 'Ahh, not for me, I'm afraid, but it does have a lot of potential.'

Colin nodded, holding onto his dog's lead as it sniffed around. 'It's a prime spot. And you've got the touch for it, from what people tell me.'

Nina let out a laugh. 'I've just been clearing out old stuff, really. But I keep imagining what it could be. I bet it was gorgeous back in the day. Some of the old stuff in the back rooms is amazing.'

'Imagination's the first step with that old place, I reckon. You turn that place around, and it could be a real gem. Holiday-makers love a place with character.'

'I was thinking along the lines of a vintage coastal style, taking into account the river, all the old boats...' Nina mused, her mind picturing the transformation. 'Keeping it really classy but comfortable and homey, you know?'

'Oh, yes. People love that kind of thing down here. Makes them feel like they're staying somewhere special,' Colin agreed. 'With the online market these days, you'd have no trouble filling it up, and it brings lots of income down our way to Lovely. Yep.'

'It's a big project for whoever takes it on.'

'Indeed. What doesn't kill you makes you stronger. So you're enjoying working for Jill now, are you?'

'I am. I'm between work at the moment, so it suited me perfectly.'

Colin chuckled, his eyes twinkling under the rim of his glasses. 'Well, Lovely Bay has a way of keeping people. You might find it harder to leave than you think.'

A gust of wind blew through; Nina shivered slightly, then smiled. 'Ahh, yes, I've heard that.'

'Anyway, as I say, if you want the vacuum, I'll drop it off. And if you need any help or advice, just ask around. We're all here to help each other.'

Nina nodded. 'Thanks, Colin. I appreciate it.'

'No problem,' Colin said, picking up his shopping bag. 'I'll drop the vacuums off later, then. Might save you some time and effort.'

'That would be great, thank you.'

'Not a problem. If you're not there. I'll pop it on the porch, there.'

'Great. See you later.'

Nina watched as Colin walked away with his dog, her mind buzzing with all sorts, but mostly how friendly everyone in Lovely Bay seemed. As she continued her walk towards the main road, she had a bit of a spring in her step. It felt nice to be recognised and to stop and chat. Nice to just have a bit of nothing talk with someone and to sort of belong. She hadn't felt that for a long time.

31

With a basket full of supplies for her recipe later, Nina strolled into the deli and smiled, and as the first time she'd walked in, she was struck by how cosy it felt. A row of classic pendant lights hung from the ceiling over the main counter, the walls, painted in soft whites, were adorned with a jumble of old photos and vintage advertisements, and little round tables were dotted here and there all around the place. The Shipping Forecast played from beside the till. At the back, where the counter ran from left to right, glass display cases were filled with sourdough, salads, and pies. On the far side, another case was stacked with piles of freshly baked biscuits.

Nina inhaled a mix of freshly ground coffee, baked goods, and something else she couldn't quite put her finger on. It was the kind of smell that made you feel instantly at home and tempted your taste buds. Just along from the counter on the wall, a length from a gigantic roll of brown paper was pulled out and fastened to a hook, and in neat, handwritten script a few specials were detailed. On the far wall, a staggering collection of assorted vintage glass jars was filled with all manner of herbs and spices. Each little jar was labelled with the same handwriting as the specials. Nina's eyes wandered along the neat rows of jars, going from the oranges of curry powder to the greens of rosemary and thyme, and then to the bright yellows of turmeric. Almost mesmerised by it all, she watched as one of the deli staff approached the shelves, selected a jar, unscrewed a lid, and then put the pot on the counter.

On the far side, a large chaotic corkboard brimmed with an assortment of notes, flyers, and personal ads. With the Shipping Forecast playing away to itself, Nina walked over and stood and read through for a minute or two; a flyer for a weekend craft fair, a charity cake sale with hand-drawn fairy cakes on its corners. A poster for an upcoming local band's gig at the lighthouse hall, a lost-and-found notice for a missing cat. On and on it went – a small card offered guitar lessons with a tear-off section at the bottom for contact details. Nina smiled as she saw that most of the tabs had already been taken. A colourful, handmade flyer announcing a book club meeting at the deli itself caught her eye. It listed the date and the book of the month, inviting any Lovelies interested to join. Nina found herself taking a picture of the notice, and she considered it for a moment, thinking it might be a nice way to meet more people in Lovely Bay. A book club? Who even was she? There was even a quirky ad from someone looking for a jogging partner, specifying 'early risers only' and 'bonus points if you like 80's music.' Nina chuckled to herself. She'd definitely give that one a miss.

The bottom corner of the board was dedicated to a small collage of thank-you notes and photographs from various community members, expressing gratitude for the support received from the deli and its patrons. Nina nodded to herself as she took it all in. It was a far cry from her local area where people put their heads down and hurried past looking down at their phones. Here, it all seemed so friendly, the community spirit alive and thriving in front of her eyes.

Nina was surprised to see Birdie come in from a back room. Birdie chuckled. 'Yes, I get around.'

Nina laughed. 'I thought you owned the chemist.'

'I am a woman of many skills.'

'Right.' Nina frowned.

'I own this place, and we're short-staffed, so it's all hands on deck. Anyway, how are you?'

'Good, thanks.'

'I saw you at the Lighthouse Drinks last night chatting away. Looked like you were having a fun evening.'

'Yes, it was really good, thank you. It was nice to be invited.'

'Ahh, we like you.' Birdie laughed.

'The view from the top was incredible.'

'I heard about your little tour to the top. Our Robby's quite the host, isn't he?' Birdie chuckled.

Nina felt a blush creep up her cheeks. 'He is. It was very kind of him to show me around.'

Birdie leaned in slightly and lowered her voice. 'You two seemed to be getting along quite well. It's always nice to see. Yes, and especially nice in his case.'

Nina wasn't quite sure how to respond or how Birdie knew she'd been up to the top of the lighthouse with Robby. 'Mmm, it was good up there.'

Birdie nodded. 'I bet it was. Anyway, how are you getting on with the hotel? It's quite the talk of the town that Jill's finally put it up for sale or is going to put it up, should I say.'

'Yikes, it's local gossip,' Nina said with her eyebrows raised.

'Oh, in a good way. Everyone's curious to see what will happen with the old place. It's been a part of Lovely Bay for so long but these past few years with the house sitters and everything. Well, I'm sure you've heard that story a few times now.'

'Bits and bobs of it, yeah.'

'Anyway, what can I get you?'

'A coffee, please.'

'Chocolate shavings?'

'From the chocolate shop?'

'You're learning fast.' Birdie chortled. 'That's how we do it here. Keep it in the family. Ha!'

Nina chuckled. 'Sounds like chocolate shavings are the way to go.'

～

Nina had thoroughly enjoyed the coffee with the shavings sitting in the little deli with the Shipping Forecast as a companion. She'd had a text conversation with her mum as she'd finished it and had relished just sitting in the window watching the world go by. Just as she was getting her things together, a little notice in the corner by the till caught her eye. A small handwritten card said the deli was seeking someone with a friendly demeanour, preferably a Lovely to help out because someone called Jenny was in hospital.

Birdie noticed Nina looking at the card. 'Fancy another job?'

Nina laughed. 'Isn't it open to Lovelies only?'

'We sometimes make exceptions.' Birdie glanced at the card and nodded. 'Our Jenny is having her ACL fixed, and she's out of action for a while. Last thing we need as the season gets close – the day trippers and trainspotters will be here soon and spending their money, and we'll be run off our feet. Officially I'm not even meant to be in here, but someone has to keep the place going.'

'I bet you'll have loads of applicants lining up in no time. Everyone seems to love this place.' Nina said, gesturing around.

Birdie smiled, her eyes crinkling at the corners. 'I wish it was that simple. I'm looking for someone who's not just about the work but also fits in with the community vibe we have here. It's not just about serving food and wiping down a few things, which is why you find *me* here.' Birdie lowered her voice. 'Then there's the whole chowder thing. It takes a certain kind of person for that.' Birdie shook her head. 'One wrong member of staff can lose us a lot of business. Ask me how I know.'

Nina nodded. 'That makes sense, actually. It's very cosy in here and such a welcoming atmosphere. I can see it needs to be a certain someone to fit in.'

'If you ever fancy trying your hand for a few shifts, I'd love to have you. I think you'd fit right in. I've got an event coming up, and it's going to be hard going without Jenny. Anyway, we'll soldier on.'

Nina laughed, surprised by the offer. 'That's very kind of you. I'm pretty tied up with the hotel at the moment, but it's certainly something to think about.'

'Of course.'

'Thank you for thinking of me.' Nina went to walk away and suddenly found herself turning around and words coming out of her mouth. 'Actually, you know what? I can give you a hand if you like. I don't have experience, but I used to waitress when I was in sixth form.'

'Done.'

'Ha, that was quick!'

'We need as many helping hands as we can. If you can load a dishwasher and smile at people, you'll be worth your weight in gold. I already know you can hold a conversation and Nancy invited you to Drinks, so that's the vetting done for me.'

Nina laughed. 'I think I can just about manage that.'

'Right, well, let's have your number, and I'll be in touch with a text.'

Nina gave her number and as she walked out and strolled along the pavement, she couldn't quite believe what had just happened. She'd gone and got herself another job.

32

Nina had spent the rest of the day clearing another of the hotel rooms, and she'd got stuck in the sitting room in the living quarters. Once she'd become sick of the sight of clutter, she'd cleaned the kitchen whilst listening to an audiobook and had prepped the curry from the old cookery book. As she pottered around, her mind constantly went back to what had happened in the lighthouse and the fact that she'd said yes to the shift at the deli. She also didn't quite know what to think about the fact that she'd heard zilch from Robby.

She tapped Sophie's number for a WhatsApp video chat. Sophie answered. 'Hi. How are you?'

'Good. I've just made a curry from that book I was telling you about. It smells amazing.'

Sophie chuckled. 'I thought it would be chowder.'

'Ha, nope, I'm not qualified to make one yet. They take it all very seriously around here. The recipes are passed down from generation to generation, apparently.'

'I've heard.'

'So, I do have a new development in my adventures in all things Lovely.'

'Oh, yeah, what? Another handsome man chatting you up? Who have you kissed now?' Sophie joked.

Nina giggled at the thought of her chat with Colin in the street. 'Not quite.'

'What have you been up to?'

'I popped into the deli for a coffee and I got chatting with the owner. There's an event coming up, and they're short-staffed. She asked if I could help out. Long story short, I said yes. I have a shift there.'

'Oh wow! Really? What made you do that?'

'I thought, why not? It's just for one event. Plus, it'll be nice to do something different and I don't know, I just said it on the spur of the moment. What's the harm in saying yes to a few things every now and then?'

Sophie laughed. 'Look at you, diving into Lovely Bay life.'

'I know, right? You said I needed a fresh start – I'm running with it.'

'All joking aside, it could be a great way to meet new people and make some friends. You've been stuck in that flat in town and in that job for way too long.'

'That's what I was thinking. I mean, I know I'm here to work at the hotel, and it's only temporary, but it doesn't hurt to branch out a bit, right?'

'Absolutely,' Sophie agreed. 'And who knows? You might end up loving it.'

'I don't know about that.'

'See, I told you good things would happen to you if you got out of that rut you were in.'

'You did.'

'You didn't want to know, even though I told you so many times. I was sick of the sound of my own voice about it in the end.'

'I know.'

Sophie made a sweeping gesture. 'So, you owe all this to me.'

'Ha, I do. I didn't realise how much of a rut I was in, actually.'

'Yeah, sometimes you need to just pop out of your life for a bit.'

'It's just a small step, but it feels good, you know? I mean, I'm hardly part of the community or anything, but I don't know, I just feel different...'

'Definitely. Plus, you never know who you might meet at the event.'

Nina's thoughts drifted to Robby, but she brushed them aside. 'Yeah, who knows? I might learn one of the town's secret recipes. Then I'll publish it online and make millions.'

'If you make millions, I want some of the money because technically the whole of this is down to me initiating it.'

'Not a problem. I'm happy to share my millions,' Nina joked.

'Anyway, what's happening at the hotel?'

Nina got up from the kitchen table, moved towards the Aga, took the lid off the curry, and stirred the pot. 'I've been clearing out another room this afternoon, deciding what to keep and what to chuck. Then I moved onto the sitting room here. It's like stepping back in time, honestly.'

Sophie chuckled. 'Sounds like a treasure hunt. Found anything interesting?'

'A few old photographs, some vintage kitchenware in a random box behind the sofa. Oh, and another load of ancient cookbooks with some wild recipes. It's all happening in my world.'

'We need one of our evenings, and you can test a recipe on me.'

Nina laughed. 'Maybe. Though I doubt you'd want some of them. Honestly, it's a real eye-opener into the taste of 1970s cuisine. Some of them literally have aspic and jellied eels.'

Sophie winced and screwed up her nose. 'Seriously, though, I need to come and stay for a night before this baby comes.'

'You do.'

'It really sounds as if you've settled in there.'

Nina paused, considering the question. 'It's different, but in a good way. I didn't expect to feel, I don't know what it is. The people are friendly, and there's a sense of something that I haven't felt in a long time. Not since, well, you know...'

'You actually sound different in your voice, and you look so much better. I knew this change would be good for you. You needed to shake things up a bit,' Sophie replied encouragingly.

'Yeah, I guess I did.'

'And there's the handsome one with the straps.'

'Ha!' Nina felt her cheeks warm. 'We're just friends, though.'

'Yeah, right! Do friends kiss in the moonlight these days, then? A new one on me! Keep me posted on that,' Sophie teased.

'I will.'

'I wonder where this will go?'

Nina felt her face flush. 'I don't know, honestly. He's great, but you know. I didn't think this would happen and to him, it's probably just nothing. Just because this is huge for me doesn't mean it is for him.'

'True. Good point. But you like him, don't you?' Sophie prodded gently.

'Who wouldn't? He's hard not to like. He's funny, and yeah, he's attractive, but at the end of the day it's nothing.'

'Hopefully not.'

'I'm just taking things as they come.'

'That's fair. Just don't close yourself off to possibilities, though. You deserve some happiness, and who knows? Robby might be a part of that.'

Nina nodded. 'I'll try to keep an open mind. I've just been so closed off and sad for so long this feels all very new, if you see what I mean?'

'Yeah, you must do.'

Nina nodded. 'I'm just going to go with the flow.'

'That's the spirit. I reckon that's always a good idea in life anyway, especially when the flow means you're invited to the top of lighthouses.' Sophie giggled.

'Works for me at the moment.'

'Seriously though, I'm really proud of you, you know. Taking on this project, making new connections. It's a big deal. It takes a lot to do what you did. I know I didn't say it at the time because I didn't want to put you off.'

'Thanks, Soph,' Nina replied, stirring the curry gently.

'I mean it, Neens. You've been through so much, and seeing you do this is so good. It's inspiring. Just shows you never know what's around the corner. I did not expect you to be kissing random men, but I'll take it.'

Nina smiled and chuckled. 'Ha, ha. I've hardly climbed Mount Everest. I guess I needed this. As you said, it's good to have a fresh start.'

'Lovely Bay is such a good place to do it.'

'It is. It's like its own little world here. Everyone knows everyone, and there's this sense of community that's just, I don't know, so comfy and nice,' Nina mused as she moved to the kitchen window to gaze out at the sky.

'That's exactly what you needed,' Sophie encouraged. 'A place where you can just be Nina, not the woman who lost her husband, not the one who's always busy with work. Just Nina. Remember, I'm the one who has known you since you were six.'

Nina's eyes pricked. 'I didn't realise how much I was hiding behind those labels. They said it in the grief circle all the time, and I always used to shake my head and say that wasn't me.'

'It's time for Neens to come out to play again.'

There was a pause as Nina let the words sink in. 'I'm trying, Sophie. And I think I'm making progress since I've been here. Yeah, things have changed.'

'You are definitely making progress! Just look at you – helping out at a deli, working on that old place, kissing amazing locals.' Sophie listed with a chuckle. 'Who is this woman, and what have you done with my best friend?'

Nina laughed. 'She's still here, just a bit more adventurous now. Someone or something gave her her mojo back.'

'I reckon Lovely gave you your mojo back.'

'It's been a bit of a rollercoaster since you sent me the link to that post, but I'm glad I'm on it. I think I am, anyway.'

'Yeah, and it's only going to get better.'

'Hope so.'

'Right, I need to skedaddle. Keep me updated on the man with the straps! I can't wait for the next instalment. Nina has sex for the first time in many years. I'll need all the juicy details. Possibly a livestream.'

Nina chuckled. 'That won't be happening! I haven't even heard from him. Yeah, I'd better finish this curry and get the rice on.'

'Keep doing what you're doing. You're finding your way back to yourself, and it's beautiful to see. I'm enjoying the ride.'

Afterwards, Nina stood and stirred the pot for ages and mused their conversation. Was Sophie right? Maybe. It was as if she was rediscovering parts of herself she had forgotten, and it was strangely exhilarating. Lovely Bay had given her a hefty old prod and made her sit up and have a dirty great look at her life. She was so up for the ride.

33

It was the next day, and Nina still hadn't heard anything from Robby. Part of her had begun to wonder if indeed she'd imagined the whole thing. She'd ventured into one of the rooms which was labelled in Jill's instructions as a junk room, and she'd realised it was not just junk but a lot of dust and spider webs too, a lot of which were now all over her clothes and in her hair. There was a lot of junk in there for sure, but also, from what she'd seen, some gorgeous old things. She'd been moving things around, sweeping and dislodging cobwebs, and made a dent in the piles of junk so that she could start to sort. Her work had been accompanied by an audiobook and as with the rest of the house, she was, in actual fact, finding the whole thing quite therapeutic. Who knew she would both enjoy and get paid for sorting out someone else's junk? She'd had worse times in her life.

She was just hauling a box of books out onto the porch from the junk room when she heard a vehicle pulling up outside. Wiping her forehead with the back of her hand, she peered towards the road, saw a dark 4x4, and didn't take much notice.

As she dragged the box along to the corner, she frowned as

she recognised the person getting out of the car. Her heart did a little flutter, but she quickly brushed the feeling aside and hastily tried to pat down her hair and dust off her clothes.

She smiled as Robby approached the gate with a broad smile, holding a box in his arms. 'Hey, how are you? I come bearing gifts.'

'I didn't recognise you in that car.'

'Oh, yeah right, I've been in one of the work vans when I've seen you.'

'Yes, you have.'

'I bumped into Colin. He sent these over for you,' Robby said with a smile on his face and raised eyebrows.

Nina realised Robby was amused at her dusty, dishevelled appearance. 'Oh, thanks. Sorry, I must look a sight. I've been clearing out rooms.' She tried to brush off some of the dust that clung to her sleeves.

Robby chuckled, placing the vacuum down. 'You look like you've been hard at work, which is always a good look in my book. This should help with the clean-up,' he gestured towards the box. 'This little guy is a bit of a lifesaver for the hard-to-reach spots, according to Colin, so there you go.'

Nina shook her head. 'I could use all the help I can get. There is just so much dust everywhere. It's like I just move it around from one spot to the other. I'm working in the junk room today, but I think there's just as much dust as junk.'

Robby leaned against the door frame, his eyes scanning the house. 'It's a big place with a lot of history. I hope Jill appreciates what you're doing for her. It's not a small job.'

'Ahh, she's paying me to clear and declutter, which I'm finding quite therapeutic, actually.'

'I guess it could be if that's what floats your boat.' Robby winked.

You are what floats my boat, Nina thought. She gestured up at the house. 'I've been thinking about all the potential it has. It could be something really special for someone. A great business.'

'Indeed.'

Nina felt as if there was a bit of awkward silence between them. She wasn't sure whether or not to mention what had happened at the lighthouse. She wanted *him* to mention it. He didn't.

Robby slipped his phone out of his pocket and checked the time. 'Right, sorry, I have to shoot. See you around.'

'Yes, okay, err, see you around,' Nina replied.

As Nina picked up the vacuum and watched Robby walk back to his car, she felt awkward and disappointed at the same time. *See you around! What did that mean?*

She felt more than stupid. He was clearly now regretting kissing her. What an idiot she'd been. He'd not even addressed it! In fact, he'd totally ignored it. She shook her head at her dusty cargo pants and old T-shirt. He'd clearly taken one look at her and thought he must have been stark raving mad to kiss her in the first place. Nina felt her heart sink. She'd thought about Robby just about every few minutes since the lighthouse. She'd daydreamed about him. She may or may not have imagined doing things with him. There might have been straps involved at some point. She closed her eyes and sighed. It was clear as day that Robby wasn't thinking along the same lines *at all*. He was just going to brush it off and leave it be. Leave her hanging in mid-air. Back to being sad.

34

Trying not to think about the fact that Robby had monumentally binned her off, Nina had decided that nothing was going to get her down, that he could go stuff himself, and she was on her way out for a run. Since the first day she'd started with the app, she'd moved on in leaps and bounds. She had progressed not only in the running app itself but her exercise gear had improved vastly. She laughed as she put her hair up and thought about the first run she'd been on along the river path in the grey-white bra that had long since lost its elasticity. After a few more outings without any support, she'd succumbed to looking for some leggings and a top whereby she wouldn't scare the locals or random boats as they passed by and had treated herself to fancy new workout clothes.

There had been a lot of toing and froing between exercise apparel websites. Workout gear had got complicated. She'd spent ages, and with a limited budget, looking for something that might help her run along the river without everything jiggling and bouncing up and down. After a lot of intensive googling and a call to Sophie, she'd ordered a pair of leggings, which had promised to sculpt and do all sorts of wonderful things. She was now standing in front of the mirror looking at said leggings. She had to give it to them, they weren't too bad. A little line of dots ran up the 7/8th legs, a reinforced panel held some of her jiggly tummy section in place, and her bottom wasn't quite as low. The seamless, ribbed, performance tank which matched the leggings held her girls in place and, like the leggings, was performing minor miracles. We're not talking Jane Fonda, but overall, a vast improvement had occurred. Nina Lavendar, in actual fact, didn't feel too bad at all. She may even have been quite pleased with herself. The fact that she'd started the running app at all was an achievement. Now here she was dressed for it and looking the part, too.

Giving herself a final once-over in the mirror, she had to admit it; the new gear had made a world of difference. Why had she not invested in herself a long time ago? She felt more confident and more prepared. It was funny how something as simple as a pair of well-fitting leggings and a supportive tank could change her outlook on exercise.

She plugged in her earphones, queued up the running app, and stepped outside into a bright morning. She took a big inhale of crisp air with a hint of brine and sea salt, and as she made her way to the river path, she was very surprised to feel a spring in her step. Was she actually beginning to look forward to running? Unbelievable but quite possibly true.

With the dawn of a nice day, the path was busier than it usually was, with a couple of joggers passing her by, a cyclist with a baby seat going the other way, and a few walkers strolling along enjoying the beautiful weather. Nina started with her brisk walk, feeling less self-conscious than she had on her first few outings. She was now used to the friendly nods and smiles from Lovelies and enjoyed being out in the fresh air.

She'd progressed with the app significantly but was still a bit apprehensive to move on to the next stage of her running journey. As the voice in her earphones instructed her to start her first run, Nina picked up the pace and noticed the difference immediately in having the correct clothes. It no longer felt as if her skin was slipping and making its way to the ground. The leggings somehow miraculously held everything in place, and the tank provided support. She was far from feeling in love with running, but now at least, she felt reigned in and no longer distracted by an exponential amount of wobbling.

The voice started to coach her in her ears, gearing her and the imaginary people who were running along beside her, up for more of a run than she'd done before. 'Three, two, one, here we go. Always feel free to start at a slower pace and then pick it up as you go. Come on, couch potatoes, let's gooooooooo!'

Nina was far from fast or enthusiastic, but she fell into a comfortable rhythm and settled into the strange thing that had started to happen to her when she got a few minutes into the running app; her mind began to clear with each step. Running along the river towards the sea, with its views and fresh air enveloping her, was becoming something she didn't actually mind. It had become a time to disconnect, not think about anything and recharge. No one was more surprised than her.

'Our goal is to increase our endurance and double our stamina. We're going to run for five whole minutes, five! You can do it! Come on, couch potatoes.'

As she ran, Nina started to go over what had happened since Sophie had sent her the post about Lovely Bay. She thought about the changes in herself, how she'd met a few new people and had even flirted with the idea of a new romance. Despite the fact that Robby had made it clear that to him it was little more than a couple of random kisses, she decided that stuff it, she would just let it be. To her, it felt like she was slowly rediscovering parts of herself that she had forgotten and neglected.

'Shoulders are back, chest is up. We want to run tall. We make sure our core is nice and tight.'

Nina still wasn't sure where her core was, if indeed she had one, but she sucked everything in anyway, and hoped for the best. Nothing in her case was nice and tight. There were still many wobbles in places she didn't know existed, but overall, she was doing well.

'Think about how far you have come and how you've grown from these runs. Think about how strong you are!'

Nina didn't feel like she'd grown, but she was panting and sweating less, so she'd take that as a plus. Her heart must be healthier, surely?

'I hope this has made you fall in love with running.'

Had she fallen in love with running? Not on your Nelly, but it was doing its job and she was achieving something.

'I hope you've fallen in love with the push, the drive, the rush you get. I want you to love that burning feeling.'

Nina wasn't sure if the person in her ears was quite right in the head, but she continued anyway. Just as she reached the final walking section of the workout, with her hair stuck to the side of her head and feeling boiling hot, she wondered if she had improved at all. She arrived at the jetty, not far from the train station. The one she'd first arrived at when the train had deposited her in Lovely Bay. As she turned, she bumped straight into Robby coming the other way.

'Oh, hi, how are you?' Nina panted, trying to slow down her breathing and embarrassed about her sweaty, hot face.

Robby looked fresh and composed and smelled as if he'd just stepped out of the shower. 'Hey, you're looking, err, energised.'

Nina self-consciously wiped her forehead with the back of her hand. 'Energised is one way to put it. More like a sweaty mess, really,' she replied with a chuckle, trying to catch her breath as she put her hands into the small of her back and tried not to pant.

Robby leaned against the railing of the jetty. 'So, you're a runner, are you? I didn't realise that. You didn't say that before.'

'Pah! No, I'm not. It's a new challenge, put it that way.' Nina shrugged, her breathing starting to normalise.

'Oh, right, I see. How are you finding it?

'It's a bit full-on, but I'm getting there. The app I'm using is pretty motivating, even if I'm not quite in love with running yet as the woman in my ears keeps telling me I should be.'

Robby nodded. 'Nice, peaceful, scenic spot for it.'

'Yeah, there is that,' Nina agreed, looking over the river and out towards the sea.

There was a brief pause as they both watched a small boat putter past. Robby seemed slightly awkward. He'd clearly not expected to bump into her and had probably hoped to avoid her since what had happened at the top of the lighthouse. He was clearly trying to make a bit of small talk so as not to be rude. 'There's a group of Lovelies who do runs over in the dunes and on the sand. Lovely Running Club.'

Nina's eyes widened at the thought. She shook her head. 'I'm not sure I'm quite there yet.'

Robby chuckled. 'Yeah, I hear they're pretty serious.'

Nina shook her head. 'Definitely not my scene.'

'Rightio, anyway, I'm heading to the train, so I'd best get on.'

'Yep, see you.'

Robby took a few steps, suddenly paused, and turned back. 'Actually, there's something else I've been meaning to ask you.'

Nina, caught off guard, turned back toward him. 'Oh, right, yep? What's that? Do you need me to help out with something for your aunt?'

Robby took a deep breath. 'No, not that at all. I was wondering if you would be interested in going out. Just as, well...'

Nina's heart skipped four hundred beats. *What in the name of goodness! Was Robby, man of straps, asking her to go out on a proper, real date?* She wasn't quite sure if she'd heard him right. She hadn't expected the question, especially not after a sweaty morning run. After he'd dropped the vacuum off, she'd convinced herself the kiss was nothing and he didn't like her. She'd told herself she could deal with that and it was just an off-the-cuff kiss at the top of a lighthouse. Other people did it and thought nothing of it all the time. She found herself momentarily lost for words, her mind racing. 'What, umm, sorry, like out-out?'

Robby frowned, 'Out-out? What does that mean?'

'Like what, you want to go out together? Like me and you?'

Robby winced. 'Ahh, sorry, honestly, no drama. I thought...'

'No! I mean, yes!'

Robby looked confused. 'Yes, or no?'

'Um, sorry, you *do* mean on like a date, right?' Nina stammered, her cheeks now flaming. 'With me, you mean?'

Robby chuckled. 'Yes, with you. I've really enjoyed our chats, and well, the other bit too. I thought it might be nice to do it properly.'

Nina was tingling from head to toe. 'I, umm, that would be really nice. Yes, I'd like that.'

'Great! I'm going away for work shortly, but how about next Friday evening? There's this little place I think you'd like. The chowder is fantastic. It's opening just for the evening. You know, as I told you.'

'Sounds perfect.'

'Brilliant. I'll pick you up at the hotel around seven. We can walk there; it's not far.'

'Fab. That's a plan. I'll see you then.' Nina beamed.

'Looking forward to it.'

After Robby hustled away in the direction of the train station, Nina plonked herself down on a bench. She wasn't sure what to think. Nina Lavendar had a date. Really? A date with Robby with the straps – who would have thought?

35

It was the day after Nina had bumped into Robby on her run. She made her way along the river and headed towards the dunes. She held her face up to the sky, inhaled and took it in – deep blue, cloudless, and full of the promise of warmer weather to come. She watched the water as it made its way out to sea and took in the curve of Lovely Bay. Somewhere up above a plane's engine droned, a boat puttered past, and she could hear a lawnmower in the distance.

She flipped over her watch to check the time and headed towards the dunes. In front of her, a couple holding hands looked at each other and smiled. In an instant, Nina felt sad. She was back with Andrew when they'd first met. In her head, she was looking at Andrew just like the young girl in front of her was looking at her boyfriend. She felt the deep, intense sadness and grief she knew so well flood through every single fibre of her body. Even now part of her still didn't believe what had happened; didn't want to believe it. She wanted to do anything but believe it. She sighed. One of the worst things about the grief was how it liked to play games. It liked to come back and poke her when she was least expecting it. It had happened many times over the years; whenever she'd thought she was feeling better and whilst not getting over but at least coming to terms with it, it decided that it would tell her who was in charge. It would rear its mean, horrid head and yell at her just so she knew she was not in control. Like now.

She forced herself not to ponder on the grief and *willed* herself not to think about Andrew. Here she was in Lovely Bay, and things were going well. She felt better than she had for ages; the sun was shining, she had a date locked in, she had a shift in a deli where the people were nice, and she'd made a couple of new friends. It was all positive, and her grief group would have said it was all part of a new existence for herself, but here was the grief again right in front of her face.

As she continued her walk towards the dunes, she focused on the here and now, trying to push away the melancholic thoughts. Determined not to be sad, she listened to the grasses rustling, the seagulls calling, and the sound of the sea in the far distance. She would not let the grief in to ruin her new start in life.

After walking for half an hour or so, she stood and took in the view of the coastline. The sea stretched out before her, an endless expanse of blue meeting the sky at the horizon. She closed her eyes for a moment, feeling the warmth of the sun on her face, and let out a long, deep breath. She then sat down on the sand, hugging her knees to her chest, and thought about the upcoming date with Robby. Part of her was scared of going but it felt like a new chapter, a step towards something different and possibly wonderful. She wasn't sure where it might lead, but the very fact that it had even come to be felt like progress.

As she started to head back across the dunes, she was lost in a world of her own when she bumped straight into Nancy, dressed in the regulation Lovely Bay wax coat with the stripy hood coming the other way.

Nancy beamed. 'Oh, hiya! How are you? What a gorgeous day, eh? Seen any otters?'

Nina shook her head. 'I don't think so.'

'You don't think so?'

'I was just crossing over there on one of the little bridges over there and I thought I saw something.'

'Ahh, if you stay around long enough, you see them.'

Nina heard herself making chit-chat with Nancy and liked how it felt.

Nancy looked down, her eyes scanning the water for any sign of otters. 'So, I hear you're doing a shift at the deli.'

Nina wondered how Nancy had got wind of it but didn't say anything. 'Yeah, just for one shift. Birdie asked if I could help out, and I thought, why not? It's something different. I'm all for broadening my horizons at the moment.'

'Good for you. Birdie's place is a Lovely Bay institution – I'm sure you've already worked that out for yourself. You'll fit right in. She more or less runs this town. Nothing gets past her and her old dad. I hope you like the Shipping Forecast.'

Nina chuckled. 'I was quite surprised when I first went in. It's like stepping into a different world in there.'

'Ah, yep. Plus, there's the family secret chowder recipe. You'll get to hear about that. Lovelies come out of the woodwork just to get a taste. Rumour has it her grandmother had a thing with one of the fishermen on the river here,' Nancy said with a chuckle.

'Ooh, how romantic.'

'I know, right?'

'Love it.'

'How are you settling into Lovely Bay otherwise? Meeting some new faces?'

Nina leaned against the railing, looking out at the water. 'You know what? It's been great, actually. I didn't expect to like it as much as I do. It's quite strange. Everyone's been really welcoming, and I don't know, just friendly. Maybe I am just too London, if you see what I mean?'

'That's Lovely Bay for you. We're a close-knit community. You never know, you might end up staying longer than planned,' Nancy said with a knowing look.

Nina smiled and contemplated for a second. 'Who knows? I've definitely felt more at home here than I expected. It's weird really...'

They stood and chatted for a second and Nina chuckled as the conversation drifted to other topics and Nancy filled her in on a bit of local gossip about Clive and his French accent. 'You'll have to come over to my cottage for dinner one night. I'm on the other side of Lovely Bay on one of the greens.'

Nina gushed. 'Ooh, I'd love that, thanks.'

From a path going the other way, June waved and called over, 'Hellooo, ladies. Gorgeous day for it.'

'Yes, I just said that,' Nancy called back.

'How are you, Nina?'

'Good, thanks. You?'

'Yes, just out stretching my legs.' June waved.

'Look at you, already part of the fabric here,' Nancy said, nudging Nina's arm. 'Next thing you know, you'll be running for town council or organising the summer fair.'

Nina laughed. 'Let's not get ahead of ourselves.'

Nancy lifted her chin towards June and then did a funny smile at Nina. 'A little dicky bird told me you're also getting on quite well with a certain nephew.'

Nina wasn't sure what to say. 'Ha.'

'You might be going on a bit of a date, if the Lovely grapevine is to be believed.'

There was no way Nina was going to broadcast her business. She made a funny sound between a laugh and a snort. 'Don't know what you're talking about.'

'It's taken a lot of us by surprise.'

Nina wrinkled up her nose. 'What does that mean?'

'Oh, nothing. Sorry.'

'Is there something I should know? Should I watch my back?'

'Gosh, no! We're just all a bit surprised. Robby normally keeps himself to himself, put it that way. Seems like you've changed that. Anyway, I must push on. I'm due at work soon and I wanted to get a walk in before I spend all day at the station.'

'Yes, me too. Well, have a nice day.'

'Will do. Same to you. We'll set a date for dinner at my place.'

'Look forward to it. See you later.'

As Nina walked away, she mulled over the small talk with Nancy. It had felt nice chatting and feeling as if she was part of something. She frowned at the odd comment about Robby. What did that even mean? She shoved it under the carpet and raised her eyebrows. She didn't really care. She was more interested in going on a date with the straps.

36

Nina felt butterflies not just swirling around a little but going rampant around her stomach as she arrived at the Lovely Bay Deli. She was feeling a mix of excitement and nervousness about her shift. The sweet little deli nestled in a row of shops, right in the heart of Lovely Bay, seemed to her, from what she'd seen so far, mostly locals popping in for coffee and homemade biscuits. Birdie had messaged her with a few instructions and as she approached along the pavement, she took in the pretty striped awning out the front, the white-painted wood, and blue accents. The Lovely flag fluttered from a flagpole poked beside the front door. She squinted down the road, trying to look for the narrow alleyway Birdie had informed her led her around the back to the entrance behind the shops. The instructions from Birdie told her to head down the alley, turn left at the bottom, and go along until she saw the gate in the brick wall with the sign for the deli on the back.

About halfway along the row of shops, she came across the alleyway similar to the one she'd been down with Robby, real-ising that she must have walked past it a few times and not even seen it. She stepped in, and instead of it being dark and gloomy as she'd been expecting, it was lit all the way along by coach lights dotted here and there. At the end, she could see another wider, cobbled alleyway running along the other way. She stopped, looked to the right, and then turned to the left as instructed. She pushed open the gate to the deli, walked through a small yard, and knocked on the back door.

Birdie hustled to the door and greeted Nina warmly. The Shipping Forecast floated between them, coming from Birdie's phone tucked on her left shoulder. 'Ahoy there! Thanks for coming. So good to see you. Ready for a fun evening at the deli?'

Nina smiled, feeling a little more at ease than she had when she'd left the house. She'd half-thought about not going. The way she was being received made her very glad she hadn't done that. 'I think so. It's been a while since I've worked in a setting like this. I hope I'm not going to let you down.'

Birdie led her through a corridor where the aroma of freshly baked bread and brewing coffee filled the air. The Shipping Forecast trailed behind her. 'It's pretty straightforward. It gets busy, but it's a good busy and that's just out the front.'

'Out the front – what's out the back, then?'

Birdie lowered her voice. 'Chowder.'

Nina's chin dropped. 'Oh gosh, am I working at one of the speakeasies?'

'I have to get you to sign a non-disclosure agreement first.'

Nina looked alarmed. 'Okay.'

'Joking.'

'Right. What does this all entail then? How does it all work?'

'Pretty simple, really. Lovelies go for chowder at various establishments around Lovely Bay all throughout the year. Tonight it's the deli's turn.'

'Yeah, but how do people know what establishment to go to if it's a secret?'

'Ahh, you just know.' Birdie tapped the side of her left temple as the Shipping Forecast broadcast away to itself.

Nina wrinkled her nose. 'How?'

'You get in the swing of it, and these days there's a secret WhatsApp group. In the old days, there was a ledger at the library, and before that, I think it was in the greengrocer's, plus people spread the word. It's prepaid, so there's no fussing with that. What in the name of goodness did we all do before technology, eh? I ask you.'

'Right, so people book in advance and then pay and just turn up?'

'Yup.'

'Is there any choice?'

'Nope.'

'What about if you want something else?'

'Tough. You don't come.'

'What if you're allergic to fish?'

Birdie stopped what she was doing and widened her eyes. 'Are you allergic to fish?'

'No, I'm not.'

'We cross that bridge when we come to it.' Birdie put her right hand up and flicked her fingers back and forth to indicate for Nina to follow her around the counter. Nina followed and stepped into a small kitchen. Birdie pointed to a long stainless steel industrial bench. 'Dishwashers under there. One for glass, one for plates. Both commercial with quick, intense washes.' She pointed to two under-bench trolleys with dishwasher baskets. 'We work on a rotation system. Very simple and highly efficient. Turn it on, fill the other baskets, and rinse and repeat. Get it?'

Nina swallowed. The kitchen was small and full to the rafters but very tidy and organised. It also smelt amazing. On an industrial cooker, a gigantic stock pot bubbled and simmered. 'Yep.'

Birdie lifted the lid from the pan. 'Chowder. My grandmother's recipe with a secret ingredient, not to be confused with my dad's. Said to be one of the best in Lovely. No pressure.'

'It smells amazing.'

'It *is* amazing.' Birdie pointed to the other side to another long, spotless, stainless steel bench. 'Bread bowls. The chowder goes in those. The whole lot goes on a plate, and you take it out and plonk it on the table.' She pointed to a huge pile of linen napkins. 'With one of those.' Birdie led the way through the narrow kitchen to another door stuck between open shelving full of herbs, spices, sauces, and all manner of condiments.

Nina gasped as she looked inside the room. A floor-to-ceiling French paned window in the middle of the far wall, a door to the right, rustic wooden bistro tables, and mismatched chairs. It was as if the chairs and tables had been squashed into a preserving room; its shelves were lined with an array of herbs in little jars, their labels handwritten, with homemade jams, chutneys, and other delicacies. Stuffed everywhere between the jars of homemade things, old photographs of Lovely Bay in frames were dotted haphazardly. The room, though small, was brimming with history and so much character, it was as if it might at any second speak. A fireplace crackled at one end; each table had a flickering tealight, jazz music played softly in the background, and piles of books were here, there, and everywhere. Nina kept shaking her head, captivated.

Birdie gestured around, her eyes twinkling with pride. 'Welcome to our little chowder speakeasy.' Seeing Nina's amazed expression, Birdie chuckled. 'Quite the surprise, isn't it? This is our haven away from it all. You thought you'd seen it all when you went to your first one with our Robby before. This is the deli version.' She lowered her voice. 'In my humble opinion, the best one in Lovely Bay.'

Nina smiled, still taking it all in. 'I had no idea this was back here. It's like stepping into another world.'

Birdie nodded. 'Yep, that's what this is all about. Locals come and enjoy a good meal, away from the bustle of Lovely. It started back in the smuggling days, or so the story goes.'

The smell of the chowder wafted through the room, a mix of seafood, fresh herbs, and a hint of something mysterious that Nina couldn't quite place. Nina inhaled and raised her eyebrows. 'It smells so good. No wonder you're busy.'

A woman with grey hair tucked into a bun wearing an apron came in from the front and beamed. 'Hi.'

Birdie gestured with her hand. 'This is Alice. She's in charge of us and keeps everyone on the straight and narrow. Alice will show you the ropes.'

'Hi,' Nina replied.

Birdie pointed around the room. 'You'll be helping with serving tonight with me out the back here. Alice will be running the rest of the show. Don't worry, it's all pretty straightforward. Our guests aren't really guests; they are here for a sit-down, good food, and maybe a little bit of Lovely Bay gossip. It's the same at all the chowder places.'

Birdie handed Nina an apron and pulled a tablet out of her own apron. 'I'll give you this. It's got the details of who is sitting where, but it's all very informal.' She slipped her phone out and scrolled. 'Yeah, everyone has paid, so that's too easy; it's pretty much serve, make sure everyone has a drink and wash up or, you know, load the dishwashers. You'll find everything you need in the kitchen, but Alice will be here anyway. Think you'll be able to handle that?'

'Yup.'

'Well, there you go. You'll be the talk of the town when it goes around that you're in here with me. The newcomer making waves in Lovely Bay.'

Nina laughed very nervously. 'Guilty as charged. I just hope I don't let you down.'

'Don't you worry about that, you won't. I wouldn't have

asked you if I had thought anything else. Just remember you keep all this under your hat. If anyone asks where you were even if they are a Lovely you say nothing. Got it?'

Nina gulped. 'Loud and clear.'

With the Shipping Forecast as background noise, Nina had worked her socks off, but as Birdie had so rightly pointed out, everything was organised and part of a highly efficient system. It had just been a case of keeping on her toes and following her nose. She'd not sat down for hours, her brain was buzzing with all things chowder, and she'd definitely earned her keep. Birdie had made it sound casual and easy, which it was for the people being entertained. For those working, though, it was go, go, go. Alice was a powerhouse.

During a moment when Nina was unloading and reloading the dishwasher, Birdie smiled.

'You're doing wonderfully, Nina. I knew you would. You're a grafter, so you've fitted right in. I spotted it a mile off.'

Nina felt a surge of gratitude. 'I've actually really enjoyed myself. I think I'm starting to understand what Lovely Bay is all about.'

Birdie pulled some mugs down from a shelf and made a few cups of coffee. She passed one over to Nina and as Alice came in, she passed one to her too. 'You're doing great. It's nice to have fresh energy around here.'

Nina took a sip of the coffee, feeling grateful. 'Thanks. It's been a while since I felt so involved in something, if you see what I mean.'

Birdie nodded. 'Lovely Bay has a way of doing that to people. It pulls you in and makes you feel like you're part of a big family, if you're the right fit, that is.'

Nina nodded. 'Hopefully, I do fit right in.'

'Well, so far so good. You survived a secret chowder night anyway.' Alice chuckled. 'Maybe you'll have to stay.'

37

The next morning, Nina finished pouring a cup of tea, grabbed a couple of biscuits, and opened the back door. A few minutes later, she was sitting at the end of the garden, dipping biscuits into her tea and looking at the view. Slipping her phone out of her pocket, she swiped up, waited for the Face ID to let her in, and pressed on the Chrome app. She'd been hesitating since the conversation with Nancy in the dunes, but curiosity finally got the better of her, and she found herself typing Robby's name into the grey search bar at the top of her screen. It was time to find out more about Robby before she went on the date.

She braced herself, wondering what she might find. Right away she was surprised as up popped numerous articles, photos, and mentions of Robby. She swallowed and shook her head. There were many more entries than she'd anticipated. As she clicked through, a picture began to form, and it wasn't at all what she'd expected. To be frank, she wasn't sure what to think at all.

Robby, it seemed, came from a lineage of maritime heritage. The O'Connors were a well-known name in Lovely Bay, who back in the day had been deeply rooted in the local community. They were known for their contributions to the town's development, philanthropy, and, most notably, their successful maritime business, which in days of old had kept a lot of the town in employment at one point in history.

The O'Connors' background was intertwined with Lovely Bay's own story. They had been instrumental in the development of the local port not far away and had various businesses along the south coast, including marinas, a shipyard, and a maritime museum in Portsmouth. Robby, it turned out, was the youngest sibling, but by the looks of the website on the marinas, didn't have anything to do with the business. Nina tapped and clicked and read. The O'Connor family had a lot of marinas. The list went on and on; Brighton, Falmouth, Chichester, Poole, Torquay, and many more, including a worldwide presence, some of which Nina had never even heard of.

Our vision for O'Connors is to be the finest operator in the marina world. We have the best marinas in amazing worldwide locations with first-class services and the marine environment as our first customer. We're exponentially passionate about our business and our seafaring heritage and continually invest in our marinas, our employees, and our surroundings. We ensure you'll be the beneficiary of efficient systems, the best customer service, green technology, and sustainable power.

Nina gulped as she scrolled down the About Us page of the O'Connor group. It seemed as if it was a whole other world. It also didn't add up. Robby hadn't given off vibes that he was part of something huge. Maybe he wasn't.

She tapped back out of the O'Connor website, found a locked-down Facebook page for Robby, and then found the page for his business. Again, she was surprised and raised her eyebrows. From what she'd seen, she'd assumed he had a smallish local business that he'd played down. He'd made out as if he cleaned a few windows for a living. His company was clearly quite a bigwig in the abseiling world. He'd not quite embellished on the whole story by the looks of what she'd found.

As Nina delved deeper, she stumbled upon an old article. As she read, her stomach turned over and over and over again. Robby had been involved in a serious accident in his twenties. His then-fiancé, Diana Austin-Jones, a marine biologist, had been involved in a tragic car accident. Nina sat back, her mind racing. She didn't really know what to think. She'd thought she'd known a little about him, but it was clear she didn't know much at all. His family was big news, he'd been involved in a tragic accident, and his business was a lot more impressive than he'd let on. She shook her head as she remembered the kiss at the top of the lighthouse and the Robby who had asked her out on a date. The Robby she'd read about felt worlds away from the one she'd seen around and about in Lovely Bay.

Closing her phone and dropping her head back, Nina let all the information she'd just taken on swirl around her brain. She shook her head and felt a twinge of inadequacy. Her life seemed so small in comparison to everything she'd just read. She was a *nothing* really. Tiny and with not much going on at all. Nina Lavender, a woman trying to find her feet again after a death that had whipped the rug out from under her and made her feel as if she would never live properly again. She didn't come from a prominent family, she didn't have a career that changed the world, and she didn't really have any hobbies or anything to write home about at all. She liked organising and decluttering and felt like running for a minute and a half was a massive achievement. She was ordinary. She was not in Robby's league whatsoever.

Closing her phone cover and snapping the magnetic closure she tutted and shook her head. She'd have to cancel the date. There was no way it was something worth spending her time and effort on. She was out of her depth with someone like Robby. She wrinkled her nose as she thought about it more. Why would someone like him ask her out in the first place? He must come across all sorts of people in his life and he'd asked her to go out-out with him. Didn't add up.

Suddenly it dawned on her; he was clearly asking her out as a bit of a joke. Maybe someone had dared him. The more she thought about it, the more she was adamant that she was going to text him and make up some excuse. What could she possibly offer a man like Robby O'Connor, owner of successful businesses and part of a family who were clearly big wigs in the world? She felt so small and so silly that a ball of nausea swirled from her stomach up to the back of her throat. Robby O'Connor clearly intended on taking her for a ride.

A couple of hours later, Nina had more or less decided she'd bow out of the date and had spent a few hours continuing with clearing the front garden. The garden was looking a lot better than when she'd started, as each day she'd chipped away at bringing it back to life. There were now defined beds on either side of the path, actual grass rather than weeds was starting to show signs of life, and a load of rose bushes on the far side looked a lot healthier than when Nina had found them.

Just as she was standing, deciding on whether or not she should prune the roses further, a voice called out from the pavement. Nina shook her head to bring herself back to the present and looked over to see June standing with a smile on her face and a blue tub in her hand. June held the tub up in the air. 'I was wondering if you would be interested in one of Pippa's chowders. She's just down here. They're one of the best.'

Nina had no idea who Pippa was but nodded anyway. The

whole chowder thing was like an unwritten code. Like when someone asks you if you want a cup of tea; whether you like it or not, you simply don't say no. The chowder code was similar to that. 'Thanks. Yes, I'd love to try it.'

June picked up that Nina didn't know who Pippa was. 'The big house down on the corner here.'

'The one with the turret?'

'The very one. She had a gathering the other night. A very small affair. I didn't go, a bit late for me, but I got a delivery. She left one for you too.'

'Aww, how kind.'

June's eyes twinkled knowingly. 'Hear you might be going out for the evening for chowder soon.'

Nina squirmed. Now she was going to have to tell June that she was going to blow Robby out. After what she'd read and having spent a couple of hours deliberating, she'd decided she'd been mad thinking about going on a date in the first place. It would never end well. She made a non-committal sound. 'Hmm.'

June chortled. 'You don't sound very sure about that.'

'Ahh...'

June's eyebrows rose. 'You're going, aren't you?'

Nina hesitated and decided to voice her doubts. 'Actually. I'm not sure.'

'What? What do you mean?'

Nina wasn't sure what to say. What were the ethics of googling the life out of someone, which was what she'd done? 'I didn't realise he was... I don't know now. Yeah, I don't think I should go.'

June frowned. 'What? You didn't realise he was what?'

Nina flicked her hand back and forth. 'Your family and everything and his business. I just...'

'Not my side of the family,' June replied firmly. 'Who told you about all that?'

Nina felt embarrassed about the Google deep-dive. 'Oh, no, no one.'

June leaned in, her voice firm. 'Don't let the O'Connors intimidate you. He's asked you out because he likes you. You.'

'Yeah, but...'

'Not your resume, not your family history. You. Trust me, I know that boy.'

'Really?'

'Yep and trust me, he doesn't ask any old one out, that's for sure. Like never. I was surprised when he told me. Not about you, but yeah...'

'Right.'

June's expression softened. 'Look, he's not one for playing games. If he's asked you out, it's because he's genuinely interested in you, if you ask me. Not that it's any of my business.'

Nina bit her lip. 'But his family, his background. I don't know, it seems so different from mine. I feel like I'm just this ordinary person who's stumbled into Lovely Bay, and I don't know...'

June chuckled. 'We're all ordinary people. The family might have a bit of history, but that's that. Anyway, Robby's made his own way, his own life. He doesn't even work for the family.'

Nina looked down at her hands, still covered in dirt from the garden. 'I just don't want to feel out of place, or worse, make a fool of myself.'

'What have you got to lose? You won't know unless you give it a chance. Besides, it's just a date, not a marriage proposal. Go out and have a bit of fun. See where it leads. No pressure. Let me tell you, if I had my time again, that's what I would do.'

Nina sighed. 'I suppose you're right. It wouldn't do any harm. I guess I'm just scared.'

'Nervous, not scared, which is totally normal. Sometimes, the best things in life come from stepping out of our comfort zones. I wish I'd taken more heed of my own advice over the years.' June chuckled. 'You live and learn, though. I'm too long in the tooth now, so take it from me, go on the date with Robby.'

Nina nodded slowly, taking in June's words. 'Thanks for the pep talk, June.'

'Anytime. Remember, Lovely Bay has a way of surprising you. You might just find what you didn't even know you were looking for. That's what they say, anyway.' June rolled her eyes. 'Another one of our weird and wonderful superstitions.' June handed Nina the tub of chowder. 'Think about it. I won't say anything.' June pressed her thumb and finger together and made as if to zip her lips. 'Soul of discretion, me. Robby is looking forward to it, that I know for a fact.'

'Thanks.'

'Enjoy Pippa's chowder. It's something special, just like everything else in this little corner of the world.'

'I will. Thanks again, June.'

As June walked away, Nina stood for a moment, lost in thought. She looked down at the tub of chowder in her hands, then back at the garden she'd been working on. Maybe June was right. She was being ridiculous, that's what Sophie would say. She'd got herself in a right tiswas because of the googling. It was time to take a chance and dip her toe into the dating world again. What could possibly go wrong? She already kissed the man twice for goodness' sake. She winced. She would go and just see where the evening took her. She would force herself to go and do what they always recommended in the grief group – give herself the chance to experience something new. She walked back into the house, put the tub of chowder in the fridge, and tried to be positive and not overthink things. She'd go for her life and simply just see where it went. There surely wasn't much to worry about in doing that, was there?

38

Nina didn't have too much time to think about the Robby issue. Just after she'd put the chowder in the fridge she'd had a call from an unknown number. Someone had called in sick at the deli, and Birdie had given her a call on the off chance to see if she could hustle around and help out in the back. Nina had said she wouldn't mind in the slightest and had hopped on the boat into town.

By the end of the shift, she was definitely feeling it. So much for the running app improving her fitness levels. Lifting dishwasher baskets was harder than working out at the gym.

Her muscles ached from the constant lifting, her clothes clung to her, and all she could smell were spices and cooking smells. The strange thing about the post-shift feeling was that it was a new kind of tiredness that Nina hadn't felt before. Not the tiredness of grief or long boring weeks in the most boring office in Britain, but sort of satisfied, muscle-ache tiredness. The whole working at the deli thing had been unexpectedly enjoyable. It had also made her appreciate the quaintness and charm of Lovely Bay even more.

Nina mulled it over as she got on the riverboat and one of

the twins, she wasn't sure which one at first, in the navy blue Lovely coat, shorts, and boat shoes smiled as she got on. After he greeted her without the aid of a faux accent, she realised it was Colin. Nina loved how feeling a bit like a local made her feel.

'Evening, Nina! Heard you were playing hero at the deli,' Colin said with a grin.

Nina laughed. 'Blimey, word travels fast around here, doesn't it?'

'You betcha! In Lovely Bay, the grapevine works faster than high-speed internet. So, how was it?'

'I was just thinking about it. Wow, they work hard in there. It was exhausting but good. It doesn't stop,' Nina said, finding a seat near the front. 'I didn't realise how much work goes into a shift at the deli. It's a whole different kind of tiredness – a good kind, I think. I'll sleep well tonight.'

Colin nodded. 'Birdie's a hard worker. Keeps all her businesses running like a well-oiled machine. And her chowder – well, that's legendary in itself. Now I come to think about it, I don't know what any of us would do without the deli or the chemist. It's like the centre of the Lovely Bay universe surrounded by the delightful tones of the Shipping Forecast, ha ha.'

Nina smiled, as the boat puttered over the water. 'Yeah, it is.'

'It sounds like you're well settled in Lovely Bay now,' Colin remarked. 'Bet you're glad you said yes to the house sitting, aren't you?'

Nina watched the lights of the town grow distant as she contemplated Colin's question. Was she? 'I think so. It's different from what I'm used to but in a good way. There's a sense of community here, or maybe I'm just imagining it.'

'That's Lovely Bay for you. We look after our own,' Colin said, his eyes on the river ahead. 'Everyone has a story, and everyone's part of the bigger picture, as it were. See, the thing with these small towns is you don't get very far if you don't work together... that's a lot of the reason why these digital nomad people never work out. They're not interested in giving back, you know?'

Nina pondered his words. 'I suppose it must be that.'

'It's just the way it is. You're obviously not used to living somewhere where everybody knows your name. That's the charm of this place,' Colin said, slowing the boat as they approached another jetty. 'Everyone's got your back. It goes back to the old days when this place survived on fishing and bartering for everything.'

Nina nodded, watching as a few passengers disembarked, and Colin called out goodbye. 'I'm starting to see that. It's nice,' she joked, 'Lovely even.'

As the boat made its way down the river and the lights on the top of the boat twinkled all around her, Nina had a strange growing fondness for Lovely Bay. Unless she was totally imagining it, the town had sort of drawn her in. She thought about Robby, the upcoming date, the shift at the deli, and the fact that she was beginning to recognise a few faces and chat with people here and there. It seemed to somehow warm the cockles of her heart.

'Here we are,' Colin announced as they reached Nina's stop. 'Nice chatting.'

'Thanks, Colin,' Nina replied, stepping off the boat. 'See you around.'

'Yep, unless next time I see you I'm my brother, which happens all the time. In which case you'll say Bonsoir.' Colin cracked up laughing.

'Yes, anyway, Bonsoir to you.'

'I'll say bye. See you.'

Nina decompressed from the shift at the deli as she ambled along back to the hotel. She'd enjoyed it in there; the conversations, the small victory of getting through the evening without any major mishaps, and also that she felt a connection to Lovely Bay. It went way beyond the picturesque views, lovely old architecture, the lighthouse, and the quaintness of the place. It was as if something was whispering to her, drawing her in, giving her a sense of belonging she hadn't felt in a long time.

As she got to the hotel, she just stood for a minute, looked upwards, and gazed at the sliver of moon hanging in the sky. What was it about this place? Soothing, that's what it was. It was easing her jagged edges. The same feeling happened as she unlocked the front door and stepped into the quiet hallway. The now familiar creak of the wooden floorboards under her feet and the smell whispered hello and made her feel at home. Shaking her head that she was beginning to lose the plot and the tiredness was getting to her, she had a shower, washed her hair and put on her dressing gown.

Then, after making a tea, she settled into the armchair by the window in the kitchen and for ages just sat and gazed out at the night, lost in thought. She reflected for a bit but mostly, she thought about the overwhelming grief that had consumed her for years. How it had seemed to swallow her whole and not let her go, and how in Lovely Bay it just didn't appear to be around as often.

For a long time, she just simply sat and thought about Andrew and felt her head turn to the side and smile as she thought about him. Something had changed: she was now not as sad as she'd always been. She had a new perspective; she was feeling memories in a different way, but what was most astonishing was that she was no longer just looking back. Lovely Bay had given her permission to move on. The view was not quite clear in front of her, and she wasn't sure where to go, but she was peering around a corner as if looking into a new world and wondering whether or not she should walk in. She was going to give it a go.

39

It was the next day and Nina had been called into the deli for another emergency shift. When she'd arrived, Birdie had asked her if she would like to go on the rota. Nina hadn't exactly felt a crushing need to be on the rota, but she'd enjoyed the work and the camaraderie with Alice and had decided to just say yes and go with the flow. She was wiping down the stainless steel food preparation counter after a busy shift, whilst the Shipping Forecast played, her mind a whirlwind of thoughts about the upcoming date with Robby. She hadn't been on a date since the days she was dating Andrew, and since she'd had the chat with June after initially feeling okay about it, now she wasn't again. Everything about it felt alien and daunting. Paranoid self-doubt whispered in her ear.

Birdie bustled around the deli. 'Everything alright? You seem quiet today.'

'Yep, fine.'

'Penny for them.'

Nina sighed and paused. 'Actually, I've got a date, and I'm a bit nervous,' she confessed, trying to sound more casual than she felt.

'Ahh, yes, I may know about your date. You don't seem too excited about it!'

Nina wasn't surprised that Birdie knew. 'I am, at least I think I am. It's just it's been so long since I've been on a date. I'm over-thinking everything. I don't even know what to wear, and I feel like I've lost touch with all of this. Yeah, I don't know.'

Birdie leaned on the counter. 'Understandable.'

'I'm just questioning everything...'

'You need a little confidence boost and to treat yourself. I've learned the hard way.'

'Treat myself? To what?' Nina screwed her nose up in question.

'Whatever floats your boat. I do it all the time, and I mean weekly. Yep, I do something every week to help with this.' Birdie mussed her hand around in front of her face. 'I have infrared saunas, facials, lasers, massages, anything and everything as long as it's something.'

'Oh, gosh. I can't even remember the last time I got my hair done, let alone done anything like a facial! It just stopped being important in a way...' Nina trailed off. She wasn't even sure if she'd had a facial ever, let alone weekly.

'Ach, that's never a good thing. Ask me how I know.'

'What sort of things do you have done?'

Birdie patted both hands on her cheeks. 'What don't I have done? I've tried everything known to man. Reiki, needling, transformation coaching, lasers, microdermabrasion – all of which I have regularly. Those are not the treaty-y things, though. I also have pampering facials and massages, masks, and full-body scrubs. Give it all to me. It's my way to give back to my body. I work hard. I also get vitamin infusions, acupuncture and osteopathy. The whole kit and caboodle.'

Nina looked very surprised. 'Wow. I really didn't expect you to say that.'

'I know it doesn't show! Ha!'

'Sorry, I didn't mean it like that.'

'I run around here like a blue-arsed fly all day long, plus I have my other delis, as you know. Then there are the pharmacies.' Birdie lowered her voice. 'I worked so hard at one point I got burnt out. It took me months to recover. Actually, it was more than a few months. It took me a few years to feel like *me* again. I will never *ever* let myself get like that again. Never again. Which is why I do weekly stuff. I take my self-care very seriously these days, especially what goes on up here.' Birdie tapped the side of her left temple.

'Oh wow, right.'

'Yep, it's not a joking matter in my case. If I do this stuff and I feel okay, I *am* okay. Plus, just having something to look forward to and lying on a bed for an hour a week does it for me.'

'I've never thought about it like that.' Nina shook her head, 'You see, I've really let myself go.' She held out her hands in front of her. 'I don't know when I had a manicure last, and what was it you said, reiki? What even is that? I don't even know what that means. It sounds painful.'

'Calming is what it is.' Birdie then tipped her head down to show Nina her parting. 'You'll never see my grey, either. I get that done religiously. I will not be letting nature take its course with me. No, no, no. I'm prepared to fight until the end.'

Nina chuckled, shaking her head. 'I wouldn't even know where to start.'

Birdie reached for her phone. 'One word: Bianca. She's a wizard with everything and does the best facials on the coast - she'll make you feel better before your date. I'll text you the website. She was in here earlier. If I'd known then I would have introduced you. She has a place in London, actually, too, but she came back to Lovely after years away. Highly sought after.'

Nina shook her head back and forth. 'No, no, sorry. It all sounds a bit much. I don't want to change anything, and I'm not up for fussing.'

'Nonsense!' Birdie waved her off. 'Consider it a little pampering. You deserve it. Just have a bit of a treat before your date with our Robby.'

'How do you know who it is?' Nina chuckled.

'I know everything.'

Nina pondered Birdie's words. She hadn't really thought about pampering herself in a long time. Since what had happened with Andrew, she'd simply not been interested. She'd been in survival mode, and for a very long time, the mere thought of indulging in self-care had seemed frivolous and a *gigantic* waste of time. As if it was for other people on the planet; ones who were not as sad as her.

'You know, come to think of it, maybe it might help.'

'I'll give her a call if you like and make sure she fits you in. If she knows you're part of the deli, she'll make sure you get in. Trust me, you'll feel like a new woman.'

'No, no. Honestly, don't worry about it. I'm not sure I have time.'

'You'll feel amazing for your date.'

Nina made a wincing face. 'Nah, I don't think it's for me and it will cost loads.'

'Tell you what. I'll pay for it as a bonus for helping me out here. Honestly, you've been invaluable. I don't know what I would have done without you, especially since the trainspotters are back.'

Nina relented. What would be the harm in someone doing something nice for her? Plus, she'd worked her socks off for Birdie and both of them were well aware of it. 'That's so kind of you.'

'We look after our own here and the longer you hang around, the more you'll get it.' Birdie joked. 'Plus, if you're going on a date with one of the O'Connors, you need to strut your stuff a little bit.'

Nina gulped. 'Right.'

Birdie wiggled her phone. 'Tell you what, I'll call her now.'

Ten minutes later, Nina was booked in with Lovely Beauty by Bianca. On the riverboat on the way home, she raised her eyebrows as she sat looking over at the evening sky painted in hues of blazing terracotta, pink and orange. She shook her head as she realised that she'd really let herself go and she needed to change that. She had neglected herself for too long. The Bianca visit was going to be another thing she did for herself. It would be part of her newfound optimism. She was quite enjoying having a new version of herself. The old one had sagged and bagged and crumpled for way too long. Time to get a life.

40

Nina stood apprehensively outside the door of Lovely Beauty by Bianca. From the outside, the building looked the same as all the other shops in the street, but unlike its pastel neighbours this one was completely and utterly white. A white and beige awning stretched out over the pavement. A beautiful decal curved across the window, and as Nina peered in, she was hit by a lot of white and a modern minimalist look. She really wasn't sure if it was her cup of tea. She'd been scarred by the white going on at The Chelsea Collective. Too late now. Taking a deep breath, she pushed the door open and swallowed. Inside, everything was pale and neutral, including a huge modern bouclé sofa that looked way too precious to sit on and a ginormous numberless white clock on the far wall.

Nina instantly felt grubby and as if she'd made a colossal mistake. It was certainly a haven of tranquillity, though, she'd give it that. Her feet seemed to make way too much noise as she crossed the room and wondered whether or not she could sit on the sofa. Eventually, she perched right on the edge, put her bag down beside her, and looked around. The walls were painted in soft, soothing hues, and the decor was so tasteful and so minimalist, Nina felt as if she stuck out like a sore thumb. The air was scented with a blend of essential oils, and soft, ambient music played in the background.

Just as Nina was seriously considering doing a runner, a woman with flawless skin, plump filler lips, and a tight midi dress in the same colour as the walls emerged from the far side of the room. 'Hello.'

'Hi, I errm, I have an appointment.'

The woman beamed. 'Yes, you must be Nina. We've been expecting you. Bianca's nearly ready. I'll get you sorted and start you with the pre-treatment elixir.'

Nina wasn't sure what to say to that. 'Thanks.'

'We have a range of pre-treatment elixirs depending on what you fancy.' The woman squinted and looked Nina up and down. 'Detox?'

Nina nodded. Great. This wasn't what she'd been hoping for. Did she look as if she needed to be detoxed? She quivered inside. 'Sounds good.'

A few minutes later, the woman was back with a glass cup and saucer with steaming beige liquid in it. 'You'll love this. It's delicious – an earthy, spiced blend, and it's anti-inflammatory. Loads of rooibos and coriander seeds in there, too. I live on the stuff.'

Nina didn't like the sound of it *at all*. She shuffled awkwardly on the bouclé sofa as the tea was put down on what looked to her like a sawn-off tree trunk. 'Thank you.'

'Right, you filled in the form online, so we're good to go on that. All you have to do is sit back and enjoy yourself. Let us do all the work.'

About five minutes later, another customer stood at the counter and paid what Nina thought was an extortionate amount for whatever she'd just had done. She stared into her rooibos tea and kicked herself for listening to Birdie. Taking a sip of the tea, she told herself to breathe, that she'd be out before she knew it, and it couldn't really be all that bad.

A couple of minutes later, Bianca, the owner, greeted Nina with a warm smile. 'Welcome to Lovely Beauty. I'm Bianca. I have heard all about you! Summer Hotel, isn't it? Plus, you're in at the deli.'

'Yes. Well, I'm helping out in both of them. I, umm, I live in London, but I'm just down here for a bit.'

'I've heard. Okay, here we go. We have a wonderful time planned for you. Birdie said you need a little bit of pampering. We are experts. When I say experts, I mean professional level. You won't be disappointed. You've got the elixir already, yes? Great. Detox? Looks like you needed it.'

Nina smiled nervously. 'Thank you. Umm, I'm not really used to this sort of thing.' She touched her hair nervously and shook her head. 'It's been a long time since I've had anything done.'

Bianca's smile was reassuring. 'Good to hear. More to work with. Honestly, don't worry in the slightest, you're in good hands. We'll take good care of you. We're all about relaxing and treatments at the same time. You're going to glow when you come out of here, but much more importantly, you're going to *feel good* inside. No need to worry at all and let me tell you we've seen it all, and I mean, *all*, in here.'

Nina followed Bianca down a long white corridor lit only by tea lights to a treatment room and felt herself relax a tiny bit as nice smells, soft lighting, and some sort of yoga music filled the room. She tried to not think about anything. She tried not to think about the fact that the most she did in beauty treatments was shave her legs and slap on some E45 cream when she could be bothered. An image of the John Lewis box of lotions and potions flashed through her mind as she removed her clothes and secured a towelling robe with Velcro at the top around herself. She tried, she really did, to just relax.

Two hours later, Nina didn't give two hoots about anything. She'd been the recipient of a treatment that had made her worries float away. It had been a long time since anyone had touched her at all, and she'd absolutely revelled in an indulgent facial under layers of starched sheets and cosy blankets. Bianca indeed was an expert.

The strangest thing had been how she'd begun to feel, as if a tight, tense coil around her jaw had started to unwind. At first, as Bianca had layered on creams and potions, she'd actually wondered what was happening to her. It was as if Bianca was actually turning a key at either side of her head, and years and years and years of stress and grief and sadness had poured out from either side of her jaw. And it just kept on getting better as Nina had lain on the bed not moving a muscle, letting all sorts of wonderful things happen to her; a head, face, neck, and décolletage massage, hot towels here, a thick cream there, and while something warm and lovely lit her face from above, another woman joined the room and Nina felt both her hands & arms and neck and shoulders being massaged at the same time. All of it had been better than she ever could have imagined. It was as if Bianca's hands knew how to move and knead and massage to create a peaceful state. It was as if the stress was melting away under Bianca's hands. As if Nina was healing.

'Your skin is responding beautifully,' Bianca commented in a whisper, as she applied a soothing serum post-treatment.

Nina whispered, feeling almost in a trance. 'Thank you. I just feel amazing. So, so good.'

By the end of the session, Nina was floating. She was also in possession of a lovely light glow, she had a set of natural-looking eyelashes, her nails were perfectly manicured, and her hair was going home with an intensive mask which she'd been instructed to wash off that night.

As she went to leave and found herself back in the reception room again, she didn't quite know what to do with herself. All she could do was keep shaking her head at how amazing she felt. 'Thank you *so* much. I can't believe how good that was. I feel like a different person. Birdie said it was good, but I didn't expect this.' She actually felt genuine gratitude at how nicely she'd been treated.

Bianca smiled warmly. 'You're welcome. We just helped to whisk away some of that stress you were wearing all over yourself.' Bianca nodded as if she was privy to some information Nina wasn't. 'I've been doing this a long time – nearly thirty years, and I felt your whole body sigh out as I was working on your face.'

'Oh my goodness, yes! I felt that too!'

'You'd be surprised what you carry around in your jaw.'

Nina felt more relaxed and lighter than she had for a long time. 'Whatever it was hiding there, I don't want to see it around and about anytime soon.'

Bianca laughed. 'You'd better make it a weekly visit then. That is, if you're intending on staying in Lovely Bay for a while.'

Nina nodded. She hadn't been intending on staying at all when she'd first arrived, but something inside had changed. Lovely Bay, it seemed, had a way of making you want to put your feet under the table and settle right in.

41

I t was the day of the date. Nina felt ridiculous and wondered if she could make an excuse that she'd picked up a mystery virus in the deli. Yes, that was what she would do; she'd pretend that she'd been sitting on the toilet all night with a dodgy tummy.

Despite the plumping and suchlike at the hands of Lovely Beauty by Bianca and the fact that she felt rejuvenated, she also still felt really, really nervous about going on a date. She just didn't *do* things like that anymore. Despite already having kissed the man, not once, but twice already, she also felt as if dates were for other people; those without lost husbands.

She stood and peered in the mirror at her reflection. Bianca and her staff clearly knew what they were talking about, or maybe the bar had been quite low to start with, so that anything that had been done to her would end up with a good result. She pulled her lips and chin down and examined her skin closely. It really did seem to have improved, it was certainly glowing from the microdermabrasion or something. The sun-kissed touch of tan on the top was so real she almost didn't believe it herself. She held her left hand out in front of her and turned it this way and that. Not only was her face good, but her hands were the recipients of a perfectly pretty rosy pink manicure and nice soft skin. The eyelashes, though, took the biscuit; they were absolutely fabulous.

Nina had very much been in two minds about the eyelashes, but she'd been persuaded by both Bianca and her assistant that they would be a game changer. As Nina had laid on the special beauty therapist's couch with lovely essential oils puffing over her in a mist, having the eyelashes put on, she'd mentally wondered how easy they were going to be to pull off when she got home. She'd had visions of two ginormous caterpillars flapping up and down in front of her and looking like something from a pantomime. What had actually happened was a very light feathering of individually applied lashes that were a tiny bit longer and thicker at the edges. The effect had been a brilliant opening up of her eyes. Boom. Perhaps the Nina Lavendar of old was back. Or maybe not.

She imagined what the grief group would say if they heard she was going on a date. She squinted and envisaged herself sitting in the grief circle with a cup of tea and a shortbread biscuit. The circle usually consisted of people sharing things that had happened to them that week, and Nina had never really had much to share. She wondered what they would say if she sat down in her usual seat in the grief circle and said, 'Well, actually, I have a date and the man I have had a date with I've already kissed twice. The second time, I was at the top of a lighthouse.'

She imagined the woman who ran the group giving her opinion and all the other people in the group offering their advice. She thought about Louisa, one of the women who was in a similar situation, albeit about ten years older, having lost her husband to bowel cancer. Louisa had been on all sorts of dates via a dating app. Most of them had not gone well, but one had resulted in her meeting a really nice man.

As she mulled everything over and was wondering whether

to pretend she had a stomach bug or not, her phone rang with a video call from Sophie. She swiped to answer and waited for Sophie to appear on the screen.

'I have been pretending that I might have a gastric bug,' Nina said, laughing.

'What? You *cannot* be serious!'

'I don't think I can go.'

'You're not pretending that, no way!'

'I'm just not sure if I can go.'

'You're going, and you are also being pathetic. It's just a date. Anyway, you're not wasting all that money you've spent on beauty treatments.'

Nina frowned. 'Technically, I didn't pay for them.'

Sophie was standing in her fancy kitchen, making a cup of tea. One of her children was sitting behind her on a stool. 'Why the doubt?'

'I don't know. What am I doing? Why am I doing this? I'm quite happy. I've not had any problems. I'm not as sad anymore. Why would I put myself through this?' she asked. 'It feels cringy.'

Sophie raised her eyebrows and smiled. 'Well, you're meant to be trying new things, and maybe it will be a good thing.'

'Yes, I know, but I'm nervous. I haven't done this for a very long time.'

'Try and look at it this way: what have you got to lose?'

Nina sighed. 'Yes, someone else said that to me. I suppose I haven't really got much to lose, have I?'

'Nope.'

Nina had overthought so much and spent too long deliberating that now, she couldn't see the wood for the trees.

'I really think you'll be fine,' Sophie reassured her. 'You just need to go and see what happens. If you don't like him, just leave.'

'No, no, it's not that I don't like him. I know that I kind of *do* like him,' Nina said, thinking about the tingles in places she hadn't felt for a long time. 'It's just that I don't know...'

'Stop it. By the way, you look fabulous. What did she do, and how much did it cost? I need to find out and go there myself.'

Nina laughed. 'What didn't she do? It was a bit complicated. I think I had microdermabrasion, then a special plumping and hydrating mask. Oh, and then I had a needling treatment, but I'm not sure on that, and I also had some kind of LED light, I think, over the top of me to set everything, all at the same time as having a lovely hand and shoulder massage, and I had a head massage with special oils, a mask, the works.'

'Wow, it sounds amazing. It must've cost a fortune.'

'Apparently, it was mates' rates.' Nina chuckled.

'I like the sound of those. I wonder if they would do them for me as well?'

'I don't know about that. It's a funny old place here.'

'Well, it works for you. You look like you haven't looked since before...' Sophie stopped mid-sentence, apologetically. 'Sorry, didn't mean to say that.'

'No, no, it's fine. I know what you mean. I *do* look better.' Nina blinked her eyelashes towards the screen. 'I mean, look at these. I thought I was going to have a couple of big slugs on my eyes and not be able to lift my eyelids, but it's the opposite. You can't even tell. When I woke up this morning, it looked like I had been lifted somehow.'

Sophie chuckled. 'You do. Meaning, you can't waste what you've had done to your face.'

'So, I guess I'll just go and see what happens.'

Sophie nodded. 'Yes, look at the worst-case scenario; you can come home.'

'Yes, good point.'

'Do you want to make some kind of backup plan?' Sophie asked.

Nina frowned. 'Like what? What sort of a backup plan?'

'Like, I don't know, I text you something at the right time. And you answer if you're okay, and then if you're not okay, I call you with an excuse that I've, I don't know, had the baby or something.'

Nina laughed.

'It gives you a get-out plan, a reason for you to get away if you need to.'

Nina pursed her lips, nodded, and thought for a second, then she shook her head. She had kissed this man twice. Why on earth was she making such a big deal out of it? She was just going to go on the date and see what happened. 'I really don't think I need that. I'm going to go. I'll be fine.'

Minutes later, Nina had finished on the phone, and she was standing in the bedroom, looking at her clothes, wondering what on earth she was going to wear. Robby had been quite elusive about the date, saying that it was sort of a surprise, but when he'd texted her confirmation, he'd said it would involve being outside and was fairly casual. Nina wasn't sure what to wear at all.

She started gathering outfits onto the bed. Did she wear jeans and a nice white shirt that could pretty much take her anywhere and on any occasion? She mulled it over for a second, but what if it was cold, then she would need a jacket, and what if it was fancier, and she wasn't able to wear jeans? Robby had said it was casual and potentially outdoors. She shook her head, thinking that jeans might be wrong. Then she started to wonder what to wear on her feet. Would she need to walk? Could she wear heels? What was the go-to for what to wear?

The problem was that for so long, Nina hadn't had to worry about things like what to wear. All she had in her life was going to work, going to the grief group, and hanging out at the weekend in the flat she owned. Her wardrobe consisted of jeans, some nice tops, nice black trousers that she wore to work, a couple of work jackets, and some fancy blouses. It really didn't get much more varied than that. To Lovely Bay, she'd brought jeans, a pair of black trousers, just in case, and one dress.

She held up the black trousers and added to them a black, high-necked top with a little ruffle at the cuffs and a soft fabric with tiny matte gold emblems on the pattern. It was a really pretty top that Nina had bought on a whim one day, as she'd been walking past a boutique next to the coffee shop where she always got her coffee. She'd seen it in the window, walked in, tried it on, thought it was quite nice, and promptly bought it.

Now it seemed that the little black top would be going out to play. She had never even worn it. It was too fancy for work, and because she hadn't been out in so long, it had just hung in her wardrobe with the tags still on. Nina tried on the trousers and the top, tucked the top into the waistband, and fluffed it over the top. As she did so, she frowned. Something was different with the waistband. She had worn the trousers to work a few times and realised that she had bought a size too small, but now the trousers seemed almost a bit too loose. What in the world?

She looked down at the waistband, making sure that she'd done the button up properly. Not only was the button done up, but it was on the second notch. She looked in the mirror again. It seemed as if Nina had lost some weight. She wrinkled her nose and wondered what had happened. She'd done nothing different, if anything, because of the physical labour she'd been doing in decluttering and clearing out the hotel, she'd actually found herself eating more. She looked down at her stomach and the fabric of the trousers. She'd definitely lost weight; before, the trousers were tight just about all over. Now they were not. Miracles did happen.

She mused for a minute and realised that it must be the running app, which she'd initially dismissed. She had continued with the running app since the day there'd been clapping on the boat. As time had gone on, she had progressed quite a bit from the initial minutes of running here and there. Now she was running for most of the sessions, and this was obviously doing something to her body that was very agreeable.

Nina couldn't believe it. The 'grief weight' was actually starting to wear off. It had taken long enough. Long may it last.

42

Nina waited anxiously in the kitchen and stood looking out the window, fiddling with the catch on her handbag. Her heart and just about everything else fluttered at the thought of the evening ahead. She wasn't quite sure why she was so ridiculously, or perhaps pathetically, nervous, or maybe she was; Robby had stirred feelings in her she hadn't experienced in a long time. The same feelings that she'd thought she'd never ever feel again.

Just as she was smoothing down her top for the umpteenth time, the doorbell went. She put her bag under her arm, clutched her phone, and as she walked across the hallway she caught sight of herself in the mirror and did a double take. Nina Lavendar had, in fact, polished up quite nicely. The black floaty top with the matte gold pattern looked lovely with the trousers. Her blow-dried hair with its natural balayage, and the aid of the mask now shone, and the eyelashes were worth their weight in gold. She'd be going back to Bianca with an open purse. Everything had miraculously come together. Nina shook her head in astonishment; she actually felt really good about herself.

She wasn't the only one who was looking good. *Goodness,*

gracious me. Nina's breath caught at the sight of Robby in chinos and a blue casual shirt. *The shoulders and the thighs, oh me, oh my.* He just looked confident, handsome, and nicely casual all at the same time.

Go with the flow. Breathe, she told herself as she smiled and Robby kissed her on the cheek. Nina swallowed as Robby chatted and she strolled along beside him.

'How have you been?'

'Good, thanks, yes. You?'

'Well. What have you been up to? You look amazing, by the way.'

I should with the amount of time I've spent primping, plumping, and getting ready for this date. 'Oh, you know, this and that. I've been at the deli again, so that's been keeping me out of mischief.'

'Ahh, you'll never get away from Birdie and the Shipping Forecast now.'

'I enjoy it, actually. If you'd told me that a few months ago, I would have said you were batty, but there we are.'

'Good to hear. Yeah, it's a nice place.'

Nina indicated along the road. 'So where are we going, then? You said the dress code was casual and we might be outdoors. I couldn't work out where.'

'Ah, you'll just have to wait and see,' Robby said with a twinkle in his eye.

'Intriguing.'

'A bit of suspense makes for a more interesting evening.'

'So, how has your week been other than working in the deli?' Robby asked.

'It's been busy, but good busy in the hotel. I feel like I'm finally breaking the back of it. It won't be long, and it will be on the market.'

'I see.'

'What about you?'

'Just the usual work stuff, launching myself down the side of skyscrapers, and as I said before, going to France to oversee that job I was telling you about.'

They turned down towards the wharf just as the boat with Colin stopped at the bottom. Nina quickened her pace and Robby shook his head. 'No, no, we're not getting on that.'

'Oh, right. Okay then. I thought because we were heading down this way…'

They watched the boat pull away, Colin waved and as they got to the wharf, Nina put her jacket on. 'What a beautiful evening.'

'Just over this side here,' Robby said, indicating to the far side of the wharf.

'Ooh, I'm intrigued. Are we getting picked up?'

'We are, indeed.'

Five minutes later, Nina watched as a beautifully lit riverboat made its way to the jetty, and her eyes widened in delight. 'Are we going on a dinner cruise? Wow.' Nina didn't know where to look first. The timber and glass cabin was completely lined with fairy lights, tiny little lanterns lit with tea lights hung everywhere, flickering light cast shadows on the water and the gentle hum of the engine sounded in the air.

Robby nodded. 'I thought it would be something different. The views are phenomenal on a night like this. I just had to keep my fingers crossed that we'd get a nice evening. I'm in luck.'

'Ooh, is this another Lovely chowder thing? It looks amazing.'

'It is. Last two tickets…'

As they boarded the boat, Nina was so glad she'd decided to bite the bullet and go on the date with Robby. She was still quite nervous but most of her apprehension had vanished as soon as she'd walked down the path. A few minutes after boarding, she was sitting opposite Robby at the back of the boat. She frowned as she saw what looked like Nancy approaching. 'Nancy? Does she work here too?'

Robby chuckled. 'She works everywhere. She must earn a fortune.'

Nancy beamed and nodded. 'Ooh, hello! Look at you two.'

'Hello, how are you? I didn't expect to see you here.' Nina chuckled.

'I get around. I only work in the establishments of Lovely Bay so that I can get the gossip on what's going on.' Nancy winked. 'I have got the gossip tonight, that's for sure. Righto, what can I get you? Bubbles, a nice mojito hand-concocted by Daureen or we have a special from the brewery.'

Nina contemplated for a second. 'The bubbles sound nice to me, please.'

'Beer, please.'

'On the way.' Nancy nodded in affirmation. 'By the way, we must get that date locked in for you to come over to mine for supper.'

Nina nodded. 'We must. Let's set a date.'

Once two drinks were on the table, Robby lifted his up in a toast. 'Here's to that sky,' Robby said and gestured upwards.

'The colours are amazing. How does nature even do that?' Nina laughed. 'Fair to say, this is another Lovely thing. The sky seems to have so many different colours here all through the day and night.'

'I don't know, but we do get some good colours out here on the water.'

Nina clinked her glass to Robby's and felt herself relax as she sat back in her chair. As they chatted, she wondered what she'd been making such a fuss about. She'd worked herself into a right old state about going on a date when really all she was doing was having a chat with a very handsome man. Things had been worse in her life.

It was as if she'd known Robby for ages. She wondered if he was going to tell her about what she'd read about in the old online article. He didn't at first, but as she asked him little bits about his business, more and more came out. Nina pretended she knew nothing and listened as Robby told her how his parents had pushed him into a degree that he'd hated with a passion. As a diversion from the boredom of numbers, he'd joined the university climbing club, and via that had seen a flyer on the noticeboard for a window cleaning company who were looking for workers who could climb and had their own gear. He'd then worked his way through the degree via abseiling down the sides of buildings cleaning windows. Once he'd got the degree, he'd decided he'd never look at a column of numbers again and had started as a one-man band contracting out to companies. Now he had lots of staff, an office he tried to avoid as much as he could, and still simply enjoyed sliding down ropes from a height whenever humanly possible.

Nina smiled as she listened. She might have thought about the straps a few times. All the time. As she asked questions and Robby told her bits and pieces about his family, she realised she hadn't said much about herself at all. The widow label was suddenly there in between them. It had decided it might like to stick itself to the outside of her forehead. Her mind flashed back in a second to when she'd walked into the funeral home to Andrew. How the undertaker man had been so nice and taken her in and patted her on the back. She shook her head to rid it of the memory and turned back to the conversation.

Robby smiled. 'So, sorry I've dominated this with stuff about me. How rude!'

'No, I've enjoyed listening. I've really enjoyed it.'

'You. What big things have you done in your life? Abseiled down the side of any buildings lately?'

'My husband died,' Nina blurted out suddenly.

Robby swore. His expression was a mix of concern and empathy. 'I'm really sorry. I didn't realise. Shit, sorry.'

Nina shook her head. 'Ahh, sorry! I didn't mean it to come

out like that! I just thought I'd better get it out in the open this evening or at some point, but not like that.' Nina smiled. 'Oops.'

'I'm *so* sorry.'

Nina found herself saying more. She answered a few questions and for some reason, maybe the champagne, the motion, the surroundings and the twinkly lights she heard herself sharing about the years since Andrew had died. As she listened to herself word-vomiting her story, she couldn't seem to stop. On and on she went, and out and out it came. She'd never told anyone the full story. It always led to pitying looks and then avoidance. Too late now.

'I don't know what to say. I'm so sorry that happened.'

'It's fine. You don't have to be sorry.' Nina heard herself repeating things that had been said in the grief group. 'It's part of my story, but not the whole story. It was a long time ago now. I'm fine.' The funny thing was that she actually was fine. To be quite honest, she'd had enough of not being fine. She was utterly bored of it. Time for Bridget Jones undies.

Robby squeezed Nina's hand. 'I know how you feel.'

Nina knew that he might know how she felt. She'd read it on the internet. She just didn't want him to realise that she knew that. She pretended she hadn't spent the best part of a morning googling the life out of him and made a non-committal sound. 'Mmm.'

'Everyone has chapters they'd rather hadn't happened. How do you feel?'

'It's been a rough journey, but life goes on, doesn't it?' She made a silly laughing noise which eased the tension. 'At least mine does; his doesn't or didn't. I can't believe I'm joking about it.'

'It does,' Robby agreed with a chuckle and a raised eyebrow. He looked away for a second. 'I had something similar...'

There it was. He was going to tell her. 'Oh?'

'A girlfriend. Well, fiancé, actually. We were in an accident. A load of us were from uni...' Robby squeezed his eyes together. 'She didn't make it. It was a long time ago now, but yeah, at the same time as if it was yesterday.' He shook his head. 'I haven't spoken about it for a very long time. Sometimes I think I'll never get over it, at the same time as never wanting to talk about it again, if that makes sense.'

Nina nodded. 'Yep, that's exactly how it feels for me too.'

'Well, that's not the sort of shared interest I was expecting.' Robby chuckled.

'Yeah, a bit morbid. We should steer the conversation back to your business, dealing with delis and decluttering.' Nina laughed and took a sip of her champagne.

'And launching oneself down the side of buildings. A lot safer topic, actually.'

'Well, I've not abseiled down any buildings, that's for sure. My life's been more about small adventures.' *Or no adventures at all,* Nina thought.

'Like running along the side of the river,' Robby joked.

'Yes, indeed. Oh gosh, that day I saw you when you were on the boat was the first attempt. I was a sweaty mess. I'm not quite a natural runner,' Nina admitted with a laugh. 'But I thought I'd give it a go.'

'Me either. I think I'll stick to dangling off buildings.'

As they chatted, Nancy returned with two plates. On each plate was a sourdough bowl filled with steaming chowder. As Nancy walked away, Nina smiled. 'Looks delicious. What does this one taste like?'

'This is a very good one.' Robby lowered his voice. 'Not as good as Birdie's, though. You didn't hear me say that if anyone asks. I'll be strung up and burned at the stake.'

'Ha. Too funny. Your secret's safe with me.'

As Nina tucked in, her taste buds exploded. The chowder wasn't too shabby to her. 'Yum, this is so good.'

'Nothing beats a meal in the sea air, though. It somehow

makes the food taste nicer,' Robby said, gesturing towards the back of the boat.

'True, this is magical. Thank you,' Nina said as the boat gently rocked and began to approach where the river met the sea.

'So, what's next for you? Any big plans or dreams?' Robby asked, his tone curious. 'I suppose coming down here was pretty big for you in light of what happened.'

Nina paused, considering. 'I haven't really thought much about it. Maybe it's time I started making big plans and dreams.'

'Maybe.'

'How about you? Any big dreams?'

Robby leaned forward. 'I don't know where the time goes. I've always wanted to travel more. See the world from more than just the side of a building, but yeah, no huge plans or dreams, really. Too busy for them.'

'Any particular place you fancy travelling to?'

'Anywhere, really. I fancy the Northern Lights, but I haven't got quite there yet. I keep threatening to go.'

'Ooh, yes, I'd love to go there too.'

'Plus, south-east Asia. Thailand looks good. I've actually been pitching for some business over there. Their economy is flying. We'll see what happens.'

'Yes, very tropical. Nice dreams.'

As the boat began its return journey, Nancy came over to the table. 'After dinner drinks are being served up on the deck if you want to pop up there.'

Robby stood up and offered his hand to Nina. 'The view as we come back is not to be missed.'

Nina followed Robby up as if she was walking on air or on cloud nine or anything just as dreamy. The lights from the shore twinkled in the distance as Nina sipped her after-dinner drink and stared at the sky lost in thought. She pulled her jacket around her against the night air as they ambled to the railing and stood looking out over the water as the boat cut through the gentle waves.

'The sky really is incredible tonight,' Nina remarked. 'So clear.'

'I always find it amazing how one minute it's oranges and pinks and now this.' Robby pointed his index finger up. 'Stars.'

'You don't get them like this where I live. It's so simple and peaceful in this part of the world.'

They stood in silence for a moment, sipping their drinks and soaking in the scene as the boat puttered along and swayed as they neared the town. Nina gazed up at the sky and then down at the water. Everything was so pretty and magical. She'd forgotten all about her nerves. In fact, she never wanted the evening to end.

An hour or so later, Nina had expected to be tucked up in bed with a cup of tea, except she so wasn't. She wasn't anywhere near her own bed at all. She was, in fact, at the end of Robby's garden, sitting beside a fire pit under a tartan blanket with a hot chocolate laced with Baileys in her hand. There was a slab of chocolate from the chocolate shop beside her. Life was very good.

Nina had to pinch herself at how she was feeling. She was happier than she'd been for ages. Sitting in the solitude at the end of Robby's garden, it was as if she'd been dropped into another world, another planet even. Just sitting with the hot chocolate and chatting, she felt as if something had shifted deep inside. She wasn't worrying or thinking or just surviving, she was actually enjoying herself. It was a revelation. It was as if this Nina Lavendar was someone else. One who wasn't bogged down in what had happened to her. She was sitting next to a nice man, looking up at the sky after having been out for a few drinks, and she was not worried or sad about anything at all. Not about what she said, what she looked like, who she was, or how she sounded. She didn't give a rat's arse about anything. It had been a long time coming.

She let out a ginormous sigh. 'Ahh, thanks for this. It's so nice.'

'No worries. Thanks for saying yes.'

'It's a funny old world, eh?'

'What do you mean?'

'Well, if someone had told me I'd be sitting under a blanket in your garden by a fire pit, I'd not have believed them.'

'Yeah, same. It's been a long time since I've been out and enjoyed myself like this.'

'Oh right, me too.'

Robby coughed. 'The first time I saw you on the road with the paprika...'

'Ha. You were snooty as! So rude!'

'The house-sitter before you was not the flavour of the month.'

'But I am?'

'You are. You've certainly made your mark in Lovely. I mean, Birdie gave you a job, that alone will go down in the history books. I remember thinking to myself you were interesting when you told me where to shove my rudeness.' Robby laughed. 'I must say, I quite liked it.'

'Would you like me to speak to you rudely again?' Nina chuckled. Robby raised his eyebrows and Nina squirmed. 'I didn't mean like that.'

'You're quite welcome to do that if you like...'

Nina wasn't sure how to react to the banter-ish flirting. She was sure that right at that precise moment Robby wasn't, as she was, tingling from head to foot. She was also acutely aware that she wanted to jump on him or do anything with him, really. She took another sip of her hot chocolate and felt a charge of tingles as he put his hand on her leg. She didn't know what to do and so did absolutely nothing and remained rooted to the spot. She was too scared to even blink. She felt as if she was in a dream which at any moment might mean that she would wake up. She did not want to wake up. She knew what she wanted as clear as day; for no longer to wear what had happened to her, to let herself go. She so badly wanted to be kissed, but she didn't want it to end there though. She wanted to go in for the kill. All the way to the moon and not look back.

Trying not to think about whether or not she was doing the wrong thing, Nina reached out and put her hand on Robby's thigh. Then she leaned forward and put her head up and kissed him. Robby kissed her back and put his hands on her back. Nina felt herself begin to spin and as she spun around and around, everything around her began to slip away.

Robby got closer, pressed hard against her, and gently moved his hands down to her waist. Nina felt overwhelmed as she ran her fingers over the hard muscles in Robby's back. This took the first kiss to a whole new level. She fizzed. She told herself to remember the moment, how it felt, and how *she* felt as she buckled up and prepared to take off to the moon. Could her evening have turned out to be much nicer? Probably not. There might have been only one thing that would make it nicer. Possibly the straps.

43

Nina Lavendar cupped her mug of tea in her hand and stared out at the little kitchen garden she'd spent a lot of time in since she'd arrived in Lovely Bay. Letting her eyes settle on the rosemary bush she'd brought back to life, she realised she was in a bit of a daze after the best deep sleep she'd had in a long time, possibly ever. That tended to happen when you tumbled into bed with a man and had the most wildly abandoned sex you'd ever had in your life. Such good sex. So good. So good that it made the corresponding sleep very deep, and the next morning everything a bit hazy and delicious and Strictly level fabulous.

She mulled over the chowder on the river, the twinkly fairy light covered boat and what had happened afterwards. Oh, how glorious it had been. It was as if something in her had left the building, but she wasn't sure what. Just like when she'd felt her jaw release in Bianca's place, things had happened to her with Robby that had released something deep inside. It might have had something to do with how excellent Robby had been at his part of the bargain. Nina had not only enjoyed it, but it had been so mind-blowing that she'd felt as if all sorts had poured out of her body as she'd lost herself in everything Robby.

With a coastal breeze wafting around her as she drank her tea, she let her mind wander over the whole evening, how they'd walked and chatted, how she'd found herself blurting out about Andrew, how she'd felt totally at ease with Robby on the boat, how they'd toasted marshmallows by the fire. How, after the initial bit by the fire pit, they'd ended up upstairs. How that had been amazing. How she'd not had any inhibitions at all. That was surprising. She'd dreamily followed Robby up to his bed, relieved herself of her clothes and underwear, and not had a care in the world. In Robby's bed, there most certainly hadn't been much sleeping going on whatsoever. In fact, she'd travelled far from that bed – to the moon and back. The trip to the moon had been one of the best she'd ever had in her life. Bring that right on.

The funniest thing about it all, she realised, as she sat and pondered, was that in the back of her head, she'd never thought she'd ever be in the situation again where she might be in bed with someone, let alone having the time of her life. It had been just so blimming well good. All the feelings she'd had at the top of the lighthouse, all the tingles, all the surges, all the fizzing had been nothing like what had happened late at night in the upstairs bedroom of Robby's house. Whatever the tingles had been, she'd wanted to bottle them, put a stopper on, and cherish them forever. Then she'd be able to dawdlingly pour them over herself whenever she fancied it.

She'd arrived home ensconced in Robby's jumper and slept in it all night. As she'd rolled over, she'd luxuriated in him over and over again. She'd loved the smell and feel of the jumper so much she'd not yet taken it off and as she sat with the cup of tea, she pulled the neck up over her mouth and nose and inhaled. It took her right back to the bed. She liked going there. She intended on being a frequent visitor.

She sat up and sipped her tea, shaking her head at what was going on in her brain as she percolated every single detail six times over. She almost couldn't fathom or believe it. It felt as if perhaps what had happened had happened to someone who wasn't actually her. Mind-blowing things, such as what had gone on the night before, didn't happen to her. Did they?

Nina pursed her lips and thought about how she'd never wanted any of it to end. She'd absolutely loved it; the intimacy, the tingles, the romance, but mostly she loved simply being touched. It had been a long time.

She smiled at a text from Sophie.

Sophie: *Morning! Spill the beans. How was the date? I've been up since like 5am with one of the children, and I've been dying to know... I couldn't stand the not knowing any longer.*

Nina: *Morning! It was surprisingly amazing.*

Sophie: *Where did u go?*

Nina: *A dinner cruise around Lovely Bay.*

Sophie: *Ooh, a dinner cruise? This gets better and better. That sounds so romantic! Tell me everything. What was it like?*

Nina: *Beautiful. The bay was stunning. We had champagne and this cosy setup on the boat.*

Sophie: *I'm swooning here! How were your nerves? Was it awkward?*

Nina: *Not at all, we talked loads. It felt really natural, actually.*

Sophie: *Any sparks?*

Nina: *Definitely sparks. There's something about him. I felt a connection, more than I expected to, honestly.*

Sophie: *This is so exciting! Then what?*

Nina sent a laughing emoticon.

Sophie: *OMG! Did you??????*

Nina: *I might have done.*

Sophie: ******** hell, Neens. I didn't expect that.*

Nina: *I know. It was fabulous.*

Sophie: *How good?*

Nina: *Like so so so so soooooooooooo good.*

Sophie: *Hoooooooray! Did you stay there?*

Nina: *No.*

Sophie: *Wow, have you heard from him?*

Nina: *Not yet.*

Sophie: *I'm so happy for you. I'm also a bit shocked hahaha-hahahaha.*

Nina: *Me too. It's been so long since I felt this way. I feel sort of guilty, though.*

Sophie: *Don't even go there. Nope. It's okay to let yourself be happy, Neens. You deserve this.*

Nina: *Thanks, you're right. It's just all so new. I'll keep you posted.*

Sophie: *I'll be waiting to hear what he says. Woohoo. I knew it! I knew something good was going to happen in Lovely Bay.*

Nina smiled as she stood up, walked back to the kitchen, made herself another cup of tea, and sliced off a piece of chocolate cake. Cake and sugar would help to bring her back down to earth. As she balanced the tea and cake and thought about what she considered to be wild sex, she suddenly cringed. The cringe was swiftly followed by a wince, then a screw-up of her whole face and a shake of her head. Suddenly she felt embarrassed, and a little doubting voice popped its head over a parapet. The voice asked her who she thought she was. What she thought she was doing. It continued to taunt her as she put piece after piece of chocolate cake into her mouth. The voice asked her if she thought Robby was feeling even remotely the same way. It mocked her, saying that he'd just been out for a good time. That he'd been on a mission to get her into bed since day one. That she'd been played. She shuddered as the voice continued to jeer; it smirked and told her she was a notch on a bedpost.

The voice said that this handsome man with the big business, lovely family, and all-around success wouldn't be thinking the same about her in any shape or form. He wouldn't be pulling jumpers over his mouth, sniffing ridiculously, and wondering if he was in a dreamy version of a Tom Hanks film. He'd be flying down the side of a building, happy that he'd had a fun, no complications, night. Nina went cold. Had she nigh-on thrown herself at the man? She absolutely had. She cringed again. What in the world?

The combination of the cake for breakfast and the horrible taunting voice made her feel nauseous. She inhaled and shook her head, resumed her position in the kitchen garden, booted the smarmy voice away, and proceeded to give herself a stern talking-to. So what if she'd ended up in Robby's bed? She'd had a fun night. She was allowed to do something off-the-cuff and enjoyable. She was allowed to enjoy herself. She was not going to worry about anything. She'd just take it for what it was: a nice evening with an even nicer ending. Quite a few of them, actually. She would be positive and breezy and oh-so-happy because, as Nina sat in the garden, she realised that the hope she'd arrived with in Lovely Bay had turned into something else. Now she was not only hopeful; she was alive. Very, very much alive.

~

Just as Nina was thinking that knowing her luck, she'd never see Robby again, a notification from him flashed on her phone. She didn't have a clue what it was going to say. She groaned, stood up, did a lap of the kitchen garden, and tapped.

Robby: *Morning. Yeah, thanks for last night. Hope you're well this morning. I am. Very, very good. x*

Nina wasn't sure what to reply. She fixated on the x for ages. *What did that mean?*

Was she good? That was too small a word to describe how she was feeling. Despite the tunnel she'd just been down because of the snarky little voice in the back of her head, she felt more than fabulous about herself, about Robby, about her entire existence, but did she let on? How did dating go nowadays? Should she be nonchalant? Or breezy? As if she did things like this all the time. The thing is, she didn't. Ever. She shook her head. No, she wasn't going to get into playing games or anything like that. She simply didn't have the energy or the inclination. Why would she pretend? She'd just be normal. What did she care if it went wrong? She cared; oh, did she care.

She decided to just answer what he asked. Keep it simple, stupid.

Nina: *Hi. Yes. I'm very good too.*

Robby: *Excellent. I'll call you. x*

Nina did laps of the kitchen table grinning like a Cheshire cat, she beat a pretend drum on top of the Aga, continued to beat on top of the shelves of the dresser and then did another lap of the table whilst punching the air. Nina Lavendar was back from a very long time away. She hadn't actually died after all.

44

It had been a few months or so since the date. Robby had definitely called her. He'd called and come round, and they'd been out loads, and there'd been a few more trips to the moon and back. Nina was, in fact, now moonlighting as an astronaut. She had been having the time of her life with Robby, and completely opposite to the taunting voice, things had only become better. She was having the best time and throwing all caution to the wind and was loving it. She'd delved headfirst into all things Robby. They'd been out all over the place, here, there, and everywhere, and mostly they were simply having a lot of fun.

Nina stood by the Aga, stirring a pot that had been simmering away all day – a gorgeous chicken chasseur recipe that had started out in her repertoire in the early days of her cooking experiments after Andrew had died. The chasseur had been on a journey with her and had started off as comfort food and now here she was cooking it in a different part of the country for someone else altogether. She replaced the lid on the pot, took out some bread from the oven, and arranged everything on a tray. A few minutes later, she was putting the tray on the table in the old conservatory where Robby was sitting with a drink. Fairy lights she'd tacked up all around the top twinkled in the night, and a soft rain pattered on the roof as Nina placed the chicken on the table along with the bread, flipped the lid off a beer, handed it to Robby, and sat down.

Nina picked up her own drink, and Robby raised his bottle, clinking it against the top of her glass. 'To more evenings like this. It's been really good these last few months, from my point of view.'

Nina nodded in agreement. 'Same here. Who would have thought I'd have so much fun moving to Lovely Bay?'

Robby raised his eyebrows. 'Oh, so you've moved here now, then? Is it permanent?'

'Ha.'

'You're not actually answering that.'

'I don't know.' Nina laughed. The truth of the matter was that she wasn't sure whether her stay was permanent or not. Part of her hoped that she wouldn't have to make the decision herself. She'd daydreamed that The Summer Hotel wouldn't find a buyer and she'd be able to stay on and see where things went. She would spend her summer mooching around the hotel keeping it going and working in the deli. She hadn't even thought much about her old job or her flat. She felt guilty that even thoughts of Andrew were becoming less and less.

It all felt quite strange, as if her flat, Andrew, and her old job existed somewhere else; in another place she wasn't sure she ever wanted to return to. That other place was filled with memories and feelings, and pain and angst. Since being with Robby – if that's what she was calling it – she realised that all those feelings had suffocated her and bound her up in horrible things. It had held her in a tight coil of grief and stress, and now with the wonderful clarity of hindsight, she could see as clear as day that she never wanted to return to it again. Sophie had been telling her for a long time that she needed a fresh start in some shape or form. Nina had resisted for so long, but now it seemed Sophie had been right all along.

'So, you're thinking of making the move?' Robby's question hung in the air for a moment, mingling with the soft sound of the rain on the conservatory roof.

Nina felt a mixture of emotions. 'I have thought about it, especially since the delays with the red tape around the hotel and Jill having the problems with the solicitors. I came here for a break, a change of scenery. But now, it feels like so much more than that. I should have done it ages ago. I was stuck in a rut I couldn't see I was in.'

Robby leaned in. 'How'd you mean?'

Nina sighed. 'It's hard to explain. It's the peace, the community, and yeah, well, meeting you.' Nina swallowed at that mention.

'Right, yeah.'

'You're a big part of it. I didn't expect to meet someone like you.'

'I *am* pretty special,' Robby joked.

It didn't feel like a joke to Nina, but she pretended all of it was just a lot of casual banter. 'No, I'm the special one.'

'Well, I'm certainly glad you decided to take a chance on Lovely Bay and on me.'

Nina chuckled, thinking of her many trips to the moon and taking a bite of her chicken. 'Yes, you were quite the gamble.'

'I hope I'm proving to be a good bet. An odds-on favourite.'

Nina felt her stomach flip-flop inside. Little did he know how much of a good bet he was. Little did he know that she was head over heels. Little did he know, Nina Lavendar was very much in love. 'You are. You really are.'

45

It had been a few weeks since supper in the conservatory. Nina had continued her ongoing tasks in The Summer Hotel, and alongside that, she'd now fallen into a bit of a routine working in the deli. Her relationship with Robby puttered along quite nicely and seemed to be blossoming beautifully. It wasn't the only one blossoming; Nina was, too.

Despite a few further meetings with the snarky voice that lived in the back of her head which had warned her to be cautious and hesitant, she'd got more and more attached to not just Robby but the fact that she was now in a relationship and part of a unit of two. She'd ceremoniously stuck her fingers up at the snarky voice she'd named Judgy Jacqui and thrown herself headfirst into what she was secretly calling in the back of her mind 'being in love'.

She'd spent a lot of time with Robby since the date, and oh how she was enjoying it and him. All of it had just been simple and easy, and most of all, comfortable. The best thing was that when she was with him, he made her feel as if things were sorted, and she wouldn't have to worry ever again. Since the date they'd spent a lot of time together; they'd been on long walks along the river, been to a few cosy chowder evenings at secret eateries, gone on the train up to London, met Sophie and her husband and had had an outing on a friend of Robby's boat. Nina was falling for Robby more and more and feeling things not only that she hadn't felt in a long time, but some things she hadn't *ever* felt at all. She was in deep and loving it hard.

But beneath the surface, because of the intense feelings, and despite the fact that she'd given Judgy Jacqui the flick, Nina's insecurities lingered every now and then. Sometimes, when she felt herself feeling happy, she suddenly also felt as if there was a shadow behind her. It trailed quietly behind her newfound happiness and sometimes poked her with little niggling doubts that perhaps Lovely Bay and Robby and the new happy Nina were just too good to be true.

Not that Robby had done anything to suggest that the shadow might be correct. Robby, for his part, seemed just as utterly smitten, and Sophie had been convinced of it. He had done loads of sweet things, little gestures here and there – a book he thought she'd like, a coffee delivery, and a spontaneous picnic on the beach on the other side of Lovely Bay, where on the way there they'd seen a little family of otters on the river. They'd even both spoken more about their not-so-nice stories from the past, and Robby hadn't even remotely made her feel as if her past was a burden when she'd talked about Andrew.

Yet, Nina couldn't help but wonder. Was it real? Was she reading too much into Robby's affections? She'd forgotten almost how emotion worked, but she'd decided that she just had to put any reservations on the back boiler and get on with living. Sometimes easier said than done.

On her way home from the deli one afternoon on a whim, Nina had decided she'd not go straight home but instead pop in to see Robby at work. She laughed to herself as she got on the boat and settled into a seat – spontaneous decisions were another thing she'd found herself doing since she'd been in Lovely Bay. As the boat puttered along the River Lovely, she chatted away with Colin and smiled as Nancy got on at the railway station.

Nancy beamed, 'Hey! How are you? What's happening with you? All good?'

'Good, thanks, yes, really good actually. The weather's helping today after all the rain we've had.'

'I know. How's our Robby?'

'Also good.' Nina nodded, exponentially pleased with herself.

'You two are quite the item, it appears,' Nancy joked. 'Not that I've been checking up on you or anything.'

Nina nodded, digesting the information around her brain. She liked the fact that Lovelies were referring to her and Robby as an item. She liked it very much. 'Yep, I guess we are.'

'How is it?' Nancy leaned forward. 'Tell me more. He's quite the catch, you know. Everyone in Lovely Bay thinks so. I'm such a nosy parker, too. I've always wondered.'

Nina blushed slightly, not sure what to say. 'We just click, you know?'

Nancy's eyes sparkled. 'I bet you do. I knew it! I could tell there was something special between you two right back in the early days.'

'Could you?' Nina felt the same way too, but she didn't want to sound too over the top.

'I'm a matchmaker, me, ha ha.'

'Ha.'

'What have you guys been up to? Where have you been on dates? Ooh, I just adore hearing about a good love story. You must come to dinner and fill me in. We've been talking about it for ages now.'

'We've been all over the place. Lots of walks along the river, the occasional chowder evening, and we popped to Southampton for the day. Oh, and we had this amazing outing on his friend's boat. Yeah, it's been really great.' Nina enthused.

'Fabulous. Happy for you and our Robby, of course. It's really nice to see.'

'Thanks. Yes, me too. I'm enjoying myself. I'm happy and, I don't know, just quite content here.'

'As you should be.' Nancy nodded.

The boat gently rocked as it continued its journey along the river. Nina looked out at the water, reflecting on Nancy's words. Should she be happy and content? It was scary letting herself go, but she needed to just get with the program and forget about the past.

'Anyway, what are you doing going this way?' Nancy said. 'You live the other way, or are you not going home?'

'I'm surprising Robby at work. Because the weather's so nice, I thought I might pop by and see if he fancied strolling to the pub down by the beach there once he's finished for the day. He's always coming to see me, and I thought it'd be nice to return the gesture. He said he's been in the office all afternoon, so I hope I haven't missed him.'

'Nice.'

'Fancy joining us?'

Nancy shook her head. 'Aww, thanks, I'd love to, but I'm working tonight.'

'Oh well, next time maybe.'

'Yes, why don't you come to dinner next week, otherwise another few weeks will go by?'

'Thanks, I'd love that. Yes, let's do it.'

'Right, well, I'll text you.'

As the boat neared the jetty, Nina picked up her bag. 'Great, yep, look forward to it.'

'Enjoy the pub.'

With a bit of a spring in her step, Nina stepped off the boat and as she walked towards Robby's office, ready to surprise him, she nodded to herself. It all felt a bit odd, like new territory for her, acting on a whim, but she was going to jolly well do more of it and enjoy it.

Lost in a world of her own as she took a small side road where a line of old fishing buildings had been repurposed as offices and looked out to sea, she sighed. The weather certainly brought Lovelies out to play – people were on the beach, she could see loads of cars in the far distance by the dunes, the river path was teeming with walkers, and the harbour was bustling with people out enjoying the sunshine

As she walked along the harbour wall and past the old fishing buildings, she got closer and closer to Robby's office and further and further away from the hustle. She turned down the alleyway to go around the back of the building, hooked her hand over the gate, and let herself in the back door. Strolling past the kitchen, she popped her head in one of the offices, saw that no one was around, and then stopped in the corridor as she heard voices from the office down the end – Robby's and someone else's, deep in conversation. Her initial plan had been to walk in and surprise him, but on hearing the serious voices, she stopped in her tracks, cocked her head to the side, and strained to hear. Edging closer, something stopped her from knocking on the door, and she stood stock still and listened.

'Yeah, not anything serious,' she heard Robby say.

The other voice agreed, 'What, you can't see the point in getting in too deep?'

'Nah. Just focus on enjoying the moment.' Robby made a strange chuckling sound Nina hadn't heard before. She didn't like it. Not one iota. 'You never want to go overboard with these things.'

'Yeah.'

'No strings attached in this case. Take it from me,' Robby said.

'You think?'

'Best way, mate.' Robby sounded very sure of himself.

'If you say so.'

'I do. Never get tied down at this stage. Just not worth it.'

'Mate, you're so right.'

Nina's heart sank to her boots and adrenaline zoomed around her body. Robby was clearly discussing *their* relationship with someone and telling whoever it was that it was nothing serious between them. She ran her fingers over her forehead, not knowing what to make of what she'd just heard. Then she felt sick. She shook her head, sighed, turned on her heels, walked the other way down the corridor, and slowly headed for the back door. The worst thing about it was how Robby had sounded so casual and not bothered.

As she stepped back outside, her mind was an absolute whirlwind of disappointment and confusion. She couldn't get over how his voice had sounded. So detached. What an idiot she'd been. The voice in the back of her head, Judgy Jacqui, had been right all along. It had warned her, told her to be more cautious, said that it was all too good to be true, and it'd been wholly correct. It was all just a bit of fun for Robby—a casual fling for him with the new house-sitter in town.

As Nina walked back in the direction of the riverboat, everything felt a bit of a blur. It was as if someone above had placed a thick layer of gauze on top of Lovely Bay, and she was trying to wade through it as emotions tangled around her legs. The snippets of conversation she'd overheard played on a loop in her mind. The few things she'd eavesdropped made her question everything, and Robby's voice had shocked her; as if she didn't know him at all.

As she strode along back in the direction of the hotel, she felt as if her body was actually physically hurting with sadness and letdown and, above all, a gigantic sense of foolishness. She berated herself for letting her guard down and for starting to believe in the possibility of fab things in her life. She wished she'd never met Robby at all.

On the painfully slow boat ride home, she mulled it over and shook her head a million times, and slowly her feelings changed. The more she thought about it, the angrier she got. How dare he even think like that about someone like her? Hurt moved swiftly to pure white-hot anger, and by the time she reached home, Robby wasn't far off a dead man walking. She'd show him about no strings attached alright. Once indoors and the recipient of a cup of tea and a lot more thinking, the anger also dissipated to a strange hollowness, a jagged heart, and a mind clouded and shrouded with doubt. She'd sailed on into something with not a care in the world, she'd strapped herself in and gone on trips to the moon, and now she was ever-so-unsure about how to navigate this new not-so-nice twist in her life in the now not-so-lovely Lovely Bay. Things were not quite as rose-tinted as they'd seemed.

46

The next few days or so were mostly a blur for Nina as she shoved the whole eavesdropping episode to the back of her mind and threw herself into her work at the hotel. However, focusing on mundane tasks to keep her mind occupied didn't really work, but she told herself to get her head down and put what she'd overheard behind her. She'd avoided Robby and made up a few excuses when he'd asked her if she wanted to come round, go out for dinner, and go for a walk. She'd pretended she was poorly and not feeling the ticket and on another occasion, she had made up a complete and utter lie about something to do with her flat.

She was on her way to Sophie's for the evening and smiled when Sophie opened the door.

'Hiya!' Sophie said and then frowned. 'Oh, everything okay? You do not look the ticket at all. Blimey, are you sick? You look green around the edges.'

'I'm fine. Do I really look that bad?'

'You do. The glow has gone. What happened?'

Nina hadn't told Sophie about what she'd overheard Robby saying. Part of her couldn't be bothered with the drama of it all;

plus, she'd not wanted the Pity Smile to make an appearance. She'd known she shouldn't have got so wrapped up in Robby in the first place. Since she'd heard what he'd said, she'd repeatedly told herself that she didn't care. She told herself that it was nothing, and she was just going to let it fizzle out. 'Nothing, I'm fine.'

'I thought you'd been a bit quiet and missing in action. Is everything okay?' Sophie asked.

Nina sighed, trying to sound nonchalant. 'Just busy with getting the last few bits together for the hotel. Finally, all the red tape stuff has been ironed out, the estate agent is coming, and yeah, then I'll be done with it.' Nina's voice totally lacked conviction.

'You don't seem right. Tea?'

Nina sighed as she sat down and swiftly changed the subject. 'Yes, love one. How are you? Have you had any appointments?'

'Yes, I saw the midwife yesterday. Everything is good.'

'Great, yeah, you're blooming. Just like you were last time.'

'Don't know about that. I'm exhausted.'

'You must be!'

'All part of the program, ha.' Sophie chuckled.

'I wouldn't know.'

Sophie frowned. 'You're not okay, Neens. You were looking so much better, too...'

'Ahh.' Nina sighed.

'Is this about Robby?' Sophie prodded.

Nina did a fake laugh. 'This isn't about anything because, as I said, I'm fine.'

Sophie rolled her eyes. 'I have known you since we were six. Do I need to remind you of that?'

'You do not.'

'Just tell me.'

'There is something.' Nina sighed. 'Ahh, I wasn't going to even bother to mention it.'

'Go on,' Sophie instructed.

'I overheard Robby talking to someone about us.'

Sophie screwed her nose up. 'Who?'

'No idea.'

Sophie frowned. 'How do you not know who he was talking to? What? Wait, what was it on the phone or something?'

'No, I was outside his office, and I heard.'

'Snooping?'

'Not at all. I don't know what to think. I thought we had something, but clearly, I was just fooling myself. I feel like *such* an idiot. I'm fine, though, which is why I haven't told you.'

Sophie leaned against the kitchen worktop and frowned. 'So, hang on, what exactly did you hear?'

'I heard him talking about not being ready for anything serious, about just having fun. It sounded like he was talking about us, our relationship. It really wasn't a very nice thing to hear, to be quite honest. I feel embarrassed.'

Sophie's eyebrows shot up. 'And you're sure he was talking about you two? He seemed all over you when we met him. It doesn't make sense.'

Nina shrugged. 'Who else would he be talking about? I don't know, but it sounded like it. I didn't stick around to hear more. I just went cold and left. In fact, the whole thing made me feel sick.'

Sophie poured the tea and handed Nina a mug. 'You left without talking to him about it?'

Nina took a sip of her tea. 'I couldn't face it. I felt so embarrassed, like I'd been making up this whole thing in my head. Maybe he's just been having a laugh at my expense. Or, I don't know, he wanted a fling or something.'

'Surely not? Maybe he wasn't even talking about you.' Sophie squinted.

Nina shook her head, her eyes brimming with tears. 'It's just been a game for him. I've sort of had that in the back of my mind. I knew I shouldn't have gone on that first date.'

'You won't know unless you talk to him, though. It's not fair to yourself or to Robby to assume things that you overheard.'

'Oh, come on, Soph! Who would he have been talking about? Nup. I think I'm just going to let it fizzle out. I've already made a few excuses. Honestly, I just can't deal with it.'

Sophie shook her head. 'You owe it to yourself to find out.'

Nina shook her head and flared her nostrils. 'I just don't want all the angst. I don't know if I can handle it.'

'You can't throw it all away because of something you over- heard that doesn't even make sense. You need to give him a chance to explain.'

'You're right, but part of me says just pull back. I don't need this… I'll be gone soon, anyway.'

'Sorry, Neens, you're being childish.'

'Am I?'

'Yeah.'

'I'm not. I just don't want to go there. You don't get it. You so don't get it.'

'I do. Whatever happens, you'll handle it. You're stronger than you think.'

Nina took a deep breath. 'Am I, though?'

'You are.'

Nina felt her voice wobble. 'Thing is, I'm sick to the back bloody teeth of being strong.'

'Tough, you have no choice. If you want to be my best friend, it's part of the deal.'

'Ha! Maybe I'll talk to him tomorrow. I just hope I'm ready for whatever the answer is.'

Nina wasn't sure what to do, but she did know that she didn't like the uncertainty. Sophie was probably right. It was time to find out where she stood, warts and all.

47

It was the next day, and Nina followed the directions in the text from Nancy. She'd already been past two greens and was now following along the road to a third green, where, according to the text, Nancy's house sat in a row of cottages at the back. She peered up at a huge conker tree as she took a narrow, winding path across the green and smiled at the long row of pretty exposed brick cottages ahead of her. She squinted to see Nancy's cottage and scanned along timber front doors and hanging baskets full of colour, moving back and forth in the breeze. She checked the text message again, worked out which cottage was Nancy's, and stared for a minute, taking it all in. Nice, very nice – a bench under the front window in a narrow cobbled front garden, a sweet white picket fence butted up to the pavement, and a black name plaque with pretty flowers to the right of the door. Little coach lights sat on either side of the entrance, and a wicker love heart hung from a tiny window in the front door.

Nina took the few steps to the front door, gripped the rope hanging from an old-fashioned doorbell, and pulled it back and forth. A few seconds later, the door opened, and Nancy, in jeans and an oversized pale blue shirt, beamed. 'Hiya, you found me! Come on in. I hope you're hungry.'

Nina smiled and turned back to look at the green and along the row of cottages. It looked even better from the doorstep. 'What a setting.' She inclined her head towards the green. 'It's so pretty here. You lucky duck.'

'I know, right.' Nancy put her right index finger to her lips. 'Shh, don't tell anyone how nice it is on this side of Lovely Bay, or they'll all be wanting a slice of it.'

Nina gestured with her hand and swept it around in front of her. 'The lighthouse and the bay look so nice from this side. All of it does, actually. What a place to live, eh? I could move right on in.'

'Yep.' Nancy pointed to the small bench under the front window and a tiny table tucked right in the corner next to the fence. 'We'll pop out here later if it's warm enough. It's a nice place to sit with a drink and watch the world go by. Come in.'

Nina followed Nancy into a tiny hallway where a white dresser with brass hooks held a couple of the Lovely coats, a mirror, and a huge white clamshell with keys and a phone charger. 'Ooh, this is nice,' she said as she looked at a steep set of timber stairs painted white where brass rods held down a seagrass runner going up the middle, a tiny door with a black door latch sat under the stairs, and a stripped and whitewashed timber floor was underfoot.

'Thank you. It wasn't like this when I moved in. I've done my best. It's tiny, literally a two-up, two-down, but it's all very much *mine*. I love it,' Nancy said as she led Nina past a compact living room with a sofa, an exposed brick fireplace, a sisal rug, and the same stripped floor. A half-step took them down to a narrow galley kitchen leading to a small area where a round white table held a gigantic vase of lilies, and a back door looked out onto a bricked patio area. Nina looked around and took in Shaker-style cabinetry painted a muted blue-green, white scalloped tiling, a white sink, and a French paned window also looking out to the small patio area. 'This is really nice,' Nina joked, 'Do you have a spare room for rent?'

Nancy smiled and ran her fingers along the tiled backsplash. 'Most of it, I did myself. I've just plugged away at it bit by bit as and when I've had the money.'

'Gosh, Jill needs you at The Summer Hotel, or whoever ends up buying it should employ you to do it up,' Nina joked.

'Not you then? You won't be buying it?' Nancy said as she placed a plate on the table.

'Ahh, nope, not me.'

'So, what are your plans, then? Your stint at the hotel is nearly done here. What next?'

'I'm not sure, to be quite honest,' Nina said as she sat down. 'I didn't expect Lovely to, well, I don't know. It was all a bit spur of the moment...'

Nancy laughed and joked, 'You're not quite sure because you didn't expect to fall into a relationship here? To fall in love?'

Nina couldn't stop a look from crossing her face. 'Actually, no, it's not that.'

'No?'

'It's not a relationship.' Nina bristled a bit.

'Oh, right, sorry, what do you mean? I thought you and Robby were a thing. It's been the talk of Lovely Bay. Did we all get the wrong end of the stick?'

Nina didn't want to embellish too much on what was going on between her and Robby. 'It's nothing really. Just casual. You know what it's like.'

Nancy stopped what she was doing, turned around, and frowned. 'I'm surprised. You don't seem like a casual fling kind of person to me.'

'No?'

'No, not at all.'

'Hmm.'

'Sorry, but has something happened? You've done a complete U-turn. You two seemed to be having such a nice time together. When I saw you last week, it was like you both had love hearts in your eyes. I was actually quite envious. It's not very often you see that.' Nancy squinted in question. 'Our Robby seemed smitten.'

Nina wasn't sure whether to say anything or not, especially as she knew her words would fly around Lovely like lightning. 'I just decided it was all going too fast, and I won't be here for long, so yeah, maybe it's best to, you know, put the brakes on.'

Nancy frowned. 'Right. Millions would believe you...'

'How can you tell?' Nina chuckled.

'I am a mind reader. It happens when you watch people and passengers all day long. Did you suddenly just get cold feet, or did something occur?'

'Ahh.' Nina decided to confide in Nancy. 'Look, don't say anything, but I overheard Robby talking the other day, and it appears he's not up for anything serious.'

Nancy made a face. 'Did you? What he said something about you, did he?'

'Yeah, umm, yes, well, no, actually, I don't know.'

'Sorry, so yes or no?' Nancy clarified.

Nina winced. 'I actually don't know if it was one hundred per cent me he was actually talking about, but he was saying it's nothing serious, etcetera.'

'Trust me, he's serious.'

Nina shook her head. 'How do you know?'

'Dunno, really, I can just tell. He's been around Lovely for a long time and had a few relationships, but you were...' Nancy stopped herself and then paused for a bit. She squinted again and contemplated. 'The way he looked at you and how you were together. It doesn't add up. You must have got the wrong end of the stick.'

'No, no, I don't think so. As I said, I overheard him at his office talking to someone.'

'Have you said anything to him?'

Nina shook her head. 'I decided to just pull back. You know? I thought I should not get myself too involved. I can back out now without too much drama.'

'Right, hmm. See, I think you need to say something. From what I know of our Robby, he wouldn't be talking about you to anyone in any capacity, let alone speaking like that.'

'Really?'

'Totally. He's just not that sort of bloke, if you know what I mean. If he were a player, a bit of a ladies' man, I'd be telling you to be cautious, but our Robby, since the accident, he's just not like that. Salt of the earth is our Robby.' Nancy wrinkled her nose in question. 'What *exactly* did you hear?'

Nina relayed the whole incident, and Nancy listened without interrupting. 'Right, so technically, he could have been discussing anyone?'

'I guess so.'

'What have you done?'

'I've been making up excuses to not see him, and I was just going to let it fizzle out.'

Nancy shook her head. 'I really think you are barking up the wrong tree with this one.'

'Do you? Do you really?'

'I do.' Nancy nodded. 'It's not our Robby's way to behave like that.'

Nina paused for a bit and then sighed. 'Even so, I think I'm going to just leave it. You know when you start to think about something, and you just think better of it? I just wondered what I'm doing...'

'Right.'

'I didn't come here looking for a relationship. I never really should have started it in the first place, and I'll be off soon anyway.'

'You're sure about that?'

Nina nodded, trying to convince both Nancy and herself. 'I am. I'm putting it to bed and leaving it at that.'

'Hmm, well, you'd better let him know.' Nancy chuckled. 'And then run fast as you get chased out of town by Lovelies in blue hooded coats.'

48

Nina put her earphones in and turned on the running app. She was on a roll with the running, and unbelievably, now, she not only wasn't too bad at it, but she kind of looked forward to it too. Stranger things had happened at sea. The wobbles were definitely still making themselves known, and sometimes she felt as if her skin was falling off as she jogged along, but she was certainly fitter, and running around the coast of Lovely Bay strangely worked as some sort of cheap and cheerful therapy that was doing her a whole lot of good. It was substantially more uplifting than the grief group, too, so that was a plus.

About five minutes into the run, Nina was on the river path heading towards the beach. She nodded and listened to the woman she now felt as if she knew, instructing away in her ears. The woman was effusively saying how proud she was, how far they'd come together, and how they were just about to have the most fabulous run together. A run to beat all runs, apparently.

'As usual, we will begin with a brisk five-minute warm-up walk. Let's go, former couch potatoes!'

Nina pounded along, and as she warmed up, she started to

think about the Robby situation and dissected it from various angles. She felt as if she was careering around Lovely Bay in free fall, wondering how she could have been so stupid. Since the overheard conversation, she'd managed to only actually see him once and speak to him only a few times because he had been away with work to oversee a project involving a huge National Trust property. When he'd arrived back, she'd pretended she was really tired and not feeling great. If Robby had noticed anything different in her attitude, he hadn't said anything yet.

As the voice instructed her to start running, she was surprised how it wasn't too hard or too bad. She was never going to love running as the voice always liked to tell her she would, but it was a trillion times better than the white gym that had filled her with fear. The voice had repeatedly told her she would have fun. That wasn't quite the word she'd use, but she'd set herself the challenge, and so far, she wasn't doing badly at all.

'Tall, soft, breath, fun,' she said to herself as she ran over a bridge and headed for one of the Lovely greens.

'You have a minute to mentally prepare your body for the next longer run. Our bodies are ready for the workout we are about to do.'

Nina nodded and thought about the Robby problem. Maybe that's what she should do with him: carry on with the relationship by mentally preparing herself for the fact that it wasn't anything serious and that there were no strings attached. She could do that, couldn't she? Too easy.

'Ten, nine, eight, seven, six, five, four, three, two, one. Keep the pace that works for you. Start running!'

Perhaps that was the key to the relationship, and she should just keep a slow pace and see where it ended up. So what if Robby wanted no strings attached? Maybe sometimes that was a good thing in life.

As she jogged around the green, she looked up at the Lovely

Bay flag fluttering high above, took in the bunting tied to everything that didn't move, and smiled to herself at how pretty it all was. A customer from the deli did a little wave of acknowledgement, and a woman pushing a pram, whom she recognised as June's neighbour, said hello.

The voice in her earphones chimed in, 'Great job! Now, slow down to a walk for one-and-a-half minutes.'

Nina obeyed, slowing her pace to a walk, and headed away from the green in the direction of the beach. She could feel her heart pounding in her chest and couldn't quite work out whether or not she liked running yet, but she didn't hate it, and the weight was falling off, so there was that.

'Guys, this is flying by! In thirty seconds, we're going to run again. Make yourself proud. You will not regret doing it. Don't quit now.'

Nina braced herself and started running again.

About twenty minutes later, she'd had enough of the jogging and the voice in her ears. Everything was trembling and wobbling. 'Last running minute coming up. Give it your best shot, guys!'

She nodded as she scooted along with a boiling face, a sweaty neck and her legs feeling like jelly. She thought that maybe giving things her best shot with Robby was the answer, too. Perhaps she should stop fannying around being vulnerable and go for the jugular and give it her best. As she ran and pushed herself, she felt as if she was going to die but was determined to finish strong. As the final minute ticked over, she allowed herself a small smile. She was doing it – really running, or plodding more like, but running for more than a few seconds and getting from A to B. Maybe she could become one of those people who actually enjoyed running. Yeah, maybe not. Just after the voice had told her to warm down and she was standing by the beach stretching, her phone pinged.

Robby: *Hey, fancy coming over tonight? xxx*

For ages Nina stared at her phone as her pulse slowed down, and her breathing got back to normal. Giving it her best shot wasn't happening – just seeing his text made her feel foolish and as if he was taking her for a ride.

Nina: *Ahh, sorry, can't...*

Robby: *Are you at the deli?*

Nina: *No. I'm going to Sophie's.*

Robby: *You've been a bit of a ghost lately. Is everything okay?*

Nina: *Just been busy, you know how it is.*

Robby: *Right.*

The little dots continued to flash. Nina put her right foot out in front of her, lifted her toes to stretch her calf, watched and waited, wondering what was going to come next. It was direct and to the point.

Robby: *Sorry, but is something wrong?*

Nina: *Not at all.*

Robby: *Not being funny, but if you've got cold feet, you know, just say. I can handle it.*

Oh dear. She hadn't seen that coming. *Always best to tell the truth in life,* Nina thought to herself. So, he was now the one with an issue. The tables had strangely turned.

Robby: *I just feel like something's changed between us. You've been distant. Is it me? If you want to call it off, let me know...*

Nina paused, her fingers hovering over the phone. She was torn between keeping up the pretence and being honest. She totally bottled it.

Nina: *It's not you, Robby. It's just that things have been a bit overwhelming lately. We've seen a lot of each other.*

Robby: *Not in the past week or so! You've clearly been avoiding me. Overwhelming? Where has this come from? That's not a word I'd use. In what way?*

Nina sighed and decided to just bite the bullet. She didn't have anything else to lose, really. She'd be leaving Lovely Bay and going back to her little flat in the not-too-distant future.

Nina: *I overheard something the other day. It made me think about us, about what this is.*

Robby: *???? Like what? What did you hear?*

Nina: *I heard you talking about not being ready for anything serious.*

Robby: *What? Not sure????? You've lost me.*

Nina: *I came to see you to surprise you before you went away for that National Trust job and you were talking to someone...*

Robby: *No idea what you're talking about. Who?*

Nina: *I don't know.*

Robby: *Right. Sorry, I'm baffled. Whatever you heard, I think you got the wrong end of the stick. Can we talk about this in person?*

Nina: *I don't know. I feel a bit silly about it all now. Maybe we should just leave it.*

Robby: *About what?*

Nina: *Look, I get it that you think this is just a bit of fun for you. Thing is I don't think that, so yeah, I don't know.*

Robby: *I don't think that at all!!!! Far from it.*

Nina: *Oh.*

Robby: *You're not making a lot of sense.*

Nina: *I suppose not...*

Robby: *Please, let's just meet up and talk. I don't want misunderstandings to mess up what we have.*

Nina: *Okay, but I'm not promising anything.*

Robby: *Fair enough. How about tomorrow evening?*

Nina: *OK, I'm working in the afternoon. I'll come over after I finish at the deli.*

Robby: *Great. I'll cook us something nice. See you then. x*

Nina put her phone away, her mind racing. So he supposedly didn't know what she was talking about? Really? He'd sounded genuine enough, but after the way what she'd heard made her feel, she wasn't sure about *anything*. She finished her stretching and started walking back, the sound of the waves in her ears and a gentle breeze nice after the run. Just as she was getting home, her phone rang with a call from Birdie.

'Hey! I don't suppose you're free, are you? John had his booster vaccination yesterday, and he's not doing well – nausea, fever, the lot. I'm run off my feet. We just need someone out the back, really.'

Nina felt quite pleased to be wanted. 'Sure. When do you need me?'

'Can you come now?'

'Just need to pop home. I've been for a run. I'll shower and head back...'

'Great, thanks. Lifesaver.'

As she walked home, stripped off her running stuff and stepped in the shower, she replayed the eavesdropped conversation in her head. Was she overreacting? What if Robby's explanation made sense? She had jumped to conclusions too quickly, possibly.

All the way to the deli, Nina deliberated what Robby had said and, more importantly, what she was going to say when she saw him. It loomed horribly in front of her, and despite what she told herself, she wasn't up for a casual fling. No way at all. Her heart was way too delicate for that. Her whole being was.

As she walked through the now familiar streets of Lovely Bay and passed by the quaint shops and friendly faces, she felt as if she had the world's troubles on her shoulders. So much for a new start in Lovely Bay. It didn't look quite as rosy when her head was swirling with emotion. She thought about her safe, cosy flat, her little ledge full of plants, her routine, and her safe job and commute. It now all appeared quite nice, affable, home... She could quite easily hop on the train and head straight back.

49

Nina had to laugh; she'd been in the handmade chocolate shop next to the deli after work and had come away with more than she'd anticipated. As she'd treated herself to a bar of chocolate with a little dash of chilli and chatted away, she'd found herself the new owner of a small chocolate melting contraption. It was a simple enough concept; the chocolate went into the top of what appeared to be a small, mug-shaped tealight holder, a candle was lit underneath, the chocolate sat on the top and Bob was your uncle.

She'd bought a slab of chocolate with the intention of having it with a cup of tea when she got home from Robby's but now with the little contraption and a punnet of strawberries in her possession, she thought she'd take it with her around to his and see what happened. She might be mightily peed off about what Robby had said, but she'd decided to pop a smile on her face and get on with it. There had to be worse things in the world and places to go than over to his house to see what was what. Plus, on top of that, chocolate, especially handmade and melted, made everything in life better.

Despite telling herself she could deal with anything because she'd lost her husband, her heart pounded and emotions swirled up and down her from head to toe as she got to Robby's house. Her hand trembled as she pushed her finger into the doorbell, and butterflies were on a rampage around her stomach. As she stood on the doorstep, Robby's voice, discussing what she thought was their relationship in dismissive tones, kept replaying in her head. She felt a knot of apprehension join the butterflies but decided what would be would be. If he *had* been talking like that, he wasn't worth her time and energy anyway.

She took a deep, steadying breath as the door swung open. The tingles started as soon as she laid eyes on him. Gorgeous and then some. Maybe she'd just take one last trip to the moon with him anyway.

'Hey,' Robby said with a smile.

'Hi.'

'Come in.' Robby kissed her on the cheek. Tingles rushed up and down Nina's body at a gazillion miles an hour.

Robby closed the door, ushered her in and gestured towards a chair. 'You okay? Drink?'

'Thanks. Gin and tonic. Half measure.'

Robby frowned. 'Pardon?'

'Yup,' Nina replied. There was no way she was getting tipsy, not on your Nelly. She was very much going to be keeping her wits about her.

Robby took a small glass shot measure out of a cupboard, poured from a bottle of Hendricks, and held it up. 'Okay? Like this?'

'Yes, thanks.'

He took a gin glass from a shelf, splashed in the half-measure of gin, and took a little cellophane parcel down from the shelf.

'What's that?' Nina asked.

'Bits and bobs for your drink.'

'Ooh, nice. Where did you get those?'

'It's from a little company called Poppy's Tipples. Birdie sells them; I'm surprised you haven't seen them.' Robby put the packet on the worktop; Nina picked it up and read the label.

'Ooh, how nice. What, so they're all different flavours? Botanicals, it says on here.'

'Yep. There are all different mixes.'

'What, you just drop them in your drink?'

'You do.'

Nina took a sip of her gin and tonic. 'Wow, that makes a difference. Nice flavour. Love it.'

'Where do you fancy eating? Right here in the kitchen, or it might be warm enough to sit outside.'

Nina couldn't have really cared less about the food, where she ate it, or how warm it was. She didn't fancy anything to eat at all. She also no longer cared about the overheard conversation or her thoughts about being in control. To be quite frank, now, as she watched Robby, all she was really interested in was repeating the night of the dinner cruise. The end bit. Definitely the end bit. Many times. It had been so good, and he was so attractive to her that she flung everything out the window. She swallowed and brought herself back to the room. 'Outside would be nice.' *Then I can remember what happened after the fire pit. I'm so doing that again.*

Robby took something out of the oven, and Nina inhaled. 'What is that?'

'Spanakopita.'

Nina giggled. 'Spana-what? Whatever it is, I like it already.'

'I can make a few things well. That's where it ends. Right, follow me. We'll sit outside. I'll put the heater on.'

Sitting outside chatting, Nina wondered if she'd dreamt the whole thing she'd heard outside Robby's office. He was so nice and so natural, she couldn't quite compute what he'd said and how he'd sounded then with how he was behaving now. As if he'd read her thoughts, he started. 'So, we need to talk about what you said in your text.'

Nina cut straight to the chase. 'I overheard you talking the other day.'

'About what?'

'About relationships. About not being serious.' Nina's voice was suddenly shaky.

Robby's expression shifted from concern to confusion. He squinted and shook his head. 'I'm not sure what you mean.'

Nina felt horrified as she felt tears prick at the sides of her eyes. She shifted in her seat, folded her arms, and then hastily took a sip of her drink. 'I came by to surprise you just before you went off to that National Trust thing, and you were in the office talking to someone. I couldn't hear it all, but to be frank, Robby, you didn't sound very nice at all.'

Robby frowned. 'Possibly Jase.'

'It sounded like you didn't want anything serious. That I was just someone you were spending time with.' Nina's body language was completely closed.

'Nup. I did not say that about us. I'm trying to remember and work out what you are talking about.'

'No strings...' Nina couldn't manage to say much else as she realised that Robby was very good at lying, by the looks of it. She needed to leave.

Robby's face showed shock, then realisation. 'What, wait? You've misunderstood.'

'No, I don't think so. See, there's not really an explanation, is there?' Nina pushed her chair out. She swore. 'I should have left it. Why did I think coming here was a good idea?'

Robby squinted. 'I think you are referring to one of the blokes at work and the girl he met on holiday. That conversation wasn't about us at all! He's going through a strange patch with her, and I was chatting it through with him.'

Nina's heart and just about everything else was a whirlwind

of emotions – hope, doubt, and she wasn't sure what. She didn't know what to believe or what to do. 'Really? Are you sure? It sounded like your issue. Your voice sounded horrible, too.'

Robby shook his head as if Nina was totally wrong. 'I am more than sure, Nina. I care about you.'

Nina tingled from head to toe. She searched his eyes. She really, really, really wanted to believe him. Plus, she very much fancied going upstairs. The moon was calling. She had a space-ship to board. 'I need to know where we stand if we, I, you know, want to…'

Robby was blunt and to the point. 'I'm not looking for a casual fling. I wouldn't even be bothering. I thought you might have ascertained that by now. I did tell you… I can't believe you even *thought* that about me.'

Robby's words hit Nina like a wave of relief. She felt a bizarre mix of embarrassment and happiness all at the same time. 'I've just been so worried about getting into something that wasn't reciprocated. I jumped to conclusions. I think I may have let my mind overthink this.'

Robby reached across the table. 'I'm serious about us. I thought that was obvious. We've hardly been apart since, well, you know what.'

'Right, yeah. I've been tying myself up in knots over this.'

Robby broke the tension in the air. 'No harm done. I can cope.'

'Ha.'

'Let's just enjoy our evening, shall we? I'm not messing around here, and I certainly wouldn't speak about you like that to anyone, let alone someone at work. Plus, I don't cook for many people, so that shows you where my allegiance lies,' Robby joked, and the mood lightened further.

Nina nodded, and she laughed, a genuine laugh of relief and happiness. 'Yep, so it definitely wasn't me you were talking about?'

'No!'

'We're not just, you know, a casual thing.'

'Not from my side of the table.'

'Mine either.'

Robby chuckled. 'Deal.'

Nina beamed, took a sip of her drink, and tucked into the food. She nodded to herself. *How long before we can go upstairs? I need a trip to the moon.*

50

Nina had been busy with The Summer Hotel and it was now ready to go. She was liaising with the estate agent to get the ball rolling on the sale. The estate agent was on her way around for a first scope and to take the photos. Nina stood in the kitchen with a cup of tea and peered out at the glistening garden. Early morning had brought with it fog, then not long after that rain, and now the garden was bathed in sunshine with a hint of a rainbow at the edges. Nina smiled to herself; she was still finding the four seasons in one day thing a funny occurrence. When she'd first arrived and heard about it, she hadn't quite believed it, but now she absolutely did. She'd become used to Lovely Bay, having all the weather in one day and being ready for it before the day even began. As she sipped her tea, she looked around and mused how she had pretty much become used to lots of things in Lovely Bay, mostly how much happier she now felt with her life.

Around the kitchen and house, too, it was as if the feel of the place had seeped into her bones. As she'd cleared, cleaned, and decluttered, the old property had let out a huge sigh and begun to breathe; Nina, along with it, felt strangely the same, as if the physical act of decluttering and elimination had emotionally prompted some sort of deep release inside. As she'd put her head down and got on with clearing out and putting the old property to rights, she had let go of many things she'd been holding onto for years. They'd floated away down the River Lovely out to sea and left her feeling as if there was hope for her and, more importantly, happiness on the horizon.

Looking around at the kitchen, she gave herself an imaginary pat on the back for a job well done. The old handmade kitchen without its worktops full of clutter now looked lovely. The open windows brought in a sea breeze, the Aga shone and the scrubbed pine table in the middle held a huge vase of flowers from the garden.

Nina pottered around and strolled into the scullery and mused how it had been full of junk and clutter and was now pristine. The washing machine had been put to good use washing all sorts. She had soaked curtains in the huge Belfast sink, and there were now bunches full of drying herbs hanging from the shelving and scenting the room.

Nina smiled as she spied the hooks by the back door, where two Lovely coats took pride of place. She had found one of them on the back of the bathroom door buried under all sorts of outerwear and the other one deep in the depths of the under-stairs cupboard. She'd thoroughly enjoyed sprucing them up. After lots of internet sleuthing on how to get them clean, she'd brushed them to rid them of dust, wiped them down with water and a sponge, hoped for the best, and left them to dry high up on the washing line in the sunshine. A chance conversation with June on how she was rescuing the coats meant a tub of wax had arrived with rewaxing instructions from Molly in the coat shop. The result had been two Lovely coats that looked almost as good as new. Nina, though, not sure that she qualified, was still yet to actually wear one in public.

Finishing off the cup of tea, she put the mug in the dishwasher and went to stand on the front path to wait for the estate agent. As she stood there looking around, she recalled the day she'd weeded the garden and come across the nest of spiders. What a long way she and it had come. Now, there was actual grass looking healthy by way of a weed and feed treatment from the garden centre, and no sign of spiders, at least none that she could see. The beds sported a now healthy mix of shrubs, roses, and hydrangea bushes, a couple of potted bay trees stood on either side of the gate, bunting tied to the porch fluttered in the breeze and the old path was jet washed, swept, and weed-free. Nina had worked hard and it showed.

As she stood admiring the old hotel and how much her handiwork had improved it, the sound of a car pulling up cut through her thoughts. She turned to see a car coming to a stop just adjacent to the gate. The car door opened, and Ella, the estate agent, stepped out with a phone in her hand, an iPad tucked into the crook of her arm, and sunglasses on her head. Her heels clicked on the pavement as she approached.

'Good morning,' Ella called out. 'The sun's out now.'

'Yes, thank goodness. Morning. Lovely to see you.'

Ella glanced around, taking in the front of the property with a practised eye. 'You've certainly been busy. The place looks transformed from the last time I saw it. It's been a while, what with all that waiting we've had to endure because of that useless solicitor!'

Nina laughed modestly. 'It's been a bit of a project. It's turned out well enough. It's amazing what a bit of graft can do.'

'I should say so.'

They walked back into the hotel, and Nina led Ella through to the old hotel rooms, each one now meticulously decluttered and cleaned. Potential seemed to look back at them from every nook and cranny.

'It's like a different place,' Ella said, appearing to be genuinely impressed. 'You've done wonders! It's going to photograph beautifully.'

'I wonder who will end up buying it? Have you had any interest so far?'

'Lots, but the restrictive clauses on the old part of the hotel that's listed have put off plenty of developers.' Ella nodded in the direction of the river. 'With the view and location, it could be a goldmine according to the people who want to knock it down and turn it into luxury flats, but that won't be happening anytime soon because of its status.'

'Good! It would be awful to see it knocked down.'

Ella nodded. 'I have to say, it's still a great investment. With the right buyer, there's so much potential here. You've probably already ascertained that for yourself.'

Nina continued to show Ella around as Ella made notes and they discussed the key selling points. Ella stopped tapping on her iPad for a second. 'It's about finding someone who appreciates this place and understands how Lovely Bay works. It's not for everyone. You might have worked out that for yourself already. It's a funny little place.'

'Yeah, I've gathered that.' Nina looked around and considered what she'd thought earlier about how Lovely Bay had done something to her. 'I love it here, though, it's been great for me.'

'Lovely Bay has a way of surprising you. Just when you think you've got it figured out, something happens. The four seasons in one day, for starters!'

Nina chuckled. 'I'm starting to realise that.'

Ella swept her hand around. 'Have you thought about taking it on? It's an absolute bargain if you can look past the listed part.'

'Me? Gosh, no! No, no.'

'Oh, right, I thought you said you had an investment property, sorry, didn't you? I assumed property was your thing. I must have got the wrong end of the stick.'

'I have, yes, but no, it's not for me.' Nina thought about how Andrew had been the one who'd pushed on the investment property.

'You said you've loved it here in Lovely.'

'True. No, it was just a temporary thing with The Summer Hotel.'

'Oh, well, what will be will be. Someone will buy it.'

'Indeed.'

'What are your plans?'

'I'm heading back to my flat, but I'll be coming down here at weekends and whatnot. I'm just going to see how it goes.'

'Nice. What on the train?'

'Yes, it's not too far. Did I say I've been working at the deli too?'

'No, you didn't.'

'I'll be staying with, well, a friend on the weekends, long weekends, I should say.'

'Sounds good to me.'

'I hope so. Best laid plans and all that.'

'Right, well, I'm about done. Initial pics are sorted and will be up on the internet later.'

'Great.'

Once Ella had finished and Nina had seen her off, she stood on the front porch feeling a mix of emotions: satisfaction in how much she'd done at the hotel, a twinge of sadness at the thought of leaving, and a strange feeling that she was actually now looking forward with hope. Her thoughts drifted to Robby and the fact they'd discussed what was going to happen and how she'd be coming down every weekend to stay with him. He'd put many suggestions on the table, but it had seemed the most agreeable one to her. She shook her head; Lovely Bay had brought a lot of things, but she hadn't ever thought that by the time she headed back to her flat that she'd be in a relationship and coming back every weekend. She shook her head and sighed, wondering quite where everything was going to go.

51

Nina zipped the front pocket of her backpack as she arrived at Lovely Bay train station. Just as Nancy had told her it would be, the station was a lot busier than on the rainy day she'd arrived clutching the river timetable on her phone. Now the weather had warmed up, the station was bustling, people were out and about and visitors were clearly in Lovely Bay for the day.

As she got to the station house itself, a blue sky greeted her from above and Nancy stood by the door in a railway uniform polo shirt, peaked cap, and navy blue trousers. Nancy beamed. 'There she is. I've been looking out for you. You haven't changed your mind then? You're leaving us?'

Nina nodded. 'I am.'

'I thought Robby might have persuaded you to stay and rent the cottage a few doors down from me.'

Nina chuckled. 'He gave it a good go.'

'And you still said no?'

'I did. I'm not far away. I'm coming back at the weekend anyway.'

'I'm going to really miss you.'

'Aww, same here.'

Nancy hugged Nina. 'Well, if Robby can't get you to stay, I definitely won't be able to.'

'Ha.'

'So what's the go-to with you two now?'

'What do you mean?'

'What will happen to the love affair of the century now you're going back to your place?'

Nina thought about her flat and how she now felt so very different from when she'd left it. How she was happier and lighter. Free. 'The love affair of the century will continue, just via a different route – I'm going to stay with him, and he's going to come to mine and go to work from there. It'll all work out.'

'Sounds like a plan. And you're still planning to work at the deli when you're here on the weekend?'

'For now, yep, while I look for a job at home. Birdie wants me, ha ha.'

'You don't argue with our Birdie.'

'I won't forget her. She's been good to me. I won't forget working alongside her listening to the Shipping Forecast either.'

Nancy turned as a sound went off behind her, and a hissing noise came from further down the track. A train pulled into the station and Nancy walked to the train door with Nina, and two minutes later Nina was sitting on the train. As the doors closed and Nina sat down by the window, she waved to Nancy and mouthed 'bye' through the window.

The train started to rumble slowly away from the station, and Nina sat back and watched as the backs of houses, the River Lovely, and then glimpses of the sea slid past the window. She looked up at the electronic display board informing her of the stations on the route, and with her chin on her hand, she gazed out the window and thought about when she'd first arrived in Lovely Bay. It had certainly been a journey. One, she hadn't realised she'd needed to be on.

Her mind mused what Robby had said to her the night before and how their relationship was going to continue; she would be back at her flat in the week and with him at the weekends in Lovely Bay. He'd told her that he would do anything she wanted to do. That he loved her. That he was more than happy to commute up and down. She nodded to herself. It was the most sensible thing.

With blurs of the River Lovely, blue sky, and the greens of the fields going past the window, her mind moved from what had happened to her in Lovely, to her flat, and the memories of her life there. Just after that, as the train trundled along, she spent a long time just simply thinking about Andrew. Images popped up as if they were on a screen in her head; him and her together on their wedding day, when they went travelling around Europe, when they'd first bought the flat, when they went on holiday to Greece, when Andrew had received a fabulous new job. A tiny tear rolled down her cheek at the memories, but despite the tear, there had been a shift. Nina Lavendar realised that she was no longer that sad. To the contrary, she was happy. Andrew was no longer a painful shroud of grief. Robby hadn't taken his place, but he'd come along and changed things and changed *her*.

So, why was she going back to the place where she hadn't been happy for a long time? Why not stay in Lovely Bay? What did she really have to lose? As the guard announced the upcoming station, it dawned on Nina that she was crazy to be going back. Why would she leave the place that had turned her life around? Suddenly, she started to grab her things in a rush. She scooped up her phone from her lap, grabbed her backpack, handbag, and suitcase, and hurried to the train door. What in the world was she thinking going back to the flat where no one cared? Where her only companion was Mrs Gilbert and Radio 4. The place where she didn't even have a job to go to anymore. In Lovely Bay, she'd found a man who loved her, a cosy little job, and she'd even made a few friends. Why would she chuck that all away?

Forty minutes later, she stepped onto the platform opposite the one she'd embarked on at Lovely Bay. Nancy did a double take as Nina lugged her stuff over the footbridge. Nina smiled, flapped her hands, and then handed her case and backpack over to Nancy. 'Can you look after these for me?'

'Err, yep. What? What's happened? Why? Where are you going?'

'I'm running for the boat.'

'What? Did you forget something?'

'Yes, yes, I did. I forgot to tell Robby that I love him, and I'm staying!'

'Oh my goodness! Yes! Way to go, Nina.' Nancy looked at her watch. 'Run! It's about to leave. I'll message Clive.'

Nina scooted along the pavement in the direction of the riverboat, her hair and handbag trailing behind her in the wind. As she turned the corner, Clive in a blue Lovely coat stood on the jetty with a beam. 'Bonjour Nina. I hear you're needing to be escorted somewhere to deliver some good news.'

Nina laughed as she hopped on the boat. 'Bonjour, Clive. I most definitely am.'

Nina read through Robby's text message as she sat on the boat. She'd messaged him just after the train had pulled away from Lovely Bay station, and he'd replied telling her he was going for a long walk and then to the deli for lunch.

After hopping off the boat, she ran past St Lovely green, past the pub where she'd first laid eyes on him and along past the chocolate shop. Birdie was standing outside the chemist chatting with June, the Shipping Forecast was playing from her left shoulder. Birdie frowned, 'What are you doing? I thought you'd be halfway home by now.'

Nina slowed and pointed towards the deli. 'I'm not going!'

'What? Not another train issue with the signals, is there?'

'No, no. I mean, I'm not leaving Lovely Bay.'

'You're not?'

'No! What in the name of goodness was I thinking? I don't even want to go back to the flat. I love it here!'

Birdie clapped her hands together and started to jump up and down. 'Hooray.'

'Have you seen Robby? He said he was going for lunch.'

Birdie shook her head. 'I haven't been in there.'

Nina turned and hustled towards the deli. 'I'll have a look.'

She pushed open the door, the little bell she'd got used to hearing tinkled, and Alice smiled from behind the counter. 'What are you doing back so soon?'

'I'm not going. I'm staying! Is Robby here?'

'He's out the back there. He wasn't very happy. I did him a chowder for one.'

Nina walked through the shop and turned into the little back room she'd come to know quite well. Robby was sitting with his back to her. He turned at the sound as she walked in. 'Hello? What are you doing?'

'I'm back.'

'Oh, no, not those train issues again. Right, okay, yeah, no dramas, I'll drive you.'

'No, no, there's not a problem with the trains.'

'And so, why are you here?' Robby frowned. 'Hang on, where is your stuff?'

'It's with Nancy.'

'What?'

'I'm staying in Lovely Bay.'

'Ahh, right. What, you're going to get a train tomorrow instead?'

'Duh, do I need to spell it out to you? I'm not going back to the flat.'

'Right. Okay, wow, I see.' Robby slowly stood up.

'I was on the train, and I just thought why am I going back to nothing when I have you here? I don't want to do some stupid part-time commuting thing.' Nina waved her hand back and forth. 'I don't know. I'll rent that cottage near Nancy's or sell the flat or something. I haven't worked that bit out yet, but I'm staying in Lovely Bay. I love you. I'm not going away. I want to be near you all the time.'

Robby beamed. 'I love you too.'

'I love you more.' Nina grabbed both Robby's hands and stood on her tiptoes and kissed him. She smiled and swooned as she felt the lever on the buckle of her seatbelt snap into place as she got herself comfy and settled in for another trip to the moon.

Wildflowers at The Summer Hotel Lovely Bay

Wildflowers at The Summer Hotel Lovely Bay

Nina Lavendar is doing rather well - a certain man and a certain small town have healed her broken heart, and she is feeling all the life feels. She loves the business that has fallen in her lap, her romance is blooming for the whole of Lovely Bay to see, and she's cleansed herself of a few things that were like a noose around her neck.

Things really are turning out to be very good indeed, and when someone proposes something she hadn't seen coming, it gets even sweeter when she jumps right on in and says yes, yes, yes.

Everything is looking on the rosy blush side of romcom perfect... that is, until something comes along and takes the wind right out of our Nina's sails. Buckle up this one is a ride and we do like a Polly ride...

An old hotel. A beach town. A romance by the sea.

'Polly Babbington is the absolute queen of romance settings. Be ready... she'll drop you into a world you'll never want to leave. If you liked Pretty Beach you will love this!'

READ MORE BY POLLY BABBINGTON

(Reading Order available at PollyBabbington.com)

The Summer Hotel Lovely Bay
  Wildflowers at The Summer Hotel Lovely Bay

The Old Ticket Office Darling Island
  Secrets at The Old Ticket Office Darling Island
  Surprises at The Old Ticket Office Darling Island

Spring in the Pretty Beach Hills
  Summer in the Pretty Beach Hills

The Pretty Beach Thing
  The Pretty Beach Way
  The Pretty Beach Life

Something About Darling Island
  Just About Darling Island
  All About Christmas on Darling Island

The Coastguard's House Darling Island
  Summer on Darling Island
  Bliss on Darling Island

The Boat House Pretty Beach
  Summer Weddings at Pretty Beach
  Winter at Pretty Beach

A Pretty Beach Christmas
  A Pretty Beach Dream
  A Pretty Beach Wish

Secret Evenings in Pretty Beach
  Secret Places in Pretty Beach
  Secret Days in Pretty Beach

Lovely Little Things in Pretty Beach
  Beautiful Little Things in Pretty Beach
  Darling Little Things

The Old Sugar Wharf Pretty Beach
  Love at the Old Sugar Wharf Pretty Beach
  Snow Days at the Old Sugar Wharf Pretty Beach

Pretty Beach Posies
  Pretty Beach Blooms
  Pretty Beach Petals

OH SO POLLY

Words, quilts, tea and old houses...

My words began many moons ago in a corner of England, in a tiny bedroom in an even tinier little house. There was a very distinct lack of scribbling, but rather beautifully formed writing and many, many lists recorded in pretty fabric-covered notebooks stacked up under a bed.

A few years went by, babies were born, university joined, white dresses worn, a lovely fluffy little dog, tears rolled down cheeks, house moves were made, big fat smiles up to ears, a trillion cups of tea, a decanter or six full of pink gin, many a long walk. All those little things called life neatly logged in those beautiful little books tucked up neatly under the bed.

And then, as the babies toddled off to school, as if by magic, along came an opportunity and the little stories flew out of the books, found themselves a home online, where they've been growing sweetly ever since.

I write all my books from start to finish tucked up in our lovely old Edwardian house by the sea. Surrounded by pretty bits and bobs, whimsical fabrics, umpteen stacks of books, a plethora of lovely old things, gingham linen, great big fat white sofas, and a big old helping of nostalgia. There I spend my days spinning stories and drinking rather a lot of tea.

From the days of the floral notebooks, and an old cottage locked away from my small children in a minuscule study logging onto the world wide web, I've now moved house and those stories have evolved and also found a new home.

There is now an itty-bitty team of gorgeous gals who help me with my graphics and editing. They scheme and plan from their laptops, in far-flung corners of the land, to get those words from those notebooks onto the page, creating the magic of a Polly Bee book.

I really hope you enjoy getting lost in my world.

Love

Polly x

AUTHOR

Polly Babbington

In a little white Summer House at the back of the garden, under the shade of a huge old tree, Polly Babbington creates romantic feel-good stories, including The PRETTY BEACH series.

Polly went to college in the Garden of England and her writing career began by creating articles for magazines and publishing books online.

Polly loves to read in the cool of lazing in a hammock under an old fruit tree on a summertime morning or cosying up in the winter under a quilt by the fire.

She lives in delightful countryside near the sea, in a sweet little village complete with a gorgeous old cricket pitch, village green with a few lovely old pubs and writes cosy romance books about women whose life you sometimes wished was yours.

Follow Polly on Instagram, Facebook and TikTok
@PollyBabbingtonWrites

PollyBabbington.com

Want more on Polly's world? Subscribe to Babbington Letters